"Am I keeping you from something?"

"No," Rachel whispered.

"Then I see no reason to rush away. Do you?" Jared lifted his hand and touched the curve of her cheek.

Her eyes met his and Rachel felt as if she were being drawn into the depths of his soul. She had no desire to pull away, although she knew she should. This wasn't a man who knew and abided by the rules. She felt sure he was going to kiss her again.

"You look as if thoughts are whirling about in your mind."

"They are," she answered. "You confuse and frighten me."

"Are you afraid of me?"

"No." Her voice was a whisper. "I'm afraid of myself."

Dear Reader,

April brings us a new title from Lynda Trent, *Rachel.* In this Victorian love story, a young, impetuous woman falls for a mysterious man with more than a few skeletons in his closet.

With her book *The Garden Path,* we welcome Kristie Knight to Harlequin Historicals. When Thalia Freemont marries a handsome sea captain to escape her scheming brother, her new husband turns the tables on her.

A courtship that begins with a poker game soon blossoms into full-blown passion in Pat Tracy's *The Flaming.* A contemporary romance author, Pat's first historical is guaranteed to please.

Be sure not to miss *Dance with the Devil* from Pamela Litton. This sequel to her first book, *Stardust and Whirlwinds,* is the story of eastern-bred Libby Hawkins and Comanchero Mando Fierro.

We hope you enjoy all our titles this month, and we look forward to bringing you more romance and adventure in May.

Sincerely,
The Editors

Rachel
Lynda Trent

Harlequin Books

TORONTO • NEW YORK • LONDON
AMSTERDAM • PARIS • SYDNEY • HAMBURG
STOCKHOLM • ATHENS • TOKYO • MILAN
MADRID • WARSAW • BUDAPEST • AUCKLAND

Harlequin Historicals first edition April 1992

ISBN 0-373-28719-4

RACHEL

Books by Lynda Trent

Harlequin Historicals

Heaven's Embrace #59
The Black Hawk #75
Rachel #119

Harlequin Books

Historical Christmas Stories 1991
"Christmas Yet To Come"

LYNDA TRENT

started writing romances at the insistence of a friend, but it was her husband who provided moral support whenever her resolve flagged. Now husband and wife are both full-time writers of contemporary and historical novels, and despite the ups and downs of this demanding career, they love every—well, *almost* every—minute of it.

The author is always glad to hear from her readers. You can write to her at: P.O. Box 1782, Henderson, TX 75653-1782.

Chapter One

Fairfield, England—1850

"Rachel?" the woman's voice called from the gate at the end of the backyard. "Rachel, do you hear me?"

"They're calling you, Miss Rachel," the groom said as he tightened the girth around the tall black horse.

"I hear them." Rachel sighed and patted the horse. He was new and she had hoped to try him out alone before her mother or any of the household staff knew what she was doing.

"I'd answer, if I was you," the groom added. He had been in the Penningtons' employ since before Rachel and her older sister were born, and he had no qualms about telling her what he thought she should do.

Rachel gave in and went to the stable door. "I'm out here, Wadkins."

The housekeeper frowned as she came through the gate and waddled down the stone path to the stable, her bulk jiggling as she hurried along. "I've been looking for you everywhere! I do wish you'd tell a person when you plan to leave the house." Wadkins had been with the family for as long as the groom, and she felt perfectly within her rights to scold her employers' daughter.

"I was only going for a ride. Harry would have known where I had gone." She smiled at the groom and tried to charm him into taking her side. Everyone on the estate, including Harry, knew she was forbidden to ride a new horse without permission before one of the younger grooms under Harry's supervision had taken it out first to determine if it was dependable.

"That will have to wait," Wadkins said. "Your father wants to see you."

"Papa? I thought he was still in London."

"He just returned. Get back into the house and talk to him. Your mother has servants running all about in search of you. It's really too bad of you to take off like this."

"You know Mama wouldn't have given me permission to ride Ebony."

Harry frowned at her. "You told me Mrs. Pennington had made an exception this time. We don't know this horse."

"It's not as if I have never ridden alone before. I've been on a horse most of my life."

"Just the same, I'll ride him about a bit while you go in and see what your papa wants." Harry lifted himself into the saddle and reined the horse toward the wide door.

Rachel had no choice but to yield to the inevitable. She had really wanted to try the animal for the first time by herself. "All right, Harry, but remember, I want to ride him as soon as I've seen what Papa wants."

She preceded Wadkins back to the house. Although the older woman's disapproval was apparent in her stiff silence, Rachel pretended not to notice. At twenty years of age, Rachel resented being treated like a child, but she knew it was her lot as long as she lived in her parents' house and had no prospect of marriage. She also knew her parents worried more about her becoming a spinster than she did herself. Rachel wasn't single because she had never been asked for, she was single because none of her suitors had made her heart race. She was determined not to settle for a dull husband as Rose, her older sister, had done.

William Pennington's frown turned to a smile when he saw Rachel enter his study. He came to her, but he stopped short of a hug. This was as close to physical affection as he ever came with his two children. "I've missed you," he said.

"I missed you, too, Papa. I thought you weren't to come home until tomorrow."

"I wanted to see the new horse I had sent here last night. I presume he arrived safely."

"Yes, Papa." Rachel didn't admit she had been about to take an unauthorized ride on him. She had always been more apt to admit her adventures to her mother than to her father, probably because Rachel knew his temperament was more like her own and that he wouldn't be as easily maneuvered as her mother. "He's a beauty."

"He should be. He cost a pretty penny, I can tell you." William went to the nearest chair and indicated the one opposite for Rachel. "Have a seat. I have good news for you."

"Oh?" She sat down and smiled at him. A dimple appeared in her right cheek. "What news?"

"You'll never guess whom I saw in London. Robert Gaston." He beamed at her.

"Beatrice said he would be coming home soon. Has he developed an American accent from studying over there?"

"No, of course not. He asked about you straightaway."

Rachel smiled, but she had already lost interest in the conversation. Although Rob Gaston was the brother of her best friend, she had not found him particularly appealing before he went to America and thought it unlikely that the experience had changed his personality. "I'm sure Beatrice and her parents will be glad to see him."

"He asked permission to call on you."

"Call on me? Whatever for?"

"As a suitor. As an admirer." William's smile began to fade. "You're not getting any younger, you know."

"I know that, Papa. I don't recall ever meeting anyone who did," Rachel parried. "Rob may call on me, but I won't give him any encouragement. I think he's dull."

"He's no such thing. I was quite taken by the way he comported himself. He would make you a good husband."

"Rob Gaston? He's like a brother to me."

"You haven't seen him for four years. There have been some changes in him, I'm sure. I gave him permission to call on Thursday."

Rachel frowned. She had no plans for Thursday, and she knew her mother would already have told her father so. "All right. I'll see him on Thursday. But I can't make any promises."

"I want you to give him a fair chance. Fairfield doesn't have an unlimited supply of young men from which to choose."

"And I'm not getting any younger. I know." She smiled and tried to tease a smile from her father. "Maybe I'll simply stay here with you and Mama and be a comfort in your old age."

William looked slightly mollified, though still doubtful. "Not unless you change a great deal. You always have been willful to a fault."

"Do you want to talk to me about anything else? I was about to go for a ride."

"No, that's all I wanted to say. Don't ride Princess too hard. She's getting on in years, you know."

"I know." Rachel kissed him on the cheek and left the room.

She all but ran back to the stable. Harry was riding Ebony in the paddock, awkwardly straddling Rachel's sidesaddle with his right leg pressed hard against the horse's side, since there was no stirrup there. The horse's muscles rippled beneath his black satin hide, and he carried his head in a proud arch. He was a far cry from old Princess, who was grazing in the pasture beyond. "I'm back, Harry."

"He's a handful, Miss Rachel. Does your father know what you're up to?"

"I told him I'm going riding, and he doesn't mind." She didn't consider omission to be the same as lying.

Harry brought the horse to the gate, dismounted and led him through. As he held the animal's head, Rachel stepped onto the mounting block and swung up onto the saddle. She could feel the horse's vitality and excitement course through her. She hadn't ridden a really spirited horse since her father had sold the chestnut that threw him the winter before. "I'll be back in an hour or so," she said as Harry released the horse and stepped back. Once Harry was clear, she nudged the horse into a trot.

Ebony moved like a dream. All his gaits were smooth, and he carried himself like royalty. Rachel wondered how she could manage to claim him for her own. Her father could be so unreasonable about which horses she was to ride, and her mother always sided with him, even though both her parents knew she was the best horsewoman in Fairfield.

Once she was out of sight, she left the lane and headed out over the open fields. Ebony wanted to run, so she let him have his head. As his muscles bunched and stretched beneath her, she lifted her head so she could feel the wind on her cheeks. She loved to ride a horse of this caliber. She enjoyed knowing her control over him wasn't a predetermined fact. Ebony was well trained but his spirit was unpredictable, and the threat of danger filled Rachel with excitement.

She let Ebony gallop until a fine sweat dampened his neck, then drew him back to a canter for several minutes, then to a trot. She didn't want to return him to the stable in a lather; from her earliest childhood Harry had taught her to respect her horse and never mistreat or overextend it. Ebony tossed his head impatiently and his black mane stung Rachel's face. She leaned forward and patted his neck. "You can run again later," she told him. "We mustn't overdo or Harry will tell Papa."

The horse snorted as if he understood what she was saying, but bowed his neck in disdainful disagreement as he picked his way over the grass as if he were walking on eggshells.

In the distance Rachel could see Ravenwood, formerly the estate of the local baron. The baron had died several months before without leaving an heir, and the estate had recently been purchased by a man from London by the name of Jared Prescott. No one knew anything of the man except that he was said to prefer being left alone and that he was rich enough to buy Ravenwood and make needed repairs to it.

No one in Fairfield had actually seen Prescott at close range, either. He had been glimpsed in his carriage and seen riding at a distance, but no one had exchanged a word with him. Even the workmen at Ravenwood had caught only glimpses of him, their work being supervised by the servants the man had brought with him from London. Rachel and her friend Beatrice had decided their new neighbor had some romantic secret or deep sorrow in his past. Most of the older residents of Fairfield were less kind in their speculation, some even hinting that he might have a darker reason for discouraging visitors.

Rachel rode beyond the boundary of her family's fields and onto Ravenwood land. She had been this way many times before, treating all this as if it were her own, even when the old baron was still alive. The old man had known but hadn't cared, and Rachel gave no thought to the fact that the new owner might mind her being there.

The wild crabapple trees were still in bloom and the pastures were carpeted with crimson clover, buttercups and oxeye daisies. May had always been her favorite month. The snows of winter were far enough behind to be recalled as picturesque and the heat of summer was still in the future. Spring, like autumn, seemed magical to Rachel, for time seemed to hover then in a special sweetness.

Up ahead, a stream flowed through the pasture, flanked on both sides by willows whose wands of foliage dropped almost to the water's surface. The place had always been one of Rachel's favorites, and she headed there with anticipation. Ebony pricked his ears forward, and she could tell as they approached the water that his eagerness to run was barely restrained. However, the closer they came to the stream, the more Ebony seemed to be agitated, as if the bubbling and gurgling of the water was bothering him. Rachel spoke to him quietly and patted his neck. She had known other horses that disliked running water, or bridges, or gates, and after taking note of his displeasure, she never gave it a second thought.

At the point where Rachel usually crossed, the stream widened and ran shallow over a sandy bottom. A few yards downstream, someone had long ago built a footbridge out of flat stone. Ebony snorted again and jerked his head up as if he distrusted these rocks as much as he did the water. Rachel nudged her heel against his side, signaling him to cross.

Unfortunately, Rachel's attention was on the clover in the pasture across the stream, which was bobbing and waving in the breeze, instead of on Ebony when the horse bolted.

Although she was caught unaware, her leg automatically tightened around the horn and she stayed upright on the saddle. Instinctively, she pulled him about and spoke sharply. Ebony responded by flattening his ears and rearing high into the air. Rachel had ridden many horses who tried this tactic, so instead of panicking, she waited for him to get all four feet on the ground before making a move. However, as soon as the hooves of his forelegs touched down, Ebony kicked as hard as he could with his back legs. Not expecting this maneuver, Rachel was pitched forward. Ebony at once sensed his advantage and lunged to one side. Rachel cried out as she found herself sitting on nothing but air. When she hit the ground the breath *whooshed* from her lungs.

In a daze she heard Ebony shy away and gallop for home. She sat up and shook her head to clear it. Cautiously she moved her arms and legs. Nothing was broken. The carpet of clover had cushioned her from serious injury. But nothing, save not having been thrown, could have prevented the wound to her temperament. She hadn't been thrown from a horse since she was twelve and she knew Harry would never let her forget this.

She stood and dusted bits of grass and clover from her skirts. Off in the distance, Ebony was growing smaller and showed no signs of slackening his pace. She muttered a few profane words she had learned as a child from stable boys and helplessly glared after her mount. There was nothing to do now but walk home. Harry would come looking for her as soon as Ebony returned, but he wouldn't know to come onto Ravenwood's grounds. Now that she thought about it, she recalled his telling her once always to stay on the Pennington estate so he could find her if necessary. As with most directives she was given, Rachel had disregarded this one as soon as it suited her to do so.

Gathering up the dark blue skirt of her riding habit, she resigned herself to the unpleasant chore ahead and began walking downstream. Her shoes, however, weren't meant for walking, and she had gone only a short distance before she was limping and her feet were aching.

"May I offer you assistance?" someone said from across the stream, startling Rachel half out of her wits.

She jumped and turned toward the voice. In the shadows of a nearby willow, a man astride a bay horse was looking sternly at her. "You frightened me. Who are you?"

"I might ask you the same, since you're on my land. I'm Jared Prescott." He nudged his horse ahead, and as he moved out of the shadow, she gazed up at him in wonder.

He was darkly handsome, and tall. His hair was as near black as any she had ever seen and his eyes were a deep brown. He sat upon the horse as if he had been born to ride. A tan top coat spanned his broad shoulders, and from the snug fit of his light gray waistcoat she could tell he was lean. A gold watch chain dangling between pockets sparkled in the sun. His legs were encased in gray trousers, several shades darker than his waistcoat.

At length she realized she was staring and decided she had better speak. "I'm Rachel Pennington, your neighbor. Welcome to Fairfield."

"This is an odd place for a social call. You overshot my house by nearly a mile. Are you here for a walk?"

Almost beneath her breath, she said, "My horse threw me." She glanced up at him suspiciously. "How long have you been watching me?"

"Long enough to ascertain you are on foot and trespassing." He fell silent, his eyes roving up and down her figure, his lips slightly upturned as if he found the scene amusing. Finally he said, "I gather your horse threw you. Are you hurt?"

Rachel was tempted to say she was, just to wipe that sardonic expression from his face. "No, I'm not. Do you have a horse you could lend me to ride home? These shoes pinch my feet, and I'll never be able to get all the way home."

"An intriguing thought. If you can't reach home, will you perish in the forest? No, too melodramatic. Perhaps you'll build yourself a house out of twigs and leaves like a bird and become a recluse. No, I'm not sure a twig house would stand up to England's harsh winters."

Rachel was sure she was being ridiculed and was anxious for the moment to pass. "Do you have a horse to lend me or not?"

"I do, but not with me." He rode across the stream and kicked his left foot free of the stirrup. "I'll give you a ride home."

"We haven't been properly introduced," she said with a lift of her chin. She had never been spoken to in this manner by anyone.

"And we aren't likely to be out here in the pasture. Do you want a ride or not? I can't leave you here alone while I go get a horse for you, and I'm not willing to give up this one and walk home myself." He held out his hand to lift her up behind him.

Rachel wished she could refuse, but her feet were in revolt. She was beginning to ache all over from her fall, and she decided she should accept his offer. She put her foot in the stirrup, took his hand and was lifted in one easy motion. Rachel threw her leg over the horse's rump and settled herself behind the saddle. She could already hear what her mother would say about her riding astride behind a stranger, but she seemed to have no choice.

As he eased his horse into a walk, he said, "You didn't tell me why you're on my land. Surely you're not lost."

"Of course not. I've lived here all my life. When the baron was alive he allowed me to ride in his pastures. This stream is one of my favorite places." She paused. "Do you mind that I'm here?"

He was quiet for a moment. She studied the way his coat lay across his shoulders and how his hair caught and swallowed the sunlight. "I suppose you've done no damage."

She frowned. "That's hardly charitable."

"I have no reason to be charitable toward you. I keep to myself and I expect others to do the same."

"In that case, why are you giving me a ride home?"

To her surprise, he chuckled. "I was just asking myself the same question. I have no good answer."

Rachel concentrated on balancing herself on the horse. Without stirrups or the horse's sides to grip with her knees, she was finding her seating precarious.

"You'll be more comfortable if you put your hands on my waist," he said as if he knew what she was thinking.

She wished she could come up with a stinging retort, but she knew he was right. Gingerly she put her hands on his waist. The sway of his body as it matched the horse's gait and the hardness of his muscles reminded her of Ebony and how he had exuded a sense of danger barely leashed. Heat from Jared's body seemed to course up her hands and arms and lodge in her middle, even though the day was pleasantly cool. She had never touched a man like this, not even one she knew well.

"I don't normally fall off my horse," she said to take her mind off the startling sensations that were being aroused by the necessity of her touching him so familiarly. "I was riding a new one."

"A black with a long tail? I saw him heading east."

"And you made no effort to stop him? Didn't it occur to you that it's unusual for a riderless horse to be traveling by?"

"Yes, it did. That's why I rode in the way he had come. Otherwise I might not have found you." His baritone voice held a note that in anyone else might have sounded tender and caring.

"I'm obliged to you." She didn't know what to think about him. From the way he had acted toward her, she wouldn't have believed he would go out of his way to come to anyone's aid.

"It wouldn't be proper to leave a body lying around."

She leaned to one side so she could see his face. He was smiling. "I had heard Ravenwood was sold. I suppose you have been so busy getting settled in that you haven't offered or accepted any invitations."

"Actually, I ignored them. I have no desire to socialize. That's one of the reasons I left London."

"But everyone visits!" She felt shocked at the idea of wanting to be so secluded. "What will people say?"

"Frankly, I don't care."

Rachel was so amazed she couldn't think of a reply. She often said she didn't care what people thought of her, but she never really meant it, certainly not to the exclusion of going to parties.

By the time they reached her house the entire household was in an uproar. The servants had alerted her parents as soon as she and the unidentified man had ridden into sight, so they were met at the front door. With a sinking feeling, Rachel noticed that neither of her parents was smiling.

"Mama, Papa," she said in as bright a voice as possible, "this is our new neighbor, Mr. Jared Prescott."

William nodded coldly. "Mr. Prescott."

Violet touched her husband's arm. "Good day, Mr. Prescott. Rachel, what are you doing on Mr. Prescott's horse?"

Rachel shifted her weight to slide off the horse. Jared caught her arm and helped her safely down. Her father

stepped forward and steadied her. "I was riding and..."
She stopped short, not wanting to admit that Ebony had
thrown her. "I got off to look at some wildflowers and my
horse ran home without me."

"You were on Ebony." William made the statement
flatly. "Princess was in the field."

She could feel Jared's eyes on her and she knew he must
be wondering at the discrepancy in her story. She hoped he
wouldn't give her away. "Princess is so old and slow. I just
took Ebony for a short ride."

"He's not a proper mount for a young lady." William
turned to Mr. Prescott. "I appreciate your bringing my
daughter home, sir. We are obliged."

Rachel frowned. It wasn't like her parents to be so cold
toward anyone, even a stranger. Their behavior was bor-
dering on rudeness.

"It was my pleasure," Prescott said.

"I do wonder, however," William continued, "how you
happened to find her, since Rachel has been told to stay on
our property when she rides."

"I happened to see her horse without a rider, and I went
to investigate." The man's voice was as cool as her father's.

"Again, I thank you." William took Rachel's arm and
turned toward the house.

Behind her, she heard Jared Prescott riding away and she
tried to look back at him, but her father pulled her into the
house. "You should have asked him in, Papa. He went out
of his way to bring me home."

Violet finally spoke up, her voice quivering despite her
soft tone. "Astride! You were riding astride as if you were
some... I don't know what! And with *that* man."

"What's wrong with Mr. Prescott?" Rachel frowned at
her parents. Something was indeed wrong here.

"We've heard talk about him," her mother said. "Unpleasant talk."

"He isn't someone we want to foster as an acquaintance," her father added.

"What sort of talk? All I've heard is that he doesn't want to socialize with anyone here. That's odd, but that's hardly a reason to condemn a person."

"We have to ask ourselves why. He's a young man and is unmarried as far as I've heard. Why doesn't he want to befriend any of us?" Rachel's mother clutched her hands nervously.

"I've heard he has reason to be ashamed in polite company," her father said. "At the club, I heard he keeps sweatshops that are the worst in London. You know how I've worked to improve labor conditions in the slums there. The mere idea of a man operating his business under such conditions is appalling. You haven't seen the things I have. It would turn your hair white overnight if you had."

Rachel's curiosity was piqued. "What sort of things, Papa?"

"Children barely old enough to leave their mothers' sides forced to work all day and into the night at jobs that would be dangerous for an adult. Men like Prescott hire children and women because they work cheap and because their hands are small enough to reach into spaces a man's couldn't. I'm telling you, it's disgraceful!"

"How do you know Mr. Prescott has a sweatshop?" Rachel asked reasonably.

"It's common knowledge at my club. We know he has something to hide or he wouldn't keep to himself so much."

Rachel knew this club. Her father and some of his cronies had taken a building in town that had once been a tavern and had tried to make it into a men's club on the order of the ones in London. The men went there in the evenings for male companionship and to solve the problems of the world and Fairfield. "But, Papa, maybe you're wrong. If he hasn't actually admitted that he owns a sweatshop—"

"That's the end of this discussion, Rachel," William interrupted. "You took Ebony out without permission, worried your mother to distraction and compounded your sin by coming home astride a stranger's horse in the most brazen fashion. You are to stay here in the house for the rest of the day and try to make it up to your mother. I'll send word to the search party to let them know you're alive—and at home."

Rachel waited until her father was out of the room, then said, "I never meant to worry you, Mama."

"I know you didn't. If only you would think about your actions, Rachel. I've never seen two girls less alike than you and Rose. If you would just think matters through from time to time . . ." Violet went to her writing desk and took out a sheet of paper. "I'll have to thank the man formally for bringing you home, but you've put me into an awkward situation of having to do so."

"Maybe you could ask him to tea, as well. Just out of gratitude?"

Violet frowned at her younger daughter. "That wouldn't be proper or necessary in this case."

"Yes, Mama." Rachel was making an effort to be as docile as Rose would have been under the circumstances, but she was thinking about Jared Prescott and wondering if he really did have some dark secret. Not that she believed that story about him having a sweatshop. It just wasn't possible for her to be at all attracted to a man of that sort, and she most certainly was attracted. She could hardly wait to see Beatrice so she could tell her friend of actually meeting him, and so they could try to figure out what his secret might really be.

Yvonne ran her hand over the tangle of her black hair and hummed a tuneless song that had crept into her mind. She liked this place, even if it was new. So far the phantoms that had followed her so closely in London hadn't found her. Although she tried to recall why she was here, she had only a vague memory of trunks and a carriage and people moving about in confusion. This didn't disturb her, not really. Yvonne was accustomed to confusion.

She went to the wall where she had found a tiny tear in the wallpaper. As she hummed she worked the sliver of paper loose and slowly tore it from the wall. It left a thin triangle through which the cheesecloth and wood could be seen. Yvonne knew she shouldn't have done this, but since she couldn't make the paper stick back into place, she folded it carefully into as small a wad as possible and hid it in the far corner of the room.

This room was nicer than the one she had lived in before. The wallpaper was pale pink and had a pattern of roses and violets. She didn't like the design along the cornice board, though—it reminded her of spiders—so she ignored it. Her bed was soft and narrow enough that she didn't feel lost in it at night. Since her Paul had died she couldn't bear to sleep in a bed large enough for two. Especially not after the phantoms began to follow her everywhere.

She had a chest for her clothes and a trunk for her dresses, although this was kept locked unless she needed to change clothes. On the washstand stood a pink basin and ewer. There were curtains at the windows, the kind she could pull shut in case anyone tried to look at her. Yvonne hated anyone to look at her.

The only door led to the adjoining bedroom. Abby lived in there. Abby always lived in the room closest to Yvonne's. It had been that way for years—for as long as Yvonne could remember on most days. Not that it had always been so. When Paul was alive, she had lived with him and she couldn't remember having known Abby then. But those days were filled with red and black and confusion, so she refused to think about them.

There was a bookcase in her room. She had not had a bookcase in her other rooms. Of course there were no books on it, but she didn't mind. Books always seemed to get torn and the phantoms had a terrible habit of throwing them on the floor. She preferred the bare shelves. They looked uncluttered and plain, the way a slate looked when it was washed clean.

Yvonne went to the bookcase and ran her hand over it. One shelf, too tall for her to see properly, even though she was unusually tall for a woman, had a rough spot. She frowned and ran her fingers over it again. It wasn't right that her plain shelf should have a rough spot. That wasn't right at all.

Her fingers pulled at the shelf and to her surprise, the whole bookcase made a faint clicking sound and pulled away from the wall.

For a moment Yvonne was afraid to touch it. Then, curiosity got the best of her and she tugged at it. The case swung out to reveal a narrow set of steps leading down. At first Yvonne thought it might be an entrance to hell, such as Abby was always telling her about, but she put out her hand and the air was cool, not hot. She paused, trying to decide what to do. Abby wanted her to stay in the room, but Abby had refused to come in and talk to her or to sing her a song, so why should she expect Yvonne to do as she said?

Yvonne carefully made her way down the steps. It was such a narrow passage that her skirts touched the sides and she could reach up and touch the ceiling. Yvonne didn't like being in large spaces, so she was quite comfortable in the passage.

The steps led down, curving back on themselves as if they were set in the walls of the house however they might fit. It was dark, yet Yvonne liked that, too. She feared the color red, and shiny, sharp objects, but such things were invisible in the darkness and therefore lost their power.

The steps ended at a door. Yvonne was rather disappointed. She had hoped they would lead on indefinitely. Her long fingers closed on the knob and she turned it. It opened easily and she found herself in a shedlike room. When she opened the door opposite her, she discovered she was out of the house and on the side lawn.

For a minute Yvonne hesitated. Were the phantoms out there? Was this one of their tricks? She listened carefully but could hear nothing except a dog barking far away. Cautiously she stepped out into the moonlight. The moon was full. She liked that. Holding out her arms, she slowly twirled in the silvery light.

In the distance she could see lights. Yvonne looked back at the house she had just left. The windows on this side were all dark. No one would miss her. She began to walk toward the town, being careful not to make any sound. She had found it was better to move about without making any sound.

Chapter Two

"Isn't it terrible?" Beatrice Gaston leaned toward her best friend to convey the importance of the matter. "She was foully murdered!"

Rachel shook her head and the cluster of dark curls piled atop it bounced. "From all I've heard of Liza Barnes, she probably met her end in a knife fight at the tavern." Rachel's parents still refused to let her out of their sight, and Beatrice had come to the Pennington house for tea.

"No, that's not the way it happened at all. Rob told me all about it, and he got his information from the men at the club. She was found in that alley between the Emporium and Flournoy's Dry Goods. Rob said she had been knifed, all right, but it was as if someone had sneaked up from behind and stabbed her in the back."

"Maybe she was losing the fight and was running away."

"Liza Barnes? Run away? It's more likely she would have gone out of her way to fight. She was infamous, Rob says."

Rachel shook her head again. "I can't imagine anyone in Fairfield doing such a thing. Why, we know every person in town. Do you know anyone who would do a thing like that? Some of the Cooper family are mean enough, and if it had been a man who was murdered, I would suspect them, but a woman? Not even the Coopers would stab a woman."

"Rob said her throat was cut from ear to ear, as well."
Beatrice shuddered but her eyes danced. "Mama and Papa
would be so upset if they knew he had told me! All Mama
said was that Liza Barnes met with a dreadful accident and
that I was to stay away from the alley where it happened.
As if I would go into an alley!"

"Our parents think we're still children," Rachel com-
miserated. "I've been told not to ride out alone until jus-
tice is done." The notion of being prohibited from riding
brought to mind her last ride. Conspiratorially, she leaned
forward, almost touching Beatrice's blond tresses with her
forehead. "You'll never guess what I did the other day! I
met Jared Prescott!"

"You didn't!" Beatrice glanced around the parlor to be
sure they were alone, even though she knew no one else was
with them. "How?"

"Come with me to the conservatory and I'll tell you."
Rachel led her friend out of the back parlor and around the
corner to the place where she had shared numerous other
secrets with Beatrice.

The room, whose curving walls were made almost entirely of glass, jutted out into the backyard. It was full of
plants. Rachel and Beatrice went to a bench beyond the
small fountain that was a replica of the one on the lawn. In
years past they had decided this was the place least likely to
be observed by family or servants. "I went for a ride on
Ebony. Remember? That beautiful horse Papa bought in
London?"

"You didn't! I'd be frightened to death of him!"

"I had to see if he had as much spirit as we thought. It
turns out he did. He actually threw me!"

"No! Were you hurt?"

"I have a bruise or two, but Mama doesn't know it. I told
Mama and Papa that I dismounted and he ran away from
me. Anyway, as I was walking home, I saw Jared Prescott
watching me." It gave her pleasure to say his given name
rather than to refer to him more formally.

"He was? What did he say to you?"

"He asked if he could give me a ride home. He was on his horse, you see."

"How gallant! He lent you his horse?"

"Not exactly. He put me up behind his saddle and we rode double."

"Double!" Beatrice looked almost as shocked as she was delighted. "You rode double? I haven't been allowed to ride that way since I started wearing long skirts."

"Neither have I."

"What did you talk about? This is even more exciting than the murder."

"Oh, this and that." Rachel was evasive in order to make it sound as if she had made a conquest of Jared. "He did say he was concerned that I might have hurt myself."

"How did he happen to be watching you?"

"I was on his property, at the stream where the willows are so pretty." At Beatrice's exclamation she added, "The baron always let me ride there. Mr. Prescott didn't say he forbade it, either, so I may go back." She grimaced. "Or I will when Papa lets me leave the house again. You don't know how lucky you are to have parents who travel so much. Servants are never as strict as parents."

"What's he like? Did he mention whether a lady has broken his heart or not?"

"On our first meeting? Certainly not." Rachel sighed. "Papa was even more upset than Mama at seeing him bring me home on the back of his horse. They were scarcely polite to him. I've been forbidden to make his acquaintance."

"That's too bad," Beatrice said in commiseration. "Especially if he's as handsome as they say."

"He's more handsome than you can imagine. He has truly black hair and his eyes are brown, and even though he was on horseback all the time I saw him, I think he would be even taller than Papa. I'll let you know if he is when I see him next time."

"But if you're forbidden—"

"Beatrice, Fairfield isn't a large town. Of course, I'll see him again. Besides, we're neighbors." She smiled and her dimple danced. "And I have every intention of getting to know him better. He's ever so mysterious and there's a sense of danger about him."

"Danger? What do you mean?"

"I'm not sure how to describe it, but I think we were right that he has some great sorrow in his past, or some terrible secret. He just has that air about him."

Beatrice's blue eyes were round. "He sounds wonderful. It's such a pity that your father won't let him call on you. Rob would be so jealous."

A cloud passed over Rachel's face. "Would you be terribly upset with me if I don't want to marry Rob?"

"No, I can't see why anyone would want to marry him. He's so dull and predictable. I had hoped he would become more interesting after spending all that time abroad, but if anything, he's worse."

"He's to call on me this afternoon. I have to be honest and tell him he has no hopes. Papa won't be pleased, but it's only fair."

"I agree. You remember when Priscilla Marsden led Wallace Cates on so shamefully. Everyone was talking about it because we all knew she didn't care a fig for him. She had to settle for James Hastings in the long run, and I think it served her right. Wallace is sweet even if he isn't very nice looking."

"I only wanted to be sure you wouldn't hate me forever."

"How could I? You're my best friend."

Rachel nodded. "I just can't settle for a man I don't love. Rose married Edwin because Papa encouraged her to, and I can't believe she's as happy as she might have been. Edwin is all right. I mean, he doesn't drink to excess or gamble, but he's *dull*."

"Like Rob." Beatrice nodded emphatically. "You have to wait for your perfect mate. I know I intend to."

Rachel smiled and patted her friend's hand. "We both will. Wouldn't it be wonderful if mine turned out to be Jared Prescott?"

As Rob Gaston sat in the Penningtons' front parlor, trying to ease the stiff collar about his silk cravat, Rachel noted that his skin was red and angry looking where the collar had rubbed it. "More iced lemonade?" she asked.

"No, thank you, Miss Rachel. I would like another of those tea cakes, however. Did you bake them yourself?"

"No, the cook did. I'm not all that fond of cooking." At that precise moment, her mother passed through the far end of the room. From the reproving look on her face, Rachel knew she must have heard her last comment. Rachel pretended not to see her. Rob had been there for half an hour, yet it felt to her as if it had been a decade.

Conversation dwindled as Rob ate the tea cake. Rachel had never liked having to make polite conversation. In fact, she resented having to come up with mundane topics to discuss with a person with whom she had nothing in common, and avoided doing so whenever she could. As Rob continued to chew, the silence grew long about them. He nodded to her as if to indicate it was her turn to speak, but she merely looked back at him as if she had no idea what he meant. However, when her mother came back into the room and sat at the opposite end near the window to work on the shawl she was making for Rachel's grandmother, Rachel forced a pleasant smile to her face and asked, "How was the weather in America?"

Rob swallowed his last bite and launched into a full description of every kind of weather he had encountered in America and at sea. Rachel pretended to be listening, but her thoughts were on the differences between Rob and Jared Prescott.

Rob was somewhat handsome. Her mother considered him to be the most handsome of the Gaston men. His hair, like Beatrice's, was blond, and his eyes were blue. Blond hair on Rob, however, looked effeminate, since the Gastons' hair tended to be as fine as silk. Blue eyes were pretty on his sister, but on him the color seemed washed out. Or at least it appeared so to Rachel. She much preferred a dark complexion. Like Jared's.

In her mind she called him Jared, not Mr. Prescott. He had been the subject of several of her dreams after that fateful day she had met him by the stream, and since in her romantic novels that usually meant the heroine had fallen in love, Rachel assumed that the same held true for her.

Rob's voice wasn't as deep as Jared's, either. Rachel had never thought much about the timbre of a man's voice, but that was before she had met Jared Prescott. Jared's resonant tones had touched a chord in her that wasn't entirely due to her imagination. As she thought about having ridden behind him and having held tight to his waist to maintain her balance, she remembered how her palms had warmed and how that heat had radiated up her arms. Moments before, her fingers had brushed Rob's as she was passing him the plate of tea cakes, but at the touch, she had felt nothing at all. Apparently Rob had been equally unmoved, since he had neither blushed nor stammered. Her novels had been very definite about that. A man in love was a man who stammered.

"I can't tell you how glad I am to be home," Rob summed up. "There really is no place like home."

"So I've heard." As her mother was still within earshot, she tried to think of another topic of conversation. Rob had been gone since before she was old enough for society, and while she knew almost everything about him, she didn't really know him at all. "Beatrice tells me you are going into business with your father."

"That's right. The sign over our bookkeeping office is being repainted to read Gaston and Son. Father says it's the proudest day of his life."

"I can imagine so." Rachel caught another of her mother's cautioning looks. "You enjoy working with numbers?"

"I hardly think enjoyment is the word." Rob sounded thoughtful as if he had never considered whether or not he liked his profession. "It's the family business. My grandfather started it with his brother. At that time the sign said Gaston and Gaston. Then, of course, Father took the reins."

Rachel tried to appear calm but she wanted to scream. Rob was even duller now than he had been as a youth.

"I'm looking for a house of my own," Rob confided. "I have one in mind. It's the old Dabney place on the street behind my parents' house. I'll be frank with you, Miss Rachel. I intend to marry in the foreseeable future."

"Oh? Anyone I know?" Rachel was determined to make this as hard for him as possible. She wished her mother would leave the room so she could tell Rob that he needn't think of her in that light.

Rob smiled and his lips puckered. Rachel thought he might be the only person she had ever known who looked worse with a smile than without one. "I have my sights on someone, but it's too early to speak of my hopes."

"I'll wager it's Pamela Driskoll!"

His smile wavered and he looked uncertain. "Pamela? No, I hadn't thought of her in that way."

"You should. She's become almost a beauty since you left home."

"I'm sure she has." He didn't sound convinced.

Violet cleared her throat and Rachel got the message, but even though she knew she was on dangerous ground, she perversely decided she must not give Rob encouragement. "You knew Priscilla Marsden and James Hastings were married? Surely Beatrice wrote to tell you. I believe you and James went to prep school together."

"Yes, I've known James quite well. I'm sure they will be very happy together."

"I hope so. Beatrice and I thought James wouldn't have her after the way she used Wallace Cates. You've never seen such blatant flirting in your life."

"A husband and family will take care of that straightaway," Rob said solemnly. "That's all she needs. Responsibility is the backbone of so many people."

"Not me. I detest responsibility. Even more than cooking," she added. "I would much rather have an adventure."

"An adventure?" Rob stared at her. "What sort of adventure?"

"I don't care as long as it's full of danger and excitement. Haven't you ever felt that way?"

"Never. Security is my hallmark. You'll feel the same when you're older."

"Why, Robert Gaston, I'm amazed at you for bringing up the subject of age with a lady!" She enjoyed his discomfort but not the way her mother shook her head in silent admonition. "Besides, you know I'm twenty, the same as Beatrice."

He looked flustered. "I didn't mean . . . I mean, I think of you as little more than a child. No, wait. What I'm trying to say, is I didn't mean to overstep my bounds."

"I should think not." Rachel sat demurely with her hands folded in her lap, her straight back the proper number of inches from the back of the chair. She tried to look as if she were only the slightest bit miffed at him, which wasn't easy since she really wanted to tell him to leave and not come back.

"Blame my brashness on my having been out of the country," he added. "You can't think how different things are outside of England."

"I'd love to travel. I want to see the world."

Rob smiled again. "It's interesting for a man, but I have to tell you it's nothing but inconveniences for a lady. On shipboard privacy is at a premium, and one never knows what one might encounter in an inn." He shook his head. "That's why I did my traveling before I wanted to settle down. I'll not drag my wife to the ends of the earth."

"Not even if she wants to go?"

"As husband, when that day comes, I'll be the master of my house. Anything else would be unnatural."

Rachel tried to keep her temper. "I'm not so sure I will agree to have a master, married or not. Especially one who—"

"Rachel," Violet broke in hastily, "did I hear you say there's an outing planned for the young people at the church? Perhaps Rob would like to attend with you. You could help him become reacquainted with all your friends."

"Yes, Mama." Rachel knew her mother could be counted on to recall something so inconvenient at a time like this. Now she was forced into being accompanied by Rob. "Beatrice and I had made plans to go in her carriage."

"Even better." Her mother's voice had sounded soft in her usual fashion, but Rachel knew she was being firm in the extreme. "Rob, would that be agreeable to you?"

"Certainly, Mrs. Pennington. Beatrice and I will call for Rachel and bring her home safely."

Rachel wished she could think of some reason that this would be impossible, but there was none. "Wonderful," she said with no conviction. "Tell Beatrice I'll wear my yellow bonnet." Beatrice would understand. Of all Rachel's bonnets, the yellow one was her least favorite.

"I think your blue one would be better," her mother said, apparently having understood her hidden meaning as well.

Rob laughed. "Surely there will be plenty of time to make these decisions. Goodness, look at the time. I've taken up half your afternoon." He stood and waited for Rachel to get to her feet.

Rachel preceded him to the foyer and opened the door for him. "Thank you for coming," she said automatically.

Rob took her hand and surprised her by placing a kiss on it. "I hope I may come again?"

"I hardly see how I can stop you."

He laughed as if she had made a witticism. "You're just as clever as I remembered. It's indeed good to be home, Miss Rachel."

She was glad to close the door with him on the other side of it. Taking a deep breath, she went back into the parlor. Her mother was waiting for her.

"You were scarcely polite," her mother scolded softly. "What has come over you lately?"

Rachel sat on the footstool beside her. "Mama, I'm twenty years old. Life is passing me by! I don't want to marry a man like Rob and spend my life in growing old. I want to meet a man like...like Mr. Prescott, who is exciting and who will take me places."

"There are no men in our circle like Mr. Prescott, thank goodness. You don't know what you're talking about. Security is much more important than you seem to believe. Where would we be if your Papa didn't have his law office? It's the mark of a good husband to provide for his family."

"But I want *more*."

"That's because you've never had to worry about a single thing in your whole life. You don't know what you're talking about."

Rachel frowned. Her mother had been raised in a family almost exactly like the one she had created with Rachel's father, and Rachel knew she had never lacked for security, either. "What if you're wrong, Mama? What if security isn't as important as excitement?"

Violet paused, and for a minute she looked as if she were examining a faraway memory. Then she shook her head. "Nonsense. I married your father and my family was pleased. We want you to marry a man like Rob. You have to depend on those who are older and wiser to help you make these decisions."

"But I don't want to marry Rob. Can't you understand?"

"I understand, but I believe you're wrong. I know twenty seems young to you, but your prospects are passing you by.

Fairfield isn't a large town, and we don't have many acquaintances in London. If you don't choose a husband
soon, you'll become a spinster like your cousin Harriet.''

Rachel leaned her cheek on her mother's lap. Neither of
her parents had ever wanted more than they had. Rachel,
however, couldn't be contented to hum when she might
sing, to walk when she might dance. She couldn't even
imagine her mother as a girl with dreams or her father
without his rounded stomach and graying hair. "I just can't
explain it. Inside me there's a gypsy aching to run free.''

Violet smiled and touched her daughter's hair. ''We all
have a gypsy in us when we're young. Or at least most of us
do. But the gypsy doesn't live forever, and it won't put food
on the table or clothes on your back.''

''You mean you once felt the way I do now?'' Rachel
asked in surprise.

Violet hesitated. ''I've always behaved in a reasonable
fashion, just as I've tried to teach you and Rose to do.''

Rachel smiled. ''At least you were successful with one of
us.''

''I'll be successful with both of you before I'm done.
Now run along and fetch your embroidery and show me
how much progress you've made on that handkerchief for
Aunt Maddy.''

Rachel did as she was told but her mind was turning over
what her mother had said. No, she told herself as she got
her sewing basket from her bedroom. Her mother had
never felt this way. That wasn't possible.

''Mark! I was beginning to wonder if your carriage had
broken down.'' Jared grinned as he shook hands with his
cousin.

''The roads between here and London are a mire after
that rain last night. I thought I'd never get here.'' Mark
Paynter gave his hat to the silent butler and looked around.
''This is nice. I should have known you'd find the perfect
house.''

"It's out of the way and that's all I insisted upon. Fairfield is down that slope to the west, but it's small and will be no problem."

"I would think a small town would be buzzing with the news of a new man in town."

"I've discouraged callers. Some noses are out of joint, I suppose, but that's a small price to pay for privacy."

Mark followed Jared into the library and read the titles of some of the books there. "I don't remember all of these."

"Some came with the house. It was in the estate of a baron and there were no descendants. I was able to buy it, furnishings and all. I kept the better books and put the rest in the attics." He laughed. "I still can't bring myself to part with a book."

"You'll never change."

"No? I feel as if I'm nothing like my old self."

Mark shook his head. "That's because you insisted on burying yourself out here in the country."

"You know it was necessary."

Mark sobered. "How is she?"

"About the same. She has her good days and her bad days. I go up to visit her every day and she usually recognizes me."

"I assume Abby is still with her?"

"Yes, thank goodness. I don't know what I would do without Abby. I was able to persuade most of my staff to move with me, so I don't have to make explanations to new people and train them as to what I require."

"That's a blessing, at least."

"I was due some good luck." Jared sat in a leather chair and motioned for Mark to take the companion one. "Is there still talk in London?"

"It's dying down. Has there been any trouble here?"

"No. Yvonne has been rather docile since the move. There were some bad times before she became accustomed to her new room, but they're behind us now."

The butler brought a tray with two sherry glasses. He offered the first to Mark.

"Thank you, Stanford."

The butler bowed slightly, then presented the tray to Jared.

"Are you here for a while?" Jared asked his cousin.

"I'm here through the summer, if you'll have me. I decided London can do without me for a season. If I'm too much trouble, you're to say so."

"You know I would. You're to consider Ravenwood your home." Jared sipped the sherry. "I can't tell you how glad I am of someone to talk with. I've let the townsfolk believe I'm a hermit, and while it was necessary, it has been lonely."

"You can't mean you've met no one in the month you've been here! No one at all?"

"Only one to speak of. A few days ago when I was riding, I discovered a young lady wandering in search of her horse. It had thrown her and she wasn't happy about walking home."

"Surely you didn't leave her to do that!"

"Of course not. I haven't become uncivilized just because I left London. I gave her a ride home behind me. Her parents looked as if they were ready to lynch me, but there was no way around it. She wasn't close to my stable, and I wouldn't trust my horse not to throw her." He frowned. "You'd think they would have been so glad to see her unharmed that they would wink at her riding double."

"Jared, Jared. What am I to do with you? There are certain proprieties that have to be followed. How old was this young lady?"

"Old enough to be interesting. She was a beauty. Dark brown hair and eyes the color of the blue in pansies."

"You seem to have been paying close attention. What was her name?"

"Rachel Pennington. She said the baron who lived here allowed her to ride in his pastures. I don't know if that's true or not, but I hinted that I wouldn't extend the same invitation. I can't have people wandering here and there over my property. What if they come too close to the house and there's a problem with Yvonne?''

"What could happen that Abby couldn't take care of? Frankly, I wouldn't want to tangle with that woman. If she ever smiled, her face would crack.''

"She doesn't care much for men, but she's good to Yvonne. That's all I care about. It's a relief to know she isn't likely to decide to marry and leave my employ. Abby would be difficult to replace.''

"I can see how that would present a problem. This Miss Pennington—it is Miss, isn't it?'' When Jared nodded, Mark continued, "Are we likely to see her again soon?''

"I can't speak for you, but I have no intention of it. I'm afraid you'll find Ravenwood boring after London, but it has to be this way.''

"I still don't agree, but I'll bow to your decision. I was only thinking how pleasant the company of a young lady is when the spring flowers are in bloom.''

Jared smiled. "Ever the romantic, Mark? I can no longer afford that luxury.''

"You must reenter society someday,'' Mark argued. "You can't expect to bury yourself alive here in the country and never speak to people again.''

"I have no such intentions. I'll return to London often, if not to my old haunts. I enjoy travel. Perhaps I'll do the Grand Tour again.''

"Someday you'll want to marry, and that requires the company of at least one young lady.''

"I'll cross that bridge when I come to it. For now my responsibility lies with Yvonne. My own needs and desires will have to come second.''

"I have to admit I admire you,'' Mark said. "Not many would do what you're doing.''

"Not many would have the need to.'' He raised his glass. "Here's to a spring and summer that is more enjoyable than I expected it to be before your arrival.''

"Hear, hear!''

Chapter Three

Rachel dressed in her best riding habit and told Harry to saddle Princess. She didn't want to push her luck when she was already about to overstep the bounds.

As soon as her mare was ready, Rachel mounted and rode away in the direction of Beatrice's house. When she was out of sight, however, she cut through the fields and cantered toward Ravenwood.

She was somewhat distressed that she was about to break several conventions, but her parents had been frustratingly stubborn about not calling on Jared Prescott, despite the fact that he had come to her aid, and Rachel felt that should be remedied.

When she reached the hill that protected Ravenwood from the north winds, she slowed her mount and traveled at a more sedate gait across the green that rolled up to the Elizabethan country house's entrance.

Ravenwood had been built in the late 1500s when a popular style was to form houses in the shape of an E in honor of the queen. Rachel had never been inside the house, but she, like most of Fairfield's residents, was curious about it. The old baron had been a bit of a recluse due to ill health, and no one could remember a time when Ravenwood entertained. Rachel thought it was sad, and as she neared the house she wondered if it somehow missed the days when women in farthingales and men in ruffs filled its rooms with laughter. She was certain that if she closed her eyes, she could see them in her mind's eye.

She dismounted and tied her horse at the post. By the time she reached the door, the butler, a man she didn't recognize, had opened it. He observed her coolly for a moment as if he knew she had no business here. "Yes, madam?" he said.

"I've come to call on Mrs. Prescott. Is she in?" Rachel, like everyone else in Fairfield, assumed there was no Mrs. Prescott, but she reasoned that Jared might not know what others' assumptions about him were.

"I'm afraid there is no such lady," the butler said in an unwelcoming voice. "It seems there has been a mistake."

"No Mrs. Prescott? Oh, dear." Rachel sighed and opened her eyes wider. "I had no idea. Otherwise I would never have come." She looked beyond the man but could only see part of the dark wood of the screens passage that formed one wall of the hall and nothing else. Her effort to see Jared again was blocked, and she knew there was nothing she could do but to leave. She fished a calling card out of her reticule and handed it to the butler. "Will you give this to Mr. Prescott along with the regards of my family?"

As she turned to go, she heard someone say, "Did I hear you talking to someone, Stanford?"

Rachel turned back hopefully. The butler stepped aside, revealing the presence of a man about Jared's age who bore a slight resemblance to him, though his coloring was lighter. "Hello," he said. "I didn't know Jared was expecting callers."

Rachel held her breath and made herself blush. "I'm afraid I've made an embarrassing mistake. I've come to call on Mrs. Prescott, and I've just discovered there is no such person."

"Allow me to introduce myself. I'm Mark Paynter. Jared and I are first cousins."

"I'm Rachel Pennington. I live on the neighboring estate. Mr. Prescott and I met briefly, and I had thought to call on his wife."

"Mark? Are you talking to someone?" she heard Jared call from down the passage.

"Come see," Mark called back. "We have a most charming visitor." To Rachel he said, "Won't you come in?"

"No, no. I couldn't possibly." She wished she could say just the opposite and step inside the passage, but without a chaperon it would have been highly improper.

Jared joined them, but his face didn't register the interest that his cousin's did. "It's you. Don't tell me you've been thrown again."

"No, I have not." Rachel felt her cheeks blaze in a real blush. "I merely came to pay my respects."

"She didn't know you have no wife," Mark supplied for her.

"Remarkable. I would have assumed that by now everyone in the village knew that, as well as the fact that I discourage visitors."

"You needn't be rude," Rachel snapped. "I was only being courteous—but perhaps you are unable to recognize such a quality."

"She has you there," Mark said with a grin.

Jared frowned at his cousin as if to silence him. Mark refused to interpret the look. "Come, let's walk in the garden," Mark suggested. "If you can't come inside, we'll come out with you."

Jared looked as if he would refuse, but then he stepped out behind Mark. Rachel gazed up at him and her heart did the fluttery dance it had done on the other occasion she had seen him. "I suppose it wouldn't do any harm to see your garden."

They walked down the drive and around the end of the house. Ravenwood's formal gardens had been designed at the same time as the house, and subsequent owners had added to them until they were truly magnificent. Nearest the house were clipped avenues of yew and bushes trimmed into the shapes of spirals, globes and pyramids. The ground was covered with paved paths and knot gardens, some fashioned with an emphasis on color, others on scents. Beyond were roses, some of which were already in bloom. In the distance behind the house, Rachel could see the corner of the maze, which was one of Ravenwood's distinctive features.

"It's lovely here," she said truthfully.

"You've never been here?" Mark asked.

"No, the baron was old and sick. He never entertained."

"I would have said that wouldn't stop you," Jared remarked. "After all, you were free enough with my pastures."

Mark looked at Jared, amazed to hear such inhospitable words come from his mouth. "What Jared means, I'm sure, is that in such a small town there must be few secrets to anyone."

"Generally speaking, there aren't." She wondered why she found Jared so much more exciting than his handsome cousin. Was it because he refused to return her flirting? Rachel had never met anyone who wouldn't flirt back with her. Then, Jared's eyes met hers, and for an instant Rachel forgot Mark's existence. She saw concern in his eyes, as if he had worries that she didn't comprehend, but she also saw a man's interest in a woman.

Feeling more in her element, she smiled and said, "If only my friend Beatrice Gaston were here. She would love to see these gardens. Next to Ravenwood, the Gastons have the prettiest garden around. Not even ours is equal to it."

"You enjoy gardens?" Mark asked when Jared refused to speak.

"I do. I suppose everyone must. Why else would every house have one?"

"A good point." Pointedly speaking to Jared, Mark added, "Don't you think so?"

"I was wondering how it can be that our lovely visitor didn't know I wasn't married. Surely, Miss Pennington, there must be talk about me in town."

"Yes, there is, but no one seems to know much about you. I had heard you might be a bachelor, but I thought that was unlikely."

"Why?" he asked.

She faltered. She couldn't say it was because he was so handsome. Not when he was refusing to flirt with her. He might think she was promiscuous. "Because you bought such a large house. When we heard it was sold, we assumed it must have gone to a large family, or at least to a couple who expected to entertain a great deal. Why else would one want such a great house?"

"Sometimes one merely wants a lovely home in which one may be left alone." Jared smiled but it didn't reach his eyes. "My family or lack of it is no one's business."

"Then you should have stayed in London where you could be anonymous, not moved to a place like Fairfield where we all know everything about one another."

"You see?" Mark asked. "My very words."

"Nevertheless, I'm here and here I'll stay. Perhaps you could all pretend the old baron is back and leave me alone."

"It's not the same. The baron was old and sick, not a hermit by temperament. In his youth he probably entertained quite often." She looked around. "This would be a lovely place for parties. Do you have a ballroom?"

Mark put in, "The old hall has been converted to a ballroom. It's quite remarkable. The house had fallen to disrepair in places, but Jared is putting it right again."

Jared frowned at his cousin as if he wished Mark would stop volunteering information to the woman. "There now. We've reached the end of the garden. As you can see, the roses are only starting to bud and there's not much to see. You should have waited until next month."

"I could come back," Rachel said, perversely hoping to make him feel more ill at ease. "And I could bring Beatrice."

"Tell me about your friend," Mark said when Jared didn't follow up with an invitation. "Is she as pretty as you?"

Rachel laughed. "I'm not pretty. You're teasing me."
She smiled up at him in a way that displayed her dimple to
its best advantage, and she lowered her dark eyelashes to
give him a flirtatious glance. "Beatrice is the real beauty in
Fairfield. She has blond hair and blue eyes and is terribly
popular with everyone."

"Your eyes are blue," Jared observed, though he seemed
to have done it in spite of himself.

Rachel didn't know quite what to say. He didn't play by
the rules. "Yes. They're blue."

"About the color of pansies, wouldn't you say, Jared?"
Mark prompted.

"Approximately." Jared seemed to think he had gone far
enough already.

"About this friend," Mark said. "Does she have a particular beau? Is she spoken for?"

"Not yet. We are both holding out for a man who will
steal our hearts away." Rachel made the truthful words
sound like banter. "No one in Fairfield fits that description."

"That's a pity. If this Beatrice is more beautiful than
you, it's a shame to leave her languishing in the country
undiscovered."

Jared made a growling sound in his throat.

Rachel ignored him. "I've enjoyed talking to you, Mr.
Paynter. Perhaps we may meet again."

"Please, call me Mark. It seems such a pity to stand on
formality so far from London."

"Mark, then." Rachel smiled up at him as if he, not
Jared, were the target of her interests. When Jared didn't
take the bait she said, "I really must be going. I had no intention of taking up so much of your time. Thank you for
showing me Ravenwood's gardens."

"You're welcome at any time." Mark made a small bow
to her. Jared glared at them both.

When they had seen Rachel back to her horse and Mark
had helped her to mount, Jared told her goodbye as briefly
as possible. As she cantered away he turned to his cousin.

"Why did you do that? You know I was trying to discourage people, and her in particular, from visiting here. You even invited her to come back again and hinted that we want to meet this Beatrice!"

"I said *I* want to meet her. You may sit here and gather moss if you like. You're making a mistake in not having any contact with your neighbors. They will be talking about you more for your eccentricities than for any other reason they might discern."

"Why can't everyone just leave me alone? That's all I'm asking."

"I told you that you should have stayed in London. A man may lose himself there."

"You know why that wasn't possible."

Mark looked up at the upper floor of the house. "Is she really so bad?"

"Why else would I have suddenly become a recluse? You know me better than that." He frowned upward as if he, too, could see past the stone walls and the reflection of the sky on the windowpanes. "I must ride to town and post a letter to the foreman of my mill in Haversham. Would you like to ride with me?"

"Of course. I'll send around for our horses."

In a few minutes they were on their way to Fairfield. Jared tried not to make eye contact with anyone as they rode into town, thereby forgoing the need to nod or to speak. Mark didn't follow his example. Fairfield was a quiet town with winding cobbled streets and houses made of the local pale gold stone. Most of the smaller houses had thatched roofs draped over them like the forelock on a pony. Each house had a garden of flowers in the yard, and most had fences with gates set beneath trellises of roses or arches of iron tracery. The shops were small and the buildings set close together with an occasional narrow wynd between. There were costermongers here and there calling out their wares, but after the bustle of London, Fairfield was sleepy and rustic.

"I rather like this place," Mark commented. "I'm finally beginning to see what drew you here."

"Ravenwood drew me here. It was for sale and was near enough London for me to stay in contact with my investments. I didn't see the village before I purchased the house."

"If I weren't so fond of you, I'd say you've become peculiar. I'll say it anyway. You're peculiar."

"Thank you for your assessment. Here's where I post my letters."

They dismounted and tied their horses. Inside the building a man with ink-stained cuffs took the letter, read the address and looked curiously at Jared. "Family in Haversham? Nice place, Haversham. I was there not three years ago."

Jared gave him a cool stare. "Here's money for the postage."

"Haversham has that river that flows through the town," the postmaster continued. "A right pretty place. My eldest brother's wife is from there. Maybe you know the family—Albright?"

"I've never met them." Jared turned to go.

"It's a real pity, what happened the other night," the postmaster added. "A real pity. I don't believe Fairfield has ever seen the like."

"What happened?" Mark asked.

"A woman was killed."

Jared stopped as if he had been turned to stone.

"A woman died, you say?" Mark asked carefully.

"Murdered, she was. Knifed. Someone cut her throat."

Jared heard a ringing in his ears. Surely it was a coincidence. "Who was she?"

"A woman by the name of Liza Barnes. You'd not be likely to know her. Old Liza was more apt to frequent the Bull and Bear than the better spots. She was fond of her bottle, was Liza."

"That explains it then," Jared said. "The Bull and Bear looks to me like the sort of place where that might happen."

"Not in Fairfield. Now I'm not saying there's never been a killing here, nor none at the Bull and Bear, but whatever else she might have been, Liza was a woman. I'd have said there's not a soul in this town that would knife a woman in the back and cut her throat for good measure. The stabbing alone would have been enough to kill her from what I hear."

Jared met Mark's eyes. Mark no longer looked so cheerful. "Does the sheriff have a suspect?"

"No, he don't. Can't nobody recall hearing Liza fighting with nobody that night. She was behaving better than usual, I hear tell. That's one reason everybody is so upset."

"Maybe somebody bore a grudge against her from a time when her behavior wasn't so exemplary," Jared said wryly. "She sounds like the sort who would nurture grudges."

"She was, for a fact, but there just isn't nobody that was mad enough at her to kill her, according to her cronies."

"Perhaps it was one of the cronies who did it." Jared looked back at Mark. "We should be going."

When they were riding out of town, Mark said, "It has to be a coincidence. She couldn't have done it."

"I keep telling myself that, but I'm not sure. He said the woman was knifed in the back and her throat cut unnecessarily. That sounds too familiar."

"How closely does Abby watch Yvonne?"

"I've never seen one without the other since the trouble in London. Abby sleeps in the room between Yvonne and the corridor. She couldn't leave without passing through Abby's room."

"Is Abby a sound sleeper?"

"No. That's one reason I'm convinced she is reliable. She says she would wake up if a feather touched the floor. I believe her."

"Then Yvonne couldn't possibly have murdered this Liza Barnes. It's a coincidence, nothing more. You have to get on with your life, Jared."

"You wonder, too."

Mark tried to deny it, but finally said, "It does seem a bit too familiar."

"As soon as we reach home, I'll go up and talk to Abby." He put his heels to his horse, encouraging it to increase its pace.

"He's wonderfully handsome." Rachel sighed. "What a pity he doesn't seem to like women."

"Surely you don't mean he's like Mortimer Cranston!"

"No, no! I mean he doesn't like *me.*" Rachel let her lower lip pout. "I gave him every opportunity to flirt with me, and he wouldn't do so much as wink."

"I still can't imagine having enough spunk to go there alone! My mother would swoon at the thought."

"So would mine, so we aren't going to let her find out." Rachel sat on the side of Beatrice's bed and toyed with the fringe on one of the pillows piled on the counterpane. "I don't know why I can't seem to get him out of my mind. He was as close to rude to me as any man I've ever seen."

"Rude? Surely not."

"Not rude in the sense that I wouldn't want to see him again, but rude in that he didn't offer me any encouragement. What do you think of a man who would do that?"

"I wouldn't know what to think. Tell me again about his cousin. You say he's handsome?"

Rachel nodded. "He has brown hair and blue eyes. He isn't quite as tall as Jared, but he must be nearly six feet."

"'Jared'? You call him by his first name?" Beatrice looked delightedly shocked.

"Only to his back. Mark insisted that I call him by his given name, however, so I don't think it's too forward of me. After all, Jared never said I shouldn't."

"I'd never have the nerve to do half of what you do. I admire you so."

"Fairfield is so boring, I have to do something. Wouldn't it be awful if we grow as old as our parents and never have an adventure of any sort? What a waste that would be!"

"My parents were never young—I'm sure of it. They seem to have no notion of what it's like to live so close to London and never visit there. *They* go. Mama and Papa are going there as soon as the party is over."

"That's right," Rachel said thoughtfully. "You are having a party next week."

"You hadn't forgotten, had you? You must come."

"Of course I will. Have I ever missed a party? I was thinking that it would be nice to add a couple of names to the list."

Beatrice's eyes widened. "I couldn't! Mama and Papa would half kill me!"

"They wouldn't know until it was too late. I think it would only be polite to invite our new neighbor and his guest."

"Mama would never agree. She would refuse."

"Did you ask her?"

"No, but . . ."

"Then we don't know that for sure. It might have been merely an oversight that Jared and Mark were left off the guest list. In that case, she would be pleased that we remembered and invited them."

"Rachel, we couldn't!"

"Do you want to meet Mark Paynter or not? I have no idea how long he may be staying. He's handsome and I'll bet he can dance."

"Do you think so?" Beatrice weakened visibly. "He's really handsome? You aren't just telling me this so I'll invite Jared? There—now you have *me* calling him by his first name and we haven't met at all."

"Mark is all I told you and more. I think you would make a wonderful couple. His coloring is slightly darker than yours, and your heights are compatible. He has probably left a string of broken hearts in London."

"If he's used to London girls, he won't be interested in me." Beatrice said the words as if she knew they weren't true. She was almost as accomplished a flirt as Rachel, and she had left enough broken hearts in her own wake to feel confident of her power over men. "How can we do it?"

"Follow me."

They left Beatrice's room and slipped into the back parlor where Mrs. Gaston did all her correspondence. As they had hoped, she wasn't in the room. Rachel went to the secretary and pulled down the desk top. Taking a sheet of paper that bore the flourishing *G* that was Mrs. Gaston's trademark, she began to write.

"There," she said when the note was complete. "Read it and tell me if it sounds like something your mother would write."

Beatrice read, "Due to an oversight on my part, your name was inadvertently left off my guest list for a party we plan to have on May 27. I hope you'll forgive my error and honor us with your company. I've heard you have a houseguest, Mr. Mark Paynter, and I look forward to meeting you both." Beatrice smiled at her friend. "It sounds exactly like Mama."

"Good. Let me sign it and you take it to whoever delivers notes for you." She signed Mrs. Gaston's name, shook sand over the ink, folded the paper and put it in an envelope. Beatrice opened a drawer and took out the thick gold seals her mother used to close envelopes and pressed it in place on the flap. "There. It's done."

Rachel handed her the envelope. "Be convincing."

For a moment Beatrice held the envelope to her breast as if she were deciding if this was really the best thing to do, then she hurried off in search of a servant.

"I did it!" she announced when she returned. "I sent the invitation to them!"

"Wonderful. Now we have to decide how to wear our hair and which dress looks best on us."

They went back to Beatrice's room and Rachel opened her wardrobe. With the familiarity of an old friend, she said, "Not the yellow one. It's not right with your hair. What about this pink one?"

"I wore it to the Flournoys' party last week."

"Mark won't know that."

"Everyone else will. Maybe the blue silk?"

Rachel pulled it out and they examined it minutely. "This will be fine. I had planned to wear my blue one, but I'll wear my rose Irish with the lace collar and cuffs."

"That looks so pretty on you. Would you like to borrow my locket?"

"The one shaped like a heart? Perfect. And I'll bring you that bunch of silk violets that I bought to go with my sarcenet shoulder cape. They will go beautifully with this shade of blue."

"What would we do without each other?" Beatrice asked with a laugh. "I would never have the daring to add names to Mama's guest list, let alone think of what to wear."

"We must dress together so we can do each other's hair. My Jane is skillful at dressing hair, but for a night as important as this, we need to look better than we ever have before."

"Come over as soon as you can get out of the house. It may take hours for us to be pleased with our hair."

"I'm going to bring silk flowers for mine," Rachel decided. "Real ones have a terrible habit of wilting and turning brown just as a party starts."

"I know. It's terrible. I'll wear silk ones, too."

Rachel hugged her friend. "Won't we be marvelous? Jared and Mark won't be able to resist us."

Beatrice nodded. "I just hope Mama isn't too angry at me."

"She won't be. Besides, they plan to leave early the next morning, and she will have forgotten all about it by the time they return."

"That's true," Beatrice said with rising spirits. "Can I borrow your blue shoes? Mine are getting worn and I want to impress Mark." She giggled. "I can hardly wait."

Chapter Four

"What's this, Stanford?" Jared asked as he took the letter from the silver card tray and studied the swirled *G* on the back of the envelope.

"It came from the Gaston house," the butler replied. "Their man is waiting for a reply."

Jared broke the seal and took out a sheet of cream-colored paper topped with another of the elaborate initials. It was an invitation to a party. "Tell the man I won't be attending." He held out the note for his butler to take, but Mark intercepted it.

"I believe you would be making a mistake not to attend this party."

"In what way?"

"I've been talking to those who know, and I've learned that Miss Pennington and Miss Gaston are particular friends. Miss Pennington is almost certain to be there."

"Talking? Talking to whom?"

Mark smiled. "To servants. They always know these things."

Jared was thoughtful for a moment. Since he had talked with Rachel Pennington in his garden, she had been in his thoughts more often than was comfortable. "I ought to avoid her above all others."

To Stanford, Mark said, "Tell their man we will both attend."

Stanford looked to his master, and on hearing no objection from him, he left to do as he had been told.

Once Stanford was out of earshot, Jared said, "You ought not to have done that. I told you I'm refusing all party invitations. That way I don't have to reciprocate. I can't have guests here. What if Yvonne was having one of her bad days? Someone might hear her."

"Still, it would be nice to hold Miss Pennington in your arms, wouldn't it? I bless the name of the man who invented dancing. I'm certain it must have been a man—it's too perfect an opportunity for a man to embrace a woman and to talk to her alone without anyone raising an eyebrow."

"And I'm equally certain for the same reasons that a woman is to credit for the custom." Jared smiled across at his cousin. He enjoyed debating with Mark. The country sometimes seemed too quiet and lonely. "I should call the man back and tell him I won't be there."

"Did you procrastinate long enough before deciding to recall him? Let me see." Mark moved to the window. "Precisely. I see him crossing the green now. Alas, but it is too late." He turned back to his cousin with a knowing grin. "I wish I had your sense of timing."

"I didn't do it on purpose," Jared protested, but he wasn't certain this was true. He would indeed like to see Rachel and to hold her in his arms, if only for a dance. He wondered how old she was. There was an untouched quality about her that he found intriguing and irritating at the same time.

"I'm surprised we were invited so late. Do you suppose Miss Pennington and Miss Gaston had anything to do with it personally?"

"I have no idea. You can ask while you are dancing with them." Jared took his pocket watch from his waistcoat and studied the engraving on the gold casing. The elegant timepiece had been given to him by his father with instructions that someday Jared was to place it in his own son's hands. He knew that behind the gesture, his father had been hint-

ing that it was time for Jared to marry and start a family.
That had been two years ago. He replaced the watch. "How
old would you say Miss Pennington is?"

Mark looked up from the globe he was inspecting beside
the library desk. "I have no idea. Nineteen? Twenty?"

"She acts younger."

"Does she? I hadn't noticed."

"I'm nearly thirty."

"You were thirty on your last birthday," Mark cor-
rected. "I will be thirty in June."

"Thank you for keeping score," Jared said wryly.

"Thirty isn't too old to marry. Our fathers have often
said that a man doesn't settle down before that age."

"I have no intention of settling down at all." Jared rose
and went to the window. Clouds were building along the
horizon. There would be rain before morning. "Perhaps if
I don't show up, the Gastons will decide not to include my
name on their guest lists in the future."

"And I will have both Miss Pennington and Miss Gaston to myself." Mark sounded pleased.

Jared smiled. He knew exactly what Mark was doing,
and he was convinced that Mark wouldn't quit trying until
he began mixing into society again. He turned to him.
"Once I'm in full demand, as you seem so convinced I
should be, how do I reciprocate? Have you given consideration to that?"

"As a matter of fact, I have. Always have dance or
chamber music when you have guests. The music will cover
any noises Yvonne might make upstairs."

"You don't think people will find it odd that I'm always
surrounded by music? That they will be followed from
parlor to table to drawing room by musicians?"

"It will take some planning, but you can do it."

Jared knew Mark was oversimplifying the problem, but
he was lonely. And he especially wanted to get to know
Rachel. "All right. I'll attend this one party. But remember—I'm not making a habit of it."

"I'll remember," Mark said with a smile.

* * *

"I'm certain Mama suspects something," Beatrice said as she pinned Rachel's hair into loops and curls. "Did you see the way she looked at me during tea?"

"It's your imagination. Do you think my hair is too curly? The rain last night made it frizz."

"No, it didn't. Mine is impossible, however." She stole a glance at her reflection in the mirror. "Look how straight it is! It will never hold the curls."

"Let me worry about that. Is my dress all right?"

"It's beautiful. That color looks good on you with your dark hair. I could never wear that shade of rose."

Rachel was still worried. She knew she had to look her best tonight because this might be her last chance. She pinched her cheeks until they were rosy. "I wish we had some rouge."

"Mama would die if she caught me wearing rouge!" Beatrice patted Rachel's hair and examined it critically. "There. Move your head and see if it feels secure."

Rachel shook her head and the curls bounced merrily. "It's perfect. I wish I had your talent with hair."

Beatrice laughed. "Move over. It's my turn."

As Rachel brushed her friend's long blond hair, she said, "I was surprised when Jared and Mark accepted the invitation. I frankly didn't think they would."

"What will Papa say when they arrive?"

"We will meet them at the door, and then he can't possibly send them away. Not that he would. Your father is the soul of hospitality. I doubt that he would tell them to leave even if he knew they weren't invited."

"No, but afterward my parents will have something to say to me."

"I'll stay and see it through with you. After all, it was my idea." She began coiling Beatrice's hair into an elegant roll that left the sides soft and flattering about her face. "I wish my hair was as manageable as yours."

"You don't know what you're wishing for." Beatrice bit her lips to bring color into them. "If I start looking too pale, be sure and give me a signal."

"I will, and you're to do the same." Her eyes met Beatrice's in the mirror. "Won't it be wonderful if we make them fall in love with us tonight?"

Beatrice smiled and her eyes lit with the thrill of the chase. "I can hardly wait to meet Mark Paynter after all you've told me. He sounds too good to be true."

By the time the first guests arrived that evening, Rachel and Beatrice were dressed and ready and hovering close to the door so they could intercept their special invitees as soon as they arrived. "What if they don't come?" Beatrice whispered to Rachel.

"Then we will have to think of some other way to get to know them." As she turned her attention back to the door, Jared and Mark stepped into the room. Suddenly, her throat went dry and excitement raced through her. In his black evening habit and white silk waistcoat, Jared Prescott was even more handsome than she remembered.

He had removed his cape and was handing it, along with his top hat and cane, to the butler. His hair was only a shade lighter than the ebony of his evening coat and he wore it soft rather than pomaded. She noted that Mark was similarly dressed and that Beatrice was staring at him in admiration. As she looked back to Jared, her eyes met his and she felt her blood warming. All her attention became centered on Jared to the exclusion of all else, and he seemed to be equally struck by her.

Beatrice punched her in the back, breaking the spell. "Papa is coming. We have to get over there!"

Rachel smoothly crossed the few yards separating them from their special guests and smiled up at Jared. "I'm glad you came."

"So am I." His voice was warm and caressing. He seemed to catch himself and remembered to smile at Beatrice. "Miss Gaston, I presume."

"How silly of me to forget you haven't met." Rachel glanced at her friend. "Beatrice, this is Mr. Jared Prescott, and his cousin, Mr. Mark Paynter. Gentlemen, this is Miss Beatrice Gaston. There now. You've been formally introduced and may dance together without any breach of propriety.'' She smiled up at Jared.

He took his cue. ''May I have this dance?''

With her heart thrumming, Rachel put her hand in his, and they were on the dance floor before Beatrice's father had time to make his way across the room.

''I'm surprised the Gastons asked me tonight,'' Jared said as he swept her into a waltz. ''I've turned down several of their invitations, and I had thought they would have given up by now.''

''They love parties, and single men are hard to find in Fairfield. At least that's what Mrs. Gaston says.''

''And I suppose you had nothing to do with it?''

''I might have had the tiniest bit of a hand in it.''

''Why? Haven't I given you enough clues to suggest to you that I don't want to be sociable?''

''Yes, but I don't believe you.''

Jared whirled her around until she was breathless. ''Why not?''

''Because your eyes don't agree with your words.''

He fell silent, and she wondered if she had gone too far. She had said only the truth. If he had wanted to be left alone, he would have refused to walk in the garden with her, and he would have been far more disagreeable. ''Why did you try to make me think you dislike me?'' she asked.

''Perhaps it's because I do.''

She didn't for a moment believe he was speaking the truth, so she waited in silence, hoping that would signal to him that she wanted him to give her an honest answer. Finally he said, ''It's because I don't want to become involved with anyone now.''

''And you think you would become involved with me?'' She smiled up at him. ''I like that idea.''

Jared felt something move within him that he had thought he never would experience. His heart was beating faster than the music. This young woman in his arms was as light as thistledown. Her head barely came to his shoulder, and he was intrigued with the way her curls bounced whenever she moved. He longed to touch the flowers in her hair to see if they were real, and especially to see if her hair was as soft as it looked.

"You could be a dangerous lady," he found himself saying.

"Could I? I've never thought of myself in that light before."

"You should stay as far from me as possible."

Rachel was quiet for a moment. "I don't think I can do that."

"Don't flirt with me. I've parried with some of the most accomplished flirts London has to offer, and I've always been the victor."

"I wasn't flirting then. I really meant what I said." Her eyes gazed up at him, and he felt himself becoming lost.

He wanted the music to last forever, yet he also wanted it to stop so he could escape while he still retained a bit of his heart. "Something is happening, and I'm not sure I like it," he said in a bemused voice.

"I feel it, too." She spoke the words so softly, he heard them more with his heart than his ears.

"I started not to come. I told Mark he would have to come without me."

"Why did you change your mind?"

"I don't know. Curiosity, perhaps. I have to confess I've thought of you often."

"Have you?" The dimple he had noticed before appeared in her cheek again.

"You're flirting again. Be honest with me."

"I've thought about you, too. Since it's honesty you want, I must confess that Beatrice and I sent you that invitation."

"You did? The Gastons weren't expecting us?" He glanced around the room but his eyes returned to Rachel. "What if they had turned us away?"

"They wouldn't have done that. You should speak to them, however. Mrs. Gaston is the lady in the pink ruffles," she said as she looked about for the party's hostess.

"Over there," she said, nodding toward a couple dancing near the musicians. "The man she's dancing with is Mr. Gaston."

Jared made a mental note of the couple she had indicated.

As the music ended, Rachel watched Beatrice and Mark leave the dance floor holding hands. "Beatrice and Mark make a handsome couple," she observed.

"They do, indeed," he agreed. "Were you matchmaking? Mark is no more suited to your friend than I am to you. He lives in London and will be gone by the end of the summer."

"He will stay so long? Wonderful." Rachel led him toward the punch bowls. "We had only hoped for a week or two."

Jared knew he couldn't win. He could easily match wits with a woman bent only on flirting, but Rachel seemed to have larger stakes in mind. He wondered if he was misreading her intentions.

He got a cup of punch for each of them, his from the men's bowl, hers from the ladies'. As he sipped his, he watched her eyes dancing as she looked about the room. When she turned back to him and made eye contact, he felt flushed. He told himself this peculiar feeling was due to the rum base of the men's punch, but he knew that wasn't so. Even before his first sip, Rachel's gaze had had that effect on him. Worse yet was that she knew it, too.

When the music began again, he put his cup on a passing waiter's tray. "Dance?"

Her smile of assent almost stopped his heart. She motioned for the waiter to take her cup and put her hand in Jared's. As he escorted her onto the floor, he decided he had better guide their conversation to a safer subject than the path his thoughts were trying to take. As he took her into his arms, he said, "I'm pleasantly surprised at the musical talent Fairfield has produced."

"The Gastons bring these particular musicians from London. Mr. and Mrs. Gaston spend most of their time in

London, and when they are home, they are constantly entertaining. Beatrice sometimes feels deserted by them. Especially when her brother was away."

"She has a brother?"

Rachel nodded and looked about the room. "That's Rob over there by the French doors. He's the one who is glaring at us."

Jared followed her glance. The young man looked angry enough to kill. "Why is he so upset?"

"Because you're dancing with me. He's jealous."

"Is that your ploy? To use me to make a suitor jealous?" He felt an unexpected stab of disappointment.

"No. I want to discourage Rob. He's unbelievably boring. We were never really friends, not even when we were children. I can't imagine how Beatrice managed to have such a dull brother. I suspect even his parents are disappointed in him, though I could be wrong about that."

"You certainly talk freely."

"I have to. I don't know when I may see you again, and I want us to get acquainted. I have to make the most of every moment."

Jared had never felt so favored, not even by the belles of London, and knew he should be resisting. "You have no business getting to know me at all." He hoped his words had sounded gruffer to her than they had to him.

"I've never met anyone who was so determined to make a bad impression as you seem to be. Why do you want me to think you dislike me so much?"

"I told you. I don't want social invitations."

"Yet, you are here, and we're dancing. You dance beautifully, by the way."

"Thank you. So do you." He whirled her, and her cheeks flushed with excitement. "I think you enjoy dancing more than any woman I've ever seen."

"Someday I plan to have a home of my own and to throw parties like the Gastons. My parents rarely entertain, and when they do, their guests are usually stuffy. In my house

there will always be music." Her dark blue eyes sparkled up
at him. "That's why I'm determined not to marry Rob."

Jared faltered. "He's asked you to marry him?"

"Not yet, but he's asked my father's permission to court
me with that goal in mind, so he might as well have. Beatrice says he told her he intends to propose."

"No wonder he's glaring at us. Will I have to fight my
way out, do you suppose?"

Rachel laughed. "Fight Rob? He wouldn't have the nerve
to so much as speak harshly to you. I told you, he's as dull
as dishwater."

"A dull man may still fight for what he believes to be his
own."

"If Rob thinks he has a claim on me, he's sadly mistaken." Rachel tossed her head and her curls bobbed. "I've
tried to dissuade him nicely, but he's stubborn. Especially
since Papa is in his camp."

Jared tried not to feel jealous and reminded himself that
he wanted no ties with any woman. "He's not bad looking
and his sister is your best friend."

"True, but you haven't talked to Rob. He was gone to
America for years, and on his return all he could talk about
was the weather there. Can you imagine? I wanted to hear
about Indians and buffalo."

Jared laughed. "What do you want to know about them?
I've seen both."

"You have? I didn't know you traveled."

"As a matter of fact, I travel a great deal. Or at least I did
at one time." He remembered Yvonne and added, "Not
anymore."

"Are Indians really red? Does the ground tremble when
buffalo walk?"

"Actually, Indians are more brown than red. And the
ground does shake when a herd of buffalo is on the move,
because the herds are so large. A buffalo is bigger than a
cow, yet they move quite fast. I saw a herd once that covered an area larger than the distance between Fairfield and
London."

"No! You're just making that up."

"No, I'm not."

She was silent for a moment. "I wonder if I'll ever see anything like that. I don't want to marry Rob or anyone like him and stay here in Fairfield all my life."

"What do you want? I thought all women wanted to marry and have a family."

"I want that, too, but I also want to see buffalo and Indians. I want to see a mountain with snow on it, and I want to sail on a ship. Not a boat—a ship. One big enough to go all the way around the world."

"That's a long way from Fairfield."

"I know. Rob is through with traveling. He doesn't like it and wants to settle down and raise dull sons like himself."

"He told you that?"

"No, Beatrice did. Look. He's coming this way."

Jared skillfully swept her across the floor away from Rob, and when they reached the other side, he said, "Do you want to step outside for fresh air?"

"No, he'll find us for sure that way. Come with me."

She took his hand and led him out of the ballroom and down a short corridor. Looking back over her shoulder, she opened a door and drew him into the library, then closed the door behind her.

In the soft, golden glow of candlelight, Jared looked around at the collection of books. Most appeared as if they never had been opened, let alone used as frequently as his own. That told him more about the Gastons than dozens of words could have. He had never trusted a person who bought books and never read them. *"Cave ab homine unius libri,"* he said.

"Pardon?"

"'Beware the man of one book.'" Jared walked to the shelves on the opposite side of the room for a closer inspection. "None of these seems to have been handled much."

"You're right. They haven't. Beatrice and I have read some of them, but Rob and his parents aren't much on reading."

"Did you enjoy the books you read?"

"Not particularly. Mr. Gaston bought them for their colors, you see, and we found them dreadfully dull."

Jared smiled. "What do you read?"

"Mrs. Radcliffe, of course. *The Mysteries of Udolpho* is my favorite book. I enjoyed *The Castle of Otranto,* too, but Walpole is more difficult to read. I could never understand why that huge helmet fell on the prince, or where it came from."

"That's in the first pages. Did you read on?"

"Yes, but it never captured me. Not like *Udolpho.* Beatrice vowed to someday have at least one adventure as exciting as some that happened to Emily."

"And as great a love?"

"You've read it, too! You know about Emily and Valancourt!"

"I confess." He laughed softly. He was enjoying himself. "Have you read Thackeray?"

"*Vanity Fair?* Of course. Have you?" She lowered her voice. "Someday I'm going to find one of Mrs. Thompson's novels and read it."

"I thought her writings were considered too scandalous for a lady's interest."

"So I've heard. That's why I'm so curious."

"You're in luck. I happen to have several of her books, and I would be happy to lend you whatever you wish to read. I have to warn you, though, she isn't as scandalous as you may have heard."

Rachel smiled. "If you lend me a book, we'll have to see each other again."

"I know." He knew he was playing with fire in more ways than one. Rachel Pennington wasn't a woman he could amuse himself with for a while, then pass over. He wasn't at all sure that he could stop seeing her once he had started. He thought it was too bad he hadn't known that before he gave her a ride home on his horse.

"I'd like to borrow a book from you. How will we manage it? I shouldn't come to your house now that it's known you're a bachelor, and I don't think Mama and Papa will welcome you at mine. Especially not if you're bringing me a copy of Mrs. Thompson." She thought for a minute. "I know! My sister Rose! She lives only a short distance from here, and we can meet there."

"Rose won't mind if you read Mrs. Thompson?"

"She isn't a reader. I doubt if she has ever heard of Mrs. Thompson. Besides, she's my sister, not my parent."

"Your first clandestine meeting, I presume?"

Rachel exclaimed with delight. "It is, isn't it! I hadn't thought of it that way."

"Good. I was hoping you hadn't."

"But now I will." She smiled at him and his heart skipped a beat. "Have you had many such meetings yourself?"

"I can honestly say that I've never met a young lady by secret means in order to give her a book." He saw her eyes widen, and he allowed her to be as shocked as she pleased. He could tell she was enjoying it and was trying hard to think of some way to ask him to elaborate.

He walked closer to her. "Rachel, I've never met anyone quite like you. You're a confusing woman."

"I am?" she asked, her voice breathless.

"You certainly confuse me. I've never known anyone who is such a contradiction of innocence and eagerness."

"I've never been called that before. Is it a compliment?" She didn't back away as he advanced.

"Yes, it is." He wondered what she would do if he kissed her. He wondered if her innocence was real or if she was more experienced than she would have him believe. There was only one way to find out.

Slowly he circled his arm around her waist and watched as her eyes widened. As he drew her to him, he saw pink spring into her cheeks and her lips part. Either she was accustomed to being kissed by men she barely knew or she was a woman made for loving. She didn't pull back. Jared lowered his head and paused a mere breath away from her lips. Rachel closed her eyes and swayed toward him.

When he kissed her, he knew with certainty this was a new sensation for her, and he was relieved. Her lips were closed, but when he touched them with his tongue she opened them hesitantly. Time seemed to hang suspended and his thoughts reeled. She was inexperienced, but she was eager to learn and had a natural talent, at least for kissing. When he raised his head he said, "How old are you?" She had a timeless quality and he didn't want to make a mistake with a child who was pretending to be a woman.

"I'm twenty, but I'm not supposed to admit it." Her eyes had grown darker and held seductive dreaminess in their depths. "How old are you? And why are you asking me this now?"

He chuckled and bent his head to her again. This time her lips opened eagerly and she returned his kiss with growing passion. Jared felt heat course through his body. He mustn't do this, he knew, but he felt powerless to stop. Kissing Rachel felt more right than anything he had ever done.

"I beg your pardon!" a man's voice exclaimed with anger. "What are you doing?"

Jared released Rachel and reflexively put his body between her and the man who had entered the library. It was Rob Gaston.

"What is going on here?"

Jared wasn't sure what to do. He could hardly upbraid a man for coming into his own library, and he couldn't blame him for being angry that another man was kissing the woman he expected to marry.

"Rachel, is he forcing himself on you?" Gaston crossed the library in quick strides. His face was pale from jealousy and his movements were stiff.

"No!" she exclaimed. "No, he's not!"

Jared heard the panic in her voice and he tensed to protect her.

"I don't believe you." Gaston put his hand on Jared's arm and tried to shove him away from Rachel. Behind him, Jared heard Rachel stumble against the desk, apparently flinching away from Gaston's unexpected move.

Rational thought left Jared, and he lashed out at Gaston, his fist landing squarely on the younger man's jaw, dropping him to the floor.

Rachel stared from one to the other as Jared shook his hand to get the feeling back in it and to ease his tingling fingers. She opened her mouth as if she were about to speak, but only shook her head. With a strangled gasp, she ran from the room.

Jared knelt beside Gaston for a moment, checking to be sure the man wasn't badly hurt, then strode after Rachel. She had already vanished into the crowd, and although he searched, she eluded him. Jared cursed himself for being a fool. Rob Gaston wouldn't have harmed her. He had struck out by instinct, and he felt like a blundering idiot. His impulsive act had possibly cost him any future contact with Rachel.

Fortunately, Mark was alone when Jared found him, and in short order, Jared told him what had happened in the library. "I think we had better get out of here before Gaston wakes up. There will be quite a scene if I'm still here."

Mark agreed. As they were getting their cloaks and hats and canes from the butler, Rob Gaston appeared in the ballroom doorway, looking about for his rival with vengeance in his eye. Jared motioned to Mark and they left quickly.

Jared was silent during the ride back to Ravenwood, but his thoughts plagued him. Of all the foolish things he could have done, this was surely the worst. Now that he would have no trouble convincing Rachel to stay away from him, he found he wanted exactly the opposite. He looked up at the stars and wondered what new tricks fate might have in store for his future. Certainly he seemed unable to control his own destiny.

Chapter Five

"Rachel did what?" William Pennington straightened and glared at the young man standing before him. "She kissed him? I don't believe a word of it!"

"I wouldn't tell you such a thing if it wasn't true." Rob Gaston bowed his head ingratiatingly to the older man.

William had already had a bad day, and he was in no mood to hear about his younger daughter's latest transgression. The new maid Violet had hired seemed to be trying to drive him crazy by breaking everything she touched, his partner at the law office had recently retired, his favorite horse had come up lame that morning and his membership was due at the club. Now this young man was wanting him to believe Rachel had kissed Jared Prescott at a recent party. "She couldn't have meant anything by it. You know how girls are. I saw her kissing a kitten just the other day. Perhaps she was playing some sort of game, like...like forfeits."

"It wasn't that sort of kiss and she was playing no game. They had gone to Papa's library alone."

William paced to the window. Heavy rain clouds had rolled in, and the day was gloomy and depressing. Dreary spring days like this always put him in a bad mood. That was why he had come to the club instead of going home. Then Rob had come bearing bad news, and he felt as if he were cornered. Like a lion in his den. He rather liked the simile.

When William didn't answer, Rob repeated, "They were alone in there."

"You must have been mistaken," William said bluntly. "Rachel isn't a trollop."

"No, no! I'm not saying anything like that!" Rob was so self-effacing he bobbed up and down like a puppet. "It's clear to me that it was all Prescott's fault."

William looked back over his shoulder. "Are you saying Prescott was forcing himself on her?" He felt anger building, and he clenched his hands behind his back. For all her faults, Rachel was and always had been his favorite.

"Well, not forcing, exactly. More like coercing. He was leading her down the garden path, so to speak."

"I'll have the man's hide!" William roared.

A faint smile popped onto Rob's features, as if this was exactly the reaction he had striven to accomplish, and William hated to be manipulated. "What do you know about this man?" he probed.

"Who knows anything about him? He's kept to himself so much since he came here, I can hardly think anything good of him. I've heard a great deal of talk that links him to a sweatshop in London where children die daily."

William wondered if Rob knew of his particular prejudice against child labor and that he made regular contributions to groups that were trying to stamp out the practice. He shook his head. The boy had no reason to use information like that even if he did know. But then, Rob had changed since he had gone to the States. William wasn't sure he liked him as well as he had thought at first. This made him feel even more uneasy, because he never allowed himself to make mistakes. Of course the lad would make a fine husband for Rachel, and he was certainly industrious. Even now he had ink on his fingers.

"There's even talk linking him to the murder of Liza Barnes."

"What's that? What did you say?" William was so shocked he thought he must have heard incorrectly.

"I heard at the office that some say Prescott may have been responsible for Liza's death. I don't have to tell you how she earned her living, such as it was."

William nodded impatiently. Liza had been notorious. He did wonder, however, how Rob had come to know so much about the young prostitute in the little time he had been back.

"There were no witnesses, but the sheriff found a partial footprint—in blood." He obviously had added the last two words for effect. "They said that footprint must have been made by the man who murdered her, since it was too large for a woman."

"It only makes sense that it was a man who did it. I can't even imagine one woman killing another," William said brusquely. "It's not something that would ever enter a woman's mind." Since he had a wife and two daughters, and was surrounded almost constantly by female servants, he fancied he knew women's minds almost as well as they did.

"I agree. I never heard of a woman murderer, and I hope I never do. Can you think of any man in Fairfield who would commit a murder? Especially a murder of a woman like Liza? She was a convenience, not a threat."

William looked at Rob closely. William would have described Liza Barnes in many ways, but referring to her as "a convenience" wasn't one of them. "Why are people linking Prescott's name to this? Is there any proof?"

"No, but in order for this sort of crime to be committed, there must be two people."

"I know that! Why Prescott?"

"He's new in the area. We know nothing about him, at least nothing good, and he has a haughty air as if he were superior to all of us."

"I've noticed that." William rubbed his lower lip absently. The bristles from his mustache tickled his thumb. "The only time I was face-to-face with him, he did have a condescending attitude." William didn't want to remember that Jared Prescott's condescending attitude that day might have been a reaction to being impolitely treated. William had been so worried about Rachel's safety when that blasted horse had come home without her that he would have snapped at the vicar himself. He had seen no way to undo what he had done, however, and he had been right to object to how Prescott had brought her home. Would it have hurt the man to walk and let Rachel ride decorously?

"It's a good thing you didn't see them kiss," Rob added. "You would have had apoplexy on the spot."

"I think that's hardly likely," William said dryly.

"You weren't there, sir, no disrespect intended. I was." Rob drew himself up and lifted his chin. "I'm willing to duel to the death for her honor. I thought you should know that."

William shook his head impatiently. "There's no reason for anyone to die for anything here." Dueling had been illegal in England for years. He frowned. "You and Prescott haven't gone and arranged to actually duel, have you?"

"Not in so many words, no."

William nodded. The young man seemed to be keeping something back. William was accustomed to cross-examining men before the bar, and he trusted his instincts on such matters. He wondered if there had been more going on than a kiss, but he couldn't come right out and ask. Not when they were discussing Rachel. Blood pounded in his temples at the idea of Prescott or any man daring to violate Rachel's body. Like most of his friends, William believed a woman to be next to saintly and that to ill-use one was practically sacrilegious. "What happened when you walked in on them?"

Rob fidgeted. "I gave him what-for! I upbraided him soundly and demanded that he leave my father's house. I wanted to strike him, but I dared not do so in front of Miss Rachel."

"I see." William studied the bruise on Rob's chin. Until now he had believed it to be a smudge or a trick of the dim light. "And you didn't fight?"

"He wouldn't have dared to lay a hand on me, I should hope. Not in my own father's house!"

William made no comment. He thought he could see now what Rob was leaving out. He had challenged Prescott's right to kiss Rachel—as was only proper—and Prescott had decked him. William disliked being lied to, but he could see why Rob would choose to do so under the circumstances. All men had their pride. "Have you seen Rachel since last night?"

"Not yet. I wanted to speak to you when there were no women about. Man to man. I'm going to call on Rachel when I leave here. With your permission, of course."

"I've already given you my permission." William tried to keep the anger from his voice, but he failed. He wanted the lad to brace up and stop giving him the impression that he was less a man than William had believed he was when he gave him permission to court Rachel. William hated the idea that he might have made a mistake. "How are things going between the two of you?"

"Splendidly, I should say. Although she left before I could speak to her last night, I daresay she is appreciative of my intervention. I only hope she isn't too ashamed to see me."

"Shame isn't one of Rachel's predominant characteristics," her father said. "She's always been headstrong."

"I'm sure she'll grow out of it, sir. She only needs a firm hand."

William uttered a noncommittal grunt. He knew a strong hand would not go far in bringing Rachel in line. He had already tried every tactic short of bodily harm or estrangement. "Perhaps, since you have brought up the subject and since I know you have matrimony with my daughter in mind, I should tell you now that I'll never condone you laying a hand on her in anger." He knew how Rachel could provoke a man, but he had his limits and it would be good for Rob to know them now.

Rob looked as shocked as William had hoped he might. "I'd never do such a thing as you're implying! Never, sir!"

"I didn't think you would. Still, it bears saying. I know men who believe that's the only way to handle a wife, but I won't have Rachel hurt."

"I'd die for her! I swear it on my honor."

"Just make her happy. That's all I want."

"I will, sir. Now if you'll excuse me, I'll be on my way." Rob hesitated at the door. "I'm going to look into Prescott's history. I have friends in London who may know him or who may have heard something about him."

"Yes." William turned thoughtfully to the window. "That might be a good idea. But Rob, be discreet."

"I will, sir. You can count on me."

William wished he felt more confidence in Rob.

William glared at his daughter across the supper table. "What do you mean you refused to see him?"

"Not at the table, dear," Violet objected. "You won't digest your food properly."

William ignored her. "Rachel, explain yourself."

"I don't like Rob, Papa. He's unbearable."

"Nonsense. He's the brother of your best friend. How can he be unbearable?"

Violet rubbed her forehead as if she were having one of her headaches. He knew she would soon make an excuse and retire for the night. Violet's headaches were a source of irritation for him, as was her insistence on separate rooms.

Rachel pushed her food around on her plate instead of answering.

William tried another tactic. "Did anything happen at the dance last night?"

Rachel's head jerked up. "Why do you ask?"

"He's only curious, dear." Violet smiled at her daughter as if she were hoping to avoid a scene by being as pleasant as possible.

"You didn't answer my question." William had almost convinced himself that Rob had been mistaken about the kiss.

"One party is pretty much like another," she evaded.

"You had a good time then?" William pursued.

"She isn't on the witness stand," Violet tried to say with a laugh. "You sound as if you're prosecuting her."

William's eyes met his daughter's across the table. His heart sank at what he saw there. Rob hadn't been mistaken.

"Papa, I've been meaning to talk to you. Jared Prescott was there last night, and I had a chance to talk to him when we danced. I really think you should get to know him."

"Why?"

"Because I like him better than I do Rob, and because I think he may want to call on me."

William felt his anger beginning to boil. "If I see that blackguard, I'll break his neck!"

Violet jumped and even Rachel looked startled. He followed up his advantage by pounding his fist on the table. "Do you fully understand me, Rachel?" There was no need for Violet to know what their daughter had been up to. It would only make her have another headache.

"Did you talk to Rob today?" Rachel countered. Her eyes were starting to blaze and her face had paled, a sure sign her temper was rising.

"I did. He says you had quite a good time at the party last night." He refused to let Rachel look away.

"That's nice," Violet said uncertainly. "Were there many people there?"

"At least one too many," William said. "I'm referring to Prescott. Why did the Gastons invite him?"

Rachel lifted her chin. "They didn't. I did."

"What?" William no longer tried to keep his voice down.

"I wanted to get to know him better, so I talked Beatrice into letting me send him an invitation."

"I can't believe you could be so forward. Your sister would never do such a thing!"

"Maybe she should have!"

"What do you mean by that?"

"Rose ought to stand up for herself. She was sweet on Philip Yardley."

"He wasn't right for her! Edwin has made her an exemplary husband."

"I have nothing against Edwin. It's just that he's as dull as Rob. I don't see why Rose isn't bored to tears every time he speaks."

"She has her children," Violet said. "Her adorable children. They're a woman's greatest happiness."

William ignored his wife. To Rachel he said, "You've changed the subject! We aren't talking about Rose." He sometimes thought it was a shame that Rachel could never be a lawyer. She had a gift for argument.

"We aren't talking about Jared, either!"

"Jared?" William shouted. "You call him by his first name?"

Violet put her pale hand on William's sleeve. "It was only a slip, I'm sure."

"No, it wasn't." Rachel's voice rose to match her father's. "I care a great deal for Jared, and I may even love him."

"That's impossible. You've only spoken to him twice." He narrowed his eyes. "That is correct, isn't it?"

"I've spoken to him three times."

"There! You can't possibly be in love with a man you've spoken to only three times. It sometimes takes years to fall in love. I know men who didn't fall in love with their wives until after the birth of their first child."

"Then I pity their wives!"

"Please," Violet said as forcibly as she was able, "think what you both are saying."

"I'm only going to tell you this once, Rachel. You're to put Prescott out of your mind and never mention him to me again. I'm your father, and I have your best interests at heart. You're to fall in love with Robert Gaston!"

"No, I won't!"

William didn't know what else to do, so he rose abruptly, causing his chair to teeter and nearly fall. He glared at Rachel from his impressive height. It was a trick he had learned in court when it was necessary to intimidate his opponent. He knew it worked on Violet because she shrank back. Rachel, however, leaped to her feet and put her hands on her hips. "You will let Rob court you, or you'll never leave this house again."

"I can't stand him!"

"Yes, you can. You haven't given him a chance. I've recently heard Prescott's name is being linked not only to child labor, but to the murder of Liza Barnes."

"Who's Liza Barnes?" Violet asked.

"I don't believe it," Rachel stated flatly.

William wished he hadn't brought up Liza's name in front of his wife and daughter. The name of a prostitute wasn't one ever to be on a husband's lips, especially not at his dinner table. His anger at Rachel increased, because she had caused his slip in propriety. "It's not up to you to believe it or not. You need only let me guide you in whom to see and what company you may keep. And I'm telling you to put Prescott out of your mind and let Rob court you properly."

Rachel crossed her arms and glared at him. "If I see Rob, you'll let me leave the house? I won't be kept inside as I was when Ebony threw me?"

"He threw you? I thought you said you dismounted, and he ran away."

"That's what I meant to say. All right, I'll see Rob, but I won't make any promises. And I won't marry anyone I don't already love!"

"That seems fair," Violet ventured.

William knew he would get no greater concessions from Rachel. "Fair enough." He tossed his napkin on the table and retreated before she could upset him further.

Rachel sat on the divan, pulling at the silk fringe on one of the decorative pillows. She wanted to be outside riding a horse or swapping speculations with Beatrice as to what Jared and Mark had thought of them. Instead she was

faced with at least another half hour of conversation with
Rob. Her mother was in evidence, though not sitting in the
room, and Rachel knew she was being left alone so romance could develop between her and Rob.

"Have you ridden out to see the fields south of town?"
Rob was asking. "The wildflowers are spectacular this
year."

"I saw them."

"I thought maybe you would like to paint them and I
could accompany you."

"Why would I want to do that? Rose keeps us well supplied with pictures of wildflowers. Or at least she did before her last child was born."

"It's hard to see how she can accomplish all she does and
still be such an exemplary wife and mother. She rather reminds me of you."

"I can't imagine in what way. Rose and I are nothing
alike. She takes after Mama and I'm more like Papa. We
don't even look alike."

"I meant in your dedication to duty."

Rachel only gave him a blank look. She had never heard
such a pack of drivel in her life. "Tell me again about the
weather in America."

"I would rather tell you how pretty your eyes are."

Rachel wished he hadn't said that. It reminded her of
Jared. He had compared her eyes to blue pansies. She had
tossed and turned for two nights wondering what Jared
thought of her for returning his kiss so brazenly. That was
why she had run away. Not because he had hit Rob. If she
had been a man, she would have hit Rob herself.

"May I compliment you?" he asked with a smile she
could only think of as simpering.

"You did. Don't do it again." She fretted with a loose
thread, unraveled a few stitches and put the pillow down
before she ruined it. "How is Beatrice today?"

"Quite well, thank you. She sends you her best. She also
said to tell you she hopes to see you tomorrow."

"Tell her I'll drop by after tea." She needed Beatrice's help in deciding what to do about Jared. What if he thought she was loose for having let him kiss her? Let him? She had kissed him back and had done so with a great deal of enjoyment. The thought of how much she had enjoyed it made her cheeks burn.

"I wish I could be there, but I'll be at the office, of course."

"Of course." She tried to think of something to say to him. "Are you enjoying your work? It must be gratifying for your father to have you working alongside him in his profession."

"It is, I'm sure. Of course, Papa seldom is at the office himself. He and my mother are often in London. He has an interest in a bookkeeping office there as well, and he says he must divide his time between them. I'm sure that in time he will make me head of the one here."

"I'm sure of it. If I were in need of a bookkeeper, you are exactly what I'd be looking for." She hid the barb she had intended behind a smile.

Rob looked as if she had given him gold. "Thank you, Miss Rachel."

A maid entered with a tray of sugar cookies and two glasses of iced lemonade. She put them on the table and silently left.

"Your mother certainly has a way with the servants," Rob observed. "I've never seen such cheeky ones as there are in America. The ones here are ever so much better."

"I think Mama only takes the ones who are quiet. I've never seen her so much as correct one." She sipped her drink. "Lemonade is one of the best parts of summer."

"I quite agree. You're fortunate not to have to watch your figure. So many women let themselves go."

Rachel tried not to snap his head off. "Perhaps I will, too, someday," she said sweetly. "After I'm married, I mean."

Rob frowned. "Surely not."

"Why not? By then I'll already have a husband." She knew she was disturbing him, and it gave her a great deal of pleasure. Perhaps she could dissuade him after all. "Or perhaps I'll decide to keep my figure and not have any children at all."

Rob looked as if he might swoon. "Really, Miss Rachel, we shouldn't be discussing this."

"Why not? I know what your intentions are. Shouldn't you know mine? Papa has already said you have matrimony in mind."

"He said that? I had thought he might leave that to me. It's too early to bring it up."

"Exactly what I told him. How do we know if we'll fall in love?"

"I must confess that I'm already in love with you."

"Nonsense. You can't possibly know that. I have it on good authority that it may take years for a man to know if he's in love."

"Years? I hadn't expected to wait that long to... What I mean is, I do love you. After you've had time to get accustomed to my company, maybe your feeling will bloom into something greater."

"Perhaps. We'll have to wait and see. I refuse to marry a man I don't love."

He smiled as if she were a precocious child. "A wife sometimes grows to love her husband after she has seen his devotion toward her for years."

"Not me. I'll never marry unless I'm sure beforehand. And you may tell Papa I said so."

"Mr. Pennington and I don't need to discuss you. That would be highly improper."

"For goodness' sake, let's not do anything improper," Rachel said with a sigh.

"Speaking of propriety, I want to say that I've decided to forgive you for... well, for what happened at the party the other night."

"You've what?"

"I'm referring to what transpired in the library."

"I know what you're talking about. You've decided to *forgive* me?" Her voice was dangerously cool.

Rob didn't notice. "I know Prescott must have forced you or led you on with who knows what in mind."

"As a matter of fact, *I* kissed *him.* What do you think of that?"

"I think you must be mistaken," he stammered. "You wouldn't do such a thing. You're a lady."

"Ladies kiss."

"Women, perhaps, but not ladies. Not a man to whom they aren't even engaged!"

"Then you're saying I'm not a lady?" She was almost enjoying this. He was so easily confused and embarrassed.

"Never!" Rob's jaw dropped and he looked stunned. "I never said that!"

"Then what did you mean by forgiving me? If you really believe it was all Jared's doing, why forgive me? I would be completely innocent. Isn't this true?"

"You're confusing me. I only meant—"

"You meant you knew I was kissing him of my own free will and you're having second thoughts about courting me?"

"No! Miss Rachel, you must stop talking like this. If your father could hear you, it would put him in his grave."

"I doubt it. Papa is made of sterner stuff."

"I'm going to forget you ever said these words. Are you trying to test my regard for you by seeing if I'll continue to forgive you? If so, don't worry. I'll forgive you for anything. Almost anything."

"Almost?"

"I don't want you to kiss Prescott anymore."

"You have no rights over me. And for that matter, why did you tell Papa? That wasn't the action of a gentleman."

"I thought he had a right to know. Men have to protect their women."

"I can protect myself. And I can kiss whomever I please, as well."

"I think I should go. I can see you're in a female humor. Melancholia sometimes takes this turn."

"I'm certainly not afflicted with melancholia! I'm angry with you!"

Rob stood and gave her a stiff bow. "I'll come back when you're feeling better. Goodbye."

She didn't walk him to the door, even though she knew her mother would reprimand her for it. Instead she let her back drop against the divan's cushions as she had when she was a child. Her whalebone corset poked her ribs, but she didn't sit up straight again. In her opinion Rob was boring to the point of making a saint curse.

Violet came into the room. "Rachel? Why, why on earth are you lying around like that? Sit up."

"Mama, Rob is such a dullard I feel as if my brain is shrinking."

Violet looked concerned. "I think he's a charming young man."

Rachel sat upright. For the first time she wondered if her parents were happy together. Her mother would have been better suited to a man like Rob. A man who had fewer passions and no bursts of temperament. Rachel reached out and patted her mother's hand. "Whatever you say, Mama." She only wished she could share her opinion.

Chapter Six

Mark thumbed idly through one of the books in Jared's library, wondering what to do with his day. Jared had gone to London, a two-hour ride, to take care of some business that demanded his attention. Mark had declined to go with him, but now he wished that he had. Ravenwood without Jared was too quiet. Mark wondered how Jared had endured being there alone before he arrived to liven things up. He was glad he had saved Jared from himself. His cousin had always taken responsibilities too seriously.

That brought Yvonne to mind. Mark had known her all their lives, but he hadn't seen her lately. Not for several months, in fact. Jared had discouraged him from going to speak to her since his arrival, and Mark had thought that odd. He decided this was a perfect time to visit her.

Yvonne was housed on the third floor in rooms that had once been used as a nursery. Jared had said the arrangement that had once kept children from escaping their nanny worked perfectly to contain Yvonne. The only access to Yvonne's room was through the nanny's room, now occupied by Abby. Jared had mentioned that when he first moved in, he had some concern about housing Yvonne in that particular location because she might be seen by an approaching visitor, but his subsequent decision to discourage callers had given him ease in that regard.

The rooms weren't hard to find. Mark knocked on the door and waited. He could hear movements inside but no one called out. After a while he knocked again. This time the footsteps came nearer and he heard the sound of a key being turned in the lock. The door opened an inch and he saw the woman he recognized as Abby. Only after he greeted her by name and reminded her who he was did she open the door.

"I've come to pay my respects to Yvonne," he said as he glanced around Abby's room. It was average size for a bedroom, but large for a servant's quarters. Abby's bed, across the room, had been made up with precision. On the wall adjacent to the door that apparently led to Yvonne's room were two chairs and a small fireplace, a concession for when there had been babies in the suite. The room was meticulously clean and tidy. So much so, it was difficult to believe anyone was living in it.

"Yvonne gets upset when she has visitors."

Mark appraised Abby. She was tall and large-boned, not fat, but rather broad. Her body, like her speech, hinted she was from farm stock. "Nevertheless, I want to see her. I'll not upset her. She knows me quite well."

Abby hesitated as if she were still considering a refusal, then shrugged. She locked the outside door of her room, a move that made Mark uneasy, before opening Yvonne's. "In here."

Yvonne's room had wallpaper with pale pink and lavender flowers, and her bed was covered with a white counterpane that should have given the room a cheerful look but only served to emphasize the opposite. In contrast to Abby's neatly kept room, this one was in disarray. Long pieces of the wallpaper had been stripped from the walls and had been folded and stacked in a corner. The curtains apparently had been pulled down from the windows leaving nothing to soften the sunlight that streamed in. The small rugs that should have covered the floor were rolled up and stacked like cordwood against one wall. There were two chairs in this room, also, but they lay on their sides and looked as if they had been dragged about. The bed was rumpled, as though someone had crawled across it repeatedly. It took Mark several moments to see Yvonne.

"Yvonne?" he asked uncertainly. "Is that you?"

She was standing between the tall dresser and the wall. When he said her name she slowly stepped out into the room. Her long black hair, once beautiful, was hanging in witch's locks down her back. Her face was still pretty, but now her eyes held a vacant stare and her smile didn't reach them. "Mark?" she asked.

"Yes. Yes, it's me." He was stunned at the change in her since the last time he had seen her. She had always been high-strung and excitable, but now sanity seemed to have left her entirely. "How are you?"

Yvonne gave him a secretive smile as she pulled a strand of her hair through her fingers. Instead of answering, she began to hum.

"She's having one of her bad spells," Abby explained, not bothering to lower her voice. "She gets like this from time to time."

Mark was speechless. Yvonne circled around him, never taking her eyes from him and continuing to hum. He recognized the tune as one he had known in his childhood. Moving slowly so as not to startle Yvonne, he righted one of the chairs and sat down. Few things had ever shocked him as much as Yvonne's appearance.

She wore a shapeless dress, but he could tell she was still slim. Like Abby, she was taller than the average woman and her movements reminded him of a cat. Her walking behind his chair was unnerving but he remained still. "Do you remember me? We were children together." Even though she had said his name, he wasn't sure she had made the connection.

"I remember." Her voice was almost in his ear.

Mark jumped and turned to face her. As she drew away, she laughed at him, but the sound wasn't happy.

"Won't you sit down? I'd like to talk to you," he said as he reached over and righted the other chair. "Do you remember how we used to talk?"

"I remember. You often wore a waistcoat I liked." Then with sudden alarm, she said, "It was red!"

"Yes, I did have a red waistcoat at one time."

"She fears red," Abby explained. "She won't let the color anywhere near her."

"See?" Mark said as he held his coat wide. "I no longer have it. Mine is tan."

Yvonne slid sideways in the chair. The smile seemed frozen on her face. "When can I go back to London?"

"You live here now." He looked around at the room. "Don't you like it here?"

"I suppose." Her eyes finally left him and she glanced about the room. "They haven't found me here yet."

"Who?" For a minute he thought she must mean the townsfolk.

"The spirits. They were after me in London, but they haven't found me here." Her eyes went to the window. "They are looking, though. I can feel them."

"What spirits?" He turned to Abby. "What's she talking about?"

Abby kept her eyes on Yvonne. "She fancies the ghosts of her husband and his fancy woman haunt her."

"Good Lord!" Mark whispered.

Yvonne's head whipped back to face him. "They say I killed them," she confided uncertainly. "They say I found them in the bed I shared with my Paul and that I stabbed them both until they were dead."

"Yes. I remember." He had never been able to wipe that terrible night from his mind. Yvonne, along with Abby, who at the time had been her maid, had been visiting an aunt in the country and had returned unexpectedly to discover not only that Paul was unfaithful, but that he was using his house as a meeting place for his trysts. "That was several years ago."

"Not so many. Three, I think, or is it eight? They won't tell me for sure and time has a way of slipping by, doesn't it?" Yvonne rose and carefully turned her chair on its side again before she went to the window. "Do you think they will find me?" she asked in concern.

"No, no. They couldn't possibly find you here," Mark reassured her. To Abby he said, "What is she like on her good days?"

"She's more rational then. We talk or I read her a story or sing her a song. She likes music. As long as I avoid mentioning Mr. Paul or the years since he died, she stays calm."

Mark rose and gazed for a minute at Yvonne. She realized he was standing and she hurriedly went to the chair he had been sitting in and turned it over on its side. "Why do you do that?" he asked.

"So the spirits won't find me and sit in these chairs. They used to sit in my chairs in London all the time. Sit there and stare at me. I hate to be stared at." She drew her hair forward so he could see only part of her face.

"I must be going now, Yvonne. Is there anything I can send up for you? Some lemonade, perhaps? You used to love lemonade."

She nodded. "Lemonade, please." She turned back to the window.

Mark backed away. When Abby had closed the door and crossed her room to unlock the door leading into the hall, she said, "When you send up the lemonade, tell Kate to bring it. She came with us from London and she is the only one belowstairs who knows about Yvonne."

Mark noticed that she no longer referred to her mistress by a formal title, but under the circumstances that was understandable. Yvonne was no longer in a position to command respect. "Is she unhappy, do you think?"

"Who can tell? She seems as blank as an egg most of the time. At times she loses control, and that's why I keep this outside door locked. She's tried to run past me at times. It's a precaution."

"I understand." Absently he added as he glanced back at the opposite door, "I would never have believed the changes I see."

"Aye. She can be a handful."

Mark looked at Abby's dour expression and wondered what sort of stories she might be able to tell Yvonne and what songs might come from that straight mouth. She was waiting for him to leave, so he stepped into the corridor. "Be kind to her, Abby," he said as the door closed.

If Abby answered, he didn't catch the words. Slowly he walked down the corridor. He understood better now why Jared had counseled him not to visit Yvonne. Seeing her this way was heartbreaking.

When they were children, Yvonne had been lovely and happy. She was Jared's stepsister, but he knew Jared had loved her as much as if she were his true kin. Yvonne had always been nervous and excitable, but Mark had never suspected she would lapse into insanity. When she married Paul, he and Jared had hoped she would be safe from life's arrows. Paul had seemed as stable and secure as anyone Mark had ever met. He was slightly younger than Yvonne, and this had caused some concern among the older relatives, but Yvonne had loved him and Jared had given her permission to marry him. By then Jared was all the close family Yvonne had left.

Almost no one but Mark and Jared knew Jared's stepmother had also gone insane and had taken her own life with a knife.

Now that he saw the same madness in Yvonne, Mark shivered. Her mother had posed no danger to anyone but herself, but Yvonne's errant behavior suggested she had taken a different turn. She had already killed Paul and his lover, and there was reason to believe she had killed at least two other women in London, though neither he nor Jared could conjure a reason as to why she would have done such a thing. Even though Mark had tried to convince Jared that Yvonne surely was innocent, he had agreed that she must be hidden for her own good. Because of circumstantial evidence against her, she could have been arrested and convicted for the women's murder. As her punishment, she would either have been hanged or, if her judge was lenient, committed to Bedlam for the rest of her life. Both men agreed that of the two, hanging would be the more humane sentence, but neither of them felt such a fate was her due.

Earlier, in the deaths of Paul and his mistress, the court had accepted Abby's eyewitness testimony as verification of Yvonne's story and had ruled that Yvonne's actions were justifiable under the circumstances. She wouldn't have been as fortunate in the case of the other two murdered women.

As Mark started down the stairs, he couldn't help but wonder if there was any connection between Yvonne and the murdered woman in the village. Jared had said that Abby was perfectly capable of keeping Yvonne under lock and key constantly, but it seemed strangely coincidental that all three murder victims were prostitutes. Prior to seeing Yvonne, he had thought such a suggestion was ridiculous. Now, he wasn't so sure. He shivered at the thought of Yvonne's belief that the ghosts of her husband and his lover would find her and sit in her chairs. He was glad to reach the main level of the house where everything seemed safe and logical.

When Jared returned later that evening, Mark was still upset. "I've seen Yvonne," he said without preamble.

Jared gave his hat to Stanford and turned to Mark. "I suppose it had to happen some time or other. How is she?"

"Abby says she's having one of her bad days. I should hope this wasn't an ordinary one. I sent up some lemonade," he added. "I know how she has always liked it."

Jared preceded him into the library and closed the doors. "Stanford and the housekeeper know about Yvonne, of course. So do the servants we brought from London, but none of the others. I would rather they not suspect anything."

"I understand. I sent Kate up with the lemonade."

"I saw Yvonne yesterday, and she seemed docile enough." Jared sat in his favorite leather chair and Mark sat opposite him. "I had hoped she would stay calm. I guess that's too much to ask."

"She said Paul and that despicable woman are haunting her!"

"I know. It's ludicrous, of course, but not to Yvonne. It can make your flesh creep when she thinks she sees them and all you see is an empty chair. At times I've actually wondered which of us was wrong."

"You can't be serious!"

"Don't worry. I'm not becoming insane. It's just that she can be so convincing. Fortunately, she says the ghosts haven't found Ravenwood yet."

"How can you be so calm? Aren't you afraid she may become violent?"

"Why else would I move from London and keep her locked up in a room? I know she can be violent. She has already killed two people at the very least—Paul and his woman. Now you know why I was so upset when it seemed likely that she stabbed those two women in London. I'm still concerned about the murder of that Barnes woman in Fairfield, yet I know Yvonne must be innocent of that. I have her securely locked away."

"She can't give Abby the slip?"

"Abby takes her job very seriously. As for Yvonne overpowering her and escaping, I'd hesitate to attack Abby. Wouldn't you?" He tried to smile, but the gravity of the situation made that almost impossible.

"Indeed I would. She reminds me of the men on the docks who load the ships."

"That's why she was hired. Everyone thought she was an odd choice for a ladies' maid, but even when Paul was alive, Yvonne had started having periods of instability. There were times when I needed Abby to prevent Yvonne from taking her own life. She had become like her mother and it broke my heart. Who knows? If her mother had lived, she might have eventually become dangerous to others as well."

"Are you sure Yvonne shouldn't be in a place where she has people watching her around the clock?"

"A place like Bedlam?" Jared's voice hardened. "Have you ever seen that place?"

"No," Mark admitted.

"I have. I would send her to hell first."

"I've heard stories about it. I think hell might be preferable."

"Yvonne is my sister. I know we aren't blood kin, but I think of her as if we were. When Papa died I promised I would always watch after her and keep her safe and as happy as possible. That's what I'm doing."

Mark was silent for a long time. "I admire you, Jared. I never realized how much until now."

"She's my sister," Jared repeated.

Only a few feet away from them, within the wall beside the fireplace, Yvonne had her ear near the cobwebby wood. She smiled when she heard Jared say he would keep her safe. That was exactly what she had been hoping to hear. She had always loved Jared and she trusted him more than she had ever trusted anyone in her life.

As she pulled back, cobwebs stuck to her hair, and she casually brushed them away. She didn't mind cobwebs. They were such soft, delicate things.

Although she would rather have slipped out into the night, Abby was still awake and Yvonne knew her absence must not be discovered. Silently she made her way back up the stairs. She wasn't sure why it was so important to Jared for her to remain in the room, but he had some reason and she wanted to obey him. The only time she had ever balked was the day soon after they had moved here when she had seen him ride away from the house. She had been afraid he was leaving her, and she had tried to get past Abby and run after him. Abby had prevented it, however, and later she had seen Jared come home. Since then she had known he always would come back, and she had felt more secure.

She let herself into the room and looked around carefully. No red had come in while she was gone. Most important of all, the spirits were still absent. She had been afraid that talking about them to Mark might somehow have let them know where she was. She laughed to herself to think of Paul and that woman searching the streets of London when she was safely here.

As had become her habit, she went to her window and stared out into the darkness. Because of the glow from the candles in her room reflecting off the glass, she could make out almost nothing outside, but she liked to pretend that she could see quite well. Now that the spirits were gone, she liked the night. Sounds were so clear then. She could hear a night bird calling, and the answer from another some distance away. Continuing to gaze at the dark panes of glass, she began to hum softly.

Chapter Seven

Rachel was about to change into her riding habit when Violet called upstairs to tell her that Aunt Maddy had come for a visit.

Rachel suppressed a moan. A visit from Aunt Maddy, who was trying under any circumstances, was as welcome this particular day as the plague. Each day for a week Rachel had wanted to ride to the hill overlooking Ravenwood and survey the house in hopes of seeing Jared, but bad weather had stifled her. And now that it was at last dry enough to ride forth, her mother's sister had come to call.

"I'll be right down, Mama." To her maid, Jane, she said, "Don't breathe a word about my plans to go riding today. Not to anyone. Maybe Aunt Maddy will take a nap during the afternoon and I can slip out then."

Jane, who was the same age as Rachel and who had been in on a number of Rachel's escapades, nodded. "Not a word from me, but why are you keeping it a secret?"

"It's best if you don't know all the details," Rachel said in a whisper. "That way you won't have to lie. Let's just say it's an affair of the heart."

Jane's eyes rounded. "You're going to meet a gentleman? How romantic!"

Rachel put her finger to her lips, warning Jane to silence. "If you hear Aunt Maddy is going to take a nap, meet me here in my room as quickly as possible. I'll say that

I'm sleepy, too, and it will be hours before anyone misses me.''

Jane nodded. Rachel smoothed her hair and fluffed her cambric skirt over her full petticoats. Aunt Maddy was so particular about appearance that Rachel always felt as if she must be prepared for a rigorous inspection during her aunt's visits.

Maddy and Violet were in the best parlor, sipping cups of steaming tea by the time Rachel arrived downstairs. ''I had a frightful journey from London,'' Maddy was saying. ''I simply must buy a better coach. The one I've been using has become so rough to ride in it is enough to bounce your eyeteeth out.'' She looked up at her niece and smiled. ''Why, here's Rachel. How good to see you, my dear.''

Rachel smiled and bent over her aunt's chair for her customary kiss. ''You're looking well, Aunt Maddy.''

An hour later Maddy had exhausted her list of ailments and was, as Rachel had hoped, ready for a nap. Even Violet, who was fond of her older sister, looked as if she needed a rest. Rachel said, ''I think I'll go up and take a nap myself.''

''A nap? You?'' Violet looked at Rachel in surprise. ''You never nap.''

Rachel hadn't counted on this. ''I'll spend the time reading, really. I'm just tired for some reason.''

Violet nodded. To Maddy she said, ''Rachel often spends hours poring over a book. Rose was almost as bad. I must confess I don't know where they got it. William reads, but never novels.''

''It's from Father's second brother,'' Maddy told her as they went to the stairs. ''Uncle Frederick did love his books.''

''He did?'' Rachel had never heard much about this uncle.

''It led to his downfall and ruined his eyes. Take care, young lady, that you read only uplifting stories. And if you feel your eyesight dimming, stop reading immediately.''

"I will." Rachel added eagerly, "What sort of downfall did Great-uncle Frederick have?"

Violet and Maddy exchanged a glance. "None that you need hear of," Violet said.

"Even his name would probably be best left unsaid," Maddy agreed. "Especially since he's off on that island somewhere in the South Seas and doing who knows what, while he has a perfectly good wife and child right here in England."

Rachel listened with great interest. Often Aunt Maddy revealed more information on a subject after she had decided she had said too much already. Great-uncle Frederick sounded like the sort of uncle that Rachel would have enjoyed knowing.

After a few minutes, Jane came to Rachel's bedroom and helped her change into a riding habit. "I won't be gone long," Rachel said in a whisper to her accomplice. "If anyone misses me and asks where I've gone, say that I left just moments before and didn't say where I was going."

"I will, Miss Rachel. You can count on me."

Rachel opened her door a crack and peered out to be sure no one was in the hall. It was almost as important for her to avoid the servants as it was to avoid her mother and aunt; not all the servants were as loyal to her as Jane. Especially not the older ones, who seemed to think Rachel already got away with more than a daughter should.

Finding the hall empty, Rachel waved goodbye to Jane, who was already busy hanging up her dress so it wouldn't wrinkle. Then Rachel slipped out into the hall and carefully pulled her door shut. Walking along the edge of the stairs where her weight was less likely to cause the boards to pop or creak, she made her way downstairs and out the front door. Once she was away from the house, she breathed easier. Violet would forbid her to ride and miss a moment of Aunt Maddy's visit, even if her aunt was asleep upstairs.

She had no difficulty with Harry at the stable and soon she was riding toward Ravenwood. Although it seemed like forever to her, it was only a short time before she reached the spot overlooking Jared's home. As she was about to dismount, she saw two riders come around the house. If she had been even a few minutes later, she would have missed them! Rachel noted in which direction they were traveling across the green and reined her horse toward the opposite side of the hill. They were heading for the village and she knew a shortcut.

Soon she reached the outskirts of Fairfield and let her horse drop back to an easy trot. It wouldn't do for anyone to know she had let him run all the way. At the point where the winding main lanes crossed, she dismounted. As she tied her horse to a hitching ring, she noticed Jared and Mark riding toward her from the end of the street.

Rachel went directly to the nearest shop window and pretended she was studying the assortment of hats displayed there. In the reflection in the glass, she watched the men draw nearer. Jared appeared to have caught sight of her, and he turned and said something to Mark. Together, they rode off at an angle.

Suppressing a frown, Rachel peered over her shoulder to see if they were looking back at her. Neither was. Did this mean Jared was intentionally avoiding her, or had she been mistaken that he saw and recognized her? Or was it that he had important business in Fairfield that demanded his immediate attention? Walking as nonchalantly as she could, Rachel crossed the street, keeping the men in sight, and determined which way they were heading. Knowing the village as well as she did her own house, she cut through a narrow wynd between buildings so she could get to the next street ahead of them.

By the time Jared and Mark turned the corner, she was walking toward them, not twenty yards away. Mark smiled and nodded a greeting to her, but Jared frowned and looked away as if he were pretending not to have seen her.

Rachel felt a chill go through her. Had he lost interest in her? She should never have kissed him. Now he thought she was forward and would avoid her! She had to talk to him and convince him that she didn't go about kissing every man she met. But how was she to do that when he wouldn't even meet her eye? If she called out to him and insisted he talk to her, it would cause a scene, and worse, Jared might take such an aggressive approach as supportive evidence that she was no lady. She would have to be subtle, but persistent. Swallowing the lump of fear in her throat, she renewed her resolve and continued her pursuit.

By the time Jared and Mark reached the market, Rachel was already there. As she pretended to peruse a merchant's wares, she watched their approach from the corner of her eye. Solemn faced, Jared was staring straight ahead in her direction, while Mark seemed to be swallowing laughter at the sight of her, yet again, in their path. She wished Jared looked as pleased. She continued browsing through the stall, keeping one eye on the men and letting them overtake her.

"Good afternoon, Miss Pennington," Mark said. "Fancy meeting you here."

She turned as if surprised to see them. "Why, hello." She tapped Mark on his arm. "I thought we were to be on a first-name basis." She smiled up at him, then at Jared. "Hello, Jared."

"Hello." His voice was cooler than the look he gave her. He had hoped to avoid her, but as Mark had pointed out on their second sighting of her, Fairfield was too small to prevent a meeting. He had decided after the party to have nothing more to do with her. Rachel was unlike anyone he had ever met, and he found himself too intrigued by those things that made her unique—and all too desirable.

To Jared's great surprise and annoyance, he heard Mark ask Rachel to permit them to walk with her. Before he had time to suggest otherwise, Rachel agreed. Jared knew that Mark meant well, but he didn't want anyone meddling in his personal affairs, and he made a mental note to upbraid Mark, when they were alone again, for putting him in such an awkward position. While Jared was thinking, Mark stepped aside and motioned for Rachel to walk between them.

Jared risked a glance at Rachel and found her smiling up at him as if he were her suitor. Then she turned her head and cast the same smile at Mark. A twinge of jealousy shot through Jared, but then he became aware for the first time Rachel was behaving in a predictable manner. She was flirting with both of them, and that was a feminine device he could understand. Feeling that he was finally on solid ground with her, he decided to take the initiative and end their relationship before it got out of hand. "I regret having caused you embarrassment at the party the other night," he boldly stated. "I will understand if you never want to speak to me again."

Rachel glanced at Mark, who was pretending to be interested in a stall where live chickens were for sale. "I would rather not talk about that, if you don't mind. That sort of thing has never happened to me before, and I would rather forget about it."

"I know it hasn't. That's why I'm apologizing." Jared felt his understanding of their relationship slipping askew again.

"How do you know?" she demanded perversely. "Didn't I do it right?"

"You did it fine. I only meant that you were inexperienced."

"How could you tell? I mean, yes, you're right. I should never have let you be so bold."

Jared felt as if he had been led into a maze and his guide had vanished, leaving no sign of the way back out. "Didn't you like it? You certainly seemed to at the time."

Rachel touched a stack of embroidered tea towels and nodded a greeting to the lady behind the counter. Looking back at Jared, she continued. "I'd really rather not talk about it. You took a great chance, you know."

"I wouldn't have if I had known Rob Gaston considered you enough his property to fight for you."

"As I told you when we were dancing, I'm not his property. I refuse to be anyone's property, and certainly not Rob's. He's my father's choice for me, not mine."

"He seems to think otherwise."

"Rob is a bore. I can't imagine why we are talking about him at all."

Jared had to smile. He was far afield from his original intent, but he was beginning to enjoy this. She might say she didn't want to talk about their kiss, but she gave no real signs of resenting the topic of conversation. "I'm trying to apologize for having resorted to violence in your presence." He noticed Mark had managed to drop far behind to give them privacy, if such could be had in a crowded marketplace. "I don't make a practice of that kind of thing."

"I never thought you did." She made eye contact with him and his heart seemed to stop.

"You have the most amazing eyes I've ever seen," he heard himself saying.

She smiled and looked away. At times she could seem so innocent, and at other times, like now, he was aware she had managed to get exactly the response from him that she wanted. She was certainly talented in the art of flirting, too much so for his taste, he tried to convince himself. He didn't want to care for a woman who wore so many hearts on her sleeve.

"What do you think of this bonnet?" she said as she picked up a cloth cap. "Is it too plain for me?"

For the first time that day, he turned his attention from who she was to what she was wearing. Her hat was the same shade of garnet as her riding habit and sported a curving black feather that drew his attention to the creaminess of her cheek. "Yes. It's too plain." He impatiently shook his head. He didn't want to play into her hand this way.

She looked up at him. "I'm afraid here in Fairfield we aren't as fashionable or as fast as your London women. It must be dull for you."

"Not anymore. It stopped being dull the day your horse threw you. But I moved here to be dull, you know."

"Why would anyone do that? For that matter, why would you leave the excitement of London to live in a sleepy place like this?"

Her questions hit too close to him for comfort. Jared parried with, "If you've never lived in London, how are you such an expert on it?"

"Everyone knows London is exciting. I read about it all the time, and I've been there for visits often. Or at least I've visited my aunt's house, and she lives in London so it's the same thing."

"There is a great difference in visiting an aunt who lives in London and in seeing London," he assured her. "A very great difference."

She looked as if she wanted to question him on that, so he stepped quickly over to a vendor selling pies and took a coin from his pocket. As was the custom in London, he wagered the toss of the coin against the pie, and when he lost, he cheerfully gave the man the coin and walked on his way.

"Why do people do that?" Rachel asked. "Wager a coin for a pie? I've seen other men do it as well."

"It's a custom. I don't know how it got started. For that matter, why are cakes always sold by men who walk about as vendors and coffee always sold in stalls run by women? Who knows when or why customs start?"

"I wonder about things like that. Don't you? I think everyone should. Otherwise, we take everything for granted and miss out on life."

"By not noticing if it is a man or a woman who is selling you coffee? I would think it would be more fascinating to wonder why coffee was discovered at all."

"I wonder about that, too. I question everything. Beatrice says I drive her to distraction at times."

"I can understand Beatrice feeling that way. You have the same effect on me."

She smiled as if she had hoped he would say that.

"Rachel, stop walking for a minute. We need to talk. I think it would be better if we didn't see each other anymore."

She stopped abruptly and stared up at him. "Why on earth would you think that?"

"We have nothing in common, for one thing." This wasn't strictly true. He, too, had an insatiable appetite for knowledge. That was why he owned so many books and why they were all well read. "And circumstances prevent me from calling on you and your family. I just think it's better if we not try to maintain a friendship."

"Well, that's just silly. What could possibly keep you from being friendly? You certainly didn't feel that way at the Gastons' party."

"You caught me by surprise. I had intended to tell you that night that we mustn't be friends."

"And that's why you kissed me? Is that a London custom?" Her voice rose and she frowned up at him in defiance.

Jared was glad Mark had separated himself from them. This wasn't going smoothly. Not when she looked so desirable even with a frown on her face. "I was wrong to do that. I must ask you to forgive me."

"No, I won't. When a man kisses a woman he must mean it. It's not a thing you can take back. Why don't you want any friends?"

"I really can't discuss it."

"Is it because you really do own a sweatshop and you're afraid for anyone to get close enough to find out?"

"I don't own any such thing. How can you think I'm such a cruel man and continue associating with me?"

"Then is it because you have a wife?" She looked away. "I've heard talk that you do."

"No. I've never been married. What else are people saying?"

Rachel hesitated. "Nothing."

He didn't believe her, but he couldn't force her to answer him. He was all too aware of the people surrounding them. "I've never married," he repeated.

"Why not? I thought perhaps you were a widower and it was your broken heart that was keeping you from society."

He had to smile at her innocence. "That's it. You've hit upon the answer."

"No, I haven't. You said twice that you never married."

"Maybe I simply want to be left alone."

"I think you need a friend."

"Whatever for? I have Mark to keep me company."

"Mark isn't from here. At the end of the summer he will go away and you'll be left alone again."

"How do you know I don't plan to have a constant stream of cousins coming out to visit me, each more interesting than the one before? I may be the least lonely man in England for all you know."

"No, I can see it in your eyes."

"What do you see in my eyes? Why do women always claim to have divine omniscience when it comes to knowing a man's unspoken thoughts?"

"I can tell you have some great concern and that you are lonely."

Jared fell silent. She had come too close with that guess, if it was one. He wasn't too sure she was only guessing. For some reason there seemed to be a link between them. He could almost read her thoughts as easily as he could discern her emotions. The idea wasn't comforting. Of all the people he could have a mental link with, Rachel Pennington was the last he would choose.

"I'm right, aren't I?" she said in commiseration. "You do have a great sadness."

"No, I don't! You can't go about saying things like that to people. It's not done!"

"It is by friends. I intend to be your friend, so it's all right for me to say that to you."

"I don't want you to be my friend," he said so forcefully that several people nearby turned to stare. He took Rachel's arm and started walking again. "Go be someone else's friend."

"You kissed me. You know you don't mean that or you wouldn't have kissed me."

"I know this is difficult to understand unless you've been there, but in London, many people kiss for many different reasons, and it rarely means that they want to be friends."

"Then why did you kiss me?"

He gazed down at her. He couldn't tell her it was because he had wanted her so much that he had been aching, or that when he looked too deeply into her eyes he felt as if his soul were touching hers. "It's something a man does from time to time."

"Rob didn't seem to think so. He apparently thought it meant a great deal more than that. So do I."

"Oh? What's your opinion?"

"I think you're falling in love with me."

Jared was so stunned he stopped in his tracks and blatantly stared at her. He opened his mouth to deny it, but found he couldn't think of the right words. Knowing he must say something, he said, "Impossible! I mean . . . I'm doing no such thing!"

"You stammered! You did!" She looked overjoyed.

"I don't understand you at all. You aren't like any woman I've ever run across in my life."

"Maybe that's why you never married."

"Now look here, you shouldn't go around saying things like that." He found he was stumbling over his own words. He drew a steadying breath. "You're too outspoken. That's one of the reasons I don't want to know you."

"What is another?"

"Another what?"

"Another reason you don't want to know me. You said that's one of the reasons. That implies there are more."

"I don't have to give you a list of reasons." He wasn't sure if the day had become unexpectedly hot or if his discomfort was due solely to this very determined young woman. He looked around for Mark, but his cousin, who had started all of this, seemed to have disappeared.

She smiled. "In that case, I'm going to befriend you whether you like it or not."

Jared didn't know what to say. No one had ever been so insistent on getting to know him. The words *love* and *marriage* had been mentioned, but she seemed particularly intent on just being friends with him. Being pursued this way was flattering, to say the least, and being just friends with Rachel probably wouldn't do anyone any harm, he rationalized. "All right. We'll be friends. But since you can't come to my house with any propriety and since your parents aren't going to invite me to your house, how do you propose for this friendship to take place?"

"We'll meet secretly. It will be even better that way. I've never had a secret friend."

To himself he thought there were times when she seemed so young, so naive. And then there were times he thought of her as worldly. "I never know what to say to you or how you'll take it."

"Do you enjoy picnics? We could meet for lunch."

He smiled at last. "I haven't been on a picnic in years."

"No? We go on them quite often around here. Beatrice even has a special basket she packs just for picnics."

"Beatrice is to come along as well? I have to be friends with both of you?"

Rachel considered for a moment. "I don't think that would be a good idea. Beatrice is good at secrets, but she is Rob's sister and she might let something slip to him. No, we should meet alone, I think."

"What about your reputation?"

"We won't do anything. You know that. You can hardly bear to talk to me, to hear you tell it. I'll be perfectly safe with you."

Jared was again stumped. Did she have any idea of what he truly felt for her? Then she smiled and he knew he had been the gullible one. "All right. A picnic it is. Where can we meet?"

She thought for a minute. "At the edge of town there's an old Roman road. You can't mistake it—it lies as straight as a knitting needle. Go down it until you come to the old orchard. I'll be waiting for you there. On Monday," she added. "At noon."

"I'll be there." He found he was actually looking forward to it. Rachel gave him another of her heart-stopping smiles and left him. Jared watched her weaving her way through the crowd. With each step she took away from him, the more he realized that becoming friends with her was the wrong thing to do. What was this hold she seemed to have over him? Why couldn't he use better judgment and leave her alone? All he had to do was to agree to several dates and not show up for them. Sooner or later, Rachel would become discouraged and leave him alone. But even as he considered it, he knew he wouldn't be able to follow through. He wanted to see her, and couldn't stop himself from speculating about what would transpire during this picnic. He would have to take great care. He was not going to allow himself to take advantage of her naiveté.

"She's gone?" Mark asked as he appeared from amid the crowd. "I had hoped you two would talk longer. You really are turning into a hermit."

Jared only smiled.

"I'm telling you, I saw her as plain as day," Hortense Bloomington said. "She was talking to him in the market."

"Rachel hasn't been to the village in days," Violet argued. Hortense was one of her best friends, but the woman had to be wrong on this point. "My sister is here and Rachel has been at home."

"Then she has a twin. I've known Rachel all her life, and I'm positive it was her. I wouldn't tell you this unless I was sure."

Violet had to admit she agreed with the woman's last statement. Hortense loved to gossip, but she was a reliable source of information. She never spread false tales. "You say she was talking to Mr. Prescott? She has been told not to speak to him at all. William was firm about that, although I don't know why, exactly."

Hortense leaned closer to her friend. "There's talk that links him to a trollop's death."

Violet was as shocked as she looked. She knew, of course, that trollops existed, but she thought they were all in London. "Here? In Fairfield?"

Hortense nodded. "They are also saying he has a mistress at Ravenwood and another in London."

"I can't believe that. If there was a strange woman in town, we would have seen her in the shops or on the street."

"Maybe she goes to London to shop. Maybe she sends a servant to see to her needs. Who knows what a mistress may do?"

"That would certainly explain why William is so against the man. Personally, I dislike his arrogance, but usually William is of a more concrete mind than that. He has to have a definite and logical reason for disliking someone."

"I can't stay. I know your sister is waiting for you, and I have to be on my way."

"Surely you'll stay for tea? You always enjoy visiting with Maddy."

"I know, but I have dozens of things to do today. Perhaps another time."

Violet nodded. As she walked Hortense to the door she said, "You'll not tell anyone else about Rachel speaking to that man, will you?"

"Certainly not! I think of her as if she were my own daughter." Hortense gave her a smile, and left.

Violet closed the door. Rachel could have slipped out. She had done it before. Hortense had said she was in the market and that only occurred once a week. On market day Rachel had claimed she wanted to take a nap, and Violet knew her daughter hadn't wanted to sleep during the day since she was a small child. She decided it was time to alert William.

She found him in his library reading a book on law. "William, we must talk."

He looked up. "I thought you and Maddy would be closeted away, exchanging recipes." He gave her a fond smile. "What do you want to talk about?"

"It's Rachel."

William's smile vanished. "What has she done now?"

"I have reason to believe she was talking to Mr. Prescott at the market yesterday."

"What? After I forbade her to have anything to do with him?"

Violet made quieting motions with her hands. This was why she so rarely confided in William. He could be so loud. "I didn't see her myself, but Hortense was just here, and she said she saw someone who could have been Rachel talking with Mr. Prescott."

"Well, was it Rachel or not? Surely she could recognize her or she wouldn't have come to you with the story."

"Hortense is convinced that it was Rachel. I'm not entirely sure."

William slammed the book shut, causing Violet to jump. "I'll speak to the girl at once. She can't be allowed to mingle with riffraff like that! Don't you have any control over her at all?"

Violet sighed. "I haven't been able to control Rachel since she was in short dresses. That's why I'm appealing to you."

"I'll see to her in short order. Where is she?"

Violet watched with relief as William went to find their daughter. If anyone could control Rachel, it was William. They were so much alike that it sometimes made her tremble. Not that Rachel was as loud as William or as forceful, but there had always been a likeness between them. She supposed that was why they had so much trouble getting along at times. She went to have tea with Maddy and to try to enjoy what remained of their visit together.

Chapter Eight

Rachel nodded at the driver to deposit her bag, and she announced to Rose, "I've come for a visit."

"With your belongings? Have you and Papa argued again?"

Rachel cast her eyes downward, unable at the moment to look her elder sister directly in the eye. "He's being entirely unreasonable." She waited for the driver to leave, then added, "It will only be for a while. I hope you don't mind."

Rose led her sister into the parlor, and after easing herself down on the fringed divan, she placed her pale hand on the curve of her stomach. "You'd better tell me all about it."

Trying to hide her nervousness, Rachel sat beside her elder sister and focused her attention on her own hands, which were clasped in her lap. She wasn't afraid of Rose, but she needed her sister's support and knew it was possible that Rose might side with their father. She inhaled deeply, hoping it would bolster her courage, then made eye contact with Rose and said, "I think I'm falling in love."

To Rachel's surprise Rose looked relieved. "With Rob Gaston? That's wonderful. Mama said they had reason to hope you might."

This was already getting started off wrong. "No. Not with Rob. With Jared Prescott."

Rose's smile faded. "Prescott? I don't think I know—"
Suddenly, she broke off her words and her eyes grew round.
"Not the Prescott who bought the baron's place."

Rose sounded astonished, but Rachel wasn't sure
whether that meant she was favorably impressed or that
their father had already filled Rose's head with his prejudice against Jared. Hoping it was the first, she brightly responded, "That's the one. Have you seen him? He's so
handsome!"

"It takes more than good looks to make a marriage,"
Rose said with prim reserve.

"You sound like Mama," Rachel snapped, then remembered she was trying to win Rose to her side. In a gentler
tone, she continued, "Jared isn't just handsome, he's intelligent, and he has traveled. He's seen buffalo and Indians!"

"I'm sure Rob has, too."

"But Rob doesn't tell me about them. Jared not only told
me about seeing them, but implied that I should go see
them myself someday. There! Doesn't that seem like he may
be falling in love with me?"

"For heaven's sake, Rachel. Put your feet on the ground!
Just because a man says he hopes you see a buffalo doesn't
mean he is falling in love with you. If you ask me, you read
entirely too many books." She pulled her shawl about her
to conceal the rounding of her latest pregnancy.

"He does care for me. I'm positive of it." She added, "I
think his cousin is fond of Beatrice, too."

"What about Rob? Where does he fit into this picture?"

"He doesn't fit in at all. That's one reason Papa is so
angry with me."

"What's another reason?"

"That busybody, Hortense Bloomington, saw me talking with Jared in the market and told Mama. Papa said I
was behaving indecorously."

"Were you?"

"We were only talking, for goodness' sake. It's not like we were kissing again."

"*Kissing?*" Rose's eyes opened wider and her mouth dropped open.

Rachel frowned. She had gotten so excited, she had again said too much. As she penitently picked at the design woven into her dimity skirt, she tried to explain. "That only happened once. At the Gastons' party. Or maybe it happened twice. Do you count the times you're kissed or the occasions?"

"Rachel! I can't imagine you doing such a thing. How forward! And at the Gastons'?" Suspicion tinged Rose's voice as she added, "Where was Rob at the time?"

"He was there, too. In fact, he walked in on Jared and me in the library. That's where the kissing took place." She smiled. "He and Jared fought over me."

"They didn't! And at Rob's own house? Why haven't I heard about this?"

"It wasn't that much of a fight. Rob pushed me—to be fair, I have to admit that it might have been by accident—and Jared knocked him down. He was wonderful," she ended softly.

"You can't have men going about fighting over you." Rose looked as shocked as their mother would have been. "What will people say about you?"

"I didn't encourage them to fight. I didn't know what was going to happen until Rob was already on the floor."

A cloud seemed to pass over Rose's features. "I wonder if Edwin would have fought for me," she said, almost to herself. Then she shook her head as if to dispel the vision. "Of course he would have. What a ridiculous thing to think."

"Philip Yardley would have," Rachel said with a smile.

Rose blushed. "I'm a married woman now, and I haven't thought of him in years."

"But don't you see? Jared is my Philip, and I don't want Rob at all. If I must choose between Rob and no one, I'll... I'll become a spinster."

"Now you're talking nonsense. Rob is a fine boy."

"Yes, but Jared is a man."

Rachel exchanged a long look with Rose. She had said her piece and now it was up to Rose. At length Rose's expression softened. "I'd like to meet this Jared Prescott. He must be quite a person to make you leave home over him."

"He mustn't know about that. I don't want him to think he was the cause of family problems. He might never speak to me again."

"From what I hear, he's not that much of a gentleman."

"Everyone is wrong about him. I don't know the details, but he has some dark tragedy in his life. Don't smile. I can see it in his eyes."

"I've looked into a great number of eyes, and I've never seen any so eloquent. You're making it up."

"No, I'm not. I'm sure of it. And I've talked to him on several occasions, and he has never acted in an ungentlemanly fashion." This was mostly true. Rose needn't know every detail of her confusing relationship with Jared. Rachel wasn't entirely sure she understood it herself. "I know how I feel when I'm with him. It's as if I've become more. Do you know what I mean?"

Rose nodded, her eyes misty. "Yes, I know." She touched her handkerchief to her eyes. "You'll have to ignore me. I get weepy when I'm in the family way."

"That's why no one will question my staying here. You should have your sister with you at a time like this."

"My unmarried sister? No, I shouldn't."

"Are you going to send me back?"

Rose sighed. "No, I'm not. You know I wouldn't. But let me be the one to break the news to Edwin. He already worries that Papa may someday decide he doesn't like him."

"There's no chance of that. I've never heard Papa say a single word against him."

"I know, but when a man works with his father-in-law, it becomes more important that the father-in-law like him."

Rose went to the bellpull on the wall and gave it two tugs. "I'll have your bag carried to the guest room. Edwin will be home at any moment now, and I want to tell him when we're alone."

Rachel stood and started for the stairs. "I'll be putting my things away. Let me know when I may come out."

Rose agreed, wishing she didn't have such a bad feeling about all this. Her father did have a temper, and Edwin was working for him in his law office. Despite what she had told Rachel, she was concerned that Edwin might fall out of favor. Not that her father would sack him. In a town as small as Fairfield, there would be no other place for Edwin to earn a living, and her father wouldn't place her in that position. But nevertheless, she knew it was important to Edwin that he maintain his father-in-law's approval.

At the sound of Edwin's footsteps on the porch, she went to meet him. Edwin smiled when he saw her. He was a young man, not much older than Rose, and was passably good-looking. His hair was slicked close to his head, and with the pomade it was darker than without. His neck was red from being abraded by his stiff collar. Rose went to him and placed a kiss on his cheek where he was trying to grow a set of muttonchop whiskers. "I'm glad you're home."

"Oh? Have the children been misbehaving again?" He put the newspaper he was carrying on the hall tree's glove box and hung his hat on a hook.

"No, all seems to have calmed down since you hired that new girl. As a matter of fact, we have company."

"We do?" He glanced past her into the parlor. "Who is it?"

"Rachel."

Edwin laughed. "Your sister doesn't count as company. She's family."

"She's come to spend a few days with us."

Edwin stopped and looked at her. "Whatever for?"

"She said she thought she should be near me at a time like this." She patted her middle and cast down her eyes demurely. Even though they were married, she felt awkward discussing pregnancy with Edwin.

He made a noncommittal grunt and tucked the newspaper under his arm.

"She's in the guest room. Are you upset?"

"No, no. Not at all." His voice sounded distracted as it sometimes did when he was upset and didn't want to admit it.

Rose was relieved. So long as he didn't express his displeasure, they could pretend he wasn't upset at all. Fortunately, Edwin had always gotten along well with Rachel. But then, he got along well with practically everybody. She glanced at her husband and reminded herself that his affability was by design and not merely because he had no firm opinion on any subject.

"Where are the children?"

"In the nursery. Would you like to go up to see them now?"

"Later. Let me read my paper in peace before they descend upon us."

Rose sat in her rocker and picked up her knitting. She needed to tell Edwin the rest of it, and she wasn't sure how to begin. He glanced at her. "Why aren't you going upstairs to make Rachel welcome?"

"There's one other small thing that you should know. Rachel and Papa have had a falling-out."

Edwin lowered the paper and stared at her. "They have? Over what?"

"It seems Rachel isn't all that taken with Rob Gaston and has set her cap for someone else. You know how Papa can be when he decides on something. He's determined that she fall in love with Rob."

"Love isn't something that can be commanded."

Rose looked at him in surprise. "I never expected you to say that. I thought you would stand with Papa."

"I do." He smiled at her. "Unofficially, however, I disagree. Take us, for example. I fell in love with you a good two years before you consented to become my wife."

"Edwin! We're in the parlor!" She felt a blush on her cheeks, but it wasn't uncomfortable. She would have said Edwin had no surprises left for her.

"The point is, I couldn't have made myself fall in love with anyone else. It's not logical, but there it is." He raised the paper again and began to scan it as he said, "Who is Rachel so taken with?"

"Jared Prescott."

This time Edwin crumpled the paper as his hands dropped to his lap. "Not the Jared Prescott who bought the baron's place!"

"I don't think there are two of them. That's the one."

"Impossible! Absolutely impossible. She will have to look elsewhere."

"But why? You were so understanding a moment ago."

"That was before I knew we were discussing Prescott."

"You've met him?"

"No one has met him. No one at all."

"Well, the Gastons must know him. He attended the party they gave the last time they were in town."

"He must have come uninvited. I know Mr. Gaston from down at the club, and he wouldn't invite such a man into his house."

Rose leaned forward. "Why? What does he have against Mr. Prescott if he doesn't know him?"

Edwin bent toward her and whispered. "They say he keeps a mistress at his house and that he may have two more in London."

"No!" Rose was shocked. "Who told you?"

"It's common knowledge at the club. Rachel should stay away from him. Tell her so."

"Me?"

"Well, I can hardly do it."

"Neither can I. What reason could I possibly give her? I can't tell my younger sister that he has a—" she glanced around to be sure no servants had come into the room "—mistress."

"Your father knows it. I'm sure that's why he won't let her change her allegiance from Rob Gaston to Prescott. He's a fair man. If there were no truth to the rumor, he would pay no attention to it."

"But how would Papa know? I'm certain he has never made Mr. Prescott's acquaintance."

"Word gets around. Haven't you heard that where there's smoke, there's fire?"

"Certainly I have, but I can't imagine Rachel fancying herself in love with a man who keeps a . . . you know."

"What does she know of love? She's still a child."

"Hardly. She's twenty years old."

"Rachel is? For some reason I always think of her as being much younger." He seemed to be pondering this, then said, "Nevertheless, Prescott isn't the man for her."

"Evidently Papa told her more or less the same thing. I didn't know she was coming until she arrived bag and baggage on our front steps. I have to send Papa a note and say where she is. Knowing Rachel, she may not have told him she was leaving."

"Surely it wasn't that serious an argument."

"I don't know. Rachel can be as stubborn as Papa."

Edwin sighed but he didn't tell her that Rachel couldn't stay. Rose waited. Edwin put aside the paper. "There's more?"

"You may as well know it all. Mr. Prescott kissed her. Rob saw them and there was a fight."

"A fight! Rob and Prescott? He kissed her?"

Rose nodded. "At the Gastons' party, in the library. Apparently Rob started the fight."

"I should think he might, if he saw his intended kissing another man, and that right in his own house."

"But Rachel says she loves Mr. Prescott. What should we do? I feel so sorry for her."

Edwin reached out and patted her hand. "We should stay out of it. If your father asks, feign ignorance. Perhaps he doesn't know all the details. I wish I didn't."

"You had to know if she's to stay in our house. I promised I'd not keep secrets from you."

Edwin sighed. "When I asked you to promise that, I had no idea you'd take me so literally. We must remain neutral or side with your father."

"Against Rachel? I couldn't. She's in love."

"Then we will take neither side. It's the best way. You'll see. In no time Rachel will see the error of her ways and return to the fold."

"I hope so," Rose said, but she thought it was unlikely.

Yvonne crept across the room and put her ear to the door. She could hear Abby moving about and knew she must be preparing for bed. With a small smile, Yvonne tiptoed to the bookcase and triggered the secret panel to open. Once Abby started to bed, she never returned to Yvonne's room.

She eased down the stairs and felt for the latch on the door. As it swung open, a cool breeze touched her cheeks, reminding her of the time when she and Jared were children and played well into the dusk behind their house. She stepped out into the darkness. Although only a half-moon hung overhead, the night was clear and she could see quite well.

Carefully she moved from shadow to shadow. Below her lay the lights of Fairfield and behind her loomed Ravenwood. She picked her way carefully down the slope toward the village.

More than an hour later, she returned. She was exhausted from her walk. After being confined in one room for so long, she tired easily. She could remember when she could shop all day long and still dance half the night. Paul had been alive then. Yvonne frowned. She had hoped he wouldn't come into her mind.

She remembered being upset in the village, too, but that memory was already growing dim. There had been a red hat in one of the windows and it had frightened her. She remembered seeing a sharp shard of glass, too. Thinking back on that was painful. When she saw the broken glass lying in the alley, she had known Paul and his woman might be near. They frequently stood near sharp objects, especially if there was red about. She tried to remember if the broken glass had been near the red hat, but she couldn't quite recall.

She stayed close to the house's shadows and ran her hand along the wall. So many textures out here. She had almost forgotten there were so many textures to touch. Her room was mostly smooth or soft surfaces and at times that was boring. She touched a vine in the dark and recoiled. Quickly she told herself that it was only a creeper clinging to the side of the house and nothing to fear. After a while she continued on.

The door was right where she expected it to be. She opened it and stepped inside. The smells of Ravenwood assailed her nostrils and she inhaled deeply. It was good to be back. She seldom slipped out at night, and when she did, it always made her appreciate coming home.

She groped her way to the first step, then climbed the rest with confidence. Although the sleeping house surrounded her with its darkness, she was quite comfortable there.

At the top of the steps, she opened the panel and let herself into the room. As always when she had been out of the room, even just into Abby's adjoining one, she checked the bed to be sure it was empty. It was and Yvonne smiled. Paul and the trollop were having some difficulty finding her this time. Maybe they wouldn't find her at all.

Yvonne undressed and shook her skirts to be sure there were no blades of grass or burrs clinging to the fabric. She was always extremely careful whenever she went out. Abby must never know.

She crossed to the door and listened. The room beyond was completely silent. Abby usually snored loud enough to wake a stone. Carefully she opened the door a crack and peered in. The room was empty.

Yvonne was so amazed, she opened the door all the way and stepped into the room. Abby was gone! For a minute she was alarmed and wondered if someone had come and taken her away. Abby sometimes told Yvonne that if she made too much noise, someone would come and take her away. Perhaps that had happened to Abby. But after some thought, she decided that was unlikely because Abby seldom made any noise at all.

She went to the door that led to the corridor and tried the knob. It turned but the door didn't open. Abby had locked it. This made Yvonne feel more secure. If it had been unlocked, it might have meant that Abby had been taken away. Had the law or whoever come for her, she would not have been allowed time to lock the door before being hauled away. Perhaps Abby had gone to the kitchen to get something to eat.

Satisfied that she had reached the right conclusion, Yvonne went back into her own room and closed the adjoining door. A glance at her bed and a more thorough look under it assured her that she was still alone. She went past the overturned chairs and climbed into bed. Wherever Abby was, she would return. She always did.

Bertha Giles's body was found early the next morning by a milkman who was making early deliveries. Like Liza Barnes, Bertha had been stabbed repeatedly in an alley and her throat was cut.

By midmorning everyone in Fairfield knew what had happened. William Pennington had gotten the news on his arrival at his law office. "Murdered? Bertha Giles?" William and Bertha Giles were the same age, though not speaking acquaintances. Nevertheless, he was shocked.

"I heard it from the servants as I was leaving the house," Edwin said. "I could hardly believe it. Two murders in as many months!"

William grimaced as he shut the door. "Was she cut up like Liza?"

Edwin nodded. "There's talk of putting her body on display at the coroner's to see if the sight of it startles anyone into confessing to the murders."

"I hardly think a man so callous as to murder two women would be stirred by the sight of his victims."

"You believe it to be the same man, then?"

"What else am I to believe? That there are two madmen in Fairfield? Of course it must be the same man. Were there any clues at the scene of the crime?"

"No, sir. Sheriff Stoddard says it must have been someone tall from the angle of the wounds. He says that rules out the possibility that it was done by a woman."

"Of course it wasn't." William impatiently went to his desk and pulled out his chair. "No woman would do such a thing. I can't imagine why people are even voicing such a thought."

"You're right, I'm sure." Edwin had followed him to the desk, and he added, "Bertha, like Liza, wasn't of the best character. She may have picked up a man in the Bull and Bear who was her undoing."

"Undoubtedly. I had thought Bertha would amount to more, but there it is." William looked at his son-in-law. "Have you nothing to do?"

Edwin immediately hurried across the room to his desk. He seated himself and began reading through a contract.

William wished he hadn't spoken so sharply to the young man. Edwin tried, and William wished that were enough. To break the silence, he said, "How are Rose and the children?"

"Fine, thank you. We plan to see you this Sunday after church if you aren't otherwise engaged."

"Sunday is fine. Mrs. Pennington is already planning the luncheon menu." In a more casual tone he said, "How is Rachel?"

Edwin looked up over the papers on his desk as if he had hoped the question wouldn't come up. "She is quite well. I've suggested that she should come see you and apologize."

"No need to do that," William said gruffly. "She did wrong and she knows it. That's enough."

"She says she won't come see you until you apologize to her and tell her she may have Mr. Prescott come calling."

"She what!" William saw Edwin flinch. "She expects me to do what?"

"Those were her words, not mine. I'm only delivering them, and I told her I didn't want to be the one to tell you. She insisted."

"You tell her... No, I want to be the one to say to her what I think of her attitude. Just wait until Sunday!"

"Rachel, well, she says she won't be there Sunday."

"What?"

"She said she plans to pine away at our house and perhaps die of a broken heart."

William was frustrated with anger. Leave it to Rachel to find a way to gammon him! What a lawyer she would have made! She knew all the ploys by instinct. "She will have to come to me if she expects there to be peace between us. You tell her that!"

"Yes, sir."

"Where does Rose stand in all this?"

"Rose and I are remaining neutral, sir."

"Good decision." William glared across the room at Edwin. "A wise decision."

He tried to concentrate on the law brief on his desk, but he found it difficult. Rachel had been stubborn since the day she was born. He could still remember her shrieking as he looked into her red face that day and wondered how he had fathered another daughter when he had so wanted a son. In the years that followed, Violet's headaches had prevented the son from being begun, and now he was entering middle age with two daughters, one of them so stubborn she would cut off her nose to spite her face, as the saying went. He thought again what a pity it was that Rachel couldn't be a lawyer or a son.

As Rachel made her way along the meandering cobblestone street toward her father's law office, she was all too aware of the heat from the stones penetrating the soles of her shoes. Summer had begun in earnest. She wished she could dispense with her petticoats and perhaps even loosen the high collar of her white blouse, but that would be a greater violation of decorum than venturing out-of-doors without a hat. All the women, even the poorer ones, wore long sleeves and dresses close about their necks. Rachel had to admit that the men, in their waistcoats and suits and shirts with unyielding collars, looked even more uncomfortable. It didn't seem right that fashion dictated that everyone be so miserable, especially during the hot months, but that was the way things were. There were a lot of things in life she didn't agree with that she had to accept because she couldn't change them—such as having to apologize to her father.

Almost without realizing she had come so far, she found herself in front of her father's office. At his door she paused. She didn't want to do this; it went against the grain. Having to admit to him that her seeing Jared Prescott was wrong was not something she could do. But she could not remain at Rose's house forever. Just this morning her sister had stated that Rachel should apologize and return home.

For another few moments, she pondered what to do, then an alternate course of action came to mind. With her head held high and a smile on her face, she went inside.

From behind his desk, William Pennington glanced up, then looked taken aback. Edwin, who was seated at a table near the rear of the room, looked even more surprised. With confidence, Rachel closed the door behind her and brightened her smile. "Good morning, Papa, Edwin," she said as if nothing at all had been wrong.

Edwin made a polite reply but her father's voice was brusque as he asked, "What are you doing here?"

"I've come to say I'm sorry. I shouldn't have left home while I was so angry. Poor Mama must feel terrible, and I know you've worried yourself sick. You have, haven't you?"

"I feel fine." He looked confused, but determined to remain angry.

Rachel went to his desk and sat in the chair nearest him. "I've missed seeing you. Have you missed me, too?" She smiled again, letting her dimple do its work.

"It's been quiet around the house with you gone. Too quiet, I should say."

"Well, I won't be gone anymore. Now that I know how much you've missed me, I'll go straight back to Edwin's and have my things put in the buggy. By the time you come home, I'll be there. Will that make you feel better?" She enjoyed watching him try to figure out why she was being so sweet and why her doing so was throwing him off balance.

After several moments of confusion, William seemed to recover his mental bearings. "We have a few things to discuss, young lady. Such as your behavior."

"I said I was sorry for making you angry and for leaving in a huff. If that's not apologizing for my poor behavior, I don't know what is."

William opened his mouth, shut it, then opened it again. "I won't have you seeing Prescott. Nothing has changed about that."

"Oh, Papa, let's not discuss that now. We're trying to make up." She lowered her eyelashes and gave him an obsequious smile. Her ploy worked. William relaxed a bit and began shuffling the papers on his desktop. He looked flustered as he always did when she had outwitted him. Rachel suppressed the smile of satisfaction that threatened to burst forth, knowing the upper hand she had over her father was tenuous at best. Any smugness on her part at this moment would turn the tables.

To Edwin she said, "I hope you won't mind my leaving before the baby arrives. I'll be back to check on Rose as often as possible."

Edwin's astonished eyes searched her face. "Rose will be quite all right, I'm sure. We'll miss you," he added.

"And I'll miss you, too," she said warmly. "My visit has been so pleasurable. I love being with my niece and nephew. Papa, don't you think young Will looks just like you? I do." She knew the boy was her father's favorite grandchild.

"I believe he does bear some resemblance to me." Even though William's voice was still curt, Rachel detected a thawing beneath the tone. She was winning.

"And little Rosemary was so adorable this morning. She said, 'When's my grandpa coming to see me?' Rose and I almost cried because it was so sweet."

"I suppose I could stop by there on my way home." He glanced at Edwin. "If it's not inconvenient."

"No, no. Not at all. You're always welcome."

Rachel smiled. She knew quite well her father had stayed away from the Jenson house because he was still angry at her, and that he had been missing his grandchildren. William never would have admitted it, but she knew he had a soft place in his heart for the children. "Well, I have to be going. I don't want to be out in the heat of the day, so I have to go back and finish packing. I'll see you tonight, Papa."

Once she was on the sidewalk and out of her father's sight, she smiled to herself. She had apologized only for the discord caused by her abruptly leaving home. She truly was sorry for that. More important, though, she hadn't admitted to any wrong where Jared was concerned, and she hadn't promised not to see him again. Facing her father on his own ground and apologizing to him without his demanding that she do so had gained her the element of surprise. She was humming under her breath when she returned to Rose's.

Chapter Nine

Rachel had considered taking Ebony for her ride, but decided that doing so would be pushing her luck too far, so she had taken Princess instead. Princess trotted obediently along the Roman road, her head bobbing at every step. At least, Rachel thought, the animal didn't look as placid as she really was.

Ahead she saw the large oak she sought and her heart beat faster. Would he be there, waiting for her? Over the past week she had admitted to herself that there was a strong possibility he would fail to show up. He had consistently said he wanted nothing to do with her, and she was beginning to believe he might mean it.

The ancient oak's limbs swept down almost to the ground. Within its bower, the shadows were dark and promised coolness but obscured the sight of anyone who might be standing there. She reined Princess off the road toward the oak, and that was when she saw a bay she recognized, tied in the shade of the enormous tree. He was here!

Anxiously she dismounted and tied Princess beside the bay. "I thought you had changed your mind," a familiar voice said as she ducked under the oak's heavy branches. When she caught sight of Jared he was smiling down at her.

"I was wondering the same thing about you," she said.

Beneath the tree he had spread a cloth on the grass and had set out a picnic. He gestured for her to sit on the cloth.

Rachel knelt, and as Jared sat beside her, she noticed a wariness in his eyes. "I didn't know what you'd like, so I had my cook prepare several things," he said. "I brought a bottle of white wine." His eyes met hers and Rachel's pulse quickened to be so close to him. Sitting within the oak's shadows, they were invisible to anyone who might pass by, and passersby were extremely unlikely. That was why she had suggested this spot.

"Why did you come?" she asked, curious about the guarded look she had seen moments before.

"I'm not sure. All week I found myself thinking about you and what it would be like to talk to you without having people all about. Twice I had convinced myself not to come. I thought that if I abandoned you, repeatedly perhaps, in time you would come to dislike me and not try to befriend me anymore."

"What changed your mind?" She was finding it hard to breathe. With Jared so close, she could see minute details, such as the texture of his skin and the way his eyelashes curved above his eyes.

"I couldn't bear the thought of not seeing you."

As she watched, Jared took a piece of baked chicken from the plate, pulled off a morsel and offered it to her just inches from her lips. Rather than back away and reach for the food with her fingers, Rachel opened her mouth and he placed the food inside. As she closed her mouth, her lips grazed his fingers, and the intimacy of the gesture made her pulse race. As she chewed slowly, he ate from the same piece of chicken.

After a moment of sensuous silence, Jared continued. "I told myself that I was daring fate, that I was a fool to encourage you when we can have no real relationship. But I've never been particularly good at listening to advice."

"Why can't we?"

"Because, my innocent, no one in Fairfield will admit me into their parlors, least of all your parents. We can't continue to meet in secluded places. Eventually we will be found out, and your father will be beside himself. He probably wants to shoot me as it is."

"Not Papa. He seldom shoots anyone." She smiled teasingly. "Besides, we are doing nothing wrong."

"Ah, but we are. We've secreted ourselves from others and are having an extremely private picnic. In Fairfield that may be a hanging offense."

"You don't know us very well."

Jared shook his head. "Not individually, perhaps, but I know you. I haven't stayed in London all my life, and I know the people in villages all seem to think alike."

"Then I'm not the first girl you've taken on a picnic?" She knew what the answer must be and she felt a twinge of jealousy.

"No, you're not. You are, however, the only one I've ever been obliged to slip out to meet. You'll find this difficult to believe, but my name isn't an anathema to all of England. There are even some parents who have encouraged, all but demanded, that I take their daughters on similar picnics."

"And did you?" She opened her mouth as he fed her another sliver of chicken.

"Rarely or never. You see, I seldom do what others expect." His eyes met hers as her lips closed over his fingers.

Rachel blushed and looked away. "I can feed myself."

"I know that, but isn't this much more fun?"

Her eyes met his again. "It feels like rather dangerous fun."

"Like an adventure, perhaps?" He grinned at her and raised an apple to his lips.

"It is, isn't it!" she exclaimed. "I hadn't thought of that."

He took another apple and handed it to her. The symbolism wasn't lost on her. She bit into it and felt daring. This was exactly the sort of thing a man would do in the romantic novels she so loved to read.

"Did anyone ask where you were going when you left home?" Jared asked as he poured them each a glass of wine.

"No, I often ride alone. Did Mark wonder where you were going?"

"Yes, so I told him."

Rachel frowned as she took the glass from his hand. "He will think ill of me."

"No, he won't. He was glad to hear about our meeting. Mark thinks I'm lonely."

"Are you?"

He hesitated, then said, "No."

"I don't believe you."

"There are circumstances that enforce loneliness. Unless I intend to alter those circumstances, and I don't, I must accept the loneliness as a natural offshoot."

"What circumstances?"

"That, unfortunately, must remain my secret."

Rachel looked down at her wine. "They say in the village that you are keeping a mistress."

"If I were, I would hardly be lonely, now would I?"

"You deny it then?"

"Of course I do. The idea is ridiculous. If I had a mistress, everyone in Fairfield would have seen her out shopping. That's the thing about mistresses—they do love to shop."

"Then you have kept one in the past?"

"I didn't move here from a monastery."

Rachel felt uncomfortably inexperienced. "You must think my questions are foolish. I don't know how to talk to a man like you."

"No? You've had no problem thus far. Does my lurid past bother you?" His smile teased her to admit it.

"No, I've just never met anyone who actually confessed to having had a mistress. You didn't even pretend or make any excuses."

"There are no excuses for having one. Mistresses don't happen to a man by accident. You don't wake up one morning and discover one has taken up residence in your back room."

"I shouldn't be talking to you about this."

"We could discuss something else."

"What are mistresses like?"

"They are no different from other women. Most are pretty, but not all. They generally have a pleasant disposition."

She tried not to feel the jealousy, but it was gnawing at her. "Was yours pretty and amiable?"

"No, she was beautiful and charming."

"You shouldn't be telling me about her. Where is she now?"

"I have no idea. She left me for a viscount."

"She left you! I would never have left—" She bit off what she was about to say.

"Yes?"

"Never mind."

"I don't regret her loss. She was my mistress, not my love, though at one time she pretended to love me."

"Maybe she did."

He shook his head. "If she had, she would never have left me. Not even for a king."

Rachel studied his face. "I've never had a man talk to me so honestly before."

"That's another reason I'm not suited for society here. I tend to speak my mind. In London my fortune is large enough that my hosts overlook it. Here I would be branded as the brash lout that I am."

She smiled. "You are no lout. Not in any sense of the word." She thought for a minute about the rumors that were speeding through Fairfield. "Tell me about your mills."

"My mills? What do you want to know?"

"I've told you what people are saying."

"I thought that must have died down by now, but I suppose Fairfield hasn't enough to occupy its collective mind. My mills are in London, Haversham and York. They are experimental in a way. I've installed windows that may be opened for fresh air, and in the winter I've had the rooms heated despite my detractors' predictions that I will burn them, and my profits, to the ground.''

''What about the children?''

''Children only work when they must in order to live. I pay my workers reasonable wages, and I employ both the husband and the wife if they both choose to work. I also have hired several women who are too old to work to watch over the small children so the mothers won't have to leave them alone at home.''

''I've never heard of such a place!''

''I said it was experimental. In return I expect my workers to do a full day's work and not to cheat me by slacking off or by pilfering the materials to sell on the sly. Everyone said my employees would steal me blind and work only when I was around, but I've proved them wrong. My mills are thriving. So, incidentally, are my workers.''

''Why don't more do this, then?''

''It costs a great deal to set up factories like this. I had them built to my specifications. I also had to interview a large number of applicants to find the ones who really wanted to do an honest day's labor. I was looking for people who already lived in the area or who were likely to want to settle there. Too often workers move on without warning, and I didn't want that. Then I had to hire good men to oversee it. Men I could trust to run the mills as I want them to be run.''

''And you found such men?''

''Yes. I drop in on them unexpectedly from time to time, but they are all more than satisfactory.''

''If everyone in Fairfield knew all this, you would be more of a hero than a villain.''

''You're assuming that I care.'' Jared moved nearer to Rachel and touched his glass to hers. ''I don't.''

Rachel knew she was staring but she couldn't help it. ''I've never met anyone who truly didn't care what people thought of him.''

"I care about some people. You, for instance."

"Why? Why do you care?"

He sobered. "I'm not sure and, frankly, it scares the hell out of me."

When he made no apology for using strong language, Rachel took a sip of her wine. Jared was certainly nothing like anyone she had ever known before.

"I have a certain freedom in my loneliness," he went on to say. "I may not have friends here, but neither do I have to bow and scrape to people I don't like. Not that I would anyway. Bowing and scraping are activities that I never mastered."

"We have a great deal in common." She wondered if the wine was going to her head or if it was Jared's presence.

"I had a feeling that we might."

Rachel put the remains of their picnic back into the basket. She felt the need to occupy her hands and thoughts. His voice seemed to touch a chord deep inside her and to move her in ways she had never experienced before she met him. When she was finished, she sat straight and put her hands in her lap. "I should be going."

"Why?"

"I mustn't keep you." Rachel found herself suddenly shy, and she felt awkward because she didn't want to go at all.

"You aren't." He put their wineglasses in the basket and sat closer beside her. "Am I keeping you from something?"

"No," she whispered.

"Then I see no reason to rush away. Do you?" Jared lifted his hand and touched the curve of her cheek.

Rachel's eyes met his, and she felt as if she were being drawn into the depths of his soul. She had no desire to pull away, though she knew she should. This wasn't a man like Rob, who knew and abided by the rules; Jared had admitted openly that he had once kept a mistress, and she would always remember their first kiss, one that had come at a time when they hardly knew each other and in a location that could only be termed foolhardy. She felt sure he was about to kiss her again.

"You look as if thoughts are whirling about in your mind."

"They are," she answered. "You confuse me and frighten me."

"Are you afraid of me?"

"No." Her voice was a whisper. "I'm afraid of myself."

Jared smiled and put his hand behind her head. As he drew her closer, her pulse quickened with anticipation. When his warm, moist lips touched hers, her heart thrummed in her throat, and the dizziness she had felt earlier was trebled. She felt as if she were being caught up in a powerful vortex that was spinning her off into another world. With no reserve at all, she kissed him back, her arms encircling him and pulling him closer. All her senses were heightened and she delighted in the experience. His coat was warmed by his body and felt slightly rough beneath her hands. Its texture was completely alien to her, and it excited her even more because she knew it was molded to fit his shape.

As the kiss deepened and Rachel learned from him how to respond, something new bloomed within her. Suddenly, and without any doubt, she knew she was in love with Jared. What had been an infatuation had now matured into an emotion that would have been frightening in its intensity if it hadn't been so wonderful.

Jared drew back, looking as moved by the kiss as she had been. He made no sound as he gazed deeply into her eyes. Rachel's newborn love swelled within her, and she tried to smile, but the emotion was still too new. She closed her eyes and swayed nearer to kiss him again.

This time Jared drew her down beside him as he reclined on the cloth. Their bodies touched from head to toe, and every nerve ending in Rachel's body was stimulated by the contact. Her small riding hat fell to one side, and she could feel the pins in her hair coming loose, but she didn't care.

All that mattered was Jared and the desire he was awakening in her.

He held her close, his breath warm against her ear. She felt his tense muscles quivering and she pulled him closer, still not daring to speak. Was he experiencing the same emotion she was? Rachel's breath came fast, and she held him tight, as if he were her anchor.

Jared raised his head and fixed his eyes on hers. The passion she had seen in him moments before now seemed to be tinged with some other emotion she didn't recognize. After a moment, he said, "It was a mistake for us to meet like this, alone, away from other people."

"A mistake?" Rachel was terribly afraid of what his next words might be.

"I want you. I think I've wanted you since the first time I saw you. And I can't have you." He touched her face, cupping it in his large hand. "You tempt me and confuse me and infuriate me and delight me. I don't know what to do or how to think when you're around. Every time I see you, I tell myself that it will be the last. That I'll get control of myself and be rational. Then I see you in a crowded street or you speak to me and I'm lost again."

"Jared," she whispered, making his name a pledge of adoration. "I love to feel your name on my lips."

"You have such an innocence. I'm afraid of harming you, and that you won't know you've been harmed. You should have some gentle man to care for you. Not someone like me."

"I don't want a gentle man." She touched his face and drew her fingertips across his lips. Every inch of him was so beloved to her. She found tiny miracles in the way his hair grew and in the darkness of his eyes. She ran her fingers through his soft, neatly trimmed hair. "I want you."

"You don't know what you're saying. You use words that you don't understand. How can I make you understand that you're playing with fire to tempt me so?"

She drew her hand over the swelling muscles of his back and marveled at the strength she sensed there. He seemed to be making a supreme effort to hold himself back. With a groan he kissed her again and Rachel responded eagerly. Jared's kiss was like fire to her veins. She wanted him in a way that she didn't fully understand, but her need was so intense that she felt herself moving beneath him by instinct.

Jared drew away and sat up. "We have to stop. If we don't, I won't be able to be strong for you, and it's clear that one of us must be."

Rachel sat up and her hair tumbled free, flowing down her back and pooling about her hips. "Have I displeased you?" She didn't understand why he had stopped kissing her. "Didn't you enjoy kissing me?"

Jared looked away for a moment, then turned back to her. Before he answered, he lifted the heavy skein of her dark hair and let it glide over his hand. "I enjoy it too much."

She took his hand and put it on her cheek. "I enjoy it, too."

"Rachel, it's more than something to merely enjoy. When I kiss you, I lose reason. Do you know what happens between a man and a woman at times like this?"

"I think so. I tried to get Rose to tell me but she refused, so I asked the scullery maid. I suppose it's the same."

"I'm sure it is. Are you so innocent that you can't see why you shouldn't tempt me like this?"

Rachel smiled. "I'm not sure any woman is that innocent. I wasn't tempting you on purpose, but I'm glad you are."

He rubbed his thumb over the corner of her lips. "I want to kiss you. I want to do much more than that. I'm not, however, that uncivilized, as it turns out. Frankly, I'm a bit surprised to learn that. I'd have said I couldn't be trusted at all."

"I trust you entirely."

"I think it's that trust that has made an honest man of me. I'm not, however, a saint. I think you should go."

Rachel felt keen disappointment. "Leave? Now?"

"If you don't leave now, I may never let you leave at all."

The import of his words touched her. She wanted to tell him that she never wanted to leave him, either, which was true. Whatever he might think or do, she knew now that he was the one she was meant to love and that she was meant to love him forever. If it took him longer to come to that realization, then she would have to wait.

She let him help her to her feet, but she swayed toward him and their bodies met. Jared's arms went about her and again he bent to kiss her. Rachel's heart was his, and he didn't seem to even know it. She tried to tell him how she felt with her kiss. He tangled his fingers in her hair and responded with an ardor that left her breathless.

"Go," he said with some difficulty. "Go now."

As she began twisting her hair back into its decorous bun, he retrieved her hairpins and her hat. She shoved the pins in securely and put the hat on her head. Without a mirror she had to go by touch. "Do I look all right?"

"You look beautiful." His eyes validated his words.

"When will I see you again?"

"I don't know. I'll send you word somehow, if we don't see each other by accident."

"I seldom trust anything important to accidents."

"I wish you were a different sort of woman. If you were, I'd take you home with me and do all in my power to make you never want to leave."

"I once overheard a footman saying there isn't much difference between a lady and a woman."

"Go home, Rachel," he said softly.

She mounted her horse and smiled down at him for one more stolen moment, then reined Princess toward home. All the way home her heart sang. Down in the woods she could hear birds singing along with her, and she doubted they had ever sung as sweetly before. She loved Jared and, whether he knew it or not, he loved her, too. If he didn't, he soon would. She might not have a great deal of experience personally, but she had a keen instinct. Jared had all the actions of a man in love. Otherwise, she would still be in his arms, and he would never have sent her away.

She left the horse at the stable and hummed as she took the path to the house. She could not recall ever having seen a prettier day. Jared had said she was beautiful. He had said he wanted her.

The first person she saw when she entered the house was her father. He glanced at her, then looked again. His brows knitted over his nose. Rachel's composure slipped. Had she pinned her hair wrong? Was her hat on backward?

"Where have you been?"

"I was out riding, Papa."

William stepped closer to his daughter and examined her in the light from the windows on either side of the door. "Were you alone?"

She hated to lie because she wasn't good at it. "Yes."

"I don't believe you." He pulled her face toward the light. "You've been kissed!"

Rachel put her fingers to her lips. They did feel bruised and swollen, and her cheek did feel slightly abraded by Jared's shaved cheek.

"There's grass in your hair!"

She lifted her hand and pulled out a strand of grass. "How did that get there?" she said with an effort at a laugh.

"You have grass on your dress, too."

Rachel tried to look over her shoulder. They had been on the coverlet all the time. How had she managed to get so much grass on her? "Princess got tired, so I stopped to let her rest. I lay down by a stream while I waited."

"Don't lie to me, girl! I'm accustomed to seeing through better liars than you are!" Her father's voice rose.

Violet rushed out from the back parlor. "What's wrong?"

William glared at his wife. "Look at our daughter!"

Violet came to Rachel. "I see nothing wrong with her," she said doubtfully. She automatically reached out and brushed the grass from Rachel's shoulder.

"Don't do that! You're destroying evidence!"

"I'm not in court, Papa," Rachel objected with matching vigor. "I told you what happened."

"I don't believe you. You've been taught how to treat a horse. Unless you were galloping her, which you've been told not to do, you haven't been gone long enough to tire Princess."

"She's getting on in years," Rachel tried to interject.

"Not that much, she isn't. Who were you with? Was it Prescott?"

"Were you riding with Rob?" Violet asked hopefully.

"Never! I detest Rob Gaston and I wish he would... would go back to America!"

"Don't you raise your voice in front of your mother," William roared.

"You are!"

"That's entirely different! Rachel, if you are to remain in this house, you must tell me who you were with and exactly what happened!"

"No!"

"That does it, miss. You are going to stay in your room until you can be civil, and you're going to marry Rob Gaston as soon as your mother can get it arranged. You're never to see or speak to this Prescott again, and I'll do whatever needs to be done in order to see that you obey. Do you understand me? This is my house and you are my daughter, and you'll do as I say!"

Rachel met his glare long enough for him to see the defiance in her eyes, then she turned and stomped up the stairs. Behind her, she could hear her mother trying to prevent her father from coming after her. She was too angry to care. All the soft gentleness from being with Jared had been replaced with anger, and that upset her even more. Why did her parents have to spend so much time trying to run her life?

Jane met her in her room. By the wideness of the maid's eyes, Rachel knew word of the argument had spread belowstairs. "Help me pack," she said.

"You're not leaving again! You shouldn't do that."

"I have to, Jane. I can't stay in a house where I'm not trusted." She threw an armload of lacy undergarments onto her bed. "Get my bag."

Without question, Jane hurried to obey, but when she returned with the bag, she said, "Your father won't keep forgiving you forever. What if Miss Rose refuses to take you in?"

"Rose would never refuse me. If she does..." Rachel thought for a minute, then brightened. "I'll elope!"

"Elope! With who? Mr. Rob?"

"Don't even say his name in front of me. No, with Jared Prescott."

"The man said to have killed those women?" Jane looked as shocked as if she knew the accusation to be well deserved.

"Jared never killed anyone. What are you talking about?" She started stuffing her things into the bag.

"That's what they are saying in the kitchen and in the village. I heard it said on my last half day off."

"Well, it's a lie. Jared is wonderful, and you can tell anyone I said so." She stopped packing long enough to say, "I love him, Jane. I think he loves me, too."

"Sometimes a man says 'love' when he means something else entirely, Miss Rachel. It's a way they have."

"Not Jared. He's honest to a fault. Do you know he even told me he once had a mistress? That's how honest he is."

Jane looked less convinced than ever. "Miss Rachel, don't do something hasty. Don't go off from here."

"I'm only going to Rose's. If there's talk, say that I'm going to stay with her until her baby is born. After the baby comes, if Papa is still being unreasonable, I'll find some other excuse to stay there."

"You're making a big mistake," Jane objected as she helped Rachel pack. "You didn't hear him going on last time you left. He was like a mad bull."

"Good. Maybe he'll come around quicker this time."
She closed the bag and handed it to Jane. "I'll carry my
jewelry box. I'll send a man up to get my trunk."

"Not the trunk, too. Miss Rachel, it's like you're moving out to stay."

Rachel looked around the room that had seen all her
years as a child. "I may be, Jane. I hope not, but there are
some things a person has to hold fast to, and this is one of
them. I love Jared, not Rob, and I won't be forced to marry
a man I don't love. After today, Papa might try to make me
do exactly that. This is better for everyone concerned." She
lifted her chin with determination. "Let's go, Jane." She
was convinced she was right, and she would let nothing de-
ter her.

Chapter Ten

"You're back!" Rose stared at her younger sister and the pile of luggage that the Penningtons' driver was depositing in her parlor. This time there was more than a simple bag.

"Yes, and you needn't tell me to make up with Papa again. This time he went too far." Rachel thanked the man and shut the door behind him.

"You can't keep doing this. Eventually he will refuse to take you back. Then what will happen to you?"

"I suppose I'll have to stay here with you forever." Rachel tried to smile, but she was too close to tears.

Rose put her arms around her sister. "I didn't mean that you wouldn't be welcome. You know that, don't you?"

Rachel nodded. "You've always been so kind to me. So has Edwin," she added. "Where is he?"

"At the club. What happened this time?"

"Papa was being unreasonable because I saw Jared again today."

"Mr. Prescott? Against Papa's orders? Rachel, what were you thinking?"

"I was thinking of Jared and myself. I love him, Rose. I really do. Before today, I only thought I did, but now I have no doubt. I have reason to believe he loves me, too."

"Have you told Papa this?"

"Yes, but I had to shout it for him to hear. You know how loud he gets when he's angry."

"Were you seen together again?"

"Not this time." Rachel went to the mantel and toyed with the fringed silk mantel scarf. As she drew her fingers through the fringe, she said, "He kissed me again."

"No! He didn't! Where were you? Not in the market-place again!"

"No, we went on a picnic. I had him meet me at the big oak beside the Roman road. Do you remember the place?"

Rose nodded. "It's so isolated! Rachel, if anyone had seen you, your reputation would have been ruined forever."

"I know. That's why I picked that spot. No one ever goes that way." She watched the fringe fall back into place as her finger tailed along. "Jared brought the food and wine. He's ever so exciting. I wish you would meet him. You'd see why I love him. When I'm with him, I feel as if I can do anything."

"So you've told me. If no one saw you, how did Papa know you'd seen him?"

Rachel turned away and went to the window. This was the question she had dreaded. "When I went in the house, I saw Papa right away. He saw that I had been kissed, and he demanded to know who I had been with. Naturally I refused to tell him."

"Then what?"

"He noticed I had bits of grass in my hair and on my shoulders. I still don't know how they came to be there. I was on a cloth, not the grass."

Rose was silent for a long time. "You lay with him?"

"It's not what you must be thinking. He only kissed me. But he kissed me again and again, and I have to admit—" her voice softened at the memory "—I wished he would do more."

"Rachel! You have no idea what you are talking about! You didn't tell him this, I should hope!"

"I didn't have to. He knew it."

"How do you have any idea what goes on between a man and a woman? I never told you, and Mama certainly wouldn't have. She didn't tell me until my wedding day."

"I heard it in the kitchen." Rachel turned back to her sister. "He makes me feel like a woman."

Rose was shaking her head. "You mustn't do that ever again. He could have ruined you!"

"I know, but he didn't. He respects me too much. He was as excited as I was, but he drew away and told me to leave."

"He did?" Rose at last sounded as if she might be seeing Jared as something other than the enemy. "It was his idea that you leave?"

"Yes. I told you that he loves me."

Rose was thoughtful. "Did you tell this to Papa?"

"No, he would never have understood. I couldn't tell him such a thing, or Mama either."

"No, don't tell Mama. That would never do at all. I'm positive she wouldn't understand."

"When Edwin kisses you, do you feel like that?"

Rose started to smile, but then shook her head as if to remind herself that such a confession would be improper. "That has nothing to do with it. The question is, what are you going to do about Mr. Prescott?"

"I don't know. He didn't propose, and naturally he doesn't know I've moved here. Even if he did, I doubt he would impose on you or try and see me here."

"I should hope not! I don't want Papa to be angry with Edwin." She put her fingers to her mouth. "Oh, dear! What will Edwin say?"

"You need not tell him everything I told you. Just say that I'm here to help you until your baby is born. That's what we were going to tell him last time."

"I know, but he didn't believe me then, and he certainly won't believe me now. Look at this mountain of things. It's obvious you've brought everything you own."

"Let's have it taken upstairs before he sees it. Once it's in my bedroom, he will never have occasion to know it's here."

"I think that would be best." Rose summoned a servant, and the sisters were silent until the man left the room to carry up the first load of Rachel's belongings.

"Rachel, have you considered the impact of your leaving home? What if Papa disowns you?"

"It's a risk I have to take."

"I know I encouraged you to marry for love, but I think now that I was wrong. You said Mr. Prescott didn't propose. In the circumstances, I think that's the least he should have done." She became quiet again as the man came back for another load. When he was out of earshot, she continued. "If he has such great regard for you, why didn't he ask you to marry him?"

"I don't know. I have the feeling that Jared doesn't do things on impulse very often. He has tremendous self-control." Rachel smiled. "I'm sure he intends to ask me."

"You can't be sure of that. How do you know?"

"If he loves me, what else would he do? He must be waiting until the moment is right."

"Rachel, be reasonable. What moment could have been better? You were alone and he was kissing you."

The man returned and shouldered the rest of Rachel's belongings.

"You have to be logical for once. What if you're wrong and Mr. Prescott doesn't love you or want to marry you? You've risked the love and affection of your parents on this gamble."

"Mama and Papa love me. They may be angry, but they won't actually disown me. That's just silly."

"No, it isn't. Rachel, you're taking a terrible chance."

Rachel hoped she was right. They had indeed been angry at her. "It's what I have to do. I love Jared, and I love him enough to risk everything." Even though her words sounded overly dramatic, Rachel meant them all.

Rose sighed and shook her head. "Whatever will I do with you, Rachel? Whatever will become of you?"

"Don't worry, Rose. Everything will be all right." She wished she were as positive as she sounded. Rose had brought up some very good questions. Why hadn't Jared proposed?

"I should never see her again," Jared fumed as he paced the length of his drawing room. "You should have seen me. I was as foolish as a boy."

Mark watched him pace. "You say nothing happened. Of a serious nature, I mean?"

"I didn't ravish her, if that's what you're getting at. I wanted to, though. Damn, but I wanted to."

"Yet you didn't lay a hand on her? Your restraint is becoming remarkable."

"I kissed her, nothing more. Mark, you've seen her, you've heard her speak. What is there about this one woman that torments me so? I've behaved disgracefully toward her. I've shown her my worst temper, I've been cold toward her, now I've kissed her as if she were some shepherd's lass, but she still seeks me out. The worst part of all is that I miss her when she isn't around, and I worry about her when she isn't constantly invading my privacy."

"Are you falling in love? It has all the earmarks, if you ask me."

"How does a man know? I think about her all the time, I can't sleep for dreaming about her, I believe I see her in every crowd and hear her voice when she is nowhere near. I'm bewitched by her."

"I've been in and out of love many times, and you can take my word for it. You are a man heading for matrimony."

"Impossible. Don't even tempt me with such a word." Jared stopped pacing and dropped into a nearby leather chair. "You know it's impossible."

"You could find another home for Yvonne. I wouldn't mind helping you. I could make inquiries of some people I know in Southend-on-Sea. That's not so far—you could see her often."

"I can't put Yvonne in a place where she might be mistreated. I would never know if she was happy or not. You know how those places tend to be. When a visit is expected, all is sunshine and good humor. When I'm not there, how will they behave toward her? No, I can't take that chance.''

"It means your happiness. I admire you for being so good to your stepsister, but there are limits.''

"She never gets past Abby in this house. Perhaps I could have a wife without her ever knowing Yvonne is here.'' He gazed thoughtfully at the paneled walls. "No, that's too farfetched. It's impossible.''

"You could forbid your wife to go into that wing.''

"Not if the wife were Rachel. She would go there before I had the words forbidding it out of my mouth.'' He got to his feet again and resumed his pacing. "I'm a fool to even consider a future with her or any other woman.''

Mark said, "You aren't cut out for this monastic life. I'm amazed you've been reclusive for this long.''

"It hasn't been easy. I'm only able to do it for Yvonne's sake.''

"It wouldn't hurt for me to make inquiries. Maybe I could find a place for her near Uxbridge or Watford. That's nearer than Southend-on-Sea, and she would be in the country.''

"She's in the country here, and I know she is well cared for as long as she is under my own roof.''

"Yes, but as long as she is, no one else can be.''

"You needn't remind me. I think of it day and night. I promised Father on his deathbed that I would always watch after Yvonne and keep her as happy as possible. She reminded him of her mother, you know. Father never really got over losing her.''

"I know. So what will you do? Sacrifice your own happiness in life for Yvonne? Your father never meant for you to do that. He loved Yvonne, but you are his son, his flesh and blood. If you don't marry, your family name will die with you.''

"I know, and Father wouldn't have wanted that, but I see no other way.''

"Yvonne is so far removed from logic that she might not know where she is or that you aren't still with her."

"No, that's not true, unfortunately. She misses me if I'm even an hour late in visiting her. Abby says she watches from the window to see me ride past and that she stands there and waits until I return. I'm the largest part of Yvonne's life. Sometimes I think I may be her last link with reality. No, I can't send her away."

"Nor would I recommend it, when you put it that way."

"But I'm falling in love with a woman and I want her with me." Jared stared vacantly at the hunting print on the wall. "In truth I think I may have already fallen."

"That was my opinion as well."

"I sent a note to her house, but I received no reply. Not that I expected one. I shouldn't have sent it in the first place. I know how her parents feel about me. They made it clear on our first meeting that I wasn't welcome there."

"That's what puzzles me. In London you are sought after by everyone. No party is complete without your name in the pot."

"Here I live as a hermit. I saw Pennington on the street the other day, and he cut me down with a glare and changed his course to avoid coming near me. Rachel must have told him that we kissed. That's why I sent the note. When I didn't see her the next few days, I was afraid her father might have done something to her."

"He's violent?" Mark asked with a frown. "I didn't know that."

"Nor do I, for certain. I only know that he has a reputation for having a temper and that he tends to be loud and rather abrasive in court. My man, Stanford, told me this. It turns out that Stanford makes an excellent spy."

"He's a man of many talents. I may hire him away from you yet."

"If I thought for a minute that Rachel was in danger, I would go to her home and force them to let me see her."

Mark shook his head. "That would seal your fate with her, I'm afraid. Pennington would certainly keep her from you if you were as aggressive as that. Do you think he has sent her away?''

"I was afraid of that, but I caught a glimpse of her in the village yesterday and was reassured. However, she was gone before I could reach the spot where she had been, and I couldn't find her again."

"She must be all right or she wouldn't have been out shopping."

"I even considered going to the Gaston house and asking Beatrice to speak to Rachel for me."

"Why didn't you?"

"It's all so convoluted. I doubt Mr. or Mrs. Gaston would welcome me after what happened at their party, and their son is also interested in Rachel. If someone other than Beatrice caught sight of me there, I would be expelled in short order."

Mark laughed. "I'd say you're like a spider caught up in its own web. I told you not to be such an eccentric."

Jared scowled at his cousin. "I don't see how I could have done anything differently, and there seems no way to undo it now. The people of Fairfield are already turned against me."

"Probably not everyone. Likely the Gastons are, because of the fight, and the Penningtons because of Rachel, but the others here have no cause to dislike you."

"Blast it, the Penningtons and the Gastons are the only ones I care about!"

Mark stood and went to his cousin. "You have to redeem yourself. Enter society, blame your previous actions on illness that has now passed, and start having parties."

"Shall I also invite Yvonne? I can't do that, as you well know."

"How about this? I'll go to Beatrice and try to intervene in your behalf."

Jared looked at him thoughtfully. "That might work."

"At the very least, it will allow me to see Beatrice again."

Jared smiled. "You sound as if you may be smitten in your own right."

"I could be at that. I seem to be experiencing the same symptoms that you described in relation to yourself."

Jared looked out his window at the sloping green below. "We have come to a pretty end when we have to court our chosen ladies so circuitously. Or should I say surreptitiously."

"True, but it may make us appreciate them more. Tell me, Jared. If you could have Rachel's hand for the asking, would you have been so intrigued?"

"Yes, I would."

"Eventually, perhaps, but at first? If I had seen Beatrice in London at one of the parties we used to attend, she would have seemed pale, though pretty, in comparison with the beauties we knew there. It was only because I saw her in her own setting that I was able to comprehend that she had more to offer than a pretty face or money."

"The Gastons are as well-off financially as the Penningtons," Jared said. "You wouldn't be settling beneath yourself."

"They are wealthy for Fairfield, but not for London. Someone as sweetly shy as Beatrice would have never survived some of the parties we've attended."

"We have indeed mellowed," Jared said with a smile. "We've sown our share of wild oats and enough for two other men as well."

"True. That's why I know we will make such exemplary husbands."

"You're thinking of marriage?" Jared couldn't keep the surprise out of his voice. "You hardly know Beatrice."

"I know her as well as you know Rachel. I haven't been sitting here idly while you've tried to intercept Rachel out riding or shopping. I've seen Beatrice several times."

"But marriage? I never thought you would settle down so early or marry anyone who wasn't the quintessence of London society."

Mark shrugged and grinned. "I see more to please me in Fairfield. Wouldn't Father be surprised? He always said I would amount to no good at all."

"I never believed it. I knew you'd settle down eventually. I just never expected it to be so soon, or for you to find the woman you would love in a place like Fairfield."

"Neither did I, and I thought the same thing about you."

"I never figured mellowing would be painful, either." Jared moved over to the mantel, then retraced his steps. "I feel like a caged lion. How can I see Rachel without compromising her? I feel guilty asking Beatrice to risk her parents' disapproval in being our liaison."

"Beatrice and Rachel are such close friends that I'm sure she would enjoy the responsibility. I'm assuming that Rachel returns your affection?"

Jared smiled. "She's as easy to see through as this glass." He tapped the windowpane. "Every thought that passes through her mind is written on her face. She cares for me."

"Did you tell her how you feel?"

"No, it was all I could do to send her on her way unharmed. You'd have been proud of me, Mark. I was as strong as a saint." He wished he hadn't regretted that strength so often since their picnic, and that his dreams hadn't shown him graphically what he had forfeited. "I only hope I can continue in my strength until she's my bride."

"Oh?"

"Rachel is a lady. I can't take advantage of her just because I would be able. I respect her too much."

"Too much respect can make for a cool courtship."

Jared laughed. "I don't need to be concerned about that. Whenever we are near each other, you can all but see the sparks in the air. No, my concern is just the opposite."

"I've known parents to give their consent freely after a seduction has taken place," Mark said.

"In London, perhaps, but not here. Fairfield has more puritanical mores. No, I must court her in the accepted fashion." He struck his fist against his thigh. "But I'm damned if I can figure out how to accomplish it."

"I'll talk to Beatrice. Will you come with me?"

"And pour out my heart in front of her as if I were some besotted shepherd? No, you go alone. I'm sure you would prefer a word alone with her. But, Mark, don't make me sound like an inept fool."

Mark grinned. "I'll try not to. I have to admit this is a side of you that I would never have guessed existed. I confess that to see you checkmated in courtship is a sight I never thought to encounter."

"Go to Beatrice while you can go in one piece," Jared suggested with exasperation. "I'm glad to hear you're so enjoying my discomfort."

Jared could hear Mark chuckling as he left the room. He brushed the heavy curtains farther to one side and gazed down the green toward Fairfield. Rachel was down there somewhere, as isolated from him as if she were in another country. Jared cursed softly at the perverseness of fate for him to have finally found a woman he could love, only to have her as inaccessible as he had been in the past to the marriageable young ladies of London.

Chapter Eleven

Beatrice glared at her brother. "I don't see why you have to be so stubborn about this. Rachel obviously doesn't want to see you."

"I refuse to believe it. Her father gave me permission to call on her, and that means he favors me as a son-in-law."

"Then court her father. Rachel isn't even under his roof. She has been staying with Rose for several weeks now."

"That has nothing to do with it. She must and will see me."

"Rob, be reasonable. People are beginning to talk about you. They think it's comical the way you're chasing after her like a terrier trying to bring down a bird. You can't have her, so stop making a spectacle of yourself."

"It's all Prescott's fault. If he hadn't come to Fairfield the way would have been open for me."

"I'm not so sure of that. You've changed a great deal. I'm not saying it's because you've lived abroad, but you're different. Harder, somehow."

"Harder? More determined, you should say. I've learned to set my sights on what I want and go after it."

"That isn't a strategy that works on women. Especially not on Rachel."

Rob scowled at his sister and crossed the parlor. "You sit there sewing and fussing and yet you dare to find fault with me? If Father were here . . ."

"He would do nothing at all. Nor would Mama. They probably think you're being foolish, too." She poked her embroidery needle into the cloth so she wouldn't misplace it, and searched in her workbasket for a different color thread. "Or at least they would if they were ever here long enough."

"Have you started finding fault with their actions as well? I should think you would at least give them their due."

"I do. I love our parents. But if I had children, I would want to spend more time with them."

"No, you wouldn't. No one does. My children will live entirely in the nursery until they are old enough to behave as adults."

"Then I'm positive that Rachel isn't the one for you. She loves children and would certainly want to be with hers as often as possible. So would I."

"That's because you haven't traveled and seen how other people live." Rob tendered a derisive laugh. "The house where I stayed in America was full of children, all running about unrestrained. It was enough to wear on anyone's nerves."

"Then you must never come to see me after I have a family," she said calmly. "My children will be very much in evidence."

"Oh? Then you have a husband picked out?"

Beatrice ignored his sarcasm. "As a matter of fact, I do."

"Who is it? Maurice Driskoll? It's not Wallace Cates, surely!"

"You're wrong on both counts. It's Mark Paynter."

"Paynter?" Rob's brow furrowed as he tried to place the name.

"You don't know him. He's Jared Prescott's cousin." She smiled as Rob's face began turning red. "I think he's ever so dashing."

"You stay away from them! If Father knew what you're up to, he would send you to our aunt's house in Wales!"

"I'm not going to tell him, and neither are you."

"No? Why are you so sure?"

"Because you can't afford to make an enemy of me."
She and Rachel had discussed ways of dealing with Rob and
had decided on this ploy. "Fairfield is too small, and our
parents are gone too often. If you tell Papa, I'll say I saw
you go into the Bull and Bear and come out with a coarse-
looking woman."

"You wouldn't!" Rob glared at her.

"Yes, I would."

"Wait a minute. How could you have seen that?"

"I didn't, but I overheard one of the servants say that he
saw you."

"Which one said that? I'll give him the sack at once!"

"I know you would and that's why I won't tell you. I like
our servants, and I won't put the man in jeopardy for being truthful." She stopped trying to thread her needle and
looked up. "Who were you with?"

"That's none of your business."

"You can't care much for Rachel if you would see other
women."

"Beatrice, you have no idea what you're talking about."

This was true, but she wouldn't give him the satisfaction
of knowing that, so she only smiled.

Looking the worse for the verbal exchange, Rob poured
himself a glass of sherry, likely in an attempt to calm himself. "How long will Rachel be visiting Rose?"

"I have no idea. At least until Rose's baby comes." Beatrice knew how permanent Rachel's lodging was at the
Jenson house, but she had promised not to tell anyone else,
especially not her brother. "She likes children," she added,
goading Rob further.

"I think I'll visit her there, whether she has invited me or
not. I know Edwin. I could call on him in the law office and
ask if I might drop by later."

"I wouldn't do that if I were you. Mr. Pennington is also
there, and it might seem odd if you ask Edwin for permission to call on Rachel."

"That's true." He bit his lower lip as he thought. "But I can't sit by and wait for Rachel to come to her senses."

"You could go to your own office and work instead," she suggested. "Papa has no idea how little work you do. Why, you haven't been to the office since they left for London."

"That's my business, not yours." He turned to her with a scowl. "Are you seeing this Paynter fellow?"

"Only now and then. You know he doesn't call on me. You're here all the time."

"I'm the head of the house when Father is away, and I forbid you to see him."

Beatrice laughed. "You can't forbid me to do anything. You're only my brother."

"You're becoming as willful as Rachel."

"Thank you."

"It wasn't a compliment." Trying to look menacing, he approached her chair. "You may not have heard, but people are linking Prescott's name with the murders of those two women. His cousin will be ostracized by association. You mustn't befriend these people. At your age, I shouldn't have to remind you of that."

"There's nothing wrong with my age."

"You're not getting any younger. Almost every woman in Fairfield marries before the age of twenty."

"Rachel is twenty, too, and she isn't married."

"She will be before the summer is up, if I have my say."

Beatrice put down her work and frowned at her brother. "I'm telling you, she will have nothing to do with you. Stop making a fool of yourself. Set your cap for someone else."

"I've known all my life that I would marry Rachel. She's the most reasonable choice since our families are so close. Once I finish work on the Dabney house, I'll have a place of my own to take a wife."

"It won't be Rachel."

"We'll see about that. You just stay away from this Mark Paynter so you don't have your name associated with his when Prescott is tumbled down."

"What's that supposed to mean?"

"Just stay away from him."

Rachel gave the Jenson house as her address to the man in the millinery store so the boy could deliver her new hat. Since leaving her father's house, she had more time on her hands than she wanted. She thought again of Princess. The horse was deplorable as a mount, but she was better than nothing. As Edwin didn't keep a saddle horse, Rachel had had nothing to ride and missed the enjoyment of the wind in her hair and the sense of freedom and excitement riding had always given her.

Preoccupied with her thoughts, she was oblivious to the world around her as she stepped out of the shop and ran headlong into a man who was trying to enter the building. Fortunately, he caught her and prevented her from falling. She looked up quickly to see who had rescued her and found herself in Jared Prescott's arms.

Time seemed suspended as she stared into his eyes, so taken aback by seeing him so unexpectedly. Once Jared seemed sure she had her balance, he released her and stepped back a respectable distance. Rachel smoothed her skirt and straightened her bonnet. Her heart was beating like a hammer. "I'm sorry. I didn't see you."

"Actually I was hoping to find you in town." Jared glanced around as if he was uncomfortably aware of the crowd. "Is there somewhere we can talk?"

"Would you like to have a lemon phosphate with me?"

He nodded with a smile and together they set out for the Emporium. As they neared their destination, Rachel cast a quick glance down the alley beside the store. "Every time I pass here, I think of that dreadful murder and how horrible it must have been for her."

"I hadn't realized this was the place."

"The first woman, Liza Barnes, was killed here. The other was found nearer the Bull and Bear."

Jared opened the Emporium door for her, and Rachel went inside. The large building smelled strongly of soaps and lavender and roses. Along the far wall was a soda fountain with stools at the counter and tables scattered about the polished hardwood floor. Rachel chose the table farthest from the man working behind the counter. "We never seem to have any privacy," she whispered. "How do people get to know each other when they must always be with other people?"

"I assume that's to keep courting couples from getting to know each other too well."

Rachel smiled. "I'm glad you're as direct as I am. It's so refreshing not to have to mince words."

"Why haven't I seen you in the past two weeks?"

"I'm staying with my sister, Rose Jenson. I foolishly left home without my riding horse, and I have no way to leave town."

"Why not simply send a man after it? That's what I would do."

"It's not that simple." Rachel broke off their personal conversation when the man came to take their order. Once they were alone again, she added, "I may be at Rose's for some time."

"What are you not telling me?"

"Rose is expecting a child soon, and I've come to town to stay with her until then and to help her out afterward until she is back on her feet. You should see my niece and nephew. They're so adorable."

"You like children?"

"Of course. Who doesn't?"

The man returned and put two lemon phosphates on the table, and Jared handed him a coin.

Once the man was again out of earshot, Jared said, "I had begun to think I wouldn't see you again." His low voice was intimate and keyed for her ears alone. "I had begun to imagine all sorts of things. I was afraid your father somehow had found out that we met at the oak and had sent you away where I might never find you."

"I would have refused to go." She put the straw to her lips and sipped the cool drink.

"Then he doesn't know we met?"

"He may have some idea," she hedged.

"What did he say to you?"

"It doesn't matter. As I told you, I'm staying with Rose for several weeks, and he will be calm again before I return home." This was true. If her father was still as angry as he had been when she left, she couldn't go back. "He doesn't approve of you, you know."

"I had gathered that. But I am curious to know what prompted him to hold that opinion of me. We have never exchanged more than a few terse sentences."

"That's just the way Papa is. He says he doesn't need to know you better for him to know he doesn't like you. I think he's being obstinate, but I thought you should understand how he feels so you won't try to contact him on our behalf." She certainly didn't want Jared and her father to talk. That would make matters worse than they already were.

"It's completely unjust! I've done nothing to warrant his negative opinion."

"No? You were the one to discourage callers. Everyone in Fairfield was talking about it."

"I had my reasons. Maybe I should call on him and explain that I care for you and that I want his permission to call on you."

"No, no. Don't do that. Papa would say no and he's already upset with me on your account."

"I'll call on your brother-in-law, then. What is his name?"

"His name is Edwin Jenson, but don't go to see him at work. He shares a law office with Papa."

"I can hardly drop in on him at home. I'm trying to follow the rules of decorous behavior as much as I can."

"That may be a mistake. Following the rules, I mean. We haven't followed them so far, and I think we've done pretty well."

"You constantly confuse me," he confessed. "Do you want me to be proper or not?"

"I did at first, but now I realize that would create more problems. You see, if Papa wouldn't want you to call on me, Edwin would have to say he disapproves as well. He goes to great lengths to please Papa."

"If I can't see you at your parents' house, and I can't call on you where you are now staying and if you have no horse to ride, how do you expect us to get to know each other?"

"I've wondered that myself. It won't be easy, will it?" She smiled, and although he continued to look distressed, she noticed the corners of his mouth turn up in the briefest hint of a smile. She longed to reach out across the polished tabletop and put her hand over Jared's, but she was too aware of the presence of the man behind the counter.

"The gentlemanly alternative would be for me to stop seeing you altogether," he said, as if to gauge her reaction.

"Then I'm glad neither of us is a gentleman."

"You don't consider me to be one?" His surprise showed in his eyes, and she laughed.

"No, I don't, but only in the nicest possible way. A gentleman would never have met me on the Roman road and kissed me under the oak tree."

"No?"

"And no gentleman would be looking at me the way you're looking at me now." She chuckled again. "I'm teasing you."

Jared grinned. "I believe you're right in your assessment of me. I was just thinking of how your lips tasted and how good it felt to hold your body close to mine."

Rachel caught her breath and glanced around to see if anyone was close enough to have overheard him.

"I was remembering how you sighed when I kissed you, and I was wondering what would happen if I kissed you again, right here."

"You wouldn't!" Her heart was pounding in her chest. "Would you?" Her voice held a hint of trepidation.

He laughed aloud, and the sound was soothing and exciting to her, all at the same time. "Now who's teasing whom?"

Rachel loosened up a bit and laughed with him for a moment, then again became serious. "I might like to be kissed again. But not here."

"No, not here." He leaned closer. "I would like to take you to Ravenwood and show you where and how I live. If only it were still fashionable, as in days gone by, for a man to kidnap his ladylove and whisk her away to his castle."

"You would do that?" she asked breathlessly.

"I would. And I can guarantee that you'd not be eager to be rescued."

Rachel couldn't speak. She was imagining what it would be like to be carried away by Jared and speculating on what delights might lie in store for her.

He continued. "I would take you to the ramparts of my castle, and we would survey the surrounding countryside for signs of your rescuers."

"Ravenwood is a country house, not a castle."

"A mere technicality. We would be able to see for miles and miles, and I would take you there on the battlements beneath the sky and the angels."

She thought she knew what he had meant, but she wasn't positive. "Take me?" she whispered in a wondering voice.

"Make love with you. And I would be certain that I made love *with* you, not *to* you. There's a big difference."

Rachel swallowed against the lump in her throat. He was very good at this game of flirting. Better, perhaps, than she was. "I would like that. Too bad you have Ravenwood and not a castle."

"Castles are too drafty. Ravenwood is snug and comfortable. There are fireplaces in every major room, no two alike, and all beautiful. In the winter we could lie on fur rugs in front of the fire and make love until the flames died into cooling embers. Then I would carry you to bed and love the rest of the night away."

"I ought to go." Rachel stood abruptly. He was much too good at word games, and he was exciting her beyond all reason.

"Don't leave." He said the words as quietly as he had said all the rest, but they were enough to stop her. She sat down again.

"I shouldn't listen to such talk."

"No? Which part bothered you? The part about making love in front of the fire?"

"No! I mean, I'm not upset, exactly."

"The part about making love on the battlements? I rather liked the idea."

"So did I," she said before she thought. "That is to say, I have no idea what you're talking about."

"Yes, you do, or you wouldn't be blushing so."

Rachel touched her hot cheeks. She was blushing, but not because she was embarrassed at what he had said. She was blushing because she wanted him to continue. "I ought to go. We can't stay here too long. People might notice us."

"Do you think they haven't already? I'm known in this village to be a recluse, and I suspect everyone is already wondering about us exchanging so much as a word."

"I'm afraid you're right."

"So if we're already the subject of their gossip, why cut our visit short?"

"You make it sound so simple. Don't you ever follow the rules of convention?"

"Rarely. I did at one time, but I found it boring. I think you know what I mean."

"I detest being bored."

"I thought you might say that. Will you meet me for another picnic?"

"Like the last one? Are you sure that would be a good idea?"

"No, it's a terrible idea. Will you meet me?"

"I mustn't." She didn't meet his eyes.

"Why not? Were you overly tempted?"

She lifted her eyes and met his gaze. "Yes. Yes, I was. Is that what you wanted me to say? It's true. I'm not skilled at this type of word game, but I can say the truth. I was tempted so much that I've regretted leaving that day."

Jared was silent for a moment. "I know. I've regretted it, too. No, we mustn't have another picnic. Not unless there are people all around us."

"And we must not have one then, because everyone would know that we are seeing each other."

"I'd say we are stymied. What's your opinion?"

"I have no opinion," Rachel said. "I only want to see you."

Jared rubbed his chin. "You play your own word game rather well. Do you mean what you're saying?"

"I say a good many things, but I rarely say anything that I don't mean."

"In that case, I think I have to continue seeing you, because I feel the same way."

Rachel paused. Was he playing with her or not? She couldn't tell. Certainly none of the men she knew would have said half he had just said to her. Certainly not in the Emporium. "How do you really feel? Tell me."

He thought for a minute. "Not here. When I tell you that, I want to be positive that no one is around and that you know I'm not playing a game."

"I have to go." She had to leave before she threw herself into his arms, Emporium or no Emporium.

He caught her wrist as she rose. "Not until you say when you'll see me again."

"I don't know." She couldn't think clearly with him touching her. Fire seemed to radiate from his fingers and flow up her arm and straight into her heart. "I don't know how to see you, much less when."

"It's damned unfair that I can't court you in the proper way. I ought to go your father and tell him so."

"No! Don't do that." She sat back down hastily. "You must not talk to Papa."

"Why not? If he's dead set against me already, I have nothing to lose by trying to convince him otherwise."

"You'll only make matters worse if you talk to him. I've told you he's determined to see me married to Rob Gaston. You don't know how stubborn he can be."

"He wouldn't hurt you, would he?" Jared's eyes grew dark with passion. "He hasn't hurt you?"

"Papa? Good heavens, no! I'm not afraid of him. It's just that once he gets his head set on something, he never changes his mind. He wants me to marry Rob, and he won't consider anyone else."

"What harm could it do for me to talk to him?"

"Believe me. It could do a great deal." If he were to discover that she and her parents weren't speaking at the moment, primarily because of him, he might decide it would be in her best interest for him not to see her again. She certainly didn't want that.

Jared continued holding her hand, and with his thumb he stroked the pulse beat of her wrist beneath the thin fabric of her shirtwaist blouse. "When I came to Fairfield and decided to keep myself apart from local society, I never thought for a moment that I would find a woman I wanted to court, or that she would be denied to me simply because I refused a handful of invitations."

"That's not it. At least it's not all of it. You have stayed so aloof. Because no one knows anything about you, your name is being linked with the most atrocious of rumors, even to the murders."

"I never so much as saw those women, let alone harmed them. I am incapable of doing such a thing."

"I believe you, but Fairfield doesn't. I'm afraid that if there's another murder, the gossip may go too far and that you could be hurt."

"Is that why you won't say you'll meet me? Because you're afraid of getting mixed up in an unpleasantness?"

"Of course not. I'm not afraid for myself. I'm afraid for you."

Jared forced a smile beyond his concern. "I like that. But how will your not seeing me prevent me from becoming involved?"

"If I'm seeing you, Rob will be certain to side against you, and the Gastons are influential in this town."

"I don't care. I have no real reason to stay in Fairfield, for that matter."

"You don't?"

He shook his head. "Only that you're here. I didn't move here to be near family holdings or for business reasons. I could move again."

"Why did you move here?" She had wondered about that many times and could find no reason.

He drew back, releasing her wrist. "I can't tell you that."

"See? Here I am trying to help you, and you won't be honest with me. It's very exasperating, Jared."

"It would be worse if I told you my reasons. You'll have to trust me about this."

"It would seem that I have to take almost everything about you on faith alone."

"Isn't that always true in relationships? Trust and faith are always an integral part."

"I really must be going. I'm sure half the town has seen us together by now, and I shouldn't wait for the other half to join the gossip."

"When will I see you again? How can I get a message to you?"

She hesitated. "Send your man to number 3 Primrose Lane. That's where Rose and Edwin live."

"Then how will I know if you need me?"

She thought for a minute. "Before you leave town, ride by the house and look at it. My room is in the front, facing the street. If I need to talk to you, I'll put a green scarf in the window."

"Green is the color of true love," he said with a smile.

"It's also the color of the scarf I own. If you must send me a message, try to send it during the hours when Edwin will be at work. All right?"

"I agree. I would prefer a more direct approach, but I can control my preferences."

She smiled but tried to hide it from him.

"I know. When you see the green scarf, meet me at our oak. That's probably the safest place."

"I'll come to town every morning and check your window. I'm looking forward to our next tryst."

"So am I," she whispered. "So am I."

Chapter Twelve

"I was so anxious to devise a method to signal Jared that I would meet him at the oak off the Roman road that I forgot I have no horse to take me there," Rachel complained to Beatrice. "I considered not putting my green scarf in the window at all, but then it occurred to me that Jared might think I didn't want to meet him if he never saw the signal. Not knowing what else to do, I put it out and left it there all one day. I'm sure he must have seen it, for he said he would come by every morning and look for it. I thought that if he saw the scarf and went to the oak, and then I didn't come, he would assume I had no way to get there and he would come up with another way to talk with me. It has been over a week and I haven't seen or heard from him at all."

"Why didn't you send me a note telling me this sooner? I'm more than happy to lend you one of our horses."

"I don't know. My thoughts are filled with longing for Jared, and I just haven't been thinking clearly these days. The day after I put out my scarf, I began watching every morning for him to come by, but he hasn't come at all. He must have seen the scarf and become angry with me for not meeting him. Or perhaps he changed his mind about seeing me because of all the inconvenience and never looked for the signal at all."

"I find that hard to believe, if he cares for you half as much as you have told me he does. He may have gone to the

oak that first day and every day since, hoping you would
find some means of getting there."

"It was a stupid idea in the first place. I don't know why
I thought it would work."

"Things like that always work in books."

Rachel sighed. "I'm discovering that a lot of things that
we've read are not a reflection of real life. Forbidden love,
for instance. It sounds so romantic, but instead it's frus-
trating!"

"We must plan a new way for the two of you to get together."

"I've thought and thought. If I can't meet him by arrangement, I'll have to wait until I accidentally run into
him. Do you know how many times I've contrived excuses
to go to a store in order to see him by chance? Rose is sus-
picious."

"I thought she was on your side."

"She is, but Edwin is afraid of making Papa angry, and
I have to admit that he's right to be concerned. If Papa
thought Rose and Edwin were making it easy for me to
meet with Jared, he would be furious at them."

Beatrice lowered her voice so she wouldn't be overheard
by a passing servant. "I'm to see Mark this afternoon. I'll
explain to him about the mix-up with the signal and ask him
to pass your regards on to Jared."

"This afternoon! Will Jared be there?"

Beatrice shook her head. "I've met Mark on several occasions and he always comes alone."

Rachel sighed and gazed sadly out the window. "It would
be best for everyone if I were never to see Jared again. Best
for everyone but me."

"Don't be melancholy. If he's your true love, everything will work out."

"I'm not so sure I still believe that. Beatrice, when I'm
with him, the whole world seems to be singing. I feel hot
and shivery, sweet and daring, all at once. I want to know
what he thinks about a dozen subjects, but when I'm with

him our time is so limited we hardly have time to talk at all."

"I know. Mark and I feel the same way. We must arrange a way to spend several hours in their company."

"What about the four of us spending the day at the old castle ruins?"

"Bittergreen?"

"Yes. Mark and Jared probably haven't been there, and you know it takes hours to climb around on it. Best of all, it's far enough from town that no one from Fairfield is likely to be there."

"That would be perfect!"

"I just hope Jared isn't upset with me over the scarf thing. He probably thinks I'm some sort of lunatic."

"No, he doesn't," Beatrice said loyally. "He's quite taken with you. Mark said so."

"He did? What did he say? The exact words."

"He said, 'Jared is quite taken with Miss Rachel.'"

"That's all? He didn't elaborate?"

"I'm sorry. I should have pressed him for details. At the time I was too busy admiring the laugh lines at the corners of Mark's eyes."

"We'll arrange the outing so that no one will have any idea where we've gone. It would be all we need for Rob to hear of it and come out to cause trouble."

"I know. My brother can be so exasperating." Beatrice inclined her head to one side. "When would be the best time to meet for this outing?"

"The sooner, the better. I have no commitments. Rose will have the baby soon, however, and I should be here when it comes. After all, that's the reason I've given everyone for my being here. I'd prefer to go as soon as possible."

"How about tomorrow?"

"That would be perfect. I don't think I can bear to wait much longer to see Jared."

"Rachel Prescott," Beatrice said experimentally. "It sounds pretty. You'll keep your same initials! I've heard that's lucky."

"I heard just the opposite. I think I'll believe your way." She closed her eyes. "Mrs. Jared Prescott. Rachel Pennington Prescott. I love the way that sounds."

"This way your old monogrammed things will still have the correct initials."

Rachel sighed. "Beatrice, do you really think it will ever work out?"

"If it's true love it will."

"Stop saying that. I can't trust myself to fate. Not on something this important. I have to make it happen somehow. I'm with him so seldom! If he were one of our crowd, it would be so much easier."

"I know. It's fairly easy to get a fellow to propose, if you know him better. I have that same problem with Mark."

"We'll just have to try harder. After all, this is for the rest of our lives!"

Beatrice's blue eyes grew round. "I never thought of it that way! You're right. We have to make it easier for them to propose. The Bittergreen ruins are just the place—romantic and secluded."

"My thoughts exactly. Now let's just hope that Jared and Mark have no plans for tomorrow."

Rachel craned her neck to see the ruins ahead. "There are their horses! They did come!" She ran her fingers over her hair to be sure every strand was in place. She wanted to be beautiful for Jared. She had chosen her prettiest straw bonnet and was wearing it tilted back so it would frame her face. Her dress was pink with sprigs of tiny yellow and white flowers and was topped off with a lacy bertha that covered her shoulders. "How do I look? I want to look perfect for him." She was as nervous as a schoolgirl.

"You look beautiful," her friend said without glancing at her. "I was so afraid they might not come."

"So was I." Rachel could feel her heart pounding. She had slept scarcely an hour all night for the excitement of spending several uninterrupted hours in Jared's company.

Rachel parked the buggy she had borrowed from Rose alongside the men's horses. As they exchanged greetings, Jared came to Rachel's side to help her down, while Mark was seeing to Beatrice. Jared put Rachel's hands atop his shoulders, then caught her by the waist and lifted her to the ground. When he did so, their bodies touched, causing Rachel to catch her breath. She had never before found it so sensuous to get out of a buggy.

"I was afraid you weren't coming," Jared said for her ears alone. "We've been here nearly half an hour."

"Beatrice was having trouble putting her hair up the way she wanted it. I had to help her."

"You look beautiful today. You're more beautiful every time I see you."

The yearning in Jared's eyes was more intense than Rachel remembered. As a blush began to color her cheeks, she felt compelled to change the subject. "Have you seen the ruins?"

"No, we waited for you. I presume you can give us a tour and explain it all?"

"Of course. I've known about this castle since I was a child." She put her hand on his arm to steady herself for their walk over the uneven ground, and he covered her hand with his.

Side by side, the two couples climbed the gradual slope that led up to the castle on the hill. Rachel saw the way Mark's eyes kept going back to Beatrice, and she made a mental note to tell Beatrice all about it. At the top of the hill, the countryside spread out below them.

"I used to come here to draw," Rachel told Jared. "My sketchbook is full of Bittergreen. Look behind us." She turned and gazed at the landscape. The fields stretching far and wide below them were divided into segments by verdant hedgerows, and a stream threaded from one farm to another like molten silver in the sunlight. Fairfield lay like a jewel in the sweeping curve of the stream. "I think whoever named the village must have done it from this spot."

"I agree." Jared gazed past the village. "There's Ravenwood."

Rachel responded. "It looks so tiny from here. I could never get it just right in my sketches."

"You were drawing what you knew, rather than what you were seeing," Beatrice commented. "From here you can see very little detail."

"It's true. I never learned to view the world as an artist," Rachel confessed. "I'm much too literal."

"Are you?" Jared asked with a smile. "I'd have said you're just the opposite."

"I'm a confusing person," she replied with a glance at him from the corners of her eyes. "Someone once told me that over a lemon phosphate."

Jared winked at her to show he remembered. "I thought the saying was, 'There is truth in wine.' I didn't know phosphates were as revealing."

Although Rachel dared not stare at Jared, she couldn't resist catching glimpses of him. The tan coat he was wearing fit him snugly, accentuating his lean waist and wide chest and shoulders. His waistcoat, like his trousers, was white, and the shirt he wore was the latest in fashion, white with narrow brown and burgundy checks. Against the pale colors of his clothing, his skin was deeply tanned and his hair was blacker than ever. She thought he was easily the most handsome man she had ever seen.

"I want to show Mark something over here," Beatrice said as she took Mark's hand.

"We'll go on to the castle," Rachel said. She and Beatrice had agreed during the ride out to the ruins that neither of their courtships would make much progress with the other couple around.

"That was neatly done," Jared commented when they were out of earshot. "Mark and I had planned more or less the same thing, only not quite so soon."

Rachel smiled up at him. "I should have played the co-
quette and waited."

"Why didn't you?"

"I was afraid you wouldn't think of a way for us to be
alone together."

"You don't give me much credit. I know how to court a
lady."

"Do you? I would have assumed that mistresses don't
require much courting," she baited as she led him up to the
ruins.

"I never should have told you about that part of my past.
I've had relationships with others besides her."

"I should hope so." She sighed. "Ladies don't have such
freedom, and I think it's a pity."

"Oh? Would you like to keep a mistress?" He couldn't
keep the laughter out of his voice.

Rachel swatted at him playfully. "I was referring to the
freedom to form relationships. We have to more or less wait
and see if the man will have the initiative on his own."

"Another contradiction. You haven't held back with me
at all. I was under the impression that you were the pur-
suer at times."

Rachel's smile disappeared. "You think I'm too forward? I was afraid of that. It's just that we have so little
time together."

"I wasn't complaining. I rather like being pursued. I can
see why the ladies enjoy it. I'm flattered that you would go
to such lengths to have my company."

When they reached the ruins at the top of the hill, Rachel paused to catch her breath. She had laced herself
tightly that morning, leaving little room for the intake of
air.

"Magnificent!" Jared observed as he walked to the
gaping hole where a door had once stood. Although much
of the structure had long since decayed, portions of the
castle walls remained intact, soaring upward like giant
monoliths against the sky. High above them a vacant round

window flanked by Gothic arches made lace of the stone wall. "Who lived here?"

"The ancient ancestors of the baron who lived at Ravenwood. When the country house was built, the castle was neglected and allowed to fall to ruin. Over the years villagers have used stone from these walls to repair the streets in Fairfield and even to build a house or two. Some of the stained glass found its way into the church."

"I'm glad some of it was preserved. It would have been a shame for something of such beauty, as I imagine it must have been, to be completely destroyed."

Rachel glanced at Jared, glad to know he appreciated things that she, too, considered valuable, although she was hardly surprised to hear him say so.

They went through the door and into what had been the great hall. Although most of its grandeur had been obliterated by the winds and the rain, Rachel's imagination always filled in the missing pieces for her and she was anxious to tell Jared all she knew of the place so he could enjoy it as much as she always did.

"The screens passage is gone, you'll notice. Legend has it that the screen, which was a movable one, was inspired by a visitation of the town's patron saint, St. Cuthbert. The man who received the vision and created the screen was a local man who never had a talent for creating anything of beauty before or after. It was one of our miracles."

"When did all this happen?"

"In the reign of Henry III. The year was about 1260, give or take a decade. People around here weren't much for keeping records then and most of this story has been passed down by word of mouth. That's why the church is named for St. Cuthbert, even though we have no evidence of his coming to this area during his lifetime."

They strolled down the length of the hall, now strewn with wildflowers and grasses where the floor stones had been removed. A blackened slab lay at the center of the room. "This must have been used for the fire," Jared observed. "If the roof was still there, we would see a smoke hole above us."

"It must have terribly smoky in here. Especially on windy days. I wonder how they stood it."

"I suppose it was a matter of being content to breathe smoke or freeze." He took her hand and helped her over a rough place on the floor. At the far end of the hall was a raised dais, the table and chair of state long ago removed. "I wonder what became of the furniture. Maybe some of it is in Ravenwood's attics."

"Wouldn't that be exciting to find? As close as we are to London and as grand a castle as Bittergreen was, King Henry himself might have sat in one of the chairs!"

"It's possible. King Henry wasn't a popular king because of the taxes and hopeless wars, but he was a man who understood buildings. Look at those pointed arches and the lancet windows. You can see his influence in the castle."

"It must have been beautiful. I wonder why it was ever abandoned. Not that Ravenwood isn't beautiful, too," she hastened to say, "but Bittergreen is so majestic."

"It was drafty as well, in all probability. Have you ever been in a castle in the winter?"

Rachel shook her head. "I've rarely been anywhere at all. When we go to London, we stay with my Aunt Maddy, who lives in a house no different from our own. Have you been in a castle?"

"I lived in one for a while. It's in Yorkshire and belongs to a relation of mine. As a matter of fact, Mark is second in line to inherit it."

"Mark? A castle! I had no idea you were from such an important family."

"I'm from an old, pugnacious family. I'm not so sure we are what you would call important."

"But you had a family castle. If people in Fairfield knew this, they might feel better toward you."

"Even though the man who built it is long since dust and was probably a scoundrel in the bargain? According to the stories my family handed down, he got most of his wealth by taking it from others.''

"I don't think I would tell that part," Rachel said. "Not in Fairfield.''

At one corner of the great hall, a crumbling stairway with stone steps hollowed by the tread of feet rose to some upper floor long since fallen to dust. "I wonder what they were like, the people who lived here," Rachel said. "Were they like us, do you think?''

"Probably. I doubt people have changed much. They must have had hopes and fears like all the rest of us. They must have fallen in love and worried that their love wouldn't be returned.''

Had he meant his last statement as a correlation to his own feelings? Rachel looked at him for a moment, but could see no evidence one way or the other. She wished she could ask him, but if he hadn't meant anything by it, she would feel foolish. "The cloister is back here," she said, leading him past the stairway and through a door behind the dais.

The cloister, like the hall, had no roof, but its more or less intact columns formed a walk that was still partially shaded by the castle wall. An ancient creeper vine, obviously having taken root after the roof gave way to the ravages of time, had wound around several of the columns as if in an effort to lend them support. At the far end of the cloister, Rachel sat on one of the lichen-encrusted benches and held her skirt aside for Jared to join her.

"I used to come here whenever I had a problem that seemed insurmountable," she confided. "I would look at these old walls and columns and realize that very little of what I did would last half as long. It always made it easier for me to make decisions.''

"What sort of decisions?''

"Whether or not to marry a beau, for instance. Up here all my suitors seemed to fade in importance.''

"Have you been faced with this decision often?''

She smiled at the hint of jealousy in his voice. "A few times. Mama and Papa are afraid I'll become a spinster and have no one to take care of me once they are gone."

"I'm only surprised that you haven't settled on someone before now."

"The right man hadn't come along." It was true. Somehow she had known she had to wait for Jared. Some part of her must have been sure he would come.

"How determined are your parents to see you marry Rob Gaston?"

"They're quite firm about it. You see, I've turned away most of the other eligible men in town, though Rob doesn't know that."

"I thought you were quite adept at flirting. I didn't realize you had had such extensive training."

She laughed. "Why, Jared, you sound jealous."

"No, I'm not." He paused. "All right, I am jealous. Do I have any other rivals besides Gaston?"

"Not any serious ones." She glanced at him to see how he was taking all this. It was one of the few times she had felt she had power over him.

Jared rose and walked to the nearest column and gazed out over the countryside. "I can see how this view would help you gain perspective. Have you been up here since you met me?"

She knew what he was asking. "No, there has been no need. I already knew what it would prove to me."

"And that is?" He turned back to her.

"Have you noticed the back garden wall?" she asked, evading his question. "Most of it has fallen down, but you can see where the herbs and vegetables were grown. And even though the kitchen is mostly gone, there are enough remnants to show where it was."

"I'm not interested in kitchens or gardens. Not at the moment."

His tone of voice was an unmistakable indication that, at the moment, she was the center of his concentration. Rachel rose and went to a column not far from his. "Papa is angry that I don't want Rob."

"I want to talk to your father."

"No."

"Rachel, how can I court you properly if I see you only by accident and by stealth? I want to walk with you and not have to worry who may see us together."

"I know Papa. Eventually, when he sees his anger has no effect on me, he will be reasonable."

"How serious is this unpleasantness between the two of you? Beatrice hinted to Mark that you may have moved to your sister's house for reasons other than the one you gave me about helping her with her children."

"She shouldn't have told Mark that." Rachel looked away.

"I had him get the information from her. I didn't think you were being entirely truthful with me."

"I see no reason why you have to talk to Papa in order to court me. Not really. I mean, here we are, all alone for all intents and purposes, and we're talking about Papa instead of ourselves."

"Don't you see that your parents' approval of me is important? What if we want our relationship to become more than friendship? What if we fall in love?"

The word lay between them, refusing to go away.

"Are you falling in love?" she asked softly.

Jared turned away and hit his palm against the column. "It goes against my grain to have to see you behind their backs. It's as if I'm ashamed of you or you're ashamed of me."

"That's not it and you know it." She went to him and put her hand on his arm. "You didn't answer my question. Are you falling in love?"

Wordlessly, Jared gazed down at her, and she could see the pain and confusion in his eyes. Finally he asked, "Are you looking for another heart to pin on your sleeve?"

Rachel backed away. "I'm not like that. I don't deliberately break hearts."

"But you don't mind cracking them a little, do you? Why else would you have had so many proposals?"

"Maybe it's because I'm well liked. Maybe it's because the boys in Fairfield know they will grow up to marry women in Fairfield and there aren't that many women to choose from." She couldn't keep the hurt from her voice. "Do you really think I flirt in order to break men's hearts?"

He refused to look into her eyes or to be swayed. "All I know is that you've managed to put yourself in my mind when no other woman has ever been able to do so. It's not comfortable, and I don't think I like it."

Rachel felt tears building. "That sounds as if you don't care for me at all."

"I guess you'll have to break someone else's heart. I'm going to keep mine intact."

"What about me? Does it matter to you that my own heart can break?"

"Can it? Has it ever been tested? In my experience, the women who leave broken hearts in their wake are seldom afflicted with the same unpleasantness."

"I wonder who told you that you're such an expert on women. It certainly couldn't have been a woman!"

"What's that supposed to mean?" He whipped his head around and frowned at her.

"I don't think you understand women at all."

"Most aren't as complex as you. Most of the time I can tell if a woman wants my company and whether she cares for me. Every time I think I know what you think or feel, you do something to prove to me that I had no understanding of you at all."

"If you can't understand me, that's not my fault. It's yours."

"Not entirely. Why can't you for once be open and stay open, or be elusive and remain that way? I went to that blasted oak three days in a row and you never showed up. Why did you hang that green scarf in the window if you didn't want to see me?"

"I did want to see you. I forgot I didn't have a way to get to the oak. I thought that when I didn't show up, you would try to make contact with me some other way. For several days, I sat watching for you to come by Rose's house, but I saw no sign of you."

"How was I to know that was what you'd expect of me? You said the oak, and that's where I went. I almost didn't come today, because I didn't know if you would be here."

"We need a new signal. The next time I hang my scarf in the window, it will mean I want to meet you at the Emporium."

"No. I've had all the signals that I want. If I can't call on you properly, I won't call on you at all."

"Is that the way you want it?" Pain and suppressed tears hardened her voice more than she had intended.

"Yes! That's the way I want it! Now what will it be? Do I get to talk to your father or not?"

"No! You may not talk to him. Is that plain enough? We must continue to meet like this or have no contact at all."

"Is this all you want from me? A secret meeting, a stolen kiss or two? Is this all I mean to you?"

Rachel wanted to cry out that he was all the world to her, but her pride prevented her confession. "That's the way it must be, Jared. Will you agree or not?"

"I will not!" He turned on his heels and went back the way they had come.

Beatrice and Mark were in the hall, and when they saw Jared striding several paces ahead of Rachel with a frown on his face, they jumped apart. Rachel noticed that Beatrice's bonnet was askew and assumed from the blush in her cheeks that they had almost been caught kissing. She hated to end Beatrice's outing, since she seemed to be making more headway with Mark than she was with Jared, but Jared was already heading for his horse.

"Jared?" Mark called. "Jared, where are you going?"

Jared made no reply, and Rachel tried to harden her heart against him. It might have worked if she hadn't seen the raw pain in his eyes and known she had put it there.

When Jared reached his horse, he mounted and galloped toward Ravenwood.

"Did you argue?" Beatrice demanded. "What could you possibly have found to argue about in this short time?"

"I'm not sure myself. I think he's angry because I won't let him ask Papa for permission to court me." Rachel made an effort to hold back her tears. "You know how Papa can be, Beatrice. He might say something to Jared that would be unforgivable."

"Is that a reason to argue?" her friend said. "Couldn't you simply have discussed it?"

Mark said, "I should go after him. It's not like Jared to behave this way. Usually he keeps his emotions strictly in check." He looked quizzically at Rachel. "Would it be so bad for him to meet your father?"

"At the moment, yes."

"Rachel has moved to Rose's because her father refuses to let her see Jared. She is almost on the verge of being disowned."

"Beatrice! I told you that in confidence!"

"If Mark doesn't know all the facts, how can he talk to Jared about it?" Beatrice demanded. "You aren't doing too well on your own."

Rachel brushed at her tears with her palm. She hated to cry when it wasn't her own idea. "You mustn't tell Jared how extreme my situation is. If he thought he was to blame for Papa acting this way toward me, he might never want to see me again."

Beatrice put her hand on Mark's arms. "Be discreet. Only tell him what you think he should know. Can we trust you?"

Mark nodded. "I'll do what I can with him." To Rachel he said, "Is it really so serious that you may be disowned?"

She silently nodded. She didn't trust herself to speak.

"And you would risk such a split with your family for Jared?"

Again Rachel nodded. There was no need to tell Mark she loved Jared. It was obvious that he already knew.

"I'll talk to him on your behalf." To Beatrice he said, "I must go. I'll see you again as soon as possible."

Rachel watched him go down the slope to his horse. She had never been so upset over a man in all her life. Nor had she ever loved one so dearly.

Chapter Thirteen

"**Y**ou can't avoid talking about it forever," Mark said.

"Yes, I can." Jared ran a practiced hand down the foreleg of the horse he was about to buy. To the stable boy he said, "Lead him around at a trot." He knelt on the ground to study the horse's movements.

Mark knelt beside him. "You've been like a wounded bear ever since we went to the Bittergreen ruins. Every time anyone speaks to you, you nearly take their heads off."

"If I'm so ill-tempered, I'm amazed that you still want to visit me. Have you forgotten the way back to London?"

"There! See? You've done it again. I wouldn't consider going back to London and abandoning you. Without my help, you're likely to become a curmudgeon."

"Does the horse seem to favor his off back leg?"

"He looks perfectly sound to me."

Jared rose and the boy brought the horse to him. As he ran his hand over the animal's satin hide, he checked for uniform warmth and soundness. Bending, he raised the animal's nearest foreleg and probed the frog of its foot. He was more than satisfied with what he saw, but he tried not to show it, because he planned to haggle over the price with the owner.

He shook his head as if displeased and walked around the animal, ostensibly checking to be sure it was carrying its weight evenly and whether its legs were straight. Jared liked the gelding's looks. The horse swished his tail and turned his head to watch him with interest, and Jared noticed the horse was curious, not wary, and likely quite intelligent. That was good.

"What do you think of him?" the owner called from near the fence. "He's a rare beauty, isn't he?"

"Passable." Jared motioned for the boy to lead the horse at a walk. "I still think he's favoring that hind leg."

"He's sounder than I am." The buyer frowned at Jared, but Jared merely gazed back. "Will you have him or no?"

Jared shook his head as if he couldn't quite decide. "I could take him off your hands for fifty pounds."

"Fifty?" The owner laughed. "His price is seventy-five."

"This horse? Seventy-five? He may be worth fifty-five, but only because I pity him."

The bargaining, thus begun, continued in earnest for several minutes. When it was done, Jared had a new horse at a fair price, and the horse's previous owner had agreed to throw in the halter for good measure. Jared paid the man and arranged for one of his stable boys to bring the animal home.

As he and Mark rode back to Ravenwood, Jared hoped Mark would refrain from again bringing up the subject of Rachel. The mere mention of her name made him ache. Not talking about her was almost as bad.

"You know, she really cares for you," Mark said.

Jared had known Mark's silence on the matter was too much to hope for. "Could we talk about something more pleasant? Plague, perhaps, or the Great Fire?"

"Don't be that way. You care for her, too. You love her."

"I'm trying to get over that. Mark, have you ever known anyone who could make you do and say things that go entirely against your nature? She's maddening."

"But that makes her all the more interesting, don't you think?"

"I did at one time."

"Then why do you look so bereft when I mention her?"

"It could be because I am trying to forget I ever met her," Jared retorted. "Or it could be because I'm coming down with a cold."

"In the summertime? Unlikely."

"You stick to your courtship of Beatrice and leave me alone."

"I'm afraid that's not possible. Beatrice and Rachel are best friends. I can't see one without the other, and I can't offend Rachel by refusing to talk to her about you without offending Beatrice as well."

"She talks about me? You've seen her since that day at the ruins?"

"Only once. I met Beatrice in town, and Rachel was with her. Rachel is being as pigheaded as you are—she has risked a great deal for your sake."

Jared gave him a frown. "What do you mean?"

"Rachel is on the verge of being disowned. That's the real reason she is staying at her sister's house."

"Disowned! Whatever for?"

"It seems she came home from seeing you and had grass in her hair. Her father saw it and became angry. I haven't met the man, but he must be formidable. At any rate, she left that day and had her belongings sent to the Jenson house."

"She told me that she is there to help with her sister's work until Rose has her baby."

"That's the story they are telling about town for propriety's sake."

"She's being disowned on account of me?" Jared was stunned. "It never occurred to me that it had come to this. Why didn't she tell me?"

"Beatrice says Rachel is too proud. She's afraid that if you know this, you will either propose out of guilt or refuse to ever see her again."

"I should speak to her father. I'll tell him that I never meant ill to come to her."

"Are you also prepared to ask for her hand?"

Jared frowned. "Marriage is a big step. I'm not at all sure I can ever take it. There is still the matter of Yvonne."

"Until you can ask for her hand in marriage, you shouldn't talk to Pennington."

"Beatrice said that?"

"No, that's my opinion. Imagine, if you will, that you go to Pennington. You tell him that you never touched his daughter. He points out that she has never come home with grass in her hair before. You admit that you kissed. He asks how that put grass in her hair. You say you were lying on the ground at the time. He asks what your intentions are toward his daughter. You can hardly say that you haven't decided."

"I see what you mean. I can't stand by and see her lose her family, though. What would you do in my position?"

"I would propose. You love her and she evidently loves you. Yvonne is a problem, but not one that's insurmountable."

"She loves me? What makes you think so?"

"Beatrice said she does. Beatrice ought to know if anyone does."

"Blast it, Mark, I don't want to play at love games as if I were a boy. I don't want to try to guess how Rachel feels by what her friend or mine said. Why can't she be straightforward about it? She's blunt enough about everything else."

"That's not a woman's way. None of them is that direct. Not about marriage."

"I thought I was an expert on women, too, before I met Rachel. She breaks all the rules."

"That's one reason I know you would be well suited for each other."

"My problem, as you well know, is that I'm not about to break the promise I made to Father about Yvonne. Even if I hadn't promised to take care of her, I wouldn't send her to Bedlam or any other place of that sort. She's my sister."

"I think that you should talk to Rachel and tell her about Yvonne. If she loves you, she will understand."

"Yes, and she will tell Beatrice and Beatrice will tell the rest of Fairfield. Then the sheriff will be at Ravenwood asking questions about the two murdered women."

"I can't believe Yvonne did that. Not even in her present state of mind."

"Neither can I, but from what I've heard, the women were of the lowest sort and that also describes the ones she might have killed in London. Even the manner in which the fatal wounds were inflicted is the same." He glanced at his friend. "What if she took it into her head to hurt Rachel?"

"I hadn't thought of that."

"I have. Lately I've had plenty of time to think, since I don't seem to be able to sleep anymore. Rachel is a refrain that resounds constantly in my mind." He added, "What about you and Beatrice? Are you considering matrimony? You have as much cause to want to marry as I do."

"As a matter of fact, I am. I've not spoken to Beatrice yet. I've only met her parents at the party and that hardly left a good impression with them. I've been trying to think of some way to get in their good graces before I propose to their daughter."

"I think she would make you a good wife. I noticed the way she was looking at you at the ruins. Unless I'm very much mistaken, she is in love with you."

Mark grinned. "I think you're right. Maybe I should consider looking for a house to buy near here."

"What about the brooding ancestral castle that will be yours some day?" Jared asked with a smile.

"I don't want to live there. Don't you remember how clammy and dreary it is in the wintertime? It's not a place for a delicate bride. Beatrice would freeze going from one chamber to another. Besides, she would rather be near Rachel, I'm certain. And her parents, of course."

"Of course."

"Provided they are still speaking to us after we are married."

"I see you really have given it some thought."

Mark nodded. "I believe our bachelor days are nearly over."

"Perhaps."

"I do think, however, you should keep it secret that I told you about the division in Rachel's family. She would be upset with us all if she knew you suspected."

"It will be a secret with me." Jared thought how like Rachel that was. She had the key in her hands that might coerce him into proposing, and she was too honest to use it. He wished understanding her was as easy as loving her.

Rose looked up from her sewing as the maid ushered Rob into the parlor. "Rob! What a surprise. I didn't expect to see you today. Is Rachel expecting you?" She knew Rachel wasn't, because Rachel had expressly told her that she wasn't seeing Rob again under any conditions.

"No, Miss Rose, she isn't. I went to see her father a while ago, and he said she is still here. Are you feeling well?"

"Well enough." She drew her light shawl about her to cover the mound of her pregnancy. She felt ill at ease discussing the upcoming baby with a man. To the maid, she said, "Go see if my sister is upstairs, won't you? Tell her, if you find her, that Rob Gaston is here to see her."

The maid bobbed a curtsy and left. Rob was looking around. "You have a beautiful home, Miss Rose. Did Rachel tell you that I've bought the Dabney house?"

"Yes, she mentioned that." Rachel had said that Rob's parents had bought the house for him and that it was probably the ugliest one in Fairfield. "Will you be moving into it soon?"

"Quite soon, thank you for asking. I'm having it refurbished. New wallpaper and paint, that sort of thing. I'm hoping to have a wife to make it into a home someday in the not too distant future."

Rose thought it unfortunate that a young man as nice looking as Rob had to spoil it all by opening his mouth. He was always so studiously polite that it made her wonder what he was really thinking. "A wife? How nice. Is she anyone I know?"

He actually blushed and his laugh could only be described as a twitter that hadn't been used very often. "I'd say so, yes. You know her quite well."

Rose smiled with as much sincerity as she could muster. When her father had decided on Edwin Jenson for her future husband, she had been disappointed in not having Philip Yardley. Now she saw that his choice had been the best, and she had grown to love Edwin in a calm, secure sort of way. She couldn't imagine Rachel ever growing to love Rob. "I remember when you were a boy," she said. "You often came over to play while our parents were visiting."

"Yes, those are some of my happiest childhood memories." He pulled awkwardly at his coat and looked as if he wasn't sure what to do to occupy his hands. "We had a grand time, didn't we?"

"Yes, indeed."

"That was a long time ago."

"Yes, it was. We've all changed a great deal. You especially." Rose hoped he would take what she said as a compliment, even though she hadn't meant it as one. All the changes in Rob were unfortunate ones. His obsequious manner as a young boy had been endearing. In a man it seemed false.

They fell silent. At last Rose heard the maid's footsteps on the stairs. Once Lizzy reported that Rachel wasn't at home, Rob would have no further reason to stay.

"Did you find Rachel, Lizzy?"

"Yes, ma'am. She said she wasn't at home."

Rose suppressed a sigh. Lizzy was new to service and, unfortunately, had her unreliable moments. To Rob, Rose said, "She must be feeling under the weather. Hot weather so often makes my head hurt. Rachel must be lying down."

"No, ma'am. She's putting on her walking shoes, and said I was to come tell her as soon as Mr. Gaston leaves."

Rose indeed felt a headache coming on. "That will be all, Lizzy." She looked at Rob. "I suppose Rachel isn't receiving company today."

He frowned and strode to the foot of the stairs as if he was considering bounding up them. "If she's here, I want to see her. I have a message for her from her father."

"You may deliver it to me, and I'll tell her."

"He said I was to tell it directly to Rachel."

Rose tried to smile. She hoped Rob wouldn't be too difficult. He had always had a temper as a boy. "I believe that's going to be impossible, since she won't come down to see you."

"It's not fair of her. I was given permission to call on her, and she is making it as difficult for me as possible."

"Well, that's her prerogative. Maybe you should think of someone else to keep company with."

"I'll have Rachel or no one!" he said petulantly. "You're her sister. You talk to her on my behalf."

"I already have. She says she will give you no encouragement. Why are you so determined to have Rachel and no one else? You hardly know each other anymore."

"That's beside the point. It is perfectly logical for me to marry Rachel. She is already practically a part of my family. She and Beatrice are close friends, and so are our parents. Mr. Pennington and I belong to the same club."

She had to smile. "Rob, there's only one men's club in Fairfield. I really think you should forget Rachel. Have you seen Pamela Driskoll lately?"

"Miss Pamela? I see her at church occasionally. She grew up to be rather plain."

Rose drew herself up. Pamela was her friend. "I think you should leave, Rob. Rachel isn't going to come down, and there's no reason for us to continue to discuss it. What was Papa's message?"

"He said that I still have his permission to court her and that she should be reasonable."

"I'll see that she gets the message." She went to the front door and held it open.

Rob remained at the foot of the stairs. "Rachel?" he called up as loudly as he dared. "I know you're up there!"

"Robert Gaston! What do you mean by shouting in my house?" Rose demanded. "I've had quite enough of this. Go home!"

"Not until I've seen Rachel."

Rachel appeared at the top of the stairs and leaned over the railing to say, "You've seen me. Now leave!"

"You come down here," he commanded. "Don't make me have to come up after you."

Rose's mouth dropped open at his audacity.

Rachel looked angry enough to tear him apart. "I wouldn't talk to you if there was a gun at my head. You can take that message back to Papa!"

"Rachel, please," Rose said. "Both of you. Stop this!" She was relieved to hear Edwin's familiar footsteps in the rear of the house.

Edwin came in, a paper under his arm and his hat in his hand. "What's going on here? I could hear you all the way to the back of the house."

"I've come to see Miss Rachel, and she is refusing to come down," Rob said. His face was flushed with anger, and he glared from Rose and Edwin to Rachel. "She's deliberately disobeying her father!"

Edwin looked up at Rachel and back at Rob. "I assume she doesn't want to see you or she would come down. Since she doesn't, I suggest you leave."

Rob looked as if he would rather fight. "Are you siding with Rachel against her father?"

Rose's breath stopped in her throat. She knew how worried Edwin already was over harboring Rachel. She also knew that he had good reason to worry. Her father's temper was legendary in Fairfield.

"I'm not siding with anyone," Edwin said firmly. "I only want order in my home. I never thought I would come home and find you shouting up at Rachel like that. Unless I'm mistaken, you were also raising your voice to my wife." His pale eyes grew hard.

Rob instantly changed his tactics. "I meant nothing by it. Why, I have only the highest regard for Miss Rose. You know that. You didn't misunderstand, did you, Miss Rose?" He tried to ingratiate himself with a smile. "Miss Rachel and I were only having a lovers' quarrel."

"We were having nothing of the sort," Rachel hurled down, "because I don't consider you to be my lover. I don't even like you!"

"All right, Rachel," Edwin said soothingly. "Rob, I think you had better go."

Rose instinctively moved closer to her husband. "Goodbye, Rob."

Rob looked as if he would refuse, but he grabbed his hat from the hall rack and slammed out the door. Rose leaned with relief toward Edwin. Upstairs she could hear Rachel slam shut the door to her room.

"I'm so glad you came home when you did."

Edwin helped her up the stairs to the room they shared. "How on earth did Rob come to be shouting in our house? Has he lost his mind?"

"It was that foolish Lizzy's fault. She can't carry any message and do it correctly." Rose felt near tears. "I had so hoped she would work out."

"I can't allow anyone to upset you, especially not at a time like this." He solicitously helped her to a chair. "Maybe you should lie down."

"Just let me sit for a moment. Edwin, you can't imagine how awful it was. He yelled at me! He actually shouted!"

Edwin sat on the chest at the foot of the bed and leaned forward, resting his elbows on his knees. "I'll have to speak to him about it. I want to be sure it never happens again. If he comes back, don't let him in."

"I didn't let him in this time. I know Rachel doesn't want to see him. Lizzy had him in the parlor before I knew he was anywhere about."

"I'll start looking for another girl to replace her. Were the children upset?"

"No, thank goodness, they are walking with Nanny. It would have sent little Rosemary into hysterics. You know how excitable she is."

Awkwardly Edwin said, "Are you feeling... Is everything all right with you?"

Rose put her hand on the swell of her unborn baby. "I'm fine. Just a bit upset."

Edwin stood and paced to the window. "We can't keep on like this, you know. It's damned—pardon, dear—it's uncomfortable working in the same office with a man when there are all these complications."

"I know it must be difficult, but what else can we do?"

"Somehow we must encourage Rachel to make up with her parents. Doesn't she realize birthrights are lost every day over less than this?"

"I don't think she cares."

"Well, she should! What will happen to her if she never marries and has nothing to inherit?"

Rose gestured helplessly. "I suppose she will stay here."

Edwin ran his hand through his hair, leaving it disarrayed. "I like Rachel better than most men like their in-laws, but I can't harbor her forever. We haven't the money, for one thing. Mr. Pennington won't stand for it for another. It could cost me my job. What would we do then?"

"I suppose you could open an office of your own," Rose said uncertainly. "What do men usually do in that case?"

"I see you aren't trying to convince me that your father wouldn't fire me," Edwin said wryly. "At least we needn't waste our breath discussing what we both know is a possibility."

"Ed, Rachel loves Jared Prescott." Rose went to him and put her hand on his shoulder. Their eyes were almost on a level. "She really seems to love him."

"Rosie, can't you see that it will never work? I can't allow him to call on her at our house without your father finding out. If he did, that would be the end for me."

Rose leaned her cheek against his shoulder, and he put his arm around her. "I hate to see her so unhappy. I've never known her to be so miserable."

"She would be happy if she obeyed her father's wishes. If she did what was right."

"Do you really believe that?"

Edwin sighed. "No. No, I don't. Sometimes I look at what is happening to Rachel and I think about us, and I'm constantly amazed that you agreed to be my wife. Why can't it be so simple with her?"

Rose smiled and kissed his cheek. She had never let him know that he wasn't her first choice. "I'm not sure that anything about love will ever be easy for Rachel. She's as hardheaded as Papa."

Edwin kissed her forehead. "I'm glad you took after your mother. I'm not sure that I could face living with a woman as stubborn as Mr. Pennington."

Rob rode toward the Pennington estate to speak with William. After his failure to convince Edwin to order Rachel to come down and talk to him, he had decided to take the matter to her father. As her formal suitor and the man chosen by her father, Rob felt his rights were being violated. He was so intent on his thoughts, he almost failed to see Prescott riding across the adjoining field.

Rob reined in his horse and watched for a moment. Prescott was heading in the direction of London, and he was alone. This might be an excellent time to follow him and see for himself where the man went in London.

He allowed Prescott a reasonable lead, then turned his horse and fell in behind. Not once did Prescott look behind him or show in any way that he suspected he was being followed. London was an easy two-hour ride from Fairfield, and as the road was one of the least traveled, Rob had no trouble keeping Jared in sight.

Prescott rode purposefully into the city as if he were well acquainted with the route. To Rob's surprise, Prescott turned away from the fashionable west end and headed into

the older section to the east. Soon the winding streets became narrower, so much so that the dwellings above the
ground-floor stores and shops on either side of the street
nearly met overhead. Rob closed his distance behind Prescott so he could keep him more easily in sight, and he
tightened his grip on his riding quirt in case he needed to
flail away some cutpurse or other unsavory character.

Following a number of twists and turns, they entered an
even more unsavory section of the city. Dark, dingy buildings hid behind enclosed and unkempt courtyards, and here
and there were derelict buildings that doubtless served as
rookeries for London's poorest and seamiest characters.
Rob was intrigued by sights such as he had never seen before, and he couldn't imagine what business Prescott could
possibly have in such an area.

Prescott rode into one of the courtyards, dismounted and
tied his horse, then disappeared into the darkness of the
doorway. Rob watched nervously from the shadows of the
overhanging buildings, feeling somewhat claustrophobic
and wishing more than the scant daylight could make its
way through to the street where he stood. From behind
came the shouts and hawkings of London's poor as they
went about their daily lives, and infusing the air was the
odor of spoiled fish and the unmistakable smell of the
nearby Thames. He hoped Prescott's stay wouldn't be long.

Nearly an hour later, Rob's patience was rewarded.
Prescott had finally emerged, and he was not alone. The
woman with him was older than he, and although her face
looked as if she had seen everything known to man, her
dress was clean and mended. In the doorway behind her, he
glimpsed a younger, prettier girl. To avoid the chance that
Prescott might see him, Rob turned his horse and melded
into the tangle of people.

After Prescott was gone, Rob gave the building where he
had spent the past hour a closer examination. It was old,
and although it had long since fallen into decay, he could
tell it had once been a large, fine house. It was better

maintained than its neighbors, but it still had the seedy look of a building that was on its last leg.

Rob stopped one of the more intelligent-looking passersby. "What building is that?" he asked.

The man glanced at the place in question. "That be Dame Webber's house."

"Dame Webber? What sort of place is it?"

The young man's face took on a sly look. "I ain't never been inside, but I've heard talk of it. Dame Webber lives there with a pack of young women."

"Young ladies? I thought I saw one I recognized at the door just now," Rob lied. "What sort of young ladies?"

The man guffawed. "None what the likes o' you is likely to meet up with, not unless you favors the girls that hangs out round the dock."

"Prostitutes? Whores live here?"

The man nodded. "I've a friend who said his girl come 'ere to live. She ain't been back to the docks in months. He said he don't think she's still in London, but I told him there's noplace else that she could go." His eyes traveled up and down Rob's expensive clothing. "If you're looking for a girl, I could fix you up."

Rob gave him a distasteful frown. "I'm only interested in the ones in that house."

"He has boys and girls there as well, if your tastes run in that way."

"Children! In a house of ill repute?" Rob was stunned. This was worse than he had thought.

The man shrugged. "You see it all around here. Young'ns have to eat same as us."

Rob tried not to show how offended he was. "Do you happen to know the name of the man who owns this place?"

"Aye. He's somebody called Jared Prescott. He bought the building several years ago. I had a pal who stayed 'ere from time to time when he was off ship. Prescott made him find other lodgings. Caused some hard feelings, it did."

Rob looked back at the house. "You've been more helpful than you know."

"If I was so helpful to you, how's about a coin for my time?"

Rob reached in his waistcoat pocket and absently tossed a coin in the man's direction. He didn't look to see if the man caught it or not. He had more important thoughts on his mind. Jared might or might not own a sweatshop, but he obviously owned something far worse. Rob almost chuckled to think what Rachel would say about this—Rachel with her fastidious manners and her attitude about wrongs needing to be righted. For that matter, what would William Pennington say? Rob thought there was a good chance that he could not only cut Prescott out of the running for Rachel's hand, but force him to leave Fairfield as well.

He would have to wait and bide his time. Eventually Prescott would cause there to be talk against him, and when that happened, Rob would be ready to step forward with information about Dame Webber and her girls. He almost laughed again at how Prescott's face would look when he was confronted with his house of ill repute. It would be almost as gratifying as the way Rachel would look. Rob could scarcely contain his enjoyment.

He reined his horse about and carefully memorized the location of Dame Webber's courtyard. He wanted to be sure he could find it again.

Chapter Fourteen

"Mark, I've decided you're right," Jared said. "At least I hope you are."

"I usually am," Mark said smugly. "But right on what count?"

"I must enter society here in Fairfield. It's the only way I can court Rachel without ruining her standing in the town."

"You're no longer worried about Yvonne?"

"Of course I'm still worried about her." Jared frowned at his cousin. "But Rachel is too important to my life for me to risk losing her. I'll begin immediately looking for a suitable home for Yvonne, but it has to have impeccable qualifications. I'll not send her to a place where she will be mistreated. And it should be in the country. She has seemed quieter here than in the city. I think the country is also healthier for her."

"No one would disagree with you on that. I know a couple near Haversham who could be perfect for Yvonne's caretakers. I know them both personally. They are responsible and tenderhearted. Shall I write them and ask if they would be interested in having her?"

"Yes, and be sure to mention that I will pay handsomely for her to have a good and kind home. Also say that Abby will be accompanying her and that I will pay Abby's keep as well. If they agree, I'll write them myself and arrange to meet them before the bargain is set."

"I'll write them today." Mark smiled at him. "You've made a good decision."

"Then why do I feel like a traitor to Yvonne?"

Mark put a firm hand on his cousin's shoulder. "I know this decision hasn't been made easily."

"Will Yvonne understand and not think I'm casting her away because I don't love her? Would Father understand?"

"Those are questions that we may never have answered. I understand, however, and I can see no way that you may do otherwise."

Jared turned and stared out the window that overlooked Fairfield, as he had done many times in recent days. Rachel was down there, not far from the steeple that was adjacent to the curiously thatched roof. "How am I to go about it? Entering society, I mean. The invitations have stopped. I can't wait until I receive another. Who knows how long that may be? If I'm to start keeping company, I want to do it right away."

"You used to have such patience," Mark teased him. "I would hardly recognize you as the Jared Prescott of London gentility."

Jared gave him a grudging smile. "I know I'll never hear the end of your teasing. Do you have an answer?"

"As a matter of fact, I do. You must throw a party. A huge one. Invite everyone who is of any importance in Fairfield."

Jared laughed. "That will hardly be a huge party, not by comparison with the ones we're accustomed to giving. But I think you're right. That way I will know Rachel is invited." His voice softened. "I want to show her my home."

"I'll get paper and we can start preparing the invitations."

"I'll meet you in the library. I'm going to go up to tell Abby of our plans. She'll need time to prepare Yvonne for visitors coming to Ravenwood and to make whatever preparations she feels necessary to keep Yvonne quiet. Even with Yvonne's room so far away, she can sometimes be heard down here when she's having one of her bad days."

Mark nodded. "I've heard the servants you hired locally say they think the house is haunted by the spirit of the old baron. That's how they explain the sounds among themselves."

"It's just as well. I don't want any of them to know about Yvonne. A servant can spread a rumor faster than anyone." He turned away from the window. "I'm sure Abby won't be any too happy knowing we're going to have a party, but I may as well tell her now and be done with it."

"Will you tell her about your plans to find them another home?"

Jared hesitated. "No, not yet. I mean to wait until all is decided. You recall how upset Abby was over moving here. She was almost as hard to handle as Yvonne. I'll wait until I know all the details before I tell her."

The next day, as Jared rode through Fairfield, he nodded a greeting to everyone he saw, but frankly had hoped for a better response than the astonished looks he got in return. Before moving here, he had never been an aloof or rude person, and until today he had paid little attention to the manner in which the locals viewed him. Apparently, they all saw him in a distasteful light, and it was more than a little uncomfortable. He knew it was his own fault that no one seemed friendly, and hoped his change in behavior would bring about a change in theirs.

As he tied his horse at the post in front of Edwin Jenson's house, he glanced at the upper window that faced the street and smiled tenderly as he recalled the green scarf Rachel had tried to use as a signal. He wondered how many of the villagers had also seen it and wondered. He loved Rachel's innocence as much as he did her complexities.

His knock on their door was answered by a maidservant. "I've come to see Miss Rachel Pennington. Is she in?"

"Aye. I'll see if she's wanting company."

He was left to wait on the steps while the young maid went to find her mistress. After a few minutes she returned. "I forgot to ask your name."

"I'm Jared Prescott."

"I'll be right back."

Jared waited with growing impatience. What if Rachel refused to see him? When he last saw her, she was furious with him. Maybe she had changed her mind about loving him.

His fears were dispelled, however, when Rachel came hurrying to the door. "Come in, come in," she said. "Lizzy should never have left you standing on the doorstep." As Rachel glanced back at the maid, Jared noticed a hint of anxiety beneath Rachel's smile.

Stepping inside, he surveyed his surroundings. Although the house was not large and the furnishings were of good, but not excellent, quality, he felt a serenity there, unlike anything he had experienced since his childhood. He instinctively knew this was not just a house, but a home. As he followed Rachel into the foyer, he gave his hat to the servant who had followed them. The girl's face was as blank as an eggshell, and if she had been scolded for not inviting him in to wait, she showed no signs of it. With a wave of Rachel's hand, the maid hung Jared's hat on the hall tree and left the room.

"I was afraid you would never speak to me again," Rachel said. "It's been more than a week."

"Yes. Nine days, to be exact." In the muted light of the foyer, she looked so sweet and vulnerable—and wary. His coming here against her wishes was obviously troubling her. He assumed her concern had something to do with the rift with her parents, but he had sworn he would not admit that he knew anything about that. "I've come to apologize for our argument. I know it was my fault, and I want to make amends."

"I shouldn't forgive you. Not only were you insufferable, but you've come here after I expressly told you not to."

"I had to come. How else could I have seen you?"

"But Lizzy will tell Rose and Rose will tell Edwin, and—" Rachel's fingers went to her lips and stopped her words.

"And Edwin doesn't like me," he finished for her. "I'm beginning to understand. People here in Fairfield have misunderstood my reclusiveness and think ill of me. I have decided to end my seclusion from society here so people will know me for who I am and not for who they thought me to be."

"It's not that Edwin doesn't... Did you say you were ending your seclusion?"

"Yes, I am. And you needn't try to hide your brother-in-law's animosity toward me. After giving this some thought, I find I have only myself to blame for the misconception my neighbors have of me."

Rachel looked puzzled. "But what about your need for privacy?"

"I'm working on an alternate solution to that." Rachel appeared somewhat bewildered by this sudden change in him, but Jared wasn't surprised. This was happening rather quickly for him as well. Although he would have preferred spending this reunion time with Rachel alone, he knew proper etiquette demanded otherwise, and without a good showing on his part, the locals—and Rachel's family in particular—would not be inclined to change their minds about him. "I would like to meet your sister and brother-in-law, if that could be arranged."

"Yes, that would be a good idea. I'm sure Lizzy has told them by now that you are here. But please understand that they may be somewhat... reserved."

Jared nodded with a smile and followed her into the parlor. Across the room, a man and a woman were seated on a sofa, one of them apparently reading to two children who were clustered about them. As the woman bore a resemblance to Rachel, although her hair was blond, he assumed them to be Rose and Edwin Jenson. When they became aware that someone had come into the room, they looked up, and from their expressions, he knew they had not been prepared to expect a visitor. He regretted that he had caught them unaware, but it was too late to correct that now.

As Edwin came to his feet, Rachel said, "Rose, Edwin, this is Jared Prescott. Jared, my sister and her husband."

Jared went to Edwin and held out his hand. After a brief pause, Edwin shook it. Jared nodded to Rose and smiled down at the children. He had always liked children and was pleased to have caught sight of them. All too often, children were closeted in the upper rooms until they were of an age to enter society. This was apparently the only advantage of his unexpected arrival. The children smiled back and the little girl reached up to take his hand.

"Children, it's time for your dinner," Rose said. "Go find Nanny, please." When they had trooped out, none too quietly, Rose said, "Won't you sit down, Mr. Prescott? You've found us unprepared for company, I'm afraid."

Rachel sat on the unoccupied sofa facing Rose, and after Jared joined her, Edwin sat down again beside his wife. Jared took the initiative with the conversation. "I should have sent word of my coming, but it was rather on the spur of the moment that I decided." He glanced at Rachel, hoping to see some sign that his new approach was reassuring her, but she still appeared somewhat perplexed and anxious. Looking back to Edwin and Rose, he added, "I've heard so much about you both. Rachel is quite fond of you two."

Rose gave her sister a level look. "Rachel tells us about you, too." Further conversation seemed to fail her, and she looked to Edwin for help.

Edwin took his cue and asked, "How are you liking our town? I imagine it must seem dull after London."

"Not dull at all." Jared could honestly say his emotions had never been subjected to such a seesaw until he met Rachel. "No, I'd not call it dull. I am, in fact, planning a party. Your invitations will arrive in a day or two, but since I'm here, I'd like to invite you in person."

"A party?" Rachel said in surprise.

"Yes. A dance in Ravenwood's ballroom."

"I'd love that!" she exclaimed.

"I don't believe we will be able to attend," Edwin said. "My wife is not going out these days."

Jared pretended not to notice Rose's automatic gesture of pulling her shawl closer to conceal her pregnancy. Because of her condition, he hadn't expected them to accept. When a woman was about to have her baby at any moment, she would leave the house only in an emergency. However, politeness had been served by his inviting them.

"When is the party to be?" Rachel asked.

"A week from this Saturday. I'm sending to London for an orchestra."

Rose spoke up. "Rachel, I don't know if—"

"Papa will never know, Rose. Besides, he isn't speaking to me anyway." Rachel caught her blunder and added, "I mean, I've seldom spoken to him since I came to stay with you."

Jared pretended not to notice. "I'm sending him an invitation as well."

"No! That is, there's no need to do that. Papa and Mama never dance."

"I have to meet them sometime, Rachel."

"You do?" Edwin lifted a curious eyebrow. "For what reason?"

Jared looked back at him. The young man seemed unprepossessing at first glance, but he had a backbone, it would seem. "I intend to ask for permission to court Rachel."

Rose and Edwin exchanged a look full of trepidation. Rachel only smiled and managed, by way of holding her breath, to blush. Jared had to struggle not to laugh at her effort to seem surprised at his words. The little actress knew his intentions were more than that.

"I'm not sure that would be such a good idea," Edwin said. "I assume that you have no way of knowing this, but

Mr. Pennington has already been approached by Rob
Prescott for the same privilege."

Jared kept his eyes fixed on Edwin's. "I assume that a
young lady of Fairfield can have more than one suitor.
That's how it's done in London."

"Yes, of course, but Mr. Pennington—" Edwin was si-
lenced by Rose putting her hand over his.

"My father is a difficult man to talk to at times," Rose
said tactfully. "Still, if you're to court Rachel, he should be
advised."

"I agree," Jared said. "I've wanted to talk to him for
several weeks."

Speaking firmly, Edwin said, "I wouldn't talk to Mr.
Pennington at this time. Since Rachel is presently living
here, I believe it's permissible for me to give my permission for her to be courted by you."

Rose frankly stared at her husband and Rachel's mouth
dropped open. Edwin pretended not to notice. "I've recently come to realize that Rob Gaston has a temper that
doesn't reflect well on his being considered for Rachel. I've
told him, in fact, not to return to my house."

Jared grinned. He could see that all this was news to the
women, as well. "So you're granting me permission to call
on Rachel?"

"Under the circumstances, yes."

"You have my heartfelt appreciation," Jared said. "If I
can ever do you any service, don't hesitate to call on me. I
never forget a kindness."

"Edwin, are you sure—" Rose started to object, but
Edwin motioned for her to stop.

"Rose, calm yourself. I've given this some thought, and
I had already decided to follow this line of action, assuming Mr. Prescott ever came calling. What Rob did the other
day was simply unforgivable, and I can't in good conscience allow him to be Rachel's sole suitor."

"What will Papa say?" Rachel asked. "I thought you
were afraid of losing your position."

"I am. I'll not lie about it. But some things are more important than a position." He cleared his throat as if he weren't used to expressing such emotions and continued. "You are my sister by law, and I owe you the protection and guidance of a brother. I wouldn't condone any sister of mine seeing a man as rude as Rob Gaston."

Rachel and Rose both appeared to be flabbergasted, but looked somewhat fearful, as well.

Jared spoke up. "I know your position with Mr. Pennington is precarious. If it should happen that you lose it because of having befriended me, I'll see to it that you are set up in a law office of your own, either here or in the place of your choice."

Edwin inclined his head in a gentlemanly manner. "Thank you, Mr. Prescott. That's a decent offer."

"Call me Jared."

Rachel and Rose stared at each other. Rachel gave an almost imperceptible shrug, as if she still couldn't understand what had just happened.

"Now that I know where we all stand," Jared said, "I'll not impose on your hospitality any longer. Again, Mr. Jenson, I thank you."

"Edwin. Call me Edwin." He again extended his hand, this time in the first gesture of genuine friendship Jared had known since coming to Fairfield.

When Jared was gone, Rachel and Rose both stared at Edwin, waiting for his answer to their unspoken but obvious question. He shifted uncomfortably. "I think I made the right decision," he said almost defensively. "Jared is a gentleman. That was obvious. After the scene Rob made here, I can't let him court and possibly win Rachel."

"Rob could never win me, even if he had the chance," Rachel was quick to affirm.

"But Edwin, what if Papa hears what you've done?" Rose said, wringing her hands in worry. "He will be furious!"

Edwin put his hand over Rose's in one of his rare public gestures of love. "Don't upset yourself, dear. It's not good for you. As for your father, well, a man sometimes has to do what he has to do, regardless of the consequences. I can't live every moment of my life trying to outguess your father and do only what will please him.''

"Edwin, even after eight years of marriage, you still amaze me," Rose said.

He smiled but glanced uncomfortably at Rachel, who was watching this exchange with undisguised interest. She realized she was staring and averted her eyes, saying, "I'm going to see Beatrice. I have to tell her that Jared has permission to call on me. She will be so pleased!"

"Be circumspect," Rose advised. "We can't throw all our hats over a windmill."

Rachel hurried out and walked as briskly as was decorous to Beatrice's house. As soon as they were closeted in the sun room, she said, "You'll never guess what Edwin has done!" When she finished telling Beatrice every detail of Jared's meeting, she sat back and watched the amazement on Beatrice's face.

"Edwin did that? We always assumed that he had no gumption at all!"

"It seems we were wrong. Maybe Rose isn't as bored with him as we thought. He was quite a hero."

"It's so hard to see Edwin in that light." Beatrice put her hands to her lips. "My, I can't picture what Rose must have looked like when he gave Jared permission to call."

"She would have fainted if she hadn't been so distracted. I'm sure of it. And Jared smiled at the children. He must like little ones. Everything is turning out so perfectly!"

"Not everything. I've tried to reason with Rob on your behalf, but he is adamant that he won't give you up."

"Edwin won't welcome him back in the house. He said so."

"Oh, dear. Rob is sure to tell your father. Edwin is taking such a chance."

"Yes, and he's doing it for my sake. I can't tell you how he has risen in my estimation. When I left, Rose still looked worried, but she also looked as if she were falling in love with him all over again. He said, 'A man has to do what he has to do.' Isn't that brave of him?''

"Indeed. Your father can be so frightening when he's upset."

"Rose has said the same thing." She thought for a minute as she tried to imagine being afraid of her father. "I can't see why. Anyway, Jared is having a ball. A real one, with an orchestra from London. I'm sure you're to be invited. What will we wear?"

"Good heavens, I don't know. Is there time to have a dress made?"

"It's to be Saturday week. There's not much time."

"I suppose invitations are sent out less formally in London."

Rachel smiled. "I think he just wanted to see me as soon as possible. What about my blue velvet? Do you think it will be too warm?"

"Velvet in the summer? You'll smother. I'll lend you my green gown."

"Thank you, but green really isn't my best color. What about my blue muslin with the velvet sash and bows?"

"Perfect. Do you have it at Rose's house?"

Rachel nodded. "I have everything I own there. I could brighten it up with some silk violets and pansies."

"I'll help you. I think I'll wear my pink gown with the rose trim."

They were interrupted by Rob coming into the room. When he saw Rachel he paused. "I didn't know you were here, Miss Rachel."

"I was just about to leave," she said hastily. "I had thought you would be at the club at this hour."

"I was about to go there."

"We won't detain you," Beatrice said. "Goodbye."

Rob came to them instead. "Since Miss Rachel is here, I'd rather stay home."

Rachel sighed. "Rob, why must you make this so difficult on all of us? I've made it plain that I don't welcome your courtship. I don't love you and I won't marry any man on the hope that I may grow to love him someday. Why, we would be miserable together.''

"I don't agree."

"I would see to it. Trust me, Rob, and give up on me. There are other girls in town who would welcome your courtship and who would be better suited to you."

Beatrice nodded. "Pamela Driskoll, for one. She's already half in love with you, and the Driskolls are a good family."

"Maybe good at one time, but I think they are going to seed. I hope to make a better match." His blue eyes traveled over Rachel in an insulting way. "Your father has encouraged me."

Rachel wanted to tell him what had just transpired at the Jenson's house, but she felt a new protectiveness toward Edwin. "Marry him, then, for I won't have you."

"It's still Prescott, isn't it?" Rob's tone was growing ugly. "He's the one you still favor, is he?"

Rachel's chin rose stubbornly. "As a matter of fact, yes. I do favor him. I've never made a secret of it."

"What if I told you there are things about him you don't know?"

"If I don't know them, you couldn't possibly know them, either."

"On the contrary. I followed him into London just the other day, and I know a great deal about him that will surprise you."

For a moment Rachel's confidence wavered. "You followed him?"

"Whatever for?" his sister demanded. "You had no right."

"I saw him go to a place that is better not named in the company of ladies." He gave Rachel a leering smile.

"If you know something, I insist that you tell me," Rachel said. "How else can I dispute it?"

"You can't dispute this on any grounds, because I saw him go there myself. He went to a rookery near the docks.

To a place such as you two have never seen before and probably didn't know existed.''

"Rob, stop being so mysterious," Beatrice demanded. "If you've got something to say, then say it."

"He went into a brothel. Forgive me, but that's what it was."

Rachel felt as if she had been punched in the middle. "Impossible! You're mistaken. You aren't familiar with London. How would you know if it's . . . what you said?"

"I know because I asked. A local man confirmed it. Not only that, but guess who owns the establishment?"

Rachel refused to lower her eyes. "Who?"

"None other than Jared Prescott."

"You're lying," she said bluntly. "I don't believe a word of it."

"Why would you make up such a thing, Rob?" Beatrice asked. "What if Mother heard you?"

"She can't hear me because she is out walking with Mrs. Bloomington. And I'm not making this up."

Rachel knew Rob wouldn't hesitate to lie, but she hadn't thought he was that good at it. Could there be a kernel of truth to this? "Jared would never own such a place."

"There can be no doubt. Naturally, he would deny it if you ask him."

"I have no intention of mentioning it to him at all. The rumors of his owning a sweatshop were false, and so were the ones about his keeping a mistress. This is false, too." She glared at him. "All the rumors probably came from the same source."

"I'm telling you that I saw the place with my own eyes. It's in an enclosed court. At one time it may have been a house with some dignity, but now it's gone to ruin. It's in an area of town that isn't safe for a gentleman even in the daytime."

"Then I marvel that you dared brave it," Rachel said with stinging directness. Rob had never shown any talent before for inventiveness or creativity. He seemed certain not only of this brothel's existence, but of details about its appearance. "How would I find this place?"

He finally looked shocked. "I'd never tell you! You couldn't consider going to such a place!"

"Rachel, you mustn't!" Beatrice echoed. "Anything might happen to you."

"If he won't tell us how to find it, we must assume it's made up entirely in his mind," Rachel pointed out. "Just as I thought."

Suddenly Rob had crossed the room and grabbed Rachel by the arm. "You press me too far," he ground out. "No one calls me a liar!"

Beatrice let out a scream, then quickly clapped both hands to her mouth to muffle it.

Rachel's arm hurt where he was gripping her, but she refused to back down. Her eyes, nearly on a level with his, glared into his. "I'm calling you a liar and worse. You're a blackguard and a scoundrel, and you won't even stop short of trying to hurt and frighten women. I don't know what's come over you, Robert Gaston, but you are sadly mistaken if you think you can frighten me into submission!"

After a long moment the sound of hurrying footsteps was heard in the hall. Servants had been alarmed by the raised voices and by Beatrice's scream. Rob blinked and released her arm. Rachel refused to give him the satisfaction of knowing he had hurt her by rubbing her arm, but it ached and she knew there would be bruises.

When the servants entered the room, she and Beatrice were talking in one corner and Rob was leaving through the far door. Rachel tried to look as calm as possible. She didn't want to be the topic of gossip in the kitchen. Beatrice quietly asked for two glasses of lemonade.

"None for me, thank you," Rachel said. "I really must be going. I've stayed too long as it is."

"I'll walk you to the door."

As soon as they were alone, Beatrice asked, "Did he hurt your arm? I'm beside myself! What could he have been thinking of?"

"It's the same way he acted at Rose's house the other evening. See what I mean about his temper? I was out of reach then, but for a minute I really thought he might hit Edwin!"

Beatrice glanced over her shoulder to be sure they weren't being overheard. "I must talk to Mother and Father about this. He can't be allowed to get away with hurting you."

"I'm not really hurt. If you tell them what happened, they may think I'm to blame."

"They never would!"

"Lately I think your mother has been a bit cool toward me. Ever since the party, in fact."

Beatrice was silent, and Rachel knew Mrs. Gaston's slight hadn't been all her imagination.

Beatrice opened the front door and Rachel stepped out. With a wry smile, she looked back at Beatrice. "Here we are in an adventure, and it's not nearly as much fun as we expected, is it? This problem with Rob, it won't harm our friendship, will it?"

Beatrice shook her head resolutely. "Never. You're my best friend and always will be. Rob was entirely to blame, and I'll tell anyone that it was through no fault of your own. We must stick together at a time like this, Rachel, or we'll never win the hearts of Mark and Jared."

Rachel nodded. "Certainly we wouldn't be worthy of their love. We must be as brave as Emily was in *The Mysteries of Udolpho*."

"Yes," Beatrice confirmed. "We will be like Emily in search of our true love. Nothing will keep us from our Valancourt."

Rachel smiled. "We will cast Rob in the role of Count Montoni."

"Rob cast himself in that role with his despicable actions toward you."

Rachel silently agreed, but since Rob was, after all, Beatrice's brother, she didn't voice her sentiments. She valued Beatrice's friendship too much to risk there being a rift between them in case Beatrice later felt she had to defend her brother.

While she walked back to the Jenson house, Rachel reflected on Edwin's change of heart. She had always assumed that he would ride the fence rather than take any firm stand if that stand would prove to be unpopular. But for the first time she saw the spunk that was needed if he was to be a good lawyer. True, he hadn't directly faced William on this issue, but he had made a good start.

When she reached the house, she was met by a wide-eyed Lizzy. "She's started birthing the baby, Miss Rachel. Mr. Edwin has gone for the doctor."

Rachel hurried up the stairs and tapped on the door of Rose and Edwin's bedroom. When she heard a soft moan, she opened it and went in. Rose lay on the bed, several quilts and a rubber sheet beneath her. Her head tossed restlessly and she murmured again.

"Are you all right?" Rachel asked as she quickly went to her sister's side.

"You shouldn't be in here. Go keep the children occupied. Take them to the park."

"I'll stay with you until the doctor arrives."

Rose's face reddened as another contraction gripped her. She held tightly to Rachel's hand. "I don't want to frighten you. Birth isn't something a young lady should be witness to." Her voice was strained.

Rachel held her hand as another pain fastened upon her. "Is it worse this time than with your others?" She was suddenly terrified that she might lose Rose.

"No. It feels the same. The doctor says I always have trouble delivering." She glanced at Rachel. "I shouldn't even be telling you this. Go stay with the children."

"I won't leave you alone." She stayed beside Rose and held her hand and tried to talk to her about calming subjects until she heard Edwin's hurried steps on the stairs.

When he came into the room, he looked as harried as a man at the end of his wits. "I can't find the doctor."

Rachel held her breath. "Did you go to the midwife?"

He nodded. "She was too drunk to understand what I was saying. I left word at the doctor's office that he is to come here straightaway when he returns."

Rose groaned and curled against the pain. "They're getting stronger, but I have several hours yet. The doctor will be back in time. You'll see."

Rachel tried not to panic, and to have as much faith in the doctor as did Rose. She knew he was sometimes away from his office for hours at a time, even overnight if one of his patients was in labor or desperately ill. There was an excellent chance that he wouldn't make it.

"Rachel," Edwin said, "go to the kitchen and ask if any of the servants knows anything about birthing." Although she knew he was trying to stay calm, Rachel could hear the fear beneath his words. She ran to do his bidding.

The news wasn't good. Rose's household staff was composed almost entirely of women who had never married. She took the news back to Edwin.

"Then it's up to us," he said in a dazed manner.

"Us? You're staying, too? Were you here before?"

"Of course not. But I helped birth foals when I was a boy." He took off his coat and rolled up his sleeves. "I hate to subject you to this, but I see no other way."

"I want to help Rose. What should I do?"

"Get the scissors that Rose uses to cut cloth. They have to be sharp."

Quickly she gathered all the things Edwin thought he might need, then positioned herself by Rose's head so she could hold her hands as the contractions became closer together and harder. By the time the doctor arrived exhausted at three in the morning, Rose already had been delivered of a baby girl, minutes before.

The doctor examined Rose and the baby and said in a solemn tone to Rachel and Edwin, "You have probably saved both their lives. Mrs. Jenson has always had a hard time birthing." Rachel and Edwin exchanged a look that would cement their bond for the rest of their lives. Together they had saved both Rose and the baby.

Now that it was all over, Edwin looked as if he were about to faint. Rachel felt exhilarated at having brought a baby into the world, although she thought the doctor might have been exaggerating Rose's danger.

"I'll never put her through this again," Edwin said, his lips turning blue.

"Edwin, sit. Put your head lower than your knees," the doctor said. "I've had enough patients for one day."

Rachel snugged the baby's soft blanket closer about her tiny, red and still puffy face, thinking that this baby was the prettiest she had ever held, then carried Rose's daughter to her.

Even though Rose was exhausted, she smiled and cuddled the baby close. "We will name her Rachel Elizabeth after you," she said.

Edwin nodded. "Rachel is the right name for her."

Rachel looked down at her namesake. Would she ever hold her own child? She was so tired that the mere idea made her feel teary. Having a baby with Jared would be beautiful indeed. She quietly left the room so Edwin and Rose could be alone with their new infant. She walked the doctor downstairs and told the sleepy maid that it was all over and she could go to bed. As Rachel climbed the stairs, she ached from head to toe and reflected that she had never felt so good.

Chapter Fifteen

As the Gastons' coach rolled toward Ravenwood, Rachel straightened the bow on Beatrice's sash. "There. You look so pretty."

"So do you." Beatrice hid her giggle behind her gloved hand. "I can hardly believe we are on our way to a ball at Ravenwood. Can you? When we were children we used to wish we could just peep inside, and I was sure it must be as grand as Buckingham Palace."

"I remember. We never dreamed we would ever be invited there. Isn't it odd, the quirks and turns life can take? So much has happened that I would never have expected."

"How is Rose?"

"She's fine now. The baby is so beautiful. She is already trying to hold her little head up. They named her after me, you know, but will call her Elizabeth so we aren't confused."

"I can't imagine how you were ever able to help deliver her. I'd have fainted dead away."

"There wasn't time." She laughed. "When it was all over, Edwin looked as if he might, though. He still says he won't put Rose through that again now that he knows what it's like to have a baby. Rose just laughs at him and pats his hand."

Beatrice paused. "Have you heard from your parents?"

"No. I'm afraid this time I've gone too far." Rachel blinked back the tears that threatened to fall. "But I can't in all honesty say that I would do it differently if I had to do it again. I love him, Bea.''

"I know. I love Mark, too. It will all work out. You'll see.''

The coach rolled to a stop in front of Ravenwood's open front doors. As Rachel was handed out by the driver, she could hear the sound of music. "They've already started to play,'' she told Beatrice.

"I don't see many coaches,'' she replied as she looked around.

Rachel saw that it was true. Although it was quickly growing dark, there was still enough light to see the green held only a few coaches. She heard Beatrice tell the driver that he need not wait, as they would be returning with Pamela Driskoll.

"Is Pamela coming?'' Rachel asked as they went up the steps.

Whispering, Beatrice said, "I have no idea. Mark is taking me home.''

A stern-faced butler took their light summer wraps and showed them up to the ballroom on the second floor. He gave their names to a man at the ballroom door, and as Rachel and Beatrice paused at the top of the steps, the doorman announced their arrival.

The ballroom was magnificent. The dance floor itself was sunken three steps below the rest. On the upper level were chairs and potted palms, and across the way a table laden with food and drink. The orchestra was located on a balcony high above the rest of the room, and Rachel already could tell it was better than any she had ever heard.

Mark and Jared met them at the bottom of the steps. Several couples were whirling around the dance floor in a waltz; the ladies' full skirts and dazzling colors looked like flowers tossed by the wind. Rachel was surprised to see how few people were there, considering the hour.

"I was afraid you weren't coming,'' Jared said as he swept Rachel into the waltz.

"I wouldn't have missed it for anything. I expected to arrive earlier, but Beatrice can never be ready on time."

"Mark tells me he is to take her home. Could I drive you?"

"I'd like that." She enjoyed the feel of being in his arms. An accomplished dancer, he made her feel as light on her feet as a fairy.

"How are Rose and Edwin?"

"Quite well, thank you. Rose has had her baby, and they named her after me." She left out the part about helping Rose deliver. She wasn't sure anyone but Beatrice would believe her.

"A little girl. That's nice. I hope all goes well with her."

"Edwin sent you his greeting. I think he and Rose would have come if the party had been at another time."

"I also sent an invitation to your parents."

"You didn't! They'll never come."

"I don't expect them, but I wanted to be aboveboard with them. It would have been impolite not to invite them under the circumstances."

Of course, he was right, but nevertheless, she felt an uneasiness that her father knew she was at Ravenwood tonight. She told herself she was being foolish.

After the waltz, the orchestra played a lively Roger de Coverly. When it was their time to dance down the middle, Jared spun Rachel around until she was laughing and breathless. She wished this night might never end so she could dance in his arms forever.

When the music ended and another dance began, Rachel and Jared went to get a glass of punch. "You have a lovely house, if this room is any indication. When we came in the front door, it took my breath away."

"Ravenwood was glorious in its day. I'm restoring it to what it was. The baron and his ancestors were lax in its upkeep, I'm afraid. I have to admit that I find it a delightful challenge. I never thought I would be so domestic."

"Domesticity isn't a trait I would have associated with you."

"No? What is?"

"You're a rogue and a pirate. I can picture you as a highwayman astride a black steed, brandishing a brace of pistols."

"You see me as a blackguard and a common thief. Interesting."

"No, there's nothing common about you at all. You're like the men Beatrice and I read about in romantic novels. I can feel the adventures all around you."

Jared laughed. "It's refreshing to talk to someone who has read something other than *The Mysteries of Udolpho.*"

"I loved *Udolpho.* Didn't you?"

"Yes, of course. Everyone does. You were to borrow some of my books. Remember? You never have."

"It's difficult when we hardly ever manage to meet. I would love to read your books. Next time you are to bring one to me."

"I'll be certain to do that."

When they finished their punch, Jared took her back to the dance floor. The orchestra was again playing a waltz and Rachel let her body move dreamily to the music. "Surely whoever invented the waltz must have been in love," she said.

"I've often thought the same thing." His voice caressed her and sent tingles of excitement through her.

"I think any woman must feel beautiful when she dances a waltz. Especially with a partner like you. At this moment I feel ravishing and glorious and free."

"I'm always amazed at the things you say. Do you always speak exactly what's on your mind?"

"Usually. Mama says it will be my undoing." She wished she hadn't thought of her mother. Violet would be appalled seeing Rachel dancing at Ravenwood, especially if she knew they had lied to the Gastons' driver about who was to bring them home.

"You stopped smiling."

"I was thinking about Mama. I do miss her so much. You know, it's funny in a way, but when I was around her every day, I seldom thought of her, but now I miss her a great deal. Rose is so much like her that she is a constant reminder."

"You must mend the rift in your family. If it will help, I'll go with you to talk to them."

"How do you know there is a rift? Did Mark..." Her voice trailed off as Jared stopped dancing and stared up at the door. She turned to follow his gaze and her breath caught in her throat. Her father and Rob stood in the doorway, William looking like a thundercloud about to erupt.

William Pennington clamped his gaze on his daughter and glared at her until Rachel dropped her eyes. Then he said in tones that stopped the orchestra, "Rachel, go to the coach and wait for me."

Jared stepped forward. "Hello, Mr. Pennington. You're welcome to my house. As are you, Mr. Gaston."

"I'm not here to be welcomed," William said. "I'm here to get my daughter."

Rob was looking for his sister, but Rachel had seen Beatrice and Mark slip out onto the adjoining terrace just moments before. She wished she, too, had been so fortunate as to be near the outside door. Beatrice's parents were in Derby for two weeks, and she had thought Rob had gone to London. Evidently he had gone instead to her father and stirred him to a fury. Rachel decided she would never speak to Rob again under any circumstances.

As Jared's guests looked from William and Rob to Jared and Rachel, tension filled the air. "You heard me, Rachel," William commanded, using his most intimidating courtroom voice. "Go to the coach. Now!"

"No, Papa." She lifted her chin and made her voice sound brave. "I won't."

William's face turned dark red with his anger, and he looked as if he was on the verge of coming after her.

"You have no reason to come here and ruin Jared's party," she said. "He has never done you any harm."

William gestured to include the entire room. "He's done you all a disservice by asking you here. This house was bought by ill-gotten gains. This man owns the worst sweatshop in all of England, and worse. He owns a brothel!"

Rachel caught her breath. Rob looked smug.

"I own a what?" Jared exclaimed. "A brothel?"

"Do you deny it, sir?" William looked down at him as if he had just won his case.

"I do indeed! My 'sweatshop' is nonexistent, and as for a brothel, why, I've never even been in one!"

"He's lying." Rob spoke up with the bravado of being partially obscured by William's bulk. "I followed him in London and saw him enter one with my own eyes. I asked, and it was common knowledge that he owns it and that one Dame Webber is the madam."

Jared's eyes lit with comprehension. "You followed me to Howard House." He grinned and relaxed visibly. "You should have followed me all the way inside."

"See?" Rob's voice squeaked in his agitation. "He admits it!"

"I admit nothing, you scurvy bag of lies. Howard House is named for my stepmother's family. I had preferred to remain anonymous, but it seems that I have lost that advantage. Howard House is a home for prostitutes, all right. Reformed prostitutes who want to learn a better way of making their living." He strolled toward the steps, Rachel close behind him. He now seemed as relaxed as if they were having a private conversation on a mundane subject.

"I bought the house where it would do the most good. Having a reform house in the fashionable west end would do no good at all. I have put out the word on the street that any woman or child who needs a home may go there and be given shelter and food. Dame Webber, or 'the madam' as you referred to her, is the widow of a clergyman who has dedicated the remainder of her life to helping me rehabilitate these people of the streets.''

He started up the steps. "Have you ever seen a child who has to go barefoot in the winter because he has no shoes? A little girl who hadn't eaten in two days and whose last meal was scrounged out of a dust bin? Have you ever looked into the eyes of a fifteen-year-old girl who has been working the docks for the past five years?''

William looked more uncomfortable with every step Jared took. "No, I have not. Here in Fairfield we take care of our own."

"It's not so in London. I saw sights worse than I can tell in the presence of ladies. Sights that would send you retching to the nearest door." Jared's voice remained calm, but there was fire in his dark eyes. "That's why I bought Howard House and repaired it, so that these people would have a refuge. Dame Webber cleans their bodies as well as their minds. She teaches all who are able to read and write. She teaches the girls and women needlework and how to cook."

"Then what happens to them? I wager they return to the streets once they have been fed and pampered." William tried to keep the hard edge to his voice, but he took a step backward as Jared reached the level he was on.

"When they have genuinely put their past behind them— and it happens with nearly all of them—Dame Webber finds them employment in another part of the city or arranges for them to be taken to America or Australia, where they may find husbands and live decent lives. Occasionally we do have failures. Some women prefer the company of low men and some children were seemingly born to be thieves. For the most part, however, we succeed."

He fixed his frown on Rob. "If you had the backbone of a man, you would have asked me about this and saved yourself this embarrassment. Now I'm afraid I'll have to ask you to leave." He stared Rob down, then turned back to William. "Because you are Rachel's father, I owe you more respect. I would still like to welcome you here if you can come in peace."

William seemed to waver, and Rachel's hopes lifted, but then he clamped his mouth shut in what she thought of as his bulldog expression and said, "I don't believe a word of it. Not a word! Rachel, go to our coach."

She knew what she must say, but she was so frightened, she was afraid the words wouldn't come out. She had never seen him so angry. Swallowing hard, she said, "No, Papa. I believe Jared." She slipped her hand into his and felt his strong fingers close over hers protectively. She lifted her chin to show she was going to be as stubborn as her father.

For a long time William glared at her, then he spoke in a chilling tone. "From this day forward, you are no longer my daughter." He turned abruptly and strode out, Rob still at his heels.

Rachel felt sick and dizzy. She had been disowned in front of many of her friends and acquaintances. Her father would never forgive her now. Jared turned to her and took both her hands. He silently gazed down at her as his guests drifted past and out the door. Soon the ballroom was empty. The members of the orchestra looked at one another as if wondering what to do. Jared gave them a dismissing gesture with his arm, and they began putting away their instruments.

Beatrice and Mark came in from the terrace. Rachel could tell by their expressions that they had heard what William had said. Beatrice came to Rachel and put her arms around her. "What will you do? Where will you go? Oh, Rachel! This is terrible."

Rachel hugged her friend, then drew away. "Beatrice, you must go home at once. Rob may not have seen you. Pretend that you've been in your room all evening. Mark, see that she gets home quickly." Her eyes pleaded with Mark, and he put his arm about Beatrice and led her out of the room.

When they were alone, Jared said, "Beatrice has a good point. Where will you go? What will you do?"

"I don't know. I never expected this. I knew Papa was mad, but I didn't think he would turn against me like this.

I can't go back to Rose's, or he will take his anger out on her and Edwin.'' She put her hands to her lips and turned away. ''I don't know what I'll do. I have no place to go.'' She still felt numbly sick and knew that the magnitude of what had happened had not yet hit her.

''Do you have an aunt, or cousins, perhaps? Surely there is someone.'' His voice was so gentle she wanted to cry.

She thought of all her relatives and shook her head. ''They will all side with Papa. What will Rose say? What about Mama?''

''Surely your mother will be able to talk your father out of such a drastic measure. He couldn't have come here with disowning you in mind.''

''Mama won't be able to sway him. Not after he said it in front of so many people we know.''

''He would rather lose a daughter than lose face? Up until now, I still had some measure of respect for him.''

''You don't know Papa. His entire reputation is built on his never backing down.''

''I'm sorry I've brought all this upon you. If I could change it, I would.''

She turned back to him and put her hand to his lips. ''No. Don't say that. I have to believe you would do it all for me again.''

''Yes. I would. I only wish it were possible to change it. You've lost everything for me.''

She could feel the tears on her cheeks, but she wasn't aware of crying. ''I would give it all up for you again and again if necessary. I love you, Jared.''

For a long moment time seemed to stand still. She knew she was taking a terrible chance in confessing her love before he had spoken of it to her. But everything had changed, and she had to know.

Jared lifted his hand and caressed away a tear. ''I love you, Rachel. I've wanted to tell you this for weeks. But I thought if I didn't, you would come to your senses, and things would not come to this end.''

"If I have to choose between you and Papa, I choose you and I have no reservations. I only wish the choice had not been necessary." She paused and asked hesitantly, "Do you really love me?"

"Yes." He put his arms around her and drew her close.

Rachel rested her cheek on his strong chest and drew strength from the contact.

"I love you with every breath I take," he said softly. "I've loved you so long that I can't recall when it began. Your love came to me like a sunrise, softly and slowly, but once it had begun, there was no turning back."

She lifted her face to him. Her heart was racing at the words he was saying and at the love in his eyes.

"If I were a gentleman, I would have refused to see you again, because I knew there would be repercussions from your caring for me. If I had known what lengths your father would go to, I would have tried to stop loving you. But I could more easily stop my heart than I could stop loving you now."

"Jared," she whispered, and his name was a word of love on her lips.

He bent and kissed her, then held her close. She held him tightly, as if she were afraid someone might try to tear them apart. "Because of me, your standing in this town is ruined. Now no one will come to your parties."

He surprised her by laughing. "You goose, I only gave the dance because I wanted to see you. I don't care a fig for anyone else in Fairfield."

She looked up at him. "You don't?"

"If we want to dance and enter society, I'll take you to London. You can have all the parties you like there."

"You'll continue seeing me?"

"Haven't you been listening? I love you."

"I know, but that isn't the same thing."

"It is with me. Rachel, I want never to be away from you again. Not for a day, not for a minute. I love you."

She pulled away from him and went to the railing that separated the upper level from the dance floor. The room was empty and seemed too large and cavernous without people. "Where will I go? I can't go back to Rose's. Papa will have gone there, more than likely, to tell them what he's done. Even if he waits until morning, he will be certain to tell them then. I can't ruin Edwin's career by having him side with me. I can't go to Beatrice's because Rob will be there."

"You can stay here."

The words were spoken quietly and hung in the air. She slowly turned to face him. "Stay here?"

"With me."

"As your mistress?"

"As my wife."

Rachel couldn't breathe. The room seemed to be rocking; she hoped she wasn't going to faint. She had never actually fainted in her life. "Your wife?"

"You aren't going to say this is too sudden, are you?" He smiled at her and caressed a wisp of hair back from her face.

"No, but it is. I only now found out you love me. After Papa's disowning me—" her voice broke on the words "—I must seem desperate to you. You may be saying this out of honor."

"I've already told you that I'm no gentleman except by birth. I should think tonight would have proved that beyond a shadow of a doubt."

"On the contrary, you are a gentleman, whatever you care to pretend. You would offer me marriage to save my reputation."

"If I did, would it offend you? You can't live in the hedgerows, and you can't stay here under any other circumstances and still go into the village with your pride intact."

"Those aren't reasons for marriage."

"I love you. Doesn't that alter anything?"

She finally smiled. "It alters my whole world. It's a miracle that I never thought to attain. But I can't marry you. Not when I'm afraid you will regret having asked me or

when you may later feel you were pressed into a proposal.''

"I'm never pressed into doing anything I don't want to
do. Ask Mark.''

"If you still feel the same way later, ask me again."

"And in the interim? Will you stay with me?"

Rachel tried to think, to be rational, but her mind was
full only of love for Jared. What he was offering her was
heaven, but heaven with a price. She had always heard that
men never married women who had given themselves to
them before marriage. She was sure that if she asked for a
room of her own, Jared would give it to her and he
wouldn't touch her. In spite of his words, he was a gentleman. "I'll stay with you."

"Are you sure? If you do, your reputation will be ruined in town. Everyone will know."

"I've already risked everything that means anything to
me in order to love you. By the time word spreads about
what has happened tonight and how I was still here after
everyone else left, my reputation will be ruined anyway."

"I've not been good for you. I'm sorry for that. I truly
am."

"I would have you no other way."

He held out his hand to her and Rachel took it. She tilted
up her chin and met his eyes. "I want to stay with you."

They went out of the ballroom and around the balcony
that overlooked the marble entryway. Rachel felt as if she
were moving in a dream. Nothing had reality for her except the warmth of Jared's hand and the way he was looking at her.

His bedroom was opposite the ballroom, and they entered it through a sitting room done in masculine colors of
maroon and dark green. He pushed open the opposite door
and she could see a large four-poster bed that dominated
the room. "Are you sure?" he asked. "You can still turn
away."

"If you love me as you say you do, I would be making
the biggest mistake of my life to turn back now. I've risked

all for you. I want to be with you all night and every night to come."

Jared took her in his arms and kissed her until her heart sang. Rachel returned his kisses and felt her body respond eagerly. Being in his embrace felt more right than anything she had ever done before. She wanted him, and she didn't care about the consequences.

Jared released her and turned the lock in the door that led to the balcony. "I don't want us to be disturbed. Especially not on our first night together."

Rachel knew she was making the right choice, and she was amazed at how easily it had been accomplished. Jared seemed to sweep away all her inhibitions as easily as he had swept her up in love. Staying with him had been so simple.

They went into the bedroom and Jared shut the door. The room seemed more intimate than any she had ever been in before. "I've never seen a man's bedroom," she said as he turned down the lamps nearest the door.

"I didn't expect that you had." He drew back the covers and asked, "Are you sure, Rachel? There are a dozen other rooms you can sleep in. I'm not offering you my bed or nothing else."

"I know." She went to him and put her arms around him. "Hold me, Jared. Kiss me and don't let me think too much."

"If you do, will you leave me? I don't want that."

"Kiss me. Please?" She tilted her head up and when he kissed her, all her doubts vanished.

Slowly he undressed her, dropping her clothes to swirl on the floor about her feet. He loosened her hair and tossed the silk violets and pansies to the nearby dresser. When he removed the pins, her hair flowed down her back. With her eyes locked on his, she stood before him in her chemise and pantalets.

As Jared began removing his own clothing, he kept his eyes on her face, and she knew he was watching to see if there was any reservation there. Her skin was cool and she felt more naked than she had ever felt in her life, but she hadn't changed her mind. Her love for him was greater than any social conditioning. She helped him release the studs that secured his pleated white shirt and realized they were made of real diamonds. He untied his cravat and opened his shirt. Reaching around her, he unfastened his cuffs.

There was no longer any thought in Rachel's mind about leaving. Seeing his bare chest had driven all caution from her mind. She put her hands on his skin and felt his warmth and strength. He caught his breath at her touch and she gloried in her ability to excite him as much as he was exciting her.

When his shirt was gone, he bent and lifted her into his arms, then laid her on the feather bed. As he gazed down at her, he removed his shoes and socks, then the last of his clothing. Rachel knew she should look away, but she couldn't get enough of seeing him. Jared was built as beautifully as her imagination had suggested. She was surprised to find he wasn't frightening in the least, not even when he stood naked before her.

Jared lay down beside her and drew her closer so that their bodies touched all the way down. She ran her hands over his bare flesh and felt his muscles tense and release beneath her. He was holding himself in check, but with an effort. The idea excited her even more.

He loosened the ribbon that secured her chemise and then each of the tiny pearl buttons down the front. Rachel was momentarily afraid. What if she wasn't beautiful to him? She had no idea what to do. What if she was too awkward?

"What's wrong? Am I frightening you?"

"No, I'm wondering if I'll please you."

Jared laughed softly. "You couldn't help but please me. Even if you weren't as beautiful as a pagan goddess, our love would show you to be. Just love me and let me teach you how to enjoy lovemaking."

She let him remove the rest of her clothing and watched his face as he drank in the sight of her. At last he said, "I had no idea you would be so beautiful. Or so soft, or that you would feel so sweet in my arms.''

He bent and kissed her neck, then trailed kisses down between her breasts. When his hand covered her breast, Rachel gasped, and a fire leaped to life in her as she buried her head in the curve of his neck. His hand caressed her and urged the bud of her breast to harden and pulse with eagerness for more. Rachel heard a soft moan and realized it had come from her own lips.

Jared smiled. "You were made for loving," he murmured. "I have a feeling you are going to take to it as wholeheartedly as you do to everything else."

"I think you're right." She tried to think, but his hands were driving all but sensation from her mind. When he bent his head lower and took her nipple into his mouth, she thought she would explode.

Gently, slowly, he taught her how to love him in return and encouraged her to explore his body as thoroughly as he was exploring hers. Rachel found that touching him was as exciting as having him touch her. Her body responded with an urgency that surprised her.

When she felt she was unable to wait any longer, he knelt between her legs and said, "This may be uncomfortable, but only for a moment. If you want me to stop, tell me."

With great care he entered her, and Rachel gasped and pulled him closer. There was a moment of discomfort that sent a bolt of fear through her, but he sensed it and stopped. Within moments she wanted him again, and she writhed her hips, urging him to move even deeper into her. Slowly he began to move, and she thought she would die from ecstasy.

As her desire built, he matched it, and when she cried out in completion, he spiraled upward with her and held her close as he gave himself to her. Rachel held him tightly and thought the sheer pleasure would rend her to pieces. Nothing existed for her except Jared and nothing was of importance except their love.

After a while the throbbing ecstasy began to drift into a deep sense of satisfaction. Jared rolled to one side and drew her head down onto his shoulder. "Was it as bad as maiden aunts claim it would be?"

Rachel laughed. "It was wonderful and beautiful and perfect. If I didn't already love you, I would fall in love with you now. Is it always so wonderful?"

"It will be between us. Love makes the difference."

"I'll have to tell Beatrice that she shouldn't fear it. We've wondered."

Jared laughed and held her close. Rachel could feel his love all about her, and she wondered if they could do this marvelous thing again and whether he would be offended if she asked him. She rubbed her cheek against his shoulder and was thankful that she had decided to match her fate to his.

Chapter Sixteen

The music had died down earlier than Abby had expected. She looked at her clock and saw that it was early for the ball to be over. Silently she opened the door to Yvonne's room and slipped in. In the darkness she could see Yvonne lying in bed, so still Abby thought she must be asleep. Skirting the overturned chairs, she went to the window.

Down below she saw the guests' buggies and coaches being brought around to the door. Women in beautiful dresses and with elegantly styled hair were being helped into their vehicles by their male escorts. Once the passengers were inside, the drivers tapped the reins on their horses' well-rounded rumps and with a muffled clatter the coaches and buggies rolled forward.

Abby leaned close to the glass for a better look, but she could see nothing to explain why everyone was leaving so early. Perhaps, she thought, it was the custom here in the country to end the evening so early. Abby had a Londoner's disdain for rural people. Yet this seemed too early even for country folk.

She again crossed the moonlit room, carefully avoiding the obstacles in her path and moving quietly so as not to awaken Yvonne, and let herself back into her room. Something was wrong downstairs and she was determined to find out what it was. She opened the door to the corridor and stepped out. For a minute she considered locking the door behind her as she was supposed to do, but Yvonne was asleep and she was such a light sleeper that the sound of the key turning the lock could awaken her. Abby hurried down the hall.

Not wanting to draw attention to herself, she moved silently and stayed close to the wall where shadows would hide her. This wasn't the first time she had left her room at night to explore; she was familiar with Ravenwood's numerous halls and stairways.

When she reached a point on the second floor from which she had a clear view of the ballroom, she hid herself in the shadows of a large tapestry so that she wouldn't be seen. As she watched, the orchestra members completed packing their things and started downstairs, shaking their heads and murmuring among themselves. Obviously they were disgruntled. Personally, Abby couldn't have cared less that something had upset them, because she had never been a proponent of dancing or any other kind of frivolous entertainment. Her family had Puritan leanings, and she was proud of the fact that her feet had never been lifted in a dance step. Nevertheless, something had upset the musicians, and her curiosity was heightened.

After what seemed to be a long time, the ballroom door opened again, and she saw Jared come out with a woman on his arm. Abby recognized the woman as the same one who had once come to Ravenwood's door and knocked upon it as bold as brass. She expected them to go down the stairs and for him to send her home.

Instead, they walked around the balcony in her direction. Abby flattened herself against the wall and tried not to breathe. She knew she had no business being here and she didn't want to lose her position. Watching over Yvonne was dull work, but it kept a fine roof over her head and the duties were relatively light. Up until now she had considered this to be a respectable household. Now she had caught the master of Ravenwood walking toward his bedchamber with a woman.

They passed so close to Abby they would have seen her if they hadn't been so engrossed in each other. The woman looked as if she had been crying, but Abby paid that no mind. There were a dozen reasons a woman might cry and still not have reason for tears.

Abby hoped they would make a complete circle of the balcony and then go down. If they did, that would vindicate Jared. She held her breath as they neared the door that she knew led to his suite. Jared opened the door and Rachel preceded him inside.

Abby clenched her fists. This was intolerable! She was so upset, she stepped out from her hiding place and took several steps toward the door, but suddenly brought herself up short. From where she stood, she could be seen by anyone below.

A glance over the rail assured her that all the guests were gone and no servants were about. Stealthily, she resumed her movement along the wall to the door to Jared's bedroom. By pressing her ear to the door, she heard the inner door click shut. There was only one thing they could be doing in there. A cold anger permeated her being, causing her to tremble.

Suddenly there was a noise behind her. Abby whirled to see Yvonne, a ghostly vision in her white nightgown, her hair loose about her gaunt face. Yvonne's black eyes seemed to glow as she came toward Abby.

Abby closed the several yards between them and grabbed her arm. "What are you doing here? You know you aren't supposed to be out of your room."

"I thought I heard Paul and that woman. Did you hear them, Abby? I'm afraid they have found me."

Abby cast a glare at the closed door. "It wasn't Paul and his mistress, though you may have heard something."

Yvonne looked past Abby at the door. "Is that where Jared sleeps?"

"Aye, though he's not doing much of it tonight."

"He's not?"

Abby knew she should not upset Yvonne, but she was too disturbed to care. "He has a woman in there. He's no better than your Paul!"

"Don't say that! Jared is much better than Paul. He's a world better!"

"Is that right? Then why does he have a trollop in there?" She turned Yvonne about and pushed her back none too gently the way they had come. Whatever Jared might be up to, her first duty was to Yvonne.

All the way back to the room, Yvonne kept up a monologue about Paul and whether he had found her. Abby ignored her. She had more important matters on her mind than whether a ghost was after Yvonne.

When they reached their rooms, Abby shut the door and pointed for Yvonne to go to her bedchamber. When she held back, Abby went to the door and opened it. "See? There's no one in here. No one, alive or dead."

Yvonne went to the room and peeked around the corner.

"Well? Do you see anyone?"

Slowly Yvonne shook her head. "They could be hiding under the bed."

Abby kept her temper with an effort. "Go look. I'll hold the light for you."

With hesitant steps, Yvonne went to her bed, looked quickly in all the corners of the room, then knelt to look under the bed. Apparently satisfied, she got to her feet. "There's no one there."

"See? I told you that they would never find you here."

As Yvonne climbed into the bed she looked at the curtainless windows. "There's a nearly full moon tonight. It's so bright out."

"You could have curtains if you wouldn't pull them down all the time. Lie down. Go to sleep."

Yvonne continued gazing at the window. "It's bright enough out to see everything. Have you ever seen such moonlight, Abby? It's almost like a dim sun."

"It's not all that bright. I said lie down."

"Why did you say Jared has a woman in his room?"

"Because it's true. Why else would I say it?"

"I thought you might be trying to upset me. To remind me of Paul and what happened to him and that woman."

Abby's eyes darted suspiciously at Yvonne. "It's late. Go to sleep."

"I'm not at all sleepy. Who was the woman? Do we know her?"

"We don't know anyone here," Abby snapped, and then she chided herself. The secret to keeping Yvonne calm was always to speak quietly. In a gentler tone, she said, "It's nothing for you to worry about. I shouldn't have told you."

Yvonne's eyes became vacant. "Paul had a strumpet. You know what happened to them."

"Yes. Now go to sleep. In the morning you will have forgotten all about this."

Yvonne shook her head. "I never forget anything. Sometimes the memories rattle around in my head so loudly that I think anyone near might hear them. Do you ever hear my memories, Abby?"

"Go to sleep or I'll set the chairs upright," Abby threatened.

Yvonne reluctantly moved to her bed and ran her hand under her pillows, as was her custom before going to sleep. Abby never knew what she expected to find there, and she didn't ask now. Yvonne lay down, and as soon as she had closed her eyes, Abby took the lamp and went out. Yvonne would stay in bed until morning, she thought. She was always afraid to step out into the darkness for fear Paul might be under the bed, waiting to grab her ankles.

Abby went back to her room and put the lamp on the shelf over her dresser. Jared was entertaining a woman in his bedchamber! She had rarely been so shocked. She had never expected to see a harlot within Ravenwood itself. All her Puritan ancestors rose up within her in horror. Abby tried to calm herself and to put her mind on something else, but it was no use.

Rachel didn't know how long she slept or what awakened her. She sat upright and for a terrifying minute she

didn't know where she was. Then she heard Jared's soft
breathing and saw him in the faint moonlight. All the
night's happenings rushed over her.

She drew the covers to hide her nakedness. What had she
done? Now Jared would never want her! She had a vague
recollection of his proposing to her, but now that seemed
to have a sinister meaning. Everyone said that a man would
do that in order to lure a woman into his bed. She had made
a terrible mistake.

As silently as possible she slid out of bed and dressed in
the darkness. She tried not to remember the ecstasy of lying in Jared's arms and of having him possess her completely. That had been like a vision of heaven, but as such,
it had no place in the real world.

She tiptoed across the room and opened the door to the
sitting room. Jared turned over and his arm stretched
across the place where she had lain. For a minute she was
tempted to go back to him, was willing to live as his mistress as long as she could stay with him. Appalled by her
thoughts, she closed the door and crossed to the one that
opened onto the balcony.

The house at night was frightening. Rachel had to clasp
her hands tightly in order to step into the darkness. What
if she encountered a ghost such as was rumored to haunt
Ravenwood, or worse, what if she fell down the stairs to the
foyer far below?

She groped for the railing and, hand over hand, felt her
way around the balcony. When she came to the stairs, she
shivered, and she had to force herself to reach out with her
toe to find the first step. Stairs that had seemed so easy to
climb in the light were now as perilous as mountainous ter-
rain.

A sound in the inky blackness made her blood freeze.
Rachel looked back the way she had come. Was someone
there? She had always been blind in the dark and couldn't
see her hand before her face. When the sound didn't come
again, she started down the stairs.

She didn't have a clear idea where to go once she was outside. Certainly she couldn't go to her parents, and Rose was out of the question, especially at this time of night. Beatrice. She would go to Beatrice. At this hour, surely Rob would be safely asleep and she could hide in Beatrice's room until she could think of somewhere else to go.

Again she thought she heard a sound, this time near the top of the stairs. Rachel whirled and gripped the banister. "Is someone there?" she whispered. "Who is there?"

Hearing no answer, she resumed her exit down the stairs as fast as she dared. When her feet touched the marble of the foyer and her footing was more assured, she moved more quickly toward the front door, which was framed in the pale moonlight coming in through the windows on either side of the door. Her fingers fumbled with the unfamiliar lock, but she managed to open it.

As soon as she swung open the door, she felt safer. Outside in the silvery light of the moon she could make out the shape of trees and the drive. She looked back at the blackness and wondered if her imagination had been playing tricks on her. Why would anyone be following her in the dark?

As quietly as she could, she closed the door behind her and made her way down the steps to the gravel drive. The crunching of the loose stones beneath her feet resounded in her ears, and for a moment she was sure it was loud enough to awaken Jared. Even though reason told her she was being foolish, she was relieved to reach the silent grass on the opposite side of the drive.

As she started down the hill toward town, she again heard the crunching noise. She froze in her tracks and strained to listen. The sound of several more steps on the gravel was unmistakable, but it suddenly ceased. Rachel tried to see behind her, but she couldn't be sure whether she was seeing ordinary shadows or the figure of a person standing perfectly still. She shivered. It had to be her imagination.

Moving as fast as she could in the dim light, she hurried down the hill, silently cursing her poor night vision. She

and Beatrice had often laughed at the fact that Rachel
could barely see by moonlight, while Beatrice could see
quite well. But it was no longer humorous. Rachel had
never been out alone at this time of night, and she was
growing more afraid by the minute. All the familiar land-
marks were altered by shadows and shapes that she was sure
weren't there in the daytime.

The walk to town was no farther than she was able to go
comfortably, but under the conditions it seemed to take
forever. Finally she saw the first cluster of houses, and although she was already breathing fast, she picked up her
pace, anxious to get to a place of safety. By the time she
started down the street of shops that led to Beatrice's house,
she had a stitch in her side.

The streets were eerie in the darkness. There were gas-
lights, but they only threw puddles of light that made the
darkness more impenetrable. She ran from streetlight to
streetlight until she realized that this made her clearly visi-
ble. She tried to keep to the shadows after that. Once she
glanced behind her and saw a shadow step out of the light.

Rachel froze. Someone was following her! She waited,
but no one stepped into the next circle of light. She forced
herself to draw a deep breath. No one was there. It was only
that the darkness frightened her.

She half ran down the street to Beatrice's house. There
was a light burning in the parlor window, and she hesitated. Was someone still up? Surely the elder Gastons
hadn't returned early. She would never be able to slip up to
Beatrice's room if someone was in the parlor.

She circled the house and stumbled over hillocks in the
grass toward the area beneath Beatrice's window. Her
friend's window was dark; if Beatrice was up there, she had
gone to bed. Rachel felt around until she found some pebbles. Taking aim, she tossed one. It clattered off the clap-
boards and dropped to the ground. She threw the next one
harder and it clicked against the window.

Rachel glanced around. The sound was loud to her ears.
Surely the neighbors would hear. A dog barked next door,

but the houses stayed dark. Rachel heard a faint rustle as if someone had brushed against the shrubbery that flanked the Gastons' house. Her heart was pounding so hard she felt ill. She threw the rest of the pebbles at the window.

This time the curtains were pushed aside and she saw Beatrice's face at the window. "Mark?" she called down.

"It's me. Can I come in?"

Beatrice brushed her hair back from her face. "Rachel? Is that you? What are you doing out there at this time of night?"

Rachel again heard the rustling sound. "Let me in!"

"I'm coming. Meet me in front."

Rachel didn't dare go back the way she had come. Not if someone was following her. Instead she ran around the back of the house and up the opposite side. She took the front steps two at a time and reached the porch just as the door was flung open. Rob stood in the doorway, and Beatrice was coming down the stairs behind him.

Rachel stopped and her mouth dropped open. She hadn't expected to see Rob. He glared at her as if she was loathsome to his sight. She knew she must have lovemaking written all over her. She had been unable to find her hairpins and she had braided her hair into a long rope that hung down her back. After being loved by Jared, she thought she must be altered in some way that was noticeable to even the casual observer.

Rob looked as if he was about to order her off the porch, when his face registered shock, then horror. Rachel was so startled she half turned to see what he was staring at.

A shape rushed at her from the dark. It was tall and something glittered in its hand. Rachel's half turn was enough to throw off the being's aim, and a knife arched and plunged into Rob's upper arm.

He shrieked and grabbed at his arm as the shape recoiled, then faded back into darkness.

Rachel stared after it, so shocked that she couldn't move or speak. Someone had tried to kill her! She knew that for certain. Only her move to one side had saved her.

She heard someone screaming and realized it was Beatrice. She was kneeling beside her brother, who was lying half in and half out of the door. Rob had obviously fainted, and his right sleeve was red with a stain that was spreading across the porch.

Rachel bent to put her hand over Rob's arm. "Beatrice! Be quiet. Go get help!" She pressed her hand against the wound to stop the flow of blood. Her actions were automatic and instinctive. In a detached part of her mind, she knew she would wonder later how she had known to do this and where she had found the courage to touch the wound. To Beatrice she repeated more sharply, "I said get help! Go wake the servants!"

Beatrice stumbled to stand, but it was unnecessary. Rachel could hear the clatter of feet as the servants came running to see what was causing the commotion. She gingerly released the pressure on Rob's arm and looked to see if the bleeding had stopped. She was reassured to see that it had. He wasn't seriously wounded if she could stop the flow of blood so easily.

"What's happened? What's going on?" the servants exclaimed as they hurried into sight of the door. "Master Robert! It's Master Robert! He's been killed!"

"He's not dead," Rachel said, "only hurt. You, girl, go fetch the doctor. You men carry him into the parlor." Another woman ran to get quilts to put under him to protect the couch from being stained with blood. "Careful! Don't bump his arm."

"It's a good thing you young ladies heard him and come down," the footman said. "He could have bled to death."

Rachel let them think she had been upstairs with Beatrice. There was no need to explain anything to them. Her eyes met Beatrice's and she knew there would be questions from her later.

"Did you see who stabbed Master Robert?" the butler asked, his normal composure shocked out of him. "Did you see him?"

Rachel shook her head. "It happened so fast. All at once she came at me. I stepped aside and she stabbed Rob by mistake."

"She?"

Rachel shook her head in confusion. "I don't know. It happened so fast. Wasn't it a woman? Beatrice, didn't you see?"

Beatrice shook her head. "Rob was between me and the door. I didn't see anything until he fell. It was a dark shape...with a knife. By then whoever it was had gone."

The doctor lived only a few houses away and was soon in the Gastons' parlor bandaging Rob's arm. "It's not serious." He looked at Rachel. "You seem to be on hand in most medical emergencies around here."

"I'm staying with Beatrice tonight." She glanced at her friend to silently ask her to back up her story.

"It's true. She's my guest." Beatrice's blue eyes were wide with questions.

"Why would anyone want to kill Master Robert?" the butler asked the footman. All the servants looked at each other.

Rachel felt faint now that the crisis was over. She stared down at the blood on her hands and party dress. Rob moaned on the couch and stirred as he began to wake up. Whoever the killer was, Rob hadn't been the target.

"He's in no danger," the doctor was saying. "You men help me get him up to his room. I'll give him a draft to make him sleep until morning. That will do him more good than anything. The cut is not deep." He again looked at Rachel as if he were wondering what part she had played in this. Rachel looked away.

"Bea, could I wash up?" She felt as if she had to wash away all the evidence of the violence directed at her or be sick.

"Of course! Come with me." Beatrice led her through the house to the kitchen.

Rachel held her hand under the pump as Beatrice worked the handle up and down. As the water sluiced over her hands, she worked at the stain.

"What happened?" Beatrice asked in a whisper. "What were you doing out at this hour of the night? Did Edwin throw you out?"

Rachel vigorously shook her head, and tears stung her eyes. "I haven't been to Edwin's house."

Beatrice's mouth rounded in amazement. "You don't mean you've been at Ravenwood all this time!"

"Hush! Don't let anyone hear you. Yes, I was." She lost her battle with the tears, which stung her eyes and coursed down her cheeks.

Beatrice stopped pumping water and came to put her arms around her friend. "There, there. It will be all right," she said in an unconvincing way.

Rachel shook her head. "It will never be all right. Nothing will ever be right again!"

"Come up to my room."

They went up the servants' steep stairs and down the shadowy hall to Beatrice's room. From below they could hear the servants locking the door after the doctor and talking in low voices as they went back to their beds.

Rachel was glad to escape into Beatrice's room. The familiar chamber with its ruffled curtains and lacy pillows and bed canopy made Rachel draw a breath of relief. Then she looked down and saw her dress stained with Rob's blood, and her tears started all over again.

"Don't cry." Beatrice went to her dresser and got a clean handkerchief for Rachel. "What on earth happened?"

"You're my best friend. I have to be honest with you. I've been with Jared."

"You let him ruin you?"

"I'm not ruined! I'm not! I never felt anything was so right before. But when I woke up, all I could think about was what would he think of me." She crumpled into the chair. "Oh, Bea, what will I do if Jared thinks less of me?"

Beatrice looked as if she was in shock. "He loves you, doesn't he? Didn't he ask you to marry him or anything?"

"Yes, yes, he asked, but he didn't mean it. I don't think he meant it. I mean, he had to say something, didn't he? Papa and Rob were so beastly and I had no place to go. He had to propose under the circumstances."

Beatrice's hand patted her shoulder, and she said in a dazed manner, "There, there. He must have meant it. If he loves you, he must want to marry you. It's only natural."

Rachel raised her tearstained face. "But that was before I... you know. Bea, have I made a terrible mistake?"

"I'm not sure. I've never known anyone who admitted to having... done that."

"It was so wonderful, Bea. Better than we thought it could be. It felt so right for him to hold me. Like I really belonged there."

"I don't think you should tell me about it," Beatrice said hastily. Then, "It really didn't hurt? You actually enjoyed it?"

Rachel nodded. "I love him so much! It's like I'm part of him and he's a part of me. Tell me you don't hate me and that you'll still be my friend."

Beatrice knelt beside Rachel's chair. "You and I have been friends all our lives, Rachel. I'll never turn my back on you. Especially not for doing something that I'm tempted to do myself. Mark and I have come closer than I've admitted to you. I was afraid to tell you for fear of losing your respect."

Rachel covered Beatrice's hand. "I understand. But Beatrice, be careful. Once done, it can't be undone. That's what frightens me so much. If he no longer respects me, there's nothing I can do to fix it."

"How terrible. Here you are, disowned and friendless and afraid of losing your true love. It's awful!"

"It really is. Can I stay here for a while? If I stay in your room and if we bribe your maid, no one will know I'm here. You could slip food up to me. I have nowhere to go and if Rob knows I'm here, he will send me away."

"Of course you can. Are you hungry now? I could go down and get you some cold roast from dinner."

Rachel shook her head. "I couldn't possibly eat. I'm too upset. Bea, Papa has really disowned me, hasn't he?"

Beatrice nodded. "I'm afraid so. Rob and I argued about it after he came home. I was able to get here first and he has no idea I was at Ravenwood. He told me all about it and how your father will never back down. He was actually gloating! He's become so despicable. I never speak to him unless I have to."

Rachel smiled weakly. "At least we know for a fact now that Jared doesn't have a mistress at Ravenwood."

"I don't see how you can joke at a time like this."

"If I don't, I'll start to cry again. You know, Bea, I still feel that there is something Jared is keeping secret from me. Twice he seemed to think he heard something and I thought that was odd." She leaned closer to her friend. "When I left, I'm almost positive I was followed. I heard sounds behind me, but I couldn't see anything. You know how I am in the dark."

Beatrice nodded. "You couldn't have seen anyone if they were standing right in front of you."

Rachel shivered. "Don't say that. You have no idea how scary it was finding my way out of that huge house and coming here in the dark."

"You've always been so brave. I'm sure I never could have done it. Not ever."

"Whoever stabbed Rob meant to kill me. I'm sure of it."

Beatrice's eyes widened. "You mean it wasn't the action of some maniac? Who on earth would want to kill you?"

"I don't know. I have no enemies. Certainly not any who would want to kill me."

"I assumed it was a random act of some madman." Beatrice looked as if she were growing more frightened by the moment. "Someone tried to kill you?"

"Someone followed me. I heard her several times. I even heard something in your yard."

"In my yard!" Beatrice rushed to her window. "I don't see anyone."

"Bea, how could you see anything down there when the light is on up here? Besides, whoever was there wouldn't have stayed around after stabbing Rob. I'm sure she's long gone now."

"You keep saying 'she.' Was it a woman?"

"I don't know. For some reason I think it was, but I didn't get a clear look. Like I said, it all happened so fast. Whoever it was, however, she was tall. Taller than most women, I would say."

"Maybe Rob saw her more clearly."

"It's possible."

"Rachel! You don't think it was whoever killed those two women!"

"I don't know. No, it couldn't be. I think I was followed all the way from inside Ravenwood." They exchanged a look.

"The murders both happened after Jared came here."

"Jared isn't the killer! How can you say such a thing?"

"I never meant that it was Jared. It might be someone in his household, though. Someone on his staff."

"It seems so farfetched. I certainly don't have any enemies at Ravenwood."

"Let's hope Rob saw her face. Or his."

Rachel nodded. The idea of the killer living at Ravenwood was a disturbing one. What if Jared was in danger? She shivered in spite of herself.

Chapter Seventeen

Early the next morning Sheriff Stoddard called on Rob to ask about the attack on him the night before.

"It all happened so fast," Rob said. He sat with his arm bandaged and a pained expression on his face.

"Surely you noticed something. Were you struck from behind?"

"No, but it was dark out."

Beatrice spoke up quickly. "I was there, too, and I didn't see anything at all. Rob fell, and I rushed to him."

Stoddard frowned and rubbed his lips as he considered. Something was wrong here, but he didn't know what. "Was anyone else present?"

"My friend was. Rachel Pennington."

"Well, where is she now?"

"She went home. She was terribly upset."

Stoddard didn't believe the girl. Beatrice wasn't very good at lying. He just couldn't see why she would need to lie about what happened. "Do you confirm all this, Mr. Gaston?"

"I do. I saw Miss Rachel on the porch, but when I became conscious again I was in my room and I presumed she was gone."

"Then you don't know for sure?"

Rob gave him a petulant sigh. "I was injured. I'm not in the habit of going from room to room to see who may be there."

Stoddard made no comment. He had never cared much for Arthur Gaston's son. It was a pity the boy was so unlikable since his parents were so popular. "When will your parents return from Derby?"

"I've sent word to them. I presume within the week."

"I'd like to talk to them when they arrive."

"I don't see why. They weren't here at all."

"Your father may have some idea who would wish you harm." Stoddard was thinking that if the lad spoke to everyone with this same surly attitude, it was no wonder that he had enemies.

"Rachel told me something I think you should know," Beatrice said hesitantly.

"Oh? What's that?"

"She said she was convinced the attack was meant for her."

"For her?" Stoddard frowned. "Why would she think a thing like that?"

"She said if she hadn't half turned away the knife would have struck her."

"Oh?" he said with more interest. He wrote a note on his pad of paper. "Who are her enemies?"

"She has no enemies."

"This is ridiculous," Rob said. "Of course the knife was meant for me. Why would anyone want to kill Miss Rachel?"

"Well, there have been two women killed in Fairfield lately," Stoddard said. "Maybe this was the same assailant.

"That's exactly what Rachel said!" Beatrice exclaimed. "She said it must have been the same person."

"Sheriff Stoddard, those women were of questionable conduct and died in alleyways. Surely you aren't impugning Miss Rachel's reputation."

"Of course not." Stoddard was surprised that Rob would jump to that conclusion. "Do you always call her Miss Rachel?"

"Certainly. It's her name."

"I know, but I had heard the two of you are keeping company."

"I hope to marry her if all goes well."

"I wish you the best of luck."

Beatrice said, "Rachel said something else. She said the person who attacked Rob was a woman."

"A woman!"

"She seemed positive of it."

Rob scowled. "I hope you're not suggesting that a mere woman could overpower me, Beatrice. As if a woman would even try."

"Did she see the culprit's face?"

"No, she barely saw her at all. She said she was wrapped in a dark cape of some sort and that she seemed unusually tall."

"You see?" Rob said with a derisive snort. "That doesn't sound like any woman I know."

Stoddard was thoughtful. There weren't many women in town that were remarkably tall. He immediately discounted the vicar's wife and Thelma Marsden, who was bedridden with a wasting disease. The dairyman's wife was tall and so was the woman who sold yarns and threads, but neither seemed to be likely candidates and he knew them well, as they had all lived in Fairfield all their lives. "Tall, you say?" He fished for more details. "Did she note the woman's coloring?"

"No, as I said, she was wearing a cape. Rachel said she was covered from head to toe."

"Odd. Very odd. The weather has been so warm lately. A cape, you say."

"I suppose she wore it to conceal herself in the darkness," Beatrice said helpfully. "I've read that it's done that way."

"My sister reads entirely too much," Rob said. "You'll have to forgive her." The brother and sister exchanged a look that held no love.

Stoddard noticed the exchange but gave no sign. He had long since discovered that he sometimes learned more by keeping quiet than he did by talking. "I get the feeling that there is something you're still leaving out. Will you think carefully?"

Beatrice's eyes widened, and she moved restlessly. Stoddard wondered what she was concealing that she didn't want him to know. Or was she keeping something from her brother? "Were you at home the entire evening?"

"I was," she said a bit too quickly.

"I was with Mr. William Pennington. We had to attend to some unpleasantness at Ravenwood."

"What unpleasantness was that?"

"I would rather not say."

Stoddard was losing his patience. "If I'm to find out who knifed you, you have to cooperate. Tell me about it."

"I want this to go no further, mind you. Miss Rachel's reputation is at stake." Rob frowned at him, then said, "She attended a party given at Ravenwood last night. Her father and I learned of it and went to take her away."

"I see." He glanced back at Beatrice. "She went, but you didn't?"

"That's right." Beatrice cast a glance at her brother.

Stoddard felt part of the mystery was cleared up. The girl must have slipped out to meet with a sweetheart while her brother was gone and she didn't want him to know of it. That was fine with Stoddard.

"In fact," Rob said thoughtfully, "that may be our man. Jared Prescott. He has ample reason to want to see me dead."

"Rob! What are you saying? Sheriff Stoddard, Rob is talking out of his head. I know Jared Prescott, and I believe him to be a man of high morals."

"You know nothing of the kind," her brother snapped.

"I certainly know him better than you do, and Jared would never try to knife anyone."

Stoddard wrote down that she called Prescott by his first name.

"Besides," Beatrice continued, "Rachel said that it was a woman, and I believe her."

Stoddard nodded. He had a great deal to think over. "I appreciate your talking with me. I'm going to leave you now, but I may have to ask you more questions later on."

"Any time," Rob said with impatience.

Beatrice merely nodded, and she didn't meet Stoddard's eyes. He wished he could talk to her alone for a few minutes. Maybe later, when her brother wasn't around, he could get more information from her.

Stoddard left the Gaston house and went directly to William Pennington's law office. As he had expected, William was there, his son-in-law seated at the other desk opposite him. When he entered the office he was aware of the tension in the air. Stoddard gave a searching look at the two men. "Good morning, William. May I have a minute of your time?"

"Of course, Darrell. Have a seat."

Stoddard lowered his bulk into the chair nearest William's desk. "This is a professional visit, I'm afraid. There was a bit of unpleasantness at the Gastons' house last night."

William frowned. "There was? Not a burglary, I hope."

"No, worse than that. Or it could have been. Rob Gaston was stabbed."

William half rose from his desk. "He was! Is he badly hurt?"

Stoddard noticed that William had no previous knowledge of the event and that he had the pallor of a sick man this morning. He also noticed that Edwin Jenson had stopped his work and was frankly listening. "No, he wasn't hurt too badly. The knife missed the important veins in his arm. The doctor told me he will have a scar, but no disability."

William sat back down. "Do you have any idea who would do this?"

"I was rather hoping you might help me decide that. Do you know of any enemies Rob might have?"

William glanced at Edwin and back at the sheriff. "I only know of one. Jared Prescott."

"He wouldn't do such a thing." Edwin sounded as if he were staying calm only by an effort.

Stoddard looked at him in surprise. "You know Prescott?"

Edwin lowered his eyes to his papers. "I've met him. We've talked."

Stoddard saw William's face suffuse with anger. There was more here than he had expected. "Why do you name Prescott, William?"

"He wants to call upon my daughter and she is being courted, with my approval, by Rob Gaston."

Stoddard wrote "jealousy" on his pad and underlined it.

Edwin raised his head to glare at his employer but he said nothing.

"I'd like to speak with your daughter, if you don't mind," Stoddard said. "With your permission I'll ride out to see her."

William looked uncomfortable. "She's not at home."

"Oh? Where may I find her?" His pencil hovered over the pad.

"I'm not entirely sure." William puffed his cheeks and said, "I hate to air personal problems, but you'll hear it sooner or later, I suppose. I disowned Rachel last night."

"You never did!" Stoddard was genuinely amazed. He knew that Rachel had always been the apple of William's eye. "Not your Rachel!"

William stood and paced to the window that overlooked the street. "I did. She backed me into a corner, so to speak, and I had no other choice."

"Well. Well, now." Stoddard stared at William, then at Edwin. "How about you? Do you know where I can find her?"

Edwin shook his head. "I didn't hear of it until this morning. Mr. Pennington told me when I came to work. We haven't seen Rachel since yesterday afternoon."

"Well," Stoddard said again, then remembered to write the date when Rachel was last seen.

"I assume she is with her friend, Beatrice Gaston." William didn't turn his head and his voice sounded strained. Stoddard could understand now why he seemed nearly ill this morning.

"I don't want to worry you, but I just came from the Gastons' house and she isn't there." He saw William's back stiffen. Edwin looked down at his papers. "Does she have another close friend?"

"She knows Pamela Driskoll rather well," William told him. "Beatrice is her closest friend, however, and if she isn't at the Gastons' house, she isn't likely to be at the Driskolls', either."

"Then where is she?"

William turned to glare at him. "Surely I don't have to spell it out for you, Darrell. Have you tried at Ravenwood?"

Stoddard could see the pain in the man's face. "You think she's there?"

William turned back to the window. "Where else could she be?"

Stoddard thought for a minute. If Rachel was at Ravenwood, Prescott would hardly be likely as a suspect for Rob's stabbing. He would have been otherwise occupied last night. He shook his head. Rachel Pennington taking up with a man! If he hadn't heard it from her own father, he wouldn't have believed it.

"I trust what I've told you will go no further," William said stiffly. "If Rachel is there, Fairfield will know about it soon enough."

"No. No, I'll tell no one. The information is confidential." He shook his head in amazement. "By the way, you should know that Miss Gaston says she has reason to believe that the person who stabbed her brother was a woman."

William turned to look at the sheriff. "A woman? What woman?"

"I have no idea. Miss Gaston says she was taller than average and was concealed in a black cape. No one saw her face." He suddenly recalled what else Beatrice had said. "She also told me that Rachel was there at the time. She couldn't have been at Ravenwood, too."

William relaxed visibly. "Thank you," he said in a stiff voice.

Stoddard stood. If Rachel wasn't at Ravenwood last night, then Jared Prescott was a suspect again. He looked at Edwin. "If Rachel comes to see you and your wife, you'll let me know?"

Edwin nodded. "And if you find out where she is, please tell me. Rose will be beside herself when she hears all this."

"If you like, I'll come by and tell her," William said.

"No, thank you. I think she will take it better coming from me."

Stoddard nodded. There was animosity brewing between Edwin and William. He hated to see a family fall apart like this, but it wasn't the first time he had seen it. He did think it was a pity, though, about Rachel being disowned. He knew the girl well and knew she had been William's favorite. But where was she?

Jared knocked on the Gastons' door, and in his impatience knocked on it again. When he woke up that morning and found Rachel gone, he had realized she must have come here. The door swung open and the maid stepped back from the dark expression on his face. "Is Miss Pennington here?" he demanded.

"Why, no, sir. I've not seen her since last night."

"Where has she gone?"

"Well, I'm not sure—"

"I'll talk to him," Beatrice said as she stepped up to the door. "Come in, Jared."

"I'm looking for Rachel. Where is she?"

Beatrice waited for the maid to leave and said in a whisper, "She's in my room."

"Why are you whispering?"

"I don't want the servants to hear. They don't know she's here and neither does Rob."

"I have to see her."

"You're fortunate to come when Rob is gone. He wouldn't let you across the threshold." Her eyes widened. "You don't know what happened last night!"

"Last night?"

"Rob was attacked."

"Attacked! By whom?"

"We don't know. In the confusion, Rachel hid upstairs in my room."

Jared strode toward the stairs. "Which room is she in?"

"You can't go up there! What if Rob comes home?"

Jared was already at the top of the stairs and opened the first door he came to. It was the wrong room, but Rachel heard him and opened the door to Beatrice's room. "Jared!" she gasped.

He went inside, Beatrice close on his heels, and shut the door. "I have to see you. Why did you leave me?"

Rachel opened her mouth but no sound came out. She glanced imploringly at her friend. Beatrice looked from one to the other and slipped out into the hall.

"Why did you leave me?" he demanded again.

"I woke up and was embarrassed. I shudder to think what you must think of me." She turned away so he couldn't see her face.

"I woke up and you were gone. I've turned Ravenwood upside down, thinking you must be there someplace. Then I realized this is where you would come. Why, Rachel? Didn't you mean the things you said last night?"

She turned to face him. "Of course I meant what I said. I *do* love you. But I'm afraid that now . . . after what happened, you won't love me. You couldn't." Tears shone in her eyes.

"Not love you!" He crossed to her and put his hands on her upper arms. "Not love you? How could I stop loving you? Why would I try?"

"Don't try to soften what you feel for me. I've lain awake all night thinking about it, and I know you must hold me in the greatest disdain."

"You're talking nonsense. I love you."

Rachel turned her face away. The tears overflowed onto her pale cheeks.

"Rachel, look at me. Don't turn away as if we've done something to be ashamed of." He put his hand to her face and turned it to him. "I'm not ashamed. Are you?"

"I should be. I ought to be."

"I didn't ask whether you ought to be. I want to know if you regret having made love with me."

Slowly she shook her head. "That's how I know I'm a trollop. I enjoyed it."

He laughed in relief and pulled her into his embrace. "God, but you had me scared half to death."

She put her arms around him and held to him as if he were a refuge in a storm. He buried his face in her hair and inhaled the aroma of soap and rose water so typical to her. "Don't you believe me when I say I love you?"

"I want to, Jared. I want to with all my heart."

"Then believe. I'm not lying to you."

"I believe you meant it last night. You loved me before you discovered you could have me. Now you must think I'm terrible."

"Rachel, listen to what I'm saying to you. I still love you. I love you more today than I did last night. I have every reason to expect I'll love you even more tomorrow. I still hold you in the highest regard. I want to marry you. Would I want to marry a trollop?"

She lifted her head quickly. "Marry me? You want to marry me?"

"Why do you look so surprised? I asked you to marry me last night."

"I know, but you didn't mean it then."

"I certainly did. You have a most deplorable habit of telling me what I think and don't think. As amazing as it must seem, I can figure it out for myself. Besides, you're usually wrong."

"I'm not."

"You're wrong about this."

"I think you proposed last night because that was all you could do under the circumstances. You knew I had no place to go and felt guilty that it was your fault. Any gentleman would have done the same."

"I'm not firm in my commitment to being a gentleman, and I don't know any man with a brain in his head who would propose marriage as a gesture of politeness."

"In all my books..."

He laughed. "Darling, I hate to tell you this, but not all books are factual."

She finally smiled. "You really want me to marry you?"

"It's not something I would say lightly. Yes, I do. You aren't going to make me go down on my knee, are you?"

"No." Her smile broadened. "I would love to be your wife."

He held her tight and released the breath he had been holding. When he had found her gone that morning, he had been afraid she had had second thoughts about him and would refuse his proposal. "I was afraid I had lost you," he murmured. "Don't ever leave me like that again."

"No. No, I'll never leave you."

He kissed her, and his pulse raced at the feel of her lips beneath his. She fit so perfectly in his arms. Love for her all but overwhelmed him.

There was a discreet knock at the door. Jared raised his head. He had forgotten all about Beatrice and where they were.

Rachel hurried to the door. "Come in, Bea. Jared and I are going to be married!"

"You are?" Beatrice's eyes widened. "He proposed to you in my bedroom? Whoever could have foreseen this?"

Jared looked around. He had never been in a young lady's bedroom in her parents' house. Suddenly he felt awkward and out of place among the pink and lace and flowery objects a young woman found so necessary. "I ought to be going."

"Not yet! I just heard Rob come in. We have to stay in here until he is in his room. That's why I knocked on the door."

He turned to Rachel. "I think we should be married today. That way, no one can speak against your reputation."

"Elope?" Rachel exclaimed. She and Beatrice exchanged a look of excitement. "I never dreamed I'd elope!"

"Under the circumstances, I think it's the best way."

She nodded and her face saddened. "I still can't think about Mama and Papa without crying."

"Then don't think about them. A bride should be happy on her wedding day."

"Eloping!" Beatrice said on a breath. "Imagine!"

Jared turned to her. "What was all this about Rob being attacked last night?"

"It was terrible!" Rachel said. "I came here and tossed pebbles at Beatrice's window to signal her to let me in. When I came up on the porch, this person lunged at me. I turned, and she stabbed Rob."

"The doctor says it's not serious," Beatrice added.

"She?" A cold dread settled in his middle. "A woman attacked him?"

"I'm positive it was," Rachel said. "She was tall for a woman, and she must be quite strong. He was cut deeply."

Jared's thought went immediately to Yvonne. She was tall, and everyone knew of the strength that accompanied madness. He was to bring a bride into a house with a dangerous madwoman? Yvonne would have to be sent away as soon as possible. "I assume the authorities have been notified?"

"I told the sheriff this morning, but I don't think he believed the attacker was a woman," Beatrice said. "He doesn't know Rachel is here. I couldn't tell him without Rob finding out as well."

"I'm amazed that you two thought you could hide under his nose and that he wouldn't suspect a thing."

"Rob and I aren't close. He has no reason to come to my room. I'm bringing food up to Rachel."

"When her parents return, I'm to hide in the wardrobe if her mother comes in. At least, that was our plan."

Jared shook his head. "I'm constantly amazed at the way your mind works."

"Is that a compliment?"

He took her hand. "I suggest we go to London to be married. The vicar here might not be agreeable, and I don't want your father barging in at an inopportune time."

"Elope to London! How wonderful!"

"I'm afraid we won't be able to take our wedding trip right away," he said, thinking of Yvonne. "There is some business I have to clear up first."

Beatrice caught Rachel's other hand and squeezed it. Happiness shone as clearly in her face as it did in Rachel's. "How romantic!"

Another thought struck Jared. If the sheriff didn't believe a woman attacked Rachel and if Rachel was known to have been here at the Gastons', then he was the most likely suspect. Everyone at the party knew he had reason to harbor ill will toward Rob Gaston. Jared was alone at the time of the attack and had no witnesses to prove he hadn't tried to kill Rob out of jealousy. He looked at Rachel and saw the happiness shining in her face. He couldn't mar her joy by pointing this out to her. There was, however, good reason to think the sheriff was looking for him to ask some questions, and this was another good reason to elope at once. Jared didn't want to take a chance on being detained by the sheriff and separated from Rachel before she had the protection of his house and name.

"We'll have to go to Rose's and get my things," Rachel was saying. "I'll have to tell her."

"I have a better idea. We'll send word to Rose that your belongings are to be sent to Ravenwood and we'll leave for London immediately."

"Now? So quickly?"

"I agree," Beatrice said. "It won't be a real elopement if your sister knows. Besides, she might feel it's her duty to tell your mother, and she would go straight to your father. No, I think you should leave now, as Jared says."

"I suppose you're right. I'll have to borrow your dress." She ran her hand over her skirt. "My gown is ruined, and I don't have anything else to wear."

"I'll gladly loan it to you. All brides need something borrowed, and it's blue as well. Here, take my prayer book. It's old. My grandmother gave it to me years ago."

"Something new will be my wedding ring," Rachel said. She looked up at Jared, her eyes shining. "Are you sure you don't have any doubts?"

"Not a single one."

Beatrice went to the door. "I'll see if Rob is in his room. You'll have to be quiet going down the stairs."

When they were alone, Jared said, "What about you? Are you sure you want to be my wife for the rest of your life?"

"I've never been so sure of anything in my whole life."

Beatrice pushed the door open and motioned for them to come out. Jared put his arm around Rachel and they started down the steps. He hadn't wanted to start his marriage in a cloak of secrecy. Rachel deserved better. He wanted to give her a wedding with orange blossoms and organ music and all her friends and family present. This was impossible, however. He hoped she would never regret their need for secrecy. His arm tightened around her protectively. He had no regrets at all about making her his wife. He did wonder, however, what she would say when she learned how wealthy they were.

Chapter Eighteen

Sheriff Stoddard looked up at the imposing facade of Ravenwood. He had lived in its shadow all his life, but he had never been inside. It sat on the slope of the hill that rambled down to Fairfield and from its green he could see the village and people, dwarfed by the distance, walking the streets. To either side were formal gardens that had been designed when his grandfather was a mere child. Stoddard wished his wife could see this. Some of the yew trees clipped into fanciful shapes had trunks thicker than her waist.

He tilted his head back and saw the pattern of clouds floating past the high rooftop. This side of the house faced east, and the sun glinted off the leaded windows. A movement caught his eye. Stoddard stepped back a couple of paces and looked at the window directly above the front door on the third floor.

A woman stood there, her long hair lifting in the faint breeze. Her dress was blue and was made of fine cloth. Embroidery softened the bodice, and the buttons were shiny so he assumed they weren't of the common bone variety. She stared down at him for a long moment, then stepped back from the curtainless window.

Stoddard was suddenly uncomfortable, but he couldn't understand why. Rumors of Prescott's mistress entered his mind, but he discounted them. The woman had an odd look about her. She wasn't the sort he would expect to become a mistress of a wealthy man. Her eyes had held a wildness.

He approached the door, and it swung silently open as he lifted his hand to knock. The butler looked as unfriendly as any man Stoddard had ever met. "I've come to see Mr. Prescott."

The butler bowed slightly and stood aside for Stoddard to enter. Stoddard tried not to stare. He had never seen so much marble and gilt. A spectacular staircase curved up to the second floor and ended in a gallery that circled the foyer. Potted plants like those on the gallery stood in the foyer among the gold and marble.

"This way, sir," the butler said.

Stoddard realized the man was waiting for him and he tried to look as if he wasn't intimidated. He tried to memorize every detail about the house to tell his wife. She would never believe it.

He was led into a study and asked to wait. Here the walls were paneled in walnut and were dark with age. Sporting prints hung on the wall and there was a rosewood desk in one corner. Several leather chairs were grouped near the fireplace, where a large fern was ensconced. The door opened and a man came into the room.

"Hello, my name is Mark Paynter. I'm afraid my cousin isn't home at the moment. Stanford wasn't aware that he is away."

"Stanford?"

"The butler. May I be of some assistance to you?"

"I hope so. Last night a man was attacked in town and I've come here to ask Mr. Prescott some questions."

Mark gave an incredulous laugh. "I can assure you Jared hasn't attacked anyone. What could he possibly know of it?"

"The man's name is Robert Gaston."

Mark's smile disappeared. "Rob Gaston?"

"I see the man is not unknown to you."

"Was he hurt badly?"

"No, not too badly, but it could have been worse. He was stabbed in the arm."

"Stabbed!"

Stoddard watched him closely. "You turned pale. Do you know something?"

Mark turned away and went to the window. "No. No, of course not. I was just surprised, that's all."

Stoddard made a mental note that Paynter had shown surprise on learning Gaston had been stabbed and not when he learned of the attack. His suspicions increased. "Do you have any idea where Prescott may have gone?"

"No. He went out riding, I assume. He was gone when I came downstairs this morning."

"Does he usually ride alone when he has guests?"

Mark glanced at him. "I'm not actually considered a guest here. As I said before, we're cousins, and I'm here for the summer. Jared often rides alone in the morning. I'm a late riser."

"I see." Stoddard watched Mark closely. He had often tricked information out of a man by merely watching him and not speaking. Mark, however, seemed buried in his thoughts. "If he isn't here, I suppose there is no reason for me to take up any more of your time." He turned to go when he recalled the woman in the blue dress. "By the way, when I was out front, I happened to see a woman at one of the upper windows. May I ask who she is?"

Mark's face became withdrawn. "A woman?"

"At a third floor window. The chamber directly above the door. She was wearing a blue dress."

"I couldn't imagine who it must have been. A servant, I assume." His voice wasn't as friendly as it had been.

"No, no. This was no servant. Her dress looked too fine for a servant, and it had that stitching ladies like to put on cloth."

"I'm not conversant with what our servants wear."

"And she had her hair down loose. No servant would be allowed to go about like that."

"I'll speak to the housekeeper about her. Is there anything else?"

Stoddard felt distinctly uncomfortable. There was something that Paynter knew that he wasn't telling. "No, I suppose that would be all." He went to the door and opened it to the foyer. "If you would be so kind, ask Mr. Prescott to drop by my office. I would like to talk to him. If he isn't agreeable to doing that, I'll come back to see him."

"I'll tell Jared you were here."

The silent butler walked Stoddard to the door and bowed slightly as he opened it. Stoddard glanced around one more time. He would have given a great deal if his wife could see this place. When he went outside, he looked up again, but the woman was gone from the window. Full of thoughts, he went to his horse and mounted for the ride back to the town.

Mark watched from the study window until he saw Stoddard ride away, then he went to Stanford. "Send word to the stable to saddle my horse and bring him around. I have to find Jared."

Stanford nodded and left. If he had any curiosity, he was too well trained to admit it.

When the horse was brought around, Mark mounted and rode away. He had no idea where Jared would have gone. A quick search of the adjoining fields proved fruitless. He reined the animal toward town. It stood to reason that Jared was with Rachel, especially after the scene at the party the night before, and if anyone knew where to find Rachel, it would be Beatrice.

He was glad to see her in the parlor of her parents' house, and he was even more glad to find her alone. "I've heard about your brother's injury. Is he all right?"

"He's resting well. He was as cross as a bear earlier, but the doctor returned and gave him some powders. I think he's asleep."

"Have you seen Jared? It's important that I find him at once."

Beatrice's smile faltered. "Jared? He's...he's with Rachel."

"I thought as much. Where can I find them?"

"I'm afraid you can't. They've gone to London."

"To London! Whatever for?"

"They've eloped."

Mark stared at her. It wasn't like Jared to be so impulsive, but Mark had never seen him so much in love. "Eloped? They've gone to be married?"

"Yes. Isn't it romantic?" Beatrice's smile returned. "He came here early this morning and I slipped him up to my room where they could talk in private."

"To your bedroom?"

"I know it sounds improper, but there was nowhere else they could talk without servants, or worse, Rob, overhearing them. You see, no one knew Rachel was here. She was quite beside herself after all that happened."

Mark shook his head. "I'm confused. I thought Rachel had..." He paused. No gentleman could tell a lady that her best friend had stayed with a man the night before.

"That she had stayed at Ravenwood? So did I. But she didn't. She came here and tossed pebbles at my window until I came down to let her in." Beatrice shivered delicately. "That's when the awful attack happened."

"Tell me exactly what happened. It's very important."

"I can only tell you what I told the sheriff. I came down to let Rachel in but Rob also heard her and he opened the door first. Someone rushed out of the shadows and stabbed him with a knife. She ran away before I could see her face."

"Her? It was a woman?" He felt a sinking feeling in the pit of his stomach. "You're sure it was a woman?"

"I didn't see her that clearly. I only saw a dark shape and the knife. It looked as long as a sword, I was so frightened, but of course it wasn't. Rachel said it was a woman."

"What did this woman look like?"

"She didn't see her face, but she said she was unusually tall and that she seemed to be terribly strong to have stabbed Rob the way she did. If the blade had struck his chest, the doctor told me today that he would be dead now."

Mark tried not to frown or to show what he was thinking. Yvonne was both tall and strong. Was she somehow escaping from Abby during the night? He shuddered to think of Yvonne roaming Ravenwood's dark halls and carrying a knife in her hand. She had been unsettling enough in the daylight and unarmed. "And no one saw her face? Not even Rob?"

"He's convinced that it was a man." Beatrice shook her head scornfully. "Rob thinks a woman wouldn't be strong enough to stab him, but I disagree. Especially if she was as tall as Rachel said. I've seen strong women before. Besides, Rachel was right beside her and she's positive of what she saw."

"Does Jared know all of this? About it being a woman, I mean?"

"Yes, Rachel told him. Why do you look so upset?"

"I'm only surprised. The sheriff never mentioned that a woman did it. I thought that was why he wanted to talk to Jared. That he suspected him of doing it after the argument last night."

"Wasn't that terrible?" Beatrice crossed her arms over her chest and hugged herself. "I dread to think what Mother and Father will say when they return from Derby. They are sure to blame Jared and even you, since you are living at Ravenwood. I'm so embarrassed to be Rob's sister."

Mark took Beatrice's hands. "We won't let them keep us apart. I love you, Beatrice, and I want you to be my wife."

Beatrice's eyes widened. "You do?"

"I know I should ask your father for your hand, but I don't think there's a single chance that he would grant it to me."

"We could elope. Like Rachel and Jared!" Her eyes sparkled.

"You'd do that for me? I know a big wedding is important to a woman."

Beatrice lowered her eyes shyly. "Not as important to me as being your wife. I can't have both, I'm afraid."

Mark smiled at her. She made him feel so protective and strong. "First we have to find Jared and Rachel. Did he say where in London they were going?"

"No, I never thought to ask that. I've been to London so seldom that I don't think of it as certain separate places. I lump it all together."

Mark thought hard. "I have no idea where to search for them. Jared sold his town house when he bought Ravenwood, but he has droves of friends that would be glad to welcome them. Or he could plan to stay in an inn."

"Oh, no, I'm pretty sure they expect to come back this evening."

"Why do you think that?"

"Rachel didn't borrow a change of clothing or a nightgown." Beatrice blushed at the mention of the last article.

Mark nodded. He doubted a bride would have need of a gown, but it seemed reasonable that she would want fresh clothing if she had a choice. "I think you're probably right. If he would be gone overnight, Jared would have sent word to me so I wouldn't worry."

"I do wish we had been able to witness for them," Beatrice said wistfully. "Rachel and I always said that we would be witnesses for each other. That's the drawback with elopements, I suppose."

"I have to find Jared and warn him that the sheriff thinks he may have been the one to attack Rob."

"He still thinks that? I told him over and over that it was a woman!"

"He came to Ravenwood looking for Jared less than an hour ago. That's why I have to find him first." Mark bit his lower lip as he tried to think what to do. Jared could clear his name by telling the sheriff about Yvonne, but knowing Jared's sense of honor, Mark wasn't sure he would expose his stepsister even under such desperate conditions. "I have to return to Ravenwood. If they come here first, tell Jared what I've told you about the sheriff's suspicions."

Beatrice nodded, her blue eyes wide and worried. "Wouldn't it be terrible if Jared was jailed for this when it wasn't even his fault?"

Mark nodded. Innocent men had been hanged before. "We have to find them," he repeated.

Rachel had been to London many times, but never without her parents or Rose. Everything looked new to her with Jared by her side. Although they were in the fashionable west end, the sky was a restless gray from the smoke of chimneys and factories. A fine soot lay on the rooftops and the smells were different from those in the country. Everywhere Rachel looked there were people. People of all shapes and ages and in all conditions of life, bustling about as if they all had somewhere important to go. There were the cries of the costermongers in the public streets as well as the rattle of carriages and the clopping of horses' hooves.

"I don't see how you could stand the peace of Ravenwood after London," she said as they passed stands selling oranges, lemons and nuts. Across the street stood a man with a brass urn, selling hot elder wine even though the day was early and the season warm.

"I value the quietness of the country. I expected to miss the city more than I have, but then, I've returned for business reasons often."

Rachel wondered what business reasons he would have that would necessitate his personal attendance. She had never understood exactly what men did when they were "at work." Her father apparently spent the day reading law records and writing papers. What did Jared do? She wanted to ask him, but she didn't want him to think she was nosy.

They rode past shops where Rachel saw hats and dresses that were far more fashionable than Fairfield offered. She wondered if Jared would someday bring her back to these places when they had time to shop.

That thought reminded her that she was soon to be Jared's wife. The idea was still so strange to her. She wondered if he was having any second thoughts, but was afraid to ask him. What would she do if he said he was? Time seemed to be rushing past faster than she could grasp it. She knew girls who had considered a proposal for weeks before they accepted. Jared had asked her to marry him only hours before, and here they were in London and on the way to a vicar.

She looked at him and her fears calmed. Jared was everything she had ever dreamed of in a husband. Best of all, he enjoyed talking to her and he didn't laugh at her daydreams and hopes. She had never expected to find a man who would actually be interested in her as a person. To love her, yes, but not to like her as a friend and an equal. She didn't know of any other man who felt that way about his wife.

"It's not much farther," Jared said. "Are you tired?"

"Goodness, no. I ride longer than this nearly every day. Are you?"

He smiled. "No. I'm not tired." He added, "Would you like to shop before we go back to Ravenwood?"

"Could I?" She thought for a minute and shook her head. "We shouldn't. No one except Beatrice knows we are here. I don't want to put her in the awkward position of having to break the news to Rose and Edwin. Mark doesn't even know where we are."

"I should have sent word to him, but I didn't think about it in time." He grinned at her. "I had something else on my mind."

"Jared, if you're having doubts, please tell me." She hated having to say that, but she couldn't in good conscience do otherwise. "All this happened so suddenly. Are you sure?"

Jared reined in and looked at her. "I'm positive. Are you? I've dreamed of this for weeks. Have I rushed you into anything you are beginning to regret?"

She shook her head. "I could never regret it." It was true. She loved him too much for there to be room for doubts. "I just wanted to be sure you weren't having second thoughts." She wished the streets weren't so full of people so she could have kissed him right there in the middle of London.

Jared smiled and his eyes softened. She knew he was following her thoughts. They rode into a part of town where the houses were more gracious than any Rachel had seen. When she had visited London with her family, they had shopped and stayed with Violet's sister, who lived in another section of town. "Did you live near here?" she asked.

"Yes, that was my house over there. The one with green shutters and the lion's head knocker."

"That was your house?" She knew he was well off or he wouldn't have bought Ravenwood, but she had somehow pictured him in a house more like her Aunt Maddy's. This one was grand enough for one of the nobility.

Jared led her down the street and around the corner to the neighborhood church. It sat with its face upon the street and a graveyard curling around the other three sides. Just beyond the gravestones other buildings crowded close. Jared dismounted and helped her off the mount they had borrowed from Beatrice.

Rachel held to him for a minute. She again had the curious feeling of time rushing by too fast for her to grasp it.

"Are you all right?" he asked.

"Yes. It's just that everything is happening so fast and that all this is so different from the way I thought it would be."

He took her hand and they went to a bench and sat down. "Rachel, it's very important for us not to make a mistake here. I know this is sudden. If you want to go back home and think it over, I'll understand."

"I have no home." Her eyes filled with tears. "I still feel shocked to think of that. I have no one to go to but you. What if someday in the future you realize that you married me only to give me a home? What if you feel pity for my circumstance and not genuine love?"

Jared laughed in relief. "Is that what's bothering you? I thought you were having doubts of your own."

"I love you, Jared. I'm not marrying you just to get a home."

"If I could make it different, I would. Do you understand that? If I could somehow make your parents see that I'm not an ogre and that I'm bent on marriage and not seduction, I would do that for you. I wish you were going to have the grand wedding you must have always dreamed of, but I see no way for it to be done. The sheriff wants to talk to me, I'm sure. I didn't want to say this in front of Beatrice, but it's a good idea for you to be my wife before I talk to him."

"But why..." Her eyes widened. "You think he will want to arrest you! But you've done nothing wrong!"

"I know. But the sheriff may think otherwise. Especially since it was Rob Gaston who was attacked. I'm frankly surprised that he didn't come to Ravenwood immediately."

"He didn't know about it until this morning. Last night we only talked to the doctor."

"So he may already be searching for me."

Rachel put her hands in his. "I won't let them take you. They can't do that."

"I know," he said soothingly. "I may be blowing this all out of proportion. I hope I am. If I'm not, however, it would be good for you to be my wife and entitled to Ravenwood and its protection."

"Don't talk like that." Her voice quivered and she felt tears rise to her eyes. "I can't live without you. If need be, I'll have Edwin defend you."

"Thank you, but I have a lawyer here in London. Mark knows his name and how to contact him." He stood and drew her up. "Are you ready?"

She nodded and made herself smile. The idea of losing Jared was of greater importance to her than the prospect of her wedding.

The church was about the size of the one she attended in Fairfield, and as in that one, the floor was paved with markers of people long dead. But there all resemblance stopped. The walls were pierced with vivid stained-glass windows that sent patterns of light and color over the pews and paving stones. The pews were padded with red velvet cushions and had brass plates to mark the names of the families that belonged in those pews. Along the sides were raised tombs with effigies of people in medieval dress and armor, some with dogs at their feet, some holding shields or psalters. The colors from the windows made the marble features bright.

At the front of the church Rachel saw a magnificent round window depicting Christ and the Virgin Mary surrounded by saints. The communion table was bright, with silver candlesticks and an ornate cross. The silence was calm and serene. Rachel moved slowly down the aisle.

As they reached the altar, a side door opened and a portly man came out. Upon seeing Jared, he smiled broadly and hurried to shake his hand. "So good to see you again! We had begun to think you would never be back to St. Giles."

Jared shook his hand and said, "I want you to meet someone. Rachel, this is an old friend of mine, Joseph McClarty. He's the vicar here. Joe, this is Rachel Pennington."

"Good to meet you." The vicar studied her curiously but asked no questions.

"We want you to marry us," Jared said.

"Marry you? I never thought I'd see the day! You must work magic, Miss Pennington."

Rachel smiled. It was easy to like this man. He wasn't nearly as forbidding as the village vicar.

"When is the grand event to be?"

"Immediately. We are eloping."

"How's that? Eloping?" He looked more closely at Rachel. "How old are you?"

"Twenty," she said. This was the first time she was glad to have so many years to her name. "I'm twenty."

"Why are you eloping?" Joseph looked more puzzled than concerned. "Forgive my asking, but I have to know."

"Her father doesn't think I'm good enough for her."

Joseph stared at Jared, then at Rachel and back again. He burst out laughing. "Not good enough?"

"Will you marry us?" Jared asked again. "I hate to rush you when I can see you are enjoying yourself so much, but we plan to return to the country tonight."

"Of course I'll marry you." He was still laughing as if he knew a joke that Rachel hadn't yet grasped. "Not good enough! Is her family directly related to the crown, perhaps?"

"What does he mean?" Rachel whispered.

"Never mind Joe. He has to have his little merriment at my expense."

"I assume you have no husband and are free to marry this blackguard," Joseph said over his shoulder to Rachel.

"I'm quite free to marry."

"So am I," Jared said.

"I realize you are. I only wish I could see the faces of some of my congregation when they hear the news."

"Just get on with it."

Rachel followed Joe to the room he used as an office and signed the papers he gave her. Jared put the pen in ink and signed his name beside her own. She still couldn't see what was so funny to the vicar, but he was still grinning.

They went back to the sanctuary and Joseph stood within the altar rail facing them. Jared took her hand and Rachel noticed his hands were warm in comparison to her cold fingers. She couldn't help being nervous. Was there something about Jared that she didn't know?

As the familiar words of the wedding ceremony were said, Rachel and Jared made the correct responses. Confidence settled over her and she found herself relaxing. She had no second thoughts. When they said "I do" for the last time, she smiled up at Jared.

"Congratulations, Mr. and Mrs. Prescott," Joseph said. "I hope you'll be the happiest of couples."

"We will be," Jared said with confidence.

They told the vicar goodbye and, hand in hand, walked out of the church. "Why did he think it so funny that Papa disapproved of you?'' she asked as soon as her feet touched the pavement outside.

"You should have asked that at the time," he said teasingly. "It's too late now. You're already my wife."

"Tell me."

"In London I am, or at least I was, considered a fine catch. There were several young ladies in this congregation who were determined to be in your shoes today."

"Oh? Did they have good reason to believe that they might be?" She couldn't help the sting of jealousy.

"No, they didn't, but that's never been a deterrent to young ladies before." He took her hand and looked down at it. "I don't even have a ring for you. I'm unforgivable as a husband."

"No, you're no such thing. I have plenty of time to buy a ring."

"Actually, I would like to give you the ring that has been in my family for several generations. If you want a newer one, I'll understand."

"I'd love to wear your family ring. What does it look like?"

"It has emeralds and diamonds on it."

She smiled. She didn't believe him for a minute. No one she knew had a ring with emeralds *and* diamonds. Most wedding rings were perfectly plain gold bands. "Whatever it looks like, I'll be happy."

Jared laughed as if her words pleased him, and walked her to where they had tied their horses.

As she was about to mount, Rachel paused. "Jared, I know you're going to say I should have asked you this before, but I have to know. Where is this house Papa and Rob were so concerned about?"

"Nowhere near here. It's on the east side, near the docks. It's not a place you should ever see."

"I want to see it. Please, Jared? If I've been there, I can say I've seen it and reassure everyone that it's not like Rob said."

"I don't need to reassure anyone. I've told the truth and that should be good enough for our friends. No one else should matter."

"Please, Jared?" She believed him, but she felt a definite need to see the house. It was one of the reasons she had been disowned and she had to see it for herself.

Jared hesitated. She put her hand on his arm. "I won't ask you for much. Just give me ammunition against your detractors."

He sighed. "Maybe it would be a good idea. You're to stay right beside me, though. That part of town is rough, and no place for a lady."

"I won't be a breath away," she promised. Excitement tingled through her. She had never been anyplace where a lady shouldn't go. "I'll stay so close to you, people will think I'm your shadow."

"We'll see." Jared didn't sound convinced.

Chapter Nineteen

As they passed through London's ancient streets, Rachel felt a sense of adventure. She was seeing a part of the city that she had never known existed. Because of London's age, there were slums and badly kept tenements near every section, but here the finer homes were becoming rare and the rookeries were more plentiful.

The people had also changed. Even the best parts of the city had their share of costermongers and men eager to hire out for menial chores. This, however, was where the majority of the costermongers and street sellers lived. Here the people were more often dressed in rags, and children were expected to go barefoot until they were old enough to earn a coin for a pair of shoes, or lucky enough to steal a pair.

The buildings crowded close together as if in a conspiracy to keep out fresh air and sunshine. Their top stories all but met over the narrow streets, and an open drain with a foul odor ran down the center of the street. They met a Cheap John with a wagon of used hardware heading for a more prosperous part of town. An old woman carrying a bucket threaded her way to gather "pure" to sell to a tanner. Rachel's horse shied away from a man who made his living as a rat catcher and who had several of his victims for display on a string. Three mud-covered boys passed on their way back to the Thames, where they earned what they could by feeling with their toes for articles lost in the river mud. Rachel tried not to stare, although everyone was openly staring at her.

Jared stayed close, his hand ready to reach out and catch her horse's reins should Rachel start to become separated from him. She was thankful for his protection and hoped they would reach their destination soon.

She could smell the Thames before she could see it. The houses were older in this section and some leaned against their neighbors as if they needed support in their great age. Looking up, she saw a ragged boy and girl framed in the open window of one of the buildings. They gazed impassively at her until a corner of another building cut off their view. Rachel felt extremely uneasy.

She rode closer to Jared. "How do they all live?" she asked. "*Where* do they all live?"

He nodded toward the decrepit buildings. "There may be two, even three families in a room. I've seen rooms so full of people that there was no space to step between them and where ceilings were so low I couldn't stand upright once inside."

"What on earth were you doing in a place like that?"

"My friends in London are certain that I've gone mad, but I couldn't live in a city and not see what's under my nose. I wandered into a part of town not unlike the one we're in now. I, too, wondered where all these people slept and what their homes must be like. I made it my business to find out. It wasn't difficult. I only waited until dark and followed a man home."

"I would never have had the courage!"

"What I saw wasn't a sight for a lady. Nor is this, I might add."

"We've come too far to back out now," Rachel said firmly. She was determined to see this venture through to the end.

"I saw mere children selling themselves on the street, boys who thought nothing of stealing and who spent their days scavenging through the sewers for anything they might

sell. I saw girls weighted down with babies, girls whose
faces were already old.''

"That's terrible!'' Rachel found his words all the more
poignant because they were passing just such people even
as he spoke.

"That's why I bought Howard House. I had made it my
business to learn about this part of town and what was
available. This house, once a fine home but by then falling
to ruin, was for sale. When I saw it, I knew it would be
perfect for my venture. I bought it and fixed it up enough
to be healthy and safe for occupation.''

Rachel glanced at him. She had thought she knew him,
but he was surprising her at every turn.

"I had to be careful and not make the place too fine.
Otherwise the street people it was meant to house would be
too intimidated to live in it and it would be a target for
every thief in London.'' He pointed to an unprepossessing
building behind a rusted and open gate. "There it is.''

Rachel didn't know what she had expected, but this
wasn't it. The building was as run-down on the outside as
were its neighbors. Straggly blades of wire-thin grass were
striving to grow between the paving stones in the small
courtyard. They entered the yard by riding under an arched
and lichen-grown tunnel that went under a part of the
house itself. Once they were inside the yard, the house surrounded them on all sides. Rachel shivered even though the
day was warm.

"Have you seen enough?'' Jared asked with a smile.

"No. I want to see inside,'' she replied with a concealed
effort. If women and children could live in this place, she
could certainly bear to look at it.

They dismounted and tied their horses at the post. Jared
ushered her to the weathered door. He knocked lightly and
in a minute the door was opened by an elderly lady, who
looked first at Rachel, then at Jared.

"Welcome, Mr. Prescott. I had no idea you'd be back so
soon.''

Jared drew Rachel into the house. "This is my wife, Rachel Prescott. Rachel, this is the woman who runs my establishment, Dame Webber."

Rachel liked the woman as soon as she looked into her eyes. She might seem formidable at first glance, but her eyes held laughter. "I hope we aren't intruding."

"Not a bit of it. I assume you'd like to look around." She made it a statement, not a question. "Ruby, show them about and mind your manners, now."

A girl who could have been as old as twelve materialized from the shadows. She didn't speak, but gazed up at Rachel and Jared as if they were gods. Then she turned and went into the interior of the house.

"Ruby here has been with us for several years," Jared explained. "She can't speak but she hears perfectly. I found her in the Thames."

"In the river?"

"We've never been able to discover if she jumped or fell in or was thrown off a bridge."

"That's terrible!"

"She's happy here and will probably stay for years, if not for the rest of her life."

Ruby turned and smiled at him and bobbed her head up and down.

When they left the dark hallway, Rachel found herself in a surprisingly clean and bright room. Several women were working at samplers such as Rachel had learned to make as a child. They looked up and, after a solemn gaze, most of them smiled.

"Dame Webber teaches them needlework in addition to their letters, and also how to cook. The ones who show the most proficiency with a needle usually find a job where they can use their skills. I have connections in York and Haversham, and I try to place them in one of those places and away from the temptations of London."

Rachel followed the silent Ruby back into the hall. The girl led them up a flight of steps and looked back to be sure they were still behind her.

"You'll find most of the people here too shy to speak," Jared said. "The brash ones usually don't stay. Howard House's tame life-style doesn't suit them. Those women we just passed are all new. This wing is for the longer residents."

"You keep them separated?"

"We found that the best way. When the women saw their sisters from the streets, it sometimes prompted them to give up learning to return to a simpler, if harsher way of life. At times a new woman is sent for by her family, or by the man who procured for her to threaten her back into the streets."

Rachel glanced at the child.

"Ruby has heard worse talk than this."

Ruby looked back and grinned. Her teeth were surprisingly white and straight.

"My house is run on the order of Urania Cottage in Shepherd's Bush."

"I've never heard of it."

"I would be surprised if you had. It was established by Charles Dickens, the writer, and a lady named Miss Angela Burdett-Coutts. I've found its example to be invaluable, though I make no effort to urge our women to immigrate as they do. I feel it's usually enough to send them to live in another part of this country."

"Why not allow them to stay in London?"

"It's too easy for them to fall in with the same company and be tempted to return to their former lives. These women are generally the ones who were sinking to the depths of depravity. There are no dollymops here." At her perplexed expression he explained. "Dollymops are girls who work as milliners, maids, shop girls and so forth, and who supplement their income on the streets."

Rachel had never heard anyone talk so plainly, and she was intrigued beyond words. "So your method works? The women become upright citizens again?"

"Usually. The doors are locked to keep the city out, not the people in. Occasionally a woman chooses to leave. We have a rule, as at Urania Cottage, that she must spend the

night in consideration before she is allowed to leave
Sometimes the children here have been separated from their
parents and may be reunited with them, sometimes they are
here because their families temporarily couldn't afford to
feed them. Occasionally their parents send for them after a
while. In these cases, once we are convinced that the family
ily is truly theirs and that the children will be cared for, they
are sent back to live with the family.''

She put her hand in his. ''If I didn't already love you, I
would fall in love with you now.''

They passed through a set of rooms and another door.
Rachel thought they must be opposite the tunnel that led to
the street now but her bearings were confused. Ruby
opened the door to another common room. These women
were talking softly, and as soon as they saw they had visitors, they smiled.

Jared greeted several by name and introduced Rachel as
his wife. The women stared at her in frank curiosity, but not
in a way that made Rachel self-conscious. To these women
Jared had been a savior and they were awed by being able
to meet his wife. Rachel, who had never seen a prostitute
other than the departed Liza Barnes, was almost as interested in them.

After a few minutes Ruby motioned for them to follow
her. She led them farther around the enclosed green and
Rachel could tell by the noise level that this was where the
children stayed. There were several women who were obviously in charge, but everywhere she saw children. Children of all ages, shapes and conditions. By the light in
Ruby's face, Rachel thought perhaps she would someday
request to be placed in charge of this area.

Rachel was, however, bothered by the children's clothing. Their garments were clean, but in many cases as
threadbare as any she had seen on waifs on the street.
''Could we send them some new things?'' she asked in a
whisper to Jared.

He shook his head regretfully. ''The children leave us too
often. We can't make them too different from the ones on

the street, or they will be robbed for their clothes if they leave the house. Or they may grow too accustomed to nicer clothing and be unduly upset if they go back to live with their parents, who would certainly not be able to keep them in that style. Cleanliness is about all we can do for them.''

''How sad!''

''It's better in the long run. They sometimes have trouble adjusting to living with their parents after being here where they don't have to scrounge for every crust of bread. We've had some refuse to leave and others who repeatedly run back here.''

''Rob is a cad to say what he did about this house.''

''He didn't have the facts. I can't blame him too much. Howard House, like my mills, is rather an experiment. Both seem to be thriving, however. In time, maybe I'll open another house nearer the warehouses.''

The tour ended in the kitchen, where Dame Webber was teaching several young women how to bake bread. She was smudged with flour from head to toe and her face glowed from the heat of the oven, but she never lost her temper with the girls.

''Most families around here can't afford an oven. Most don't even have a brazier. They have to buy bread already baked or arrange to rent an oven. Most of the women and children who come here have never seen a complete meal cooked or tasted meat and vegetables at the same time.''

Rachel was shocked. Even though she would never be expected to actually cook a meal, her mother had instructed her in how to do it since she was a small child. Rose had been taught in the same fashion. Violet contended that her daughters couldn't properly supervise a staff unless they understood what the servants were expected to do.

Dame Webber showed the girls how to place the bread in the oven and then wiped her floury hands on her apron. ''How is Miss Yvonne? Faring well, I take it?''

Rachel had never heard of anyone called Yvonne, so she was surprised when Jared said, ''She's quite well, thank you. So is Abby.''

Dame Webber shook her head. "Poor, simple thing. She was such a pretty girl. Yvonne, I mean." She laughed. "I don't suppose anyone would ever say that about Abby."

"Probably not. Yvonne seems to like her, however, and that's all that's important to me."

Rachel stared at her new husband. How many more secrets did he have in store for her? "Who are Yvonne and Abby?"

Dame Webber and Jared exchanged a glance. "It doesn't matter, Webber. She would have to know sooner or later." To Rachel he said, "Yvonne is my stepsister and Abby is her keeper. I'll tell you more about them as we ride back to an inn."

Dame Webber glanced at the window. "Aye, it's growing late. You'll not want to be in these streets after dark."

They said goodbye and thanked Ruby for the tour. The girl smiled shyly and bobbed a curtsy. Rachel wondered if there wasn't something more that could be done for her, like a place at Ravenwood, for instance, where the air was better. She let Jared help her onto her horse, and when he was mounted, she rode close beside him onto the street.

"I should have told you about Yvonne long before this," he said. "She's the reason I moved to Ravenwood."

"You have a sister at Ravenwood? Why have I never seen her?"

"She's my stepsister. The reason I emphasize that is because she suffers from a certain madness that runs on her side of the family."

"A madness?"

"Her mother had it before her. It led to her killing herself. My father didn't know of it when they married, but he doted on her and I don't think it would have made any difference if he had known. They had no children. Yvonne is from an earlier marriage. We are almost the same age, and as children we were as close as true brother and sister."

Rachel rode as close as possible to hear his words and to take her mind from ragged men who were eyeing her clothes and reticule with interest. "Where is she now?"

"At Ravenwood. That's the reason I was determined to have no one visit me. I was afraid they would learn of Yvonne. She stays with Abby in attendance on the third floor in a part of the house that's rarely used, but on her bad days she can be heard in the rooms below." He smiled without mirth. "The servants apparently believe the sounds are made by a ghost. They are more careful than ever to avoid that wing of the house."

Rachel stared at him. "Why didn't you tell about her before? Did you think I was so small-hearted that I wouldn't have compassion for her?"

"No, love. That wasn't it. Several years ago Yvonne seemed as sane as anyone. She was always high-strung, but she was within the limits of normalcy. Her husband was named Paul Rowse. He was a bit of a rake, but she loved him and I gave my consent to their marriage. That was a mistake.

"Paul began almost at once to see other women. I hoped Yvonne would never find out, but she came home unexpectedly one day and found him in bed with one of his lovers. At this time Abby Mansard, the woman who is now Yvonne's attendant, was her companion. Abby once lived at Howard House and held the position Dame Webber now holds. Abby had lived in the streets herself and had an understanding of those women. She and Yvonne, amazingly, hit it off so well that Yvonne asked her to become her companion. It was always an incongruous match, but Yvonne was happy with it, so I hired Dame Webber to take over Howard House.

"Abby was with Yvonne when she discovered Paul and his mistress. What happened next I know only through Abby, because Yvonne has never been sane since that day. Yvonne apparently grabbed her sewing shears from a nearby table and fell upon them. They were stabbed to death. By the time the constables and I arrived, Paul and the woman were dead on the bed and Yvonne was cowering in a corner. Abby was able to coax her out and to stand with her during the trial. The judge was lenient in view of

Yvonne's obvious insanity, and he granted her freedom in my custody."

"And that's when you came to Fairfield. If only I had known about this. The people of Fairfield would have understood if you had said you couldn't enter society because of your stepsister."

"Would they? I wonder. But there's more to my story. All went well for a time. Yvonne showed a distinct aversion to sharp, shiny objects—presumably because they reminded her of the shears she used on Paul and his lover. She couldn't abide the color red to be in the same room with her, I assume for the same reason."

"That's certainly understandable for a woman in her unstable condition."

"Then some women were murdered."

"Murdered?" Rachel felt suddenly cold.

"They had all been residents at Howard House and had all gone back to the street. We do have some failures, I have to admit. They were found near my house across town, and they had been stabbed."

"Yvonne?" Rachel whispered.

"I don't know it for a fact, but what else could it mean? These were all women who had been known to her, and she had already killed two people. She might have seen them to be like Paul's mistress, who knows? At any rate, I couldn't take the chance, so I found a place in the country and moved her there."

"What about the women who were murdered in Fairfield?"

"It has to be a coincidence. Abby is with Yvonne every moment. The only way out of Yvonne's room is through the one Abby uses, and she is an extremely light sleeper. I don't think it could have been Yvonne."

Rachel hoped he was right. She was having some difficulty adjusting her thoughts to sharing her new home with a madwoman. The thought was selfish, so she shook her head impatiently. Jared said Yvonne was under lock and constant supervision. If there was any danger, he would never have married her. "Perhaps I could be of some comfort to her," she said uneasily. "Maybe if she had a woman's companionship—other than this Abby, I mean—she might be improved."

"I never meant to begin our marriage with so low a note. You should be happy today, not worried about Yvonne. I promise that she will never harm you. She is never aggressive, even on her bad days. Her madness is characterized by fear, not anger."

"When we return to Ravenwood I think I should meet her."

"Perhaps you should." He pointed to the lowering sun. "We won't be there tonight, however. I think we should find a room and go home tomorrow."

That reminded her that the sheriff was probably looking for Jared and that this could be the only night they would have together for a while. "I agree. Tomorrow will be soon enough."

Jared took her back into the fashionable and safer side of town. He knew this area well and stopped at an inn with a courtyard enclosed behind a white wall. Its roof was tiled in slate, and its sign proclaimed it to be the Molly Angel.

"What an odd name," she said as she dismounted. "Why is it named that, do you suppose?"

"I have no idea. It's been named that all my life."

He took her inside and spoke to the proprietor, who greeted him by name. "We've not seen you in our pub lately."

"I've moved to the country," Jared said with a smile. "I came to town to be married." He put his arm about Rachel and she blushed but smiled.

"A beautiful bride! Welcome to the Molly Angel. I'll give you my best room."

Rachel followed the man up the winding stairs, with Jared close behind her. She was still having trouble believing the events of the day and that she was now a married woman. It seemed daring to go to a room with Jared. The proprietor didn't see any reason for embarrassment, however, and he kept up a conversation with Jared about people whose names she didn't recognize but whose titles made her wonder. Evidently Jared traveled in high circles.

When they were alone, Rachel clasped her hands together to hide their trembling. This room seemed even more intimate than Jared's large bedroom at Ravenwood. She was as shy as if she had never given herself to him before.

He came to her and put his arms around her. "You're trembling."

"So much has happened today. I feel dazed."

He kissed her lightly. "Come to bed. I never should have taken you to Howard House or told you about Yvonne. Not yet. I've gone too fast."

"I wanted to know." She looked up at him. "The sheriff won't take you away, will he?" She was afraid to voice the question that had troubled her all day.

"If he does, he won't keep me. I didn't harm anyone. No one can prove that I did. English courts are still just, even in Fairfield." He drew in a deep breath as his next words caused him pain. "If necessary, I'll tell the court about Yvonne. I don't want to do it and I feel that it would be wrong, but if she is, indeed, murdering people, she can't be allowed to continue. I've had Mark write to several people he knows to find her another place to live, assuming that I don't have to reveal her presence. She won't be at Ravenwood much longer."

Rachel tried to hide her relief. Guarded or not, this Yvonne sounded dangerous. "I can't bear the thought of Sheriff Stoddard taking you in. Isn't there anything I can do to prove your innocence? I was there. I'm sure the attacker was a woman."

"We'll cross that bridge when we come to it." He began to unbutton her dress. "For now, let's put it all from our minds. It may be a long while before I can lie beside you again, and I don't want to waste a single minute."

Rachel helped him loosen her clothes and he taught her how to remove his own. Her fingers were awkward on the buttons and cuff links and the knot if his cravat, but she was an eager learner. Soon they stood naked beside the bed.

"Rachel, so much has happened in the past twenty-four hours." He reached up to stroke her cheek while his other hand rested on the bare curve of her hip. "I promise you that I'll never do anything to make you regret the haste of our actions."

"I'll never regret them at all. I love you, Jared, and I don't love halfway. I must seem impetuous to you, but it's only because I'm able to make my mind up quickly. I knew I wanted you the first time I ever saw you."

"I wasn't kind to you that day." His dark eyes were soft with love.

"I could see right through your mask and I liked what I found there. It's a good thing I did, or we wouldn't be here now."

"I'm not so sure of that. You crept into my heart before I ever put you behind me on my horse."

Rachel smiled and lay on the bed. Silently she held out her arms to him, and all her shyness vanished. Jared gazed down at her for a moment, then lay beside her. Rachel drew in her breath at the contact with his naked flesh. "I love to feel you. Perhaps I'll hide all your nightshirts as soon as we reach Ravenwood."

He laughed softly. "I don't own any."

Unlike the night in Jared's room, their lovemaking was slow and leisurely, as if they had all the time in the world. Rachel trembled under his touch and wished on one hand that he would rush with her to their satisfaction, and on the other that this night might last forever.

Jared kissed her breasts and ran the tip of his tongue over her taut nipples until she arched her back to offer herself to him. He obliged by drawing her nipple into his mouth and lathing it with his tongue. His fingers replaced his mouth and he moved lower, sampling and tasting every inch of her.

Rachel had never felt such ecstasy. She was no longer aware of the room or of any of the myriad problems awaiting them in Fairfield, but knew only the touch of his hands, the warmth of his kisses and the heat of his body against hers.

She explored him in return. His skin was smooth and warm, and she could feel hard muscles and sinews beneath the surface. His hands, while smooth, were hard and masculine, driving her wild. She licked the warm pulse in the hollow of his neck, and Jared moaned with pleasure. Encouraged, she ran her tongue over his shoulder and down his chest, enjoying the taste of him.

Her hands curved over his buttocks and circled his thighs. Jared seemed as sensitive to her touch as she was to his. She was enjoying the different textures of his body while offering him her own. As he touched her in places she ached to have touched, she let herself drown in pure pleasure.

When he entered her, she half expected to feel the stab of pain, but this time there was only pleasure. She held him tightly and moved in rhythm with him. Her body seemed to be keenly tuned to match his. As his body moved faster, hers responded. Rachel held to him and let him carry her spiraling up to the summit of passion.

All at once she was there, and pleasure became her entire soul and being. She existed only for him and he only for her. Lights and colors seemed to flash in her mind as she rode the waves of sheer ecstasy. She cried out in her pleasure and was answered by him as he met and joined her in fulfillment.

For what could have been an eternity or only moments their souls entwined and became one. Then slowly, softly, Rachel became aware of the bed beneath her and the strange room around her. She opened her eyes to find Jared watching her, a smile on his lips. She smiled and ran her fingers down his chest.

"I love you, Rachel Prescott," he murmured.

"I love you. I never dreamed I would enjoy being a wife to such an extent."

He grinned. "Didn't I tell you that you were made for loving? I think we've discovered your best talent."

Happily she rubbed her cheek against his chest and breathed in the warm, clean scent of his body. "I really make you happy? Truly?"

"Really and truly." He laughed softly and stroked his hand over her hair. "Happier than I've been in all my life."

Rachel kissed his chest and snuggled as close to him as was possible. She had never been happier either.

Chapter Twenty

When Rachel awoke, she still lay in Jared's arms. She felt warm and safe, and she smiled to remember how Jared had made love with her the night before. She looked up at him and found he was watching her. "You're awake," she said softly.

"I've been watching you sleep."

Nothing else he could have said would have touched her so deeply. Tears of happiness came to her eyes. "I love you so much."

They made love again, slowly and with the sureness of lovers beginning to learn the pleasures of each other's body. Rachel had never felt so loved and secure. She knew Jared was feeling the same way. "I can hardly believe no one has snapped you up before now," she said when she again lay quietly beside him.

"I didn't want to be snapped up. You couldn't tell it from our courtship, but I was quite good at evasion."

"I noticed, but I didn't let that stop me."

"Thank goodness." He kissed the tender area behind her ear.

Rachel wrapped her arm and leg over his body to hold herself as close to him as possible. "Our entire bodies are kissing," she observed. "That's what it feels like."

He laughed and stroked her hair. "We have to go back," he said after a time. "You know we do."

"I know. I was trying to pretend it wasn't so."

"The longer we stay gone, the more it will look as if I'm guilty."

She sat up at once, the sheet pooling in her lap. "Then we should go at once."

He smiled as he gazed at her. She had lost her shyness with him during the night. "I never want to leave here. You know that, don't you?"

"I know."

They dressed, and Rachel combed her hair into an attractive bun high on her head. As she did the familiar things she did every morning, she couldn't quell a growing sense of dread. What if Jared was taken from her? Her hands trembled and she set her jaw. He wouldn't be. Somehow she would prevent it.

They ate at a small bakery Jared knew, then started for home. She glanced down at her bare left hand. If she had a wedding ring, she would feel better. Yesterday was already beginning to seem like a dream. Had she really married Jared, and was she now truly his wife? It had happened so quickly she had to keep reminding herself. She looked at her husband, so tall and straight in the saddle, and knew she had no regrets.

When they arrived at Ravenwood they saw a horse tethered out front. Rachel swallowed and said, "It belongs to Sheriff Stoddard. I recognize it."

A muscle moved in Jared's cheek. He gave Rachel a long look. "Remember that I love you. That I would never leave you of my own volition."

She nodded. She didn't trust herself to speak.

They dismounted and went into the house. Stanford, the butler, was coming to meet them, and for the first time Rachel saw a look of dismay on his usually passive features. "The sheriff is here, sir. Sheriff Stoddard."

"I know. We saw his horse."

Stanford straightened. In a whisper he said, "He's in the back parlor with Mr. Mark. If you were to leave again, he'd never know."

Jared smiled and clapped the man on the shoulder. "I never run away," he said. He took Rachel by the hand and led her down the foyer to the back parlor.

Stoddard and Mark looked up when Rachel and Jared entered the room. For a minute they stared at each other. Stoddard spoke first, his eyes on Rachel. "You! I never expected to find you here."

"We were married in London yesterday," Jared said calmly. "Rachel is my wife and the mistress of Ravenwood."

She lifted her chin as she did when she knew she would have to argue a point. "Why are you here? I'm sure Beatrice told you Rob was attacked by a woman. Do you suspect one of Ravenwood's servants?"

"No, I started thinking after I talked to Miss Gaston. There were some odd things that didn't make sense. If the attacker was whoever killed those two women in town, who were known to be bawds, why would the same person be after you? Even better, why would this person stab Mr. Gaston? It didn't make any sense. So I asked myself, who was likely to want you dead?"

"I have no enemies. Certainly not any murderous ones. Beatrice must have told you that."

"Aye, she did. So I asked myself, who would want to see Mr. Gaston dead? I came up with a jealous lover."

"I had no reason to be jealous," Jared said quietly. "As you can see, Rachel has married me. Not Rob Gaston."

"Yes, but did you know she would at the time of the knifing? That's what we have to ask ourselves."

"Jared doesn't look like a woman," Rachel argued. "A woman stabbed Rob."

"So I heard. But Mr. Gaston was so confused by it all, he's not the best of witnesses. Miss Gaston is your best friend and is likely to believe whatever you tell her."

"You're saying I lied?" Rachel gasped. "No one has ever accused me of lying!"

"Now let's not put ugly words to it," Stoddard said in a calming manner. "I just have to do my duty."

"Which is?" Jared asked.

"I have to take you into custody for the attempted murder of Mr. Robert Gaston and to hold you until your trial."

Mark took a step forward. "Jared, you have to tell him. If you don't, I will."

Jared paused and drew a long breath.

"What's he talking about? Tell what?"

"I don't live here alone," Jared said reluctantly. "I have a stepsister who stays on the third floor."

Stoddard rubbed his chin as if he were considering. "The third floor? Why is it nobody in the village knows about her?"

"She's hopelessly mad. I've confined her to her room in the care of a woman whose only duty is to see to her."

"If she's under supervision, how can she make any difference in this matter?"

Mark said, "She was always unstable. She went mad when she came home to find her husband in bed with a whore. Her mind snapped and she killed them both."

Silence ticked long in the room. At last Stoddard said, "She killed them?"

Jared nodded. "She stabbed them with a pair of sewing shears."

Stoddard looked uncertain. "That's hard to believe. I've never heard a whisper of this before, and all the rumors in town pass through my office eventually."

"Not this one. No one in Fairfield knows. I brought servants with me from London. The ones I hired here are never allowed near the third floor. Even the staff don't know about Yvonne."

Rachel stepped nearer Jared and put her hand in his. She could feel the pain behind his words. To tell the sheriff about Yvonne was putting him in anguish. "Jared meant the best for his sister," she said in his defense.

"She stood trial, didn't she?" Stoddard demanded.

"Yes, of course. She was found guilty, but not responsible for her actions. You'll understand when you see her. Yvonne is hopelessly mad.

"There's more," Jared continued. "Before we moved here from London, some women were found stabbed not far from where we lived. They, like the two women in the village, were of low morals, and they were known to Yvonne through a connection that has no reason to be explained. I brought her here where I thought I could more easily keep her under lock and key."

"At first I thought the murders were a coincidence," Mark said. "I couldn't see how Yvonne could get past Abby. But the chances of it being another woman seem unlikely. You see, Yvonne is tall and strong—just as Rachel described the woman who attacked Rob."

"On the night Rob was stabbed, I thought I heard a sound in the hall outside my room," Jared said. "At the time, I thought it was only my imagination, but it must have been Yvonne. I don't know how she is getting away from her keeper, but she must be doing exactly that."

Stoddard stared from one to the other. "I think you'd better take me up to her. I have to see for myself if all this is true."

Jared looked down at Rachel and she tightened the grip on his hand. "I'm going up with you. I have to meet her sometime."

He reached up and untied the red ribbon that decorated the neck of Rachel's dress. "We never wear red in her presence. It overly excites her."

Rachel felt herself pale but she refused to waver. She put the ribbon aside and said, "Which way do we go?"

Silently they went up the stairs. On the balcony they passed the closed doors to the ballroom and Rachel tried not to look at the door that led to Jared's chamber. She wondered if the sheriff believed they were married or if he was labeling her as no better than a mistress. They started up the next flight of stairs.

The third floor was silent and had the feel of rooms in disuse. Rachel took Jared's hand, for her own fortitude this time. He gave it a reassuring squeeze.

Halfway down the hall, Jared stopped at a door. He tapped lightly. Inside Rachel could hear footsteps and muffled voices. At last the door opened a crack. "Open up, Abby. We've come to see Yvonne."

The woman did as she was told, but her mouth hardened into a line when she saw Rachel and Stoddard. "She'll be upset if she sees all of you. She's not used to so much company."

"It's necessary for the sheriff to meet her."

Abby's eyes widened and she stared at Stoddard. "She'll have one of her spells."

"It can't be helped." Jared led the others into the room. Abby closed the door behind them.

He went to the door opposite and knocked softly. "Yvonne? I've brought you some guests."

Rachel heard a murmured response but she couldn't make out the words. Jared opened the door and went in. Rachel followed close on his heels. At first she thought the room was empty and that it had been torn apart. The chairs all lay on their sides. There were no curtains at the windows. The wallpaper had been pulled away in strips, and there were none of the small odds and ends that a woman would enjoy having about.

"Don't be afraid," Jared said as he held out his hand toward a dark corner.

Hesitantly a woman stood from where she had been crouching in the shadow between the bed and the wall. Her dark eyes were frightened and wild, and her hair hung about her shoulders. Slowly she edged nearer Jared.

"May I present my stepsister, Yvonne Rowse?" Jared said as calmly as if they were still in the parlor. "Yvonne, this is my wife, Rachel. And this is Sheriff Stoddard."

Yvonne was studying Rachel. Hesitantly she reached out and touched the lace on Rachel's dress. Her eyes met Rachel's and held. Rachel found herself losing her fear of the woman. This was someone to pity. How could this timid creature kill anyone?

"They came last night," Yvonne whispered to her, then to Jared. "They've found me after all!"

"Who?" Rachel asked before Jared could stop her.

"Paul. Paul and his whore. They were moving about on the green. I saw them through my window. They were looking for a way into the house." Her voice was worried and it was clear that she believed every word she said.

"That's why she keeps the chairs turned over," Jared said to Stoddard. "She believes that if they are left up-right, her dead husband and his woman come and sit in them. It keeps her quiet if we humor her in this." To Yvonne he said, "I'll have extra locks put on the doors. They can never get in."

Yvonne gave him a faint smile and her face became almost pretty. She reached out and patted his chest as if that were her way of saying thank-you.

"Mrs. Rowse," Stoddard said reluctantly, "I have some questions I have to ask."

Jared glared at him but didn't speak. Rachel could see why he was so protective of the poor woman. Yvonne was like a frightened child, not a person to fear.

"Someone tried to kill Mr. Robert Gaston two nights ago. Do you know anything about it?"

Yvonne's head snapped toward Abby. "You said that name to me! That's the name! You said I hurt someone else. Did you tell on me?"

Abby remained as silent as marble. Stoddard looked as if he wished he could leave it alone. "Then you did attack him?"

"No! I wouldn't hurt him. I don't even know him."

"You're lying, Yvonne," Abby spoke up fiercely. "You did it. Just like you killed those other women."

"How did you know about the murders?" Jared asked.

"Tell them, Yvonne. If you don't, I will!" Abby glared at her charge.

Yvonne wavered as if she wasn't certain what to do. "I must have killed them. Abby said I did."

Stoddard sighed. "Then I have no choice but to arrest you for the murder of Liza Barnes and Bertha Giles, and for the stabbing of Robert Gaston."

"Stabbing?" Yvonne whispered.

"That's impossible," Jared said as if something had suddenly occurred to him. "Yvonne is terrified of knives or of anything that resembles one. The sight of blood sends her into a state approaching catatonia. She couldn't have stabbed anyone, especially not over and over as I've heard the women were stabbed!"

"She must have!" Stoddard said. "If it wasn't her, it had to be you!"

"It was Yvonne!" Abby shrieked. "I'm telling you it was Yvonne!"

They turned at her outburst. Rachel didn't like the expression she saw in Abby's eyes. This woman was far more frightening than Yvonne.

Yvonne turned away and knelt beside the bed. Rachel thought she was hiding in fear, but Yvonne drew something out and held it out to her. "Abby's," she said.

Rachel took the black cloak, her eyes questioning Yvonne's. The sheriff took it from her and carried it to the window.

"I'm sorry, Abby," Yvonne said. "I had to hide it. There was red on it. I couldn't let it stay out in the open."

Stoddard looked up. "There's dried blood here."

Abby suddenly grabbed Rachel and yanked her back against her body. Rachel was choking under Abby's grip, but when she felt the cold blade beside her throat she froze.

"I'll not let you take me," Abby said. "Those whores had it coming. They should have stayed decent! They should have listened to me at Howard House!"

"What's she talking about?" Stoddard whispered, as he prevented Jared from rushing to Rachel's aid.

Jared restrained himself. "Those women were in London, Abby, not here."

Abby jerked her head. "A whore is a whore." She began backing up, Rachel still held in front of her.

Rachel was afraid to breathe. She tried to see behind her, to find some way to escape. She knew that if she could dodge away from the knife, Jared and Stoddard would be on Abby before she could grab her again. The blade stung her neck. She didn't dare try to wrestle away.

She was aware of movement, but she was too frightened to question it. All she knew was that she was nearer death than she had ever been before. By the expression on Jared's face she knew Abby wouldn't hesitate to kill her. Mark and Stoddard seemed almost as upset as Jared. Rachel's steps faltered as she was forced to walk backward and Abby tightened the knife against her throat. Rachel had never been so frightened in her life.

They crossed Abby's room and she felt Abby release her arm to fumble for the doorknob. Out of years of habit, however, she had locked it and the door didn't budge. Abby spit out a street curse and yanked on the door.

Unexpectedly, Yvonne stepped out from the corner where she had run to hide at the first sight of the knife. She touched Abby's shoulder. Abby cried out and spun to face what she thought was a new attacker. Rachel twisted away and threw herself toward the bed. She had a blurred impression of the men lunging at Abby, but her eyes were on Yvonne.

Abby growled like a trapped animal and lashed out at Yvonne. The knife impaled the woman's chest. Yvonne's widened eyes glazed over as she sank to the floor. Abby's arm was raised to stab her again, when Jared reached her and wrenched her backward.

Mark knelt by Yvonne, but it was already too late. Her face had lost its pinched and nervous expression and was relaxing in death.

Stoddard and Jared easily subdued Abby, and Jared took the knife from her. "Rachel! Are you hurt?"

Rachel's lips moved, but it took a moment for her to make a sound. "No. I'm not hurt."

Mark took a cord that bound the curtains on the bed and helped Stoddard tie Abby's hands. All the time Abby was shouting curses and vile threats at them. Rachel could only stare at her. She had come so close to death she was still unable to think clearly.

Before Stoddard took Abby away, Jared said to her grimly, "I have to know. Did Yvonne kill Paul and that woman, or was that you, too?"

Abby glared at him, her eyes nearly on a level with his. Then she smiled and turned away.

Jared stared after her until Rachel came to him. "She must have done it," she said softly. "Yvonne wouldn't hurt anyone."

They gazed down at the woman on the floor. Jared said, "I'll stay with her. Mark, go tell Stanford what has happened and that he is to send for the undertaker."

He looked at Rachel, his eyes full of his pain at all that had happened. She silently went to him and held him close.

Rachel sat in the back parlor and held Jared's hand. Even though the danger was all over and Yvonne's body had been taken away, she still felt as if everything could tumble down around her head. Jared smiled and patted her hand. "It's over, love. I won't have to leave you now."

She nodded. There was no way she could make him understand that she was almost as upset now as she had been during the crisis.

Mark came into the room and smiled at them. "So you're married. Beatrice told me you had gone to London to elope."

"Sorry you couldn't have been there," Jared said. "With matters the way they were, we thought it best not to wait." He looked at Rachel. "I only wish it could have been more festive. A woman plans these things half her life, if my female cousins are to be believed."

Rachel smiled. "I would rather be married to you in secret than have a royal wedding with anyone else."

Mark said, "I don't know if this is the best time to tell you or not, but Beatrice has agreed to be my wife."

"She has!" Rachel leaned forward happily. "How won derful!"

"I suppose you'll insist on dragging her away to tha drafty old castle of yours," Jared teased.

"Only occasionally. I thought I might possibly find house similar to Ravenwood and not too far from here. Ou brides might not forgive us for separating them."

"Wouldn't that be perfect if you two would live clos by?" Rachel was almost as happy for Beatrice as she wa over her own marriage. She touched Jared's shoulder t reassure herself that he was there and safe.

There was a discreet knock at the door. Stanford en tered and said, "Two gentlemen to see you, sir."

"Not Stoddard again!"

"No, sir. It's Mr. Pennington and Mr. Jenson."

"Papa and Edwin?" Rachel exclaimed. "What can the want? Jared, they can't force me to leave you, can they?'

"Never. You're my wife." He rose and helped her to he feet. Rachel felt faint. He said, "Show them in, Stan ford."

Mark also stood and kept himself near Jared and Ra chel, as if to show his support. When William and Edwi came into the room, Rachel lifted her chin defiantly. Sh might be afraid, but there was no reason to show it.

"Rachel," William said in way of greeting. "Prescott. He nodded his head in Mark's direction. "I assume you ar well," he said to Rachel.

"Quite well, Papa."

"Stoddard came to the house and told me all that hap pened." He frowned at Jared. "It would seem I owe you a apology."

"I accept your apology." Jared's voice sounded almos as stiff as William's.

Edwin smiled at Rachel. "Rose says she misses you We've worried about you ever since you left."

"I didn't expect to desert you like that," Rachel said. " didn't know Rob would cause so much trouble or to dra Papa into it. Is the baby well?"

"She's perfect and misses her aunt. All the children do."

William cleared his throat as he did when he was about to make a telling point in court. "As matters stand, I've decided, your mother and I, that is, that if you two are determined to be married, we won't stop you."

Edwin added, "Mrs. Pennington says to tell you she can begin right away on a trousseau. Rose is practically designing it now."

"A trousseau?" Rachel said in amazement. "But we're already—"

Jared cut off her words. "Don't say anything to change his mind, love. It would seem that you are to get the wedding you've always wanted."

Rachel opened her mouth, and Jared's laughing eyes cautioned her to think first. "Are you giving us your blessing, Papa?"

William frowned at her, but he nodded. "I am. Prescott, I assume your intentions are still honorable?"

Jared suppressed his smile. "Entirely, sir. I want nothing more than to be married to your daughter."

"Perfect!" Edwin exclaimed with some relief. "Then it's done."

William turned his frown on his son-in-law. "Not so fast. I want to be sure that this man loves Rachel and that he will be good to her."

Jared smiled down at Rachel. "I love her with all my heart, and I would do anything to keep her safe, even if it meant giving my life for her."

"It's not likely to come to that, now is it?" William asked rhetorically. "Rachel, do you still want him?"

She couldn't keep the laughter from her voice. "I want him very much, Papa."

"Then it's done." William announced to Edwin with a firm bob of his head. He crossed the room and held out his hand to Jared.

After a pause, Jared took it and they shook. "I'll be good to her. She will never want for a thing."

"See that she's happy. I'm still her father and I always will be."

Rachel felt happy tears rising, and she couldn't stop them. They traced down her cheeks, and Jared wiped them away with his fingers. "A bride shouldn't cry," he said softly.

"It's only that I'm so happy." She hugged him, then her father. She had never thought to be able to see them both in the same room again, let alone that William would do what he had. She had never known him to apologize for anything. Around his shoulder, she caught Edwin's eye and he winked. Rachel winked back. Edwin, whom she had always thought ineffectual and weak, had been instrumental in William's turnabout. She could hardly wait to ask Rose what Edwin had said to cause it.

"You had better come home with me now," William was saying. "Your mother is beside herself. You know how she gets."

Rachel didn't want to leave Jared, but he smiled and nodded at her. "It's best this way," he said. "It's right that you should go to her and reassure her. Plan your wedding, love. We have all our lives to be together."

Rachel smiled back in return. "Will we now be able to go on a wedding trip?"

"To the moon, if you wish it." Jared's eyes laughed into hers.

"I would really like to see a buffalo," she said. "Also, I'd like to talk to an Indian."

"I happen to know an Indian who would be glad to oblige."

Rachel put her hand on William's arm. "Let's go, Papa. The quicker Mama, Rose and I start planning the wedding, the sooner it can take place." She smiled over her shoulder at Jared and winked.

* * * * *

◈ Harlequin®

JANELLE TAYLOR

Valley of Fire

HARLEQUIN IS PROUD TO PRESENT *VALLEY OF FIRE* BY JANELLE TAYLOR—AUTHOR OF TWENTY-TWO BOOKS, INCLUDING SIX *NEW YORK TIMES* BESTSELLERS

VALLEY OF FIRE—the warm and passionate story of Kathy Alexander, a famous romance author, and Steven Winngate, entrepreneur and owner of the magazine that intended to expose the real Kathy "Brandy" Alexander to her fans.

Don't miss VALLEY OF FIRE, available in May.

Following the success of WITH THIS RING, Harlequin cordially invites you to enjoy the romance of the wedding season with

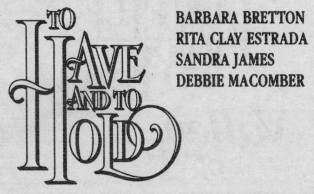

BARBARA BRETTON
RITA CLAY ESTRADA
SANDRA JAMES
DEBBIE MACOMBER

A collection of romantic stories that celebrate the joy, excitement, and mishaps of planning that special day by these four award-winning Harlequin authors.

Available in April at your favorite Harlequin retail outlets.

Harlequin Regency® Romance™

WHO SAYS ROMANCE IS A THING OF THE PAST?

We do! At Harlequin Regency Romance, we offer you romance the way it was always meant to be.

What could be more romantic than to follow the adventures of a duchess or duke through the glittering assembly rooms of Regency England? Or to eavesdrop on their witty conversations or romantic interludes? The music, the costumes, the ballrooms and the dance will sweep you away to a time when pleasure was a priority and privilege a prerequisite.

If you are longing for the good old days when falling in love still meant something very special, then come to Harlequin Regency Romance—romance with a touch of class.

RRG

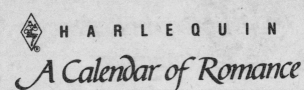

H A R L E Q U I N

A Calendar of Romance

Be a part of American Romance's year-long celebration of love and the holidays of 1992. Celebrate those special times each month with your favorite authors.

Next month, we salute moms everywhere—with a tender Mother's Day romance.

MAY

S	M	T	W	T	F	S
					1	2
3						
10						16
	1		21	22	23
24/31	25	26	27	28	29	30

**#437
CINDERELLA
MOM
by Anne Henry**

Read all the books in *A Calendar of Romance*, coming to you one per month, all year, only in American Romance.